FLOOD OF PASSION

Kissing Hawk was like being caught up in a flash flood, unexpected and overpowering.

She was ecstatic. Jubilant. Exultant. Hawk wanted her as much as she wanted him. She had to calm down before she did something to drive him away. "I came here tonight hoping you liked me well enough to let me stay. I never dreamed you liked me that much." She was petrified she wouldn't be able to control her feelings for him but was determined she wouldn't let this opportunity to experience something close to love slip from her grasp.

"I never dreamed you'd want to stay with me," Hawk said.

"I can't imagine why any woman wouldn't want to spend the night in your arms."

"I've never wanted just any woman."

But he wanted her. She could see it in his eyes and hear it in his voice. She could practically feel his heat despite the cooling of the night air around her. The scent of the river and sagebrush weren't nearly as strong as the scent of a man burning up with his need for a woman.

Other books by Leigh Greenwood:

THE RELUCTANT BRIDE
THE INDEPENDENT BRIDE
SEDUCTIVE WAGER
SWEET TEMPTATION
WICKED WYOMING NIGHTS
WYOMING WILDFIRE
SCARLET SUNSET, SILVER NIGHTS
THE CAPTAIN'S CARESS
ARIZONA EMBRACE

The *Night Riders* series:
TEXAS HOMECOMING
TEXAS BRIDE
BORN TO LOVE

The Cowboys series:
JAKE
WARD
BUCK
DREW
SEAN
CHET
MATT
PETE
LUKE

The *Seven Brides* series:
ROSE
FERN
IRIS
LAUREL
DAISY
VIOLET
LILY

CRITICS ARE RAVING ABOUT
LEIGH GREENWOOD!

"Leigh Greenwood continues to be a shining star of the genre!"
—*The Literary Times*

"Leigh Greenwood NEVER disappoints. The characters are finely drawn...always, always, a guaranteed good read!"
—*Heartland Critiques*

"Leigh Greenwood remains one of the forces to be reckoned with in the Americana romance sub-genre."
—*Affaire de Coeur*

"Greenwood's books are bound to become classics."
—*Rendezvous*

THE RELUCTANT BRIDE
"Leigh Greenwood always provides one of the year's best western romances, but his latest tale may be the best in an illustrious career. ...Once again Mr. Greenwood will have one of the sub-genre top guns of 2005."
—Harriet Klausner

THE INDEPENDENT BRIDE
"Leigh Greenwood unfolds his Westerns like an artist.... Like his other books, *The Independent Bride* should be placed among the western classics."
—*Rendezvous*

BORN TO LOVE
"The characters are complex and add a rich element to this western romance."
—*Romantic Times*

TEXAS HOMECOMING
"Leigh Greenwood raises the heat and tension with *Texas Homecoming*. Few authors provide a vivid descriptive Americana romance filled with realistic angst-laden protagonists as this author can."
—*The Midwest Book Review*

The Mavericks

LEIGH GREENWOOD

LEISURE BOOKS NEW YORK CITY

A LEISURE BOOK®

December 2005

Published by

Dorchester Publishing Co., Inc.
200 Madison Avenue
New York, NY 10016

ISBN 0-8439-5237-7

Visit us on the web at www.dorchesterpub.com.

The
Mavericks

The Family of Jake Maxwell and Isabelle Davenport
(m. 1866)

Eden Maxwell b. 1868

Ward Dillon m. Marina Scott 1861
       Tanner b. 1862
       Mason b. 1869
       Lee b. 1872
       Conway b. 1874
       Webb b. 1875

Buck Hobson (Maxwell) m. Hannah Grossek 1872
       Wesley b. 1874
       Elsa b. 1877

Drew Townsend m. Cole Benton 1874
       Celeste b. 1879
       Christine b. 1881
       Clair b. 1884

Sean O'Ryan m. Pearl Belladonna (Agnes Satterwaite) 1876
       Elise b. 1866 (Pearl's daughter by previous marriage)
       Kevin b. 1877
       Flint b. 1878
       Jason b. 1880

Chet Attmore (Maxwell) m. Melody Jordan 1880
       Jake Maxwell II (Max) b. 1882
       Nick b. 1884

Matt Haskins m. Ellen Donovan 1883
       Toby b. 1868 (adopted)
       Hank Hollender b. 1870 (adopted)
       Orin b. 1872 (adopted)
       Noah b. 1878 (adopted)
       Tess b. 1881 (adopted)

Pete Jernigan m. Anne Thompson 1886

Luke Attmore m. Valeria Badenburg 1887

Hawk Maxwell m. Suzette Chatingy 1888

Zeke Maxwell m. Josie Morgan 1888

Bret Nolan

Will Haskins

Chapter One

Arizona Territory, 1888

The small but powerfully built bay mare walked with surefooted confidence along the rock-strewn trail, her head swaying from side to side with each stride, her gaze sweeping the ground ahead for obstacles to be avoided by her unshod hooves. Her bulging sides bore evidence that it would soon be time to drop her foal. Without warning, she stopped, threw her head up, and whinnied softly.

"What's wrong, girl?" Hawk Maxwell's hand drifted to his rifle stock as his gaze swept the rocky hills in the distance. "You looking for a place to have your baby?"

The mare whinnied again, shook her head vigorously. Behind her, eight mares halted, their tails busy driving away flies, their heads hanging low as they patiently waited for their leader.

"You talk to that mare like she was your woman," Zeke Maxwell shouted from his position at the rear of the small band of horses.

"She's more faithful than any woman I ever had," Hawk said.

"She's certainly prettier than the last one." Zeke would like to see what had upset Dusky Lady, but they were following a narrow game trail along the San Pedro River through a thicket of willow and cottonwood saplings. Pulling out to look ahead was virtually impossible.

"Well, you're too old to have a kid," Zeke said. "Even a four-legged one."

"I'm only thirty-six," Hawk said, "two years younger than you."

"We're both too old for kids or wives. I guess that limits us to a shady lady now and then."

"I'm sticking with Dusky Lady. She hasn't deserted me yet."

With her Morgan blood, the mare was the most costly horse they'd ever bought. They hoped she'd be the linchpin of their plan to breed quality stock. They already had twenty-one horses, mares, new foals, and yearlings, at a run-down ranch they'd bought about twenty miles from Tombstone. Now they were trying to get this last and most expensive group of mares to the ranch as quickly and safely as possible.

"Wait until she gets a look at that stud horse Hen Randolph sold us. You won't even be a distant memory."

The mare started forward, but this time she kept her head high and sniffed the wind. The horses negotiated the rocky ground closest to the riverbed cautiously, taking care not to set their feet down on a stone that could strain a ligament or bow a tendon. As the trail turned away from the river and the land rose, rocks gave way to sandy soil, making the footing easier, but the navigation more difficult. The horses were forced to push their way through banks covered with tamarisk thickets interspersed with mesquite, ironwood, and several kinds of cactus. The bright yellow flowers of the senna plant helped compensate for the unpleasant odor of the creosote bush, which had been intensified by recent rains.

"What do you think she scented?" Zeke called to Hawk.

"I'll ride ahead and have a look." Hawk spurred his horse forward. "The old girl is better than a watchdog, but scent can't tell her whether what's up ahead is friendly or not."

Over the years, Hawk and Zeke had roamed most of the West together, gradually drifting into a relationship that was closer than most married couples. They practically operated from the same mind. It was an advantage on the trail, but a real handicap when it came to women.

While Hawk rode ahead, Zeke scanned the countryside for clues as to what might have startled the mare. They had passed through the rough landscape of the Salt River—an easy place for rustlers to waylay them—into the relatively open and flat desert. Due to unusually heavy and lingering winter rains, a trickle of water meandered along the often dry bed of the upper San Pedro River. Despite the danger of exposure to attack, they had decided to follow the river because it offered water and forage for the horses.

The horses were too calm for there to be a dangerous wild animal in the vicinity. But then, the most dangerous animal in the West was man. Zeke and Hawk had survived without serious injury because they were always ready to back each other up, whether fighting with fists or guns. They'd established a reputation as a tough combination, one most men were reluctant to tackle, but there was always someone who didn't know anything about them or was young and foolish enough to want to build a reputation by taking on somebody other men stayed away from. As Zeke often said, he hadn't reached the age of thirty-eight by relaxing his guard.

Zeke was glad they'd finally decided it was time to settle down and stop wandering from place to place. They planned to raise quality horses to sell to wealthy ranchers who—

A rifle shot broke the silence.

Zeke jerked his rifle from its scabbard, dug his heels into his mount's sides, and shouted, "Watch the horses!" to Dusky Lady as he galloped past. He and Hawk had expected that someone would try to steal their horses. Blooded mares were worth a small fortune in Arizona. He found Hawk crouched behind a clump of cholla cactus and bailed out of the saddle to join him.

"Who is it? Where are they?"

"They're women," Hawk said, "and they're camped on a sandbar on the other side of the bend in the creek." Zeke stood, trying without success to see through a tangle of blossoming paloverde.

"Women! What the hell are they doing out here, and why are they shooting at you?"

"*They* didn't. Just one mighty pretty black woman. The rest of them were hiding under the wagon."

"What did you say to them?"

"I didn't get a chance. She took one look at me and opened fire."

Zeke laughed. "I told you to stop wearing that damned feather. You look like some white man playing at being an Indian." Despite Zeke's constant ridicule— and complaints—Hawk liked to wear a single feather as a headdress.

"I'm not a white man."

"You're not a Comanche, either." It was an old argument. "Let me talk to her. Maybe she won't shoot at me."

When he was around Hawk, Zeke found it easy to forget he was an ex-slave. But whenever he met a stranger, he was certain to be reminded of the color of his skin.

"I'll go back to the horses and let the *lady's man* take over," Hawk said.

That was another bone of contention. Zeke refused to have anything more to do with women than buying drinks or buying sex. As a boy he'd been a slave to a woman who'd abused him. More than twenty-five years later, he still hadn't forgiven her sex.

Returning his rifle to its scabbard, Zeke dismounted. "Take my horse," he said to Hawk. "Give me about five minutes, then ride in."

"You think they're gonna let a big, ugly black man walk right into their camp?"

"I don't plan on asking," Zeke replied.

"Watch out. That woman knows how to use a rifle."

5

Holding his hands well away from his sides and dragging his feet to make as much noise as possible, Zeke started toward the bend in the creek that flowed into the San Pedro River. The shallow streambed would normally have been dry this time of year, but Arizona was green this spring. He just needed to get these women moving so he and Hawk could go on their way before anybody with an itching to own fine horseflesh figured out where they were.

Zeke pushed his way through a thicket of tamarisk. A nonnative plant that probably came to Mexico in hay from Spain, the bushes grew in dense thickets. Several stalks branched out from the base of the plant and towered over his head. Dense growth and thousands of tiny leaves made it impossible to see where he was going. Pushing limbs aside as he walked, he felt like he was moving blindly toward an unknown reception. The moment he pushed aside the last branch and stepped into the shade of an ancient and twisted cottonwood, a woman's voice rang out.

"Hold it right there."

"We're not here to cause trouble." Zeke didn't stop, but he did slow down. "We just want to move our horses past you, and we'll be on our way."

"How do I know you're telling the truth?"

He couldn't see the speaker. Her voice seemed to be coming from an area choked with mesquite.

"If you'll wait a few minutes, my partner will bring the horses up."

"Is that Indian your partner?"

"He's only half Indian."

"I don't trust him."

6

"If you'll hitch up your wagon and move on, you won't have to trust him."

Moving closer to the stream, Zeke rounded the mesquite thicket and came face to face with the most beautiful black woman he'd ever seen. Even as his brain registered that she couldn't be more than half black, his body registered its instantaneous response to a vision that would have caused a more world-weary man than Zeke to be rendered breathless.

"We can't move on," she said. "A wheel came off our wagon."

Zeke fought to force his brain to focus on what she was saying. He was too old to allow a beautiful woman to befuddle his wits. He was also well acquainted with what such beautiful women wanted from a man, and he knew he didn't have it. Yet this woman had the kind of beauty that could cause even the most sensible male to betray himself.

"I'll take a look," Zeke said, forcing himself to remember that this woman was an obstacle to his and Hawk's goal—getting their horses safely to their ranch. "Maybe Hawk and I can fix it."

For a moment she looked as though she wasn't going to let him pass. "Our camp is just ahead," she said before turning to lead the way.

Though she looked like the kind of woman who'd never been more than twenty feet from a mirror, she walked across the rock-strewn ground with a confident gait. Her tan skirt hugged her hips suggestively before flaring out to accommodate her stride. Though the sleeves of her blouse reached her wrists and the collar brushed her chin, any attempt at modesty was foiled by the way it fitted snugly across her breasts and tapered down to her slim waist.

"My name's Zeke Maxwell." Zeke had to get his mind off her body. "What's yours?"

"You won't be here long enough to need it."

"Maybe not, but it's common courtesy to introduce yourself, especially if someone offers to give you a helping hand." He could understand her not trusting him, but her rudeness was something else.

"It's Josie." Her tone didn't invite any comment.

The women had made camp on a sandy bank only a short distance away. It was shielded from view by another thicket of tamarisk and mature cottonwoods. The wheel had apparently come off when they pulled the wagon out of the creek. The vehicle listed at a crazy angle, the wheel leaning against its side. Three women occupied various positions near a small fire. A tall blond woman stood, feet well apart, as though ready to face any danger. The second woman, a brunette with hair halfway down her back, looked up momentarily before returning her attention to something she was cooking over the fire. The third, another brunette, lay on a blanket close to the fire. She propped herself up on her elbows when Zeke approached.

"Who's the blonde with the attitude?" Zeke asked.

"Suzette."

"How about the one cooking?"

"Anna."

"Why is the other woman covered with a blanket?"

"Laurie's been having chills for the last two days."

Going over to the wagon, Zeke saw immediately

what was wrong. "You lost the linchpin. Didn't any of you see it when it dropped?"

"What's a linchpin?" Suzette asked.

In the twenty-three years since the end of the war, Zeke had met hundreds of men and women coming West. Why didn't they realize they had to learn to do things for themselves? At the very least, they could learn something about the equipment and animals on which their lives depended. "It's the piece of wood that goes through the end of the axle to hold the wheel on. It looks like this," he said, pointing to the linchpin on the front wheel.

"It just looks like a piece of wood," Anna said. "Why would we notice it?"

Zeke wondered why women who knew so little thought they could start out on a journey like this by themselves. Either they were fools or they were running from something. Or someone.

"Can you fix it?" Josie asked.

Zeke turned to Suzette. "With Hawk's help, I can get the wheel on in less than a minute. It may take a little longer to find a suitable piece of wood to form the linchpin."

"There's wood all over the riverbanks," Suzette pointed out.

"Cottonwood is soft. Mesquite is better, but I'd prefer something hard like oak or hickory."

"You won't find that around here," Josie said.

"I'll probably have to cut a piece out of the wagon."

Suzette and Josie looked at each other, their doubt apparent.

"Don't worry. I won't hurt your wagon. I'll go get Hawk. We'll be back in a few minutes."

* * *

"Do you trust him?" Suzette asked.

Josie didn't answer right away, because she wasn't sure she knew the answer. She hadn't hesitated to shoot when she saw the Indian. She wasn't stupid enough to think all Indians were trying to kill her, but this was southeastern Arizona where the Apache had been at war until four years ago. Yet, it wasn't the Indian that concerned her. It was Zeke. Josie was used to men being attracted to her. In fact, she depended on it. She was a dancer and singer. If men weren't attracted to her, she didn't make money. What confused her was her attraction to Zeke. She was never attracted to men, not even handsome men. What was it about Zeke, a down-at-the-heels cowpoke, that could possibly hold her attention, much less her interest?

"I don't trust anybody," Josie said. "I intend to make sure those men leave as soon as they fix the wagon wheel."

"I think we ought to invite them to supper," Anna said.

"I want them gone before dark," Josie said.

Josie didn't like being attracted to Zeke. It made her feel vulnerable. That feeling brought back painful memories she'd sworn to forget. She would never allow herself to feel vulnerable again. Never.

"I agree with Anna," Laurie said.

"And what are you going to do when he tries to crawl into your bed?" Josie demanded.

"He won't be interested in me, not with you and Suzette around."

"Thanks," Josie snapped, "but I don't want him in my bed."

"He won't try. He's not that kind of man."

"You don't know anything about him," Josie fired back. But her anger lacked conviction because she felt the same thing. Entertaining men was her business; being able to judge character was a skill she'd acquired through experience. Zeke's physical attraction to her was strong, but he was the kind of man who would never allow his desires to overpower his will. Despite herself, that self-restraint intrigued Josie. What kind of man could deny his physical need when his body shook from the force of it?

The kind of man who would feel comfortable in the desert, who would know all about linchpins, and who wouldn't be intimidated by her rifle. She looked around and shivered with disgust. She hated the heat, the bugs, the dirt, the effort it took to wrest a living from the hostile earth of the desert. Why would anyone want to live here? The land was covered with plants that offered little shade and came equipped with thorns that were sometimes poisonous as well as painful. She dug her foot in the sand and kicked a smooth pebble into the riverbed. The flow of crystal-clear water was so meager it filled only a few feet of the thirty-foot-wide riverbed. Grass, the ever-present willow, and some small yellow flowers Josie couldn't identify had sprouted in the dry portions of the riverbed. Despite the clusters of flowers, she didn't like the desert.

"I intend to keep my eye on him every minute," Josie said.

"Me, too," Suzette added.

"You'd better keep your eye on the other one," Laurie cautioned. "I don't trust Indians."

"He's a half-breed," Josie pointed out.

Laurie remained unconvinced. "That's even worse. He doesn't belong on either side."

Having a white father who'd married his former slave, Josie knew how that felt. The sound of hooves against rocks caused the women to turn. Josie felt a shiver go through her when Zeke appeared astride an Appaloosa gelding. She didn't know a lot about horses, but she knew all about men who looked magnificent in the saddle. She couldn't deny that watching him ride toward her stirred something deep inside, but she had learned long ago to throttle any such attraction. Married or not, men wanted only one thing from a woman.

And that was the one thing Josie was determined no man would ever get from her.

Excitement began to build inside Suzette when she saw one mare after another follow Zeke around the bend in the stream. Bay, dun, sorrel, and one with the distinctive markings of an Appaloosa followed in the footsteps of their leader. "You didn't tell me they had horses," she exclaimed. "That first mare looks ready to foal. I wish I could be there when she does."

"If you want a horse, you can buy one when we get to Tombstone," Josie said.

Suzette knew Josie didn't understand her attachment to animals. Josie had grown up on a farm and hated anything to do with animals, but Suzette's young years had been spent in very different circumstances. The stepdaughter of a wealthy man, she'd been allowed to have virtually any pet she wanted—cats, dogs, and rabbits—but she'd been especially fond of her horses. She'd been devoted to a Morgan mare she was given on her sixth birthday. But everything had changed abruptly for her and her sister after their mother's death. Since then she'd never had the opportunity to do more than adopt a stray cat or feed and care for an injured dog.

"I can't afford a horse. Besides, it's not practical." Maybe the men would let her watch the horses while they put the wheel back on the wagon.

"Don't go wandering off looking at those horses while they're here," Josie said.

Suzette counted nine horses, all mares, before the second man appeared. Having grown up in the East and having heard numerous stories of the barbarous cruelty of Indians, Suzette tensed when she saw the single feather hanging down the back of the man's neck. He didn't look like the Indians she'd seen in Colorado. His skin was dark and his hair as black as a raven's wing, but his features were finely chiseled rather than rounded and blunt. Even though he was seated in the saddle, she could tell he was as tall and powerfully built as the black man.

While the horses fanned out to drink, the two men rode up together.

"I'm Zeke Maxwell," the black man said, introducing himself.

"I'm Hawk Maxwell," the other one said. He glanced at the wagon. "It shouldn't take but a minute to fix that wheel."

He must have realized all of them were staring, a question in their minds.

"We were adopted," Zeke explained.

13

"Adopted? You two?" Josie asked.

Suzette didn't understand why Josie had to be so abrupt with men. Suzette wasn't thrilled to have these two intimidating strangers so close, yet she couldn't help feeling a little sympathetic to them. It couldn't be easy being an outsider wherever you went.

"Yes, by a couple crazy enough to adopt eleven orphans at once," Zeke said, his manner as brusque as Josie's. "Now, do you want to keep poking around in something that's none of your business, or do you want us to fix that wheel?"

Suzette decided Zeke Maxwell was about as friendly as a prickly-pear cactus. Since she was a little afraid of Hawk, she agreed with Josie in wanting the men to leave as soon as possible. Not even the opportunity to be around the horses was enough to make her want them to stay past supper.

"Fix the wheel," Suzette said. "In return, you can eat with us." She couldn't make herself say she *wanted* them to stay.

"I don't eat with people who shoot first and ask questions later," Hawk said.

"If you don't want to be taken for a savage, you shouldn't go around wearing a feather in your hair," Josie said.

"If you don't want to be taken for a strumpet, you shouldn't go around in the desert wearing so much rouge," Hawk responded.

Familiar with the way Josie's temper could blaze out of control at the slightest provocation, Suzette intervened before the exchange could escalate into a full-fledged argument. "I think we all understand each other a little better now. First impressions can be misleading."

"Or they can be right on the mark." Zeke's grin was wide and insincere. "Too bad we won't get to know each other well enough to know which applies in this situation."

Zeke turned away abruptly. He and Hawk walked over to the wagon, apparently deciding how to handle their tasks without the need of words. Josie followed close on their heels, her rifle still in her grasp, her gaze riveted on the pair. Suzette wondered if Josie thought they might try to steal something from inside the wagon. She could have told her they wouldn't. They were the kind of men who would give, but never feel comfortable taking.

Suzette would have preferred that the women fix the wheel themselves, but she knew that none of them could have held up the wagon the way Zeke did by putting his shoulder under it. Or lifted up the wheel as though it weighed hardly anything as Hawk did. The bulging muscles in Zeke's back, shoulders, and legs belied his calm expression. He talked to Hawk as though holding up a wagon single-handedly was something he did every day. Hawk acted like it was nothing to pick up a wheel so heavy it had taken three of the women just to lean it against the wagon.

"All I need to do now is find a piece of wood I can make into a linchpin, and you can be on your way," Zeke said.

"Where's he going?" Suzette asked when Hawk walked away without a word.

"To see to the horses," Zeke said.

"Would he mind if I went, too?" Suzette asked. "I used to have two horses," she explained when Zeke looked surprised. "I miss them."

"Go if you want," Zeke said. "If Hawk doesn't want you around, he'll let you know quick enough."

"Are you always this rude?" Josie asked Zeke.

"Actually, I'm being very well-mannered. Isabelle would be proud of me."

Suzette didn't know who Isabelle was, but she didn't have a high opinion of the woman's notion of what constituted good manners. Suzette's stepfather had been a member of Quebec society, so she knew all about suitable behavior. As far as she was concerned, neither Zeke nor Hawk had a nodding acquaintance with it, but she decided a chance to be with the horses was worth a brush with a prickly personality.

Chapter Two

Hawk wasn't happy when he turned to see Suzette following him. He didn't mind helping the women, but that didn't mean he wanted to have anything more to do with them than necessary. Thirty-six years had given him no reason to believe a woman was anything but trouble.

Hawk studied the ground as it changed from sandbar to riverbank to desert, looking for a good place to picket Dusky Lady. The other mares didn't need to be hobbled, because they wouldn't leave without their leader. They needed to graze, and the abundant growth along the river would be enough to last them through the night.

"What do you want?" He didn't mean to sound rude or angry, but he didn't bother to modulate the tone of his voice.

"I love horses." Suzette's expression softened as she looked at the mares. "I miss having some of my own."

"You don't look like a woman who spends much time around horses."

Hawk had seen enough saloon women to recognize one the moment he saw her. Their clothes were different. It wasn't just the colors or even the style. It was the way the material clung to their bodies, accentuating their breasts, hips, legs, and shoulders. It was also the way saloon women wore their clothes, like they were part of their personalities, as if they were never able to take time off from the business of attracting men and seducing them into spending time and money on them. This woman didn't look like she'd ever saddled her own horse, much less cleaned up behind one.

"I had two horses when I was growing up," Suzette said. "They would take sugar or apple pieces right out of my hand."

"I don't make pets out of my horses."

"Mine were riding horses, one a Morgan very much like that mare."

Hawk looked at Dusky Lady and his anger subsided. "She's the best horse we own. She's in foal to a stud with Morgan blood. I'm hoping she'll drop a filly so I can breed them both to our new stud horse."

"What are you planning to do with these horses?"

"Breed quality horses for sale."

"I could never sell them if they were mine."

"Then you'd go broke and the bank would sell them for you."

Hawk didn't understand why some women seemed unable to think logically about animals that they depended on for a livelihood. If you had a product—no matter what the product was—you had to sell it if you wanted to make money. It was probably a good thing Suzette was a saloon girl. That way she only had to sell herself.

"I'd raise cows for money," Suzette said. "I'd keep the horses for myself."

She walked up to Dusky Lady and reached out to pat her neck. The mare raised her head from the scarce grass and thrust her muzzle against Suzette's chest. Suzette's peal of laughter sounded as out of place as an exotic bird; the look on her face was near bliss. She looped her arm around the mare's neck and leaned against her. Moments later she stepped back and walked around the mare, her fingers trailing along her sides, probing, caressing, all the while murmuring softly.

"She's going to have twins," Suzette announced.

"How do you know?" Hawk didn't want twins. He wanted a single, strong, sturdy foal.

"A woman knows."

How many times had Hawk heard that before? It translated as *There's no logical reason to support my opinion, but I'm going to stick with it because it's how I want things to be.* What was it about females that told them when another female—regardless of the species—was pregnant? Maybe it was the same kind of instinct that told a man when he was facing an enemy even before the other man said or did anything.

"Maybe they'll both be fillies," Suzette said.

She wandered among the horses, going from one to the other without fear or hesitation. Entranced, she talked to them, patted them, stroked them, hugged them.

"All the mares are in foal," Hawk told Suzette. "We're hoping to get to our ranch before they start dropping their foals. Travel isn't easy on new foals or nursing mares."

"Are these all the horses you have?"

"We have more at the ranch, but these mares are the best we've bought so far. We've followed back trails all the way from the Mogollon Rim to keep thieves off our track. That's part of the reason we were surprised to see your wagon. There must be easier ways to get where you're going."

"I'm sure there are." Though she responded to his questions, Suzette's attention was still focused on the horses. "But we didn't want anyone to follow us, either."

"Where are you headed?"

"To Tombstone. We hope to work at the Birdcage."

Tombstone had once been the biggest city between St. Louis and Los Angeles, but the town had begun to slip into decline after water started filling the silver mines four years earlier.

"Do you know how to get there?"

"Follow the San Pedro River."

That directive wouldn't get them to Tombstone, but they'd be close enough to make it the rest of the way. He couldn't imagine why they had started on such a journey in a wagon. It would have been much easier and faster on horseback. This woman certainly seemed more comfortable around horses than around him. She continued to weave among the mares like she was one of them.

"Zeke said your name was Suzette."

"That's right."

"That's an unusual name for an American."

"My parents were French Canadians."

Dusky Lady ambled over to Hawk, nipped at his sleeve. He glanced at Suzette, who was still talking to one of the mares. After his remark about not making pets of his horses, he didn't want her to see him feed Dusky Lady the sugar she'd come to expect from him each evening. He was certain Suzette would take it to mean he was a sucker at best, a liar at worst. But his loyalty was to the mare, so she got her sugar. While she lapped it up with her rough tongue, Hawk ran his hands over her sides, trying to feel the foal she carried inside. How did Suzette know she carried twins? Could she feel two sets of legs, two heads? The sugar gone, Dusky Lady nickered softly—her way of showing her appreciation—then turned back to graze. Hawk would let her seek out a favorite spot, then stake her out for the night. The sun had about two hours before it would sink over the horizon, but he knew it would be pointless to travel further today. It was unlikely they'd find a better camp spot. Even with the generous rains, it was difficult to find enough graze for eleven horses.

Curiosity drew Hawk's attention back to Suzette. She'd stopped moving among the horses and seemed content to watch them graze as she leaned against the trunk of a cottonwood. Occasionally she raised her hand to brush away a strand of blond hair a gust of wind had blown across her face. He wondered if she ever put a bandana over her hair. For some reason, the image appealed to him.

"Where did you grow up?" Hawk asked.

"Quebec."

21

He walked over to join her in the shade of the cottonwood. Briefly, her gaze turned to him. Apparently deciding he hadn't come too close, she turned back to watch the horses. She looked relaxed, even content, despite the fact that he knew she didn't trust him. He didn't know if he felt any different about her, but he did know he was attracted to her. Any man would have been. She wasn't as beautiful as Josie, but there was something earthy about her, a kind of simplicity that made her look at home under a tree in the middle of the desert. The movement of her hand capturing an errant strand of hair, the billowing of her skirt in the sudden gusts of wind, even the steady rise and fall of her chest as she slowly breathed in the warm, dry air contributed to the sense of rightness about her being here. Hawk decided it was good that they would be going their separate ways soon. He found far too much to like about this woman.

"How did a French Canadian from Quebec end up in Arizona?" he asked.

When she turned toward him, he saw that her eyes were a deeper blue than he'd first thought. He'd always associated deepening eye color with passion, but that couldn't be true in this case. She found the horses more attractive than him.

"My father died when I was a child." Suzette spoke softly but without hesitation. "Unfortunately, he was as improvident as he was handsome and charming. Having no means to support herself and her two daughters, my mother married the first man who offered for her, an austere Scot." She turned her gaze to a sorrel mare. "I don't know why he married my mother. He made it clear from the beginning that he thought the French were a godless lot. When my mother died, he married me off to the first man who would have me. My husband brought me out West and went off to the gold fields, where he had the bad luck to die of cholera. Having been reared to be a lady, I had no skills. It soon became clear that I would have to marry again, or work in a saloon, or become a soiled dove. Having had a father, stepfather, and husband who thought more of their breakfast than of me, I decided against marriage. Fortunately, I met Josie, who convinced me to work with her. Now, what's your story?"

Her gaze wandering back to the horses, Suzette moved out of the shade to pick flowers from some rabbit brush. She sniffed for fragrance but showed no reaction. She rubbed the flowers against her cheek as she looked for more. She appeared totally uninterested in whether Hawk would answer her question or not. Inexplicably, it was this apparent lack of curiosity that made it easier for Hawk to speak.

"My father was a Comanche chief, my mother a woman he captured. I lived with the Comanche until I was eleven and my mother was retaken by white men. After she and my sister died, nobody wanted me. Even my father thought I had become a spy for the white man. I became so rebellious, no one would have me. I didn't *want* anyone to want me until Isabelle grabbed up eight orphans like me, and we ended up on Jake's ranch. Next thing you know, we're taking his cows to Santa Fe." He chuckled softly, shook his head at the memory of the cattle drive that changed his life. "By the time we got there, he and Isabelle were crazy about each other and determined to adopt all of us. Zeke and

I have trailed cows over most of the West, hired out as guards, cowhands, drivers, gunmen, just about any job you can do out here."

"Where's the rest of your family?"

"Back in Texas."

"Why aren't you back there with them?"

That was something Hawk didn't mean to share with a stranger. He unwound the picket rope from his waist and headed to where Dusky Lady was grazing. She barely lifted her head for him to loop the rope around her neck before going back to cropping the sparse grass that grew in tufts among the cactus and under the outstretched branches of the mesquite and cottonwoods. He played out the rope and tied it to a stake he'd pounded into the ground with a rock. Satisfied that Dusky Lady wouldn't pull it up during the night, he turned his gaze to Suzette, who had wandered farther in her search for flowers. She had a handful now, some paintbrush, what looked like a lily or a poppy, and more yellow flowers.

"Last year we found a ranch we liked when we were running cows up from Mexico," Hawk continued, "so we bought it. It's a little run-down, but getting it cheap allowed us to put more money into buying quality horses."

She didn't have to know that he and Zeke had saved quite a bit of money over the years, or that Jake had tried to buy the ranch and the horses for them.

"You married?" Suzette asked.

"No."

"Zeke?"

"Him, neither."

"A man rich enough to own a ranch is rich enough to have a wife."

That statement irritated Hawk, but she didn't seem to attach any importance to it. She had paused on the shady side of a mesquite bush and appeared to be searching some vines for fruit, possibly grapes. She moved the leaves aside with a gentleness that was startling in such a harsh land. She was more likely to find a bird's nest than anything edible.

"Best not to linger in shady places during the day," Hawk said. "Could be a snake has curled up there out of the sun."

She jumped back so abruptly, she dropped some of her flowers. Feeling guilty, Hawk walked over, picked them up, and handed them to her. "I didn't mean to frighten you," he said. "Most snakes out here aren't poisonous."

"One of the boys who used to come to the saloon died of a rattlesnake bite," she said, her eyes still wide and unsettled. "He looked awful when they brought him in. His leg was black and swollen so bad the skin had cracked." She shuddered. "He was so nice and sweet, the girls used to argue over who would get to dance with him or sit with him while he drank his beer. It's a shame that snake didn't bite one of the other men."

Whether a woman served food, brought drinks, danced, or kept men company at the tables, working in a saloon was a rough life because they served rough men. Many men were engaged in a life-and-death struggle with Mother Nature to wrest her riches from the earth—as well as a life-and-death struggle with other men to keep what they found. They worked hard, played hard, and often died hard. They had little use for women other than as company when they drank or as a release for their sexual energy.

"Why haven't you married again?" Hawk asked. "As pretty as you are, I'm sure you've had more than one chance."

When Suzette's gaze met his, he saw none of the softness he'd seen in her eyes when she'd wandered among the horses or searched for flowers. Her eyes were bright, even hard, and her gaze steady. He could almost believe she was squaring up to face an adversary.

"None of the men who were interested in me showed any desire to provide for a family. Nor were they swayed by any moral obligation to be a good provider. Out of necessity I learned I could do better on my own."

Her gaze held his; the challenge remained. If she was waiting for him to argue with her, she'd be disappointed. He didn't want a wife any more than she wanted a husband.

She heaved a sigh and turned to him. "I ought to be getting back. Josie is liable to come looking for me soon."

"Why?"

Her lips twisted in a faint smile, and she held her hair away from her face with her right hand. "Josie doesn't trust men. She'll probably figure the only reason I've stayed away from camp this long is because you forced me."

"I didn't ask you to follow me."

"That wouldn't make any difference to her."

"That's stupid."

26

Suzette's expression turned hard. "Not if you knew what happened to Josie." She walked past him before turning back. "You're invited to eat with us," she said. A lazy smile played across her lips, but her eyes were full of caution. "We could never have fixed that wheel on our own."

"Someone would have come by sooner or later."

"Maybe, but I'm glad it was you."

She turned and walked away without giving any indication what she might have meant by those last words. She probably referred to the horses. That she preferred them over him seemed obvious, but there was something else in her manner that Hawk couldn't identify. He had no trouble identifying what it was about her that attracted him: everything, even the view of her as she walked away. Her stride was long and fluid, swinging easily from the hips in a manner that caused them to sway gently from side to side. He was acutely aware of the body hidden beneath the layers of material. Telling himself he should turn away, he continued to watch until she disappeared around a willow thicket. For several moments he continued to stare, his mind filled with images of her wandering among the horses, pressing yellow flowers against her cheek, her hand pulling her hair away from her face.

An uncomfortable tightness in his jeans brought him back to the present. He cursed as he rearranged himself. It was useless to let his physical attraction for Suzette get to him. Even if there had been an opportunity to act on it, she'd made it clear she wanted nothing to do with him. Wishing for anything else would be stupid beyond belief.

* * *

"That was a mighty good supper," Zeke said to Anna. "There's a lot to be said for traveling with a wagonload of supplies."

"Those supplies wouldn't have done us much good if you hadn't come along to fix the wheel," Anna said.

"And cut up the wagon in the process," Josie added.

"It was only one rib," Anna said. "You can hardly notice it's gone."

"I noticed," Josie snapped.

Zeke had found the perfect wood for his linchpin in one of the ribs that supported the canvas cover of the wagon. Josie had been furious when he removed the rib despite her objections. She hadn't been any more pleased when he said all the linchpins needed to be replaced. The rib had provided him with enough wood for spares, but Josie hadn't been mollified.

Zeke and Hawk sat crossed-legged in the sand about twenty feet back from the fire. Suzette sat with her feet under her, a position that made Zeke uncomfortable just looking at her. Anna sat with her feet out to the side, Laurie, leaning up on her elbow. Josie had been too agitated to sit and had eaten her meal standing up. Even now, her stew lay unfinished in her bowl, as she shifted her weight from foot to foot, occasionally moving a few feet before pausing again. Zeke felt certain she was itching to tell them they'd been amply repaid for their courtesy and it was time to leave. He felt the same way, but watching her practically bite her tongue to keep from telling them to vanish made him want to stay just to see if she'd put her thoughts into words.

"You ought to stay on flat ground as much as possible," Zeke said. "Losing a linchpin isn't a big problem. Breaking a spoke or a wheel would be."

"We tried," Anna said, "but sometimes the only way was to use the riverbed."

Zeke knew that. He and Hawk used riverbeds as often as they could. Despite being littered with rocks, they were usually more level than existing trails and offered a more direct route. In addition, the water would cover their tracks when they didn't want to be followed.

"You shouldn't be out here by yourselves," Zeke said. "Why didn't you hire a man to drive you?"

"Anna is perfectly capable of driving," Josie said.

"I was thinking more of protection."

"I know how to use a rifle."

"Nevertheless, it's not a good idea for women to travel alone in this territory. There are too many things that could happen to you."

"Like losing a wheel."

Zeke couldn't understand Josie's belligerence. He could see no reason for her to argue with everything he said. He was just trying to help her stay out of trouble. And a woman as beautiful as Josie was bound to run into difficulty. If her temper didn't cause it, her beauty would. She was the kind of woman men couldn't stay away from even when they knew being close to her was dangerous.

"Somebody would have come along, or we'd have figured it out," Josie said.

Hell, he wasn't going to argue with a woman who refused to listen to reason. He'd be better advised to talk to his horses. At least they acted like he knew what he was talking about.

"What are you doing out here in the first place? I'd have thought there was plenty of work in Globe."

"There was until the fine ladies of the town decided dancing girls were a danger to their husbands' morals." Josie's snort of indignation was loud and rude. "Even a cracked mirror should have told the wives their *appearance* was the greatest obstacle to marital fidelity."

"Don't tell me they tried to close down the saloons." Zeke had heard of women trying but not of any succeeding.

"They realized men have to eat and drink," Suzette explained. "They just didn't think the customers needed to be entertained at the same time."

"We didn't do anything but sing and dance," Anna said, "but they didn't believe us."

"They needed somebody to blame," Josie said, "so they picked us."

"They picked *you*." Laurie's voice was too weak to convey any of the anger or animosity she might have felt.

Apparently, the conversation had stirred up Josie's resentment at her treatment. She talked with her hands, flinging the last bits of her stew into the air with one particularly angry gesture. Some pieces landed in the fire and sizzled noisily before bursting into tiny flames and leaving the unpleasant smell of burned meat.

"Forget about it," Suzette said with a shrug. "We got our money, and we'll be able to find jobs in Tombstone. I don't like to stay in one town too long, anyway. The men get used to your act and start to want something else from you."

"Do you want some more stew?" Anna asked. "There's still a little bit left."

Zeke and Hawk both got up and took their bowls over for the remainder. Zeke didn't like to eat until he was uncomfortably full, but he couldn't see any reason to waste good food.

"Whoever saw a man who didn't want more to eat?" Josie asked with a sharpness that would take the edge off any man's appetite. "Why don't you just give them the pot and let them finish what's left?"

"Isabelle says a gentleman never eats out of the pot," Zeke said, his irritation at Josie's jibes beginning to get to him. "Hawk and I eat out of bowls even when we're on the trail by ourselves. Just because we're camping outdoors doesn't mean we don't know how to act." Zeke handed his bowl to Anna, then turned to Josie, waiting for her reply. She glared at him, shrugging her shoulders in a manner that suggested she didn't believe a word Zeke said.

"I met a man once who had lovely manners," Laurie said. "He said he was the son of an earl."

"And you believed that?" Josie asked.

"Hawk and I took some blooded bulls up to Monty Randolph's ranch in Wyoming a few years ago," Zeke said before Laurie could reply. "He had an earl and a couple of younger sons of a Scottish duke staying with him. They wanted Monty's advice on buying a ranch in Montana."

Zeke doubted that Josie knew of Monty Randolph or the reputation of the Randolph family, but she didn't challenge his statement.

"I think as many men know good manners as

31

women," Anna said. "It just seems men can do without them easier."

"If you spent a winter in a mining camp or on some cattle drive, you'd understand," Zeke said.

Zeke decided the conversation was getting too heavy, the tension in the air too strained. He ate the rest of his stew standing up. "Thanks for the food and the coffee," he said. "If you don't mind, Hawk and I will say good night. We plan to head out at daybreak, so we'll try not to wake you."

"We're heading out at the same time," Suzette told him. "We want to get to Tombstone as soon as we can."

"Just keep the river in sight and you can't miss it."

"Suzette said you have a ranch only a few miles from Tombstone," Anna said. "Since we're all going practically to the same place, why don't we go together?"

Four women started to speak at the same time, but Josie's voice rose above the others'. She moved so close to the fire, Zeke could see its flames reflected in her eyes. "We don't need anybody to protect us," she said.

"I'm sure they'll want to travel as fast as possible," Suzette said. "It'll be better if the mares reach the ranch before they start dropping their foals."

Zeke turned to Anna. "Thanks for the invitation, but Josie and Suzette are right. You don't need us to protect you, and we do need to get to the ranch as soon as we can."

Anna frowned, clearly unhappy with Josie. "Something could happen to the wagon."

"If you have to, you can ride your mules," Zeke said.

"I don't ride mules," Josie declared.

It was on the tip of Zeke's tongue to ask what made her so uppity, but he figured he already knew. Any woman who looked like Josie got pretty much what she wanted. It must have really put her nose out of joint to be driven out of town by a bunch of dowdy housewives, but it was no use taking her anger out on Hawk and him. If she had turned it on the women who'd attacked her, she might still have a job.

But looking at Josie as she glared at him across the fire made him wonder if she would ever be able to keep any job for long. She seemed so angry, so determined to attack anyone who disagreed with her, that he was sure she'd either be fired or walk out after a few months. Even beauty like hers could compensate only so long for a cantankerous personality.

"I'm sure you'll manage without our help," Zeke said. He bent down and picked up the pot Anna had used to cook the stew. "Since you cooked, we'll clean up. Give Hawk your bowls."

Three women readily accepted his offer. Only Josie seemed reluctant, but she handed Hawk her bowl after a brief hesitation.

Zeke was relieved to walk away from the camp. He could feel the tension ease a little bit with each step he took into the darkness. By the time he and Hawk reached the riverbed, the camp was only a red glow in the distance. Zeke squatted down and began to scour the inside of the pot with sand. "I don't know what's bothering Josie, but I'm surprised the men didn't run her out of town without waiting for the women."

"Some man has given her a rough time."

"Hell, some man has given every woman a rough time, but it hasn't turned all of them into man haters."

"You shouldn't judge her until you know what happened," Hawk said. "It could be that—"

Hawk broke off at the unmistakable sound of a horse approaching. Both men dropped their work, drew their guns, and headed back to the camp on silent feet.

Chapter Three

Josie hated to admit it even to herself, but the moment she heard the horse approach, she looked toward the river to see if Zeke was returning. She could even feel his name rising in her throat before she forced it back down. She wasn't going to depend on any man to protect her. "I think we ought to get out of sight," she said.

"I'm not sure I can move." Laurie grimaced as she tried to sit up.

Josie saw Anna's eyes dart fearfully to the campfire. "Whoever it is will see our fire," Anna said. "I think we ought to call Zeke and Hawk."

"We can take care of ourselves." Josie had retrieved her rifle from where she'd propped it against the wagon. She turned, pointing it in the direction of the sounds that were coming closer all the time.

"Suppose it's a bunch of men come to carry us off?" Anna said.

"It's just one." Suzette's features had turned hard. "But I can only guess his purpose."

"Move away from the campfire."

Zeke's voice came from the shadows. It made Josie angry to realize she felt better just knowing he was there.

"If you need help, just say so," Zeke said when Laurie was slow to get to her feet.

"I'd be obliged," Laurie said.

Materializing out of the dark like a shadow, Zeke picked Laurie up and lowered her into the wagon, then pulled Anna behind it. "Nobody comes out until I say so."

"Where's Hawk?" Suzette asked.

"Guarding the horses. Until we know who's out there, we don't know what he's after."

Suzette had retreated into the deep shadows, but Josie hadn't budged.

"Don't stand there," Zeke hissed. "Move."

"I'm not afraid of any man," Josie said. "I've got my rifle. I'll—"

Zeke didn't wait for her to finish her sentence. Nor did he try to persuade her to change her mind. He simply walked up behind her, clamped one hand over her mouth and the other around her waist, picked her up, carried her to where Suzette stood, and set her down.

"If you want to risk getting yourself killed, do it when you won't endanger other people," Zeke snapped.

"If you ever do anything like that again, I'll shoot you." Josie's body shook with such fury, she could hardly form the words. "I don't need you to—"

"Look," Zeke said, interrupting her. "I won't tell you

what to do when you sing and dance in a saloon, and you don't tell me what to do out on a trail. I was guarding cattle from rustlers before you were born."

"That doesn't make you—"

"It sure as hell does. Now be quiet. No point in telling whoever is out there that you'd rather shoot me than him."

"I *know* you. I don't know him."

"You don't know me, either."

Josie choked back a sharp response. Just because Zeke was a man didn't mean she knew him. She'd have been incensed if he'd said he knew her simply because she was a woman. Besides, she wasn't sure she knew just how she felt about him. Despite being so mad at Zeke she wanted to bang her rifle stock against his hard head, she could still feel his hands on her waist, still feel the lingering sensation of his hard muscles against the length of her body. Rather than feel distaste or repugnance, her skin had come alive with almost painful sensitivity. How could this man do that to her when she didn't even like him?

"What are you going to do?" Laurie asked Zeke in a small, frightened voice.

"I won't know until I see who's coming and find out what he wants."

"He can't be friendly, can he? I mean, he wouldn't be riding about in the dark if he was."

"Sure he might," Zeke replied. "He could be hungry and looking for a meal. He could be lonely and looking for a little company for the night. He's not trying to hide. He's riding straight in and letting his horse make plenty of noise."

Josie had seen too many men who on first appearance seemed to be friendly. Later, when they saw something they wanted, their attitude changed. If this stranger wanted company, he could bed down with Zeke and Hawk.

Moonlight cast the rider into silhouette. He was alone, riding with one hand on the reins and the other held up to show he wasn't holding a weapon.

"Hold up," Zeke called. "What's your name and what do you want?"

"My name's Ben Norman." He spoke from where he'd pulled up about twenty feet from the campfire. "I'm looking for a woman named Anna. She used to sing at the Golden Slipper in Globe."

"What do you want with her?" Zeke asked.

"That's my business. She was traveling with three other women. If you haven't seen them, I'll be on my way."

"If I do see her, what message should I give her?" Zeke asked.

"Just tell her Ben Norman's looking for her. She left Globe before I could tell her something important."

"Ben, I'm here," Anna said, her voice choked with excitement as she moved from behind the wagon.

"What are you doing here with that man?" Ben asked as he walked his horse closer to the campfire.

Ben's tone was sharp and accusing, probably because he could see only Anna and Zeke. Josie stepped from behind the wagon.

"We're all here," she said to Ben. "This man and his friend stopped to help us fix a wagon wheel that came off."

Ben's gaze returned to Anna. "Why did you leave? I told you I was coming back as soon as I could."

"Some ladies got us fired because they thought we were undermining their husbands' morals. What good would your coming back do? You couldn't make them change their minds."

Ben dismounted, ground hitched his horse, and started toward Anna, a warm smile on his face. "I don't care about those women. I only care about you. I want to marry you."

Josie's surprise was nothing compared to Anna's. Her mouth fell open. She turned white, then red. Zeke reached out to steady her before Ben took his place.

"Are you sure?" Anna asked. She gazed into Ben's eyes as if she hoped to find the answer to her question written there.

"Of course I'm sure," Ben said, a touch of impatience in his voice. "I'd be a fool to sell my claim if I wasn't."

"You sold your claim?" Anna asked in disbelief.

"Yep. Got a real good price for it, too."

"But you've been working that claim practically night and day for a year."

"Hell, it's just a claim. I was only working like a fool so I could get the money to buy a ranch like I always wanted, like we talked about."

Anna gazed up into Ben's eyes with what Josie thought was a mooncalf look. She was disgusted to see her friend so ready to throw herself into the arms of a man, ready to blindly entrust her future to him.

"I thought you were just making up stories like everybody else," Anna said.

"I sorta was until I met you." Ben looked almost as lovesick as Anna. "Then everything started to make sense."

A whimper caused Josie to turn around. Laurie was

leaning against the wagon, staring at Anna and Ben, tears running down her face. "They're perfect for each other," she whispered.

Josie wasn't sure there was any such thing as a man who was perfect for a woman, but she tried to be pleased for Anna. They'd all done their best to keep her from falling in love with Ben—falling for a miner was just about the most stupid thing a woman could do—but they hadn't been able to stop her. Anna had tried to hide it, but they all knew she cried most of the night before they left Globe. From the looks of things, she was about to start crying again.

"You know this man?" Zeke asked Josie.

"He was a regular at the saloon. I knew he liked Anna, but I never thought he'd want to marry her."

"Why not? She's pretty, and she can cook."

"Just like a man! Concerned only with his physical needs."

"No. I just haven't had time to learn much else about her except that she seems nice, easy to get along with, and not prone to falling into hysterical fits. That's important. Men hate hysterical women, because we never know what's wrong with them or how to fix it."

"Since it's nearly always a man who is the cause of the hysterics, you might begin by getting as far away as possible."

"Now, when did you ever know a woman who was that easy to figure out?"

Josie wished the moon was full and bright. She had the feeling the expression on Zeke's face would tell her something very important, but she couldn't see anything in the shadows.

"Will you marry me?" Ben was holding Anna's hands in his, pressing them against his chest.

"You know I will."

"Do you want a wedding?"

"No. There's nobody except Suzette, Josie, and Laurie I'd want to come."

"They can come back with us."

Josie was sure Ben didn't care whether they took part in Anna's marriage or not. "You two go back alone," she said. "If we come, it'll just cause trouble."

"But I want to share my happiness with you," Anna protested.

"We can share it tonight." Suzette emerged from the dark to walk over and embrace Anna. "You can't leave until morning, so we've got all night."

With Josie's help, Laurie joined Suzette and Anna. In a moment Ben found himself closed out of the circle of women.

Zeke crossed over to Ben. "You might as well come sit with me. There's something about weddings that makes women close out the man who's making it all possible."

Ben didn't look at all happy about spending time with a black man he'd never seen before instead of the woman he'd trailed fifty miles.

"Don't worry. It only lasts until the marriage vows are said. After that, she'll be impatient to be alone with you."

"You been married before?" Ben asked.

"No, but there've been a lot of weddings in my family."

Ben continued to stare at Anna, who seemed com-

41

pletely absorbed in sharing her happiness with her friends. Occasionally she'd glance up at Ben, cast him a broad smile, then turn her attention back to her friends. Zeke thought this closing of the circle around the prospective bride was akin to a primitive rite. Maybe it was some sort of mysterious channeling that changed her from a girl into a woman. Whatever it was, it was clear that men had no part in it.

"Do you have any liquor in your saddlebags?" Zeke asked.

"One bottle. Why?" Ben asked.

"You might as well break it out. It's going to be a long night. Come on. I need to tell my partner you're not trying to steal our horses. If you're gone for a while, maybe Anna will start to miss you."

Ben left to get the liquor, and Zeke turned back to the women. They were standing in a circle, their arms entwined, their heads inclined toward the center. Occasionally a laugh rose above the soft murmuring of voices. Moonlight reflecting on Anna's hair caused it to stand out in marked contrast to the others. It was almost as though the cosmos was proclaiming that she was the woman of the moment, that the whole world should stop and take note of her happiness.

"Sounds like you've found a good spot and have a good plan," Zeke said after they'd listened to Ben's enthusiastic description of his new ranch. "With a little luck, you ought to do quite well."

"I know finding silver was a stroke of luck," Ben said, "a one-time thing. I don't mean to waste it."

The three men were sitting in a small clearing that enabled them to keep an eye on the horses and still keep the women's campsite in view. About half of the bottle was gone, thanks mainly to Ben. Zeke drank little, Hawk none. Zeke had encouraged Ben to tell them about his plans for his ranch. Zeke and Hawk offered a few suggestions, but mostly they let Ben talk to take his mind off the fact that he'd effectively been banished from the company of the woman he loved. It wasn't much of a bachelor party, but it was the best they could do.

"I think I'd better turn in," Ben said. He wasn't drunk, but his speech was beginning to be a little slurred. Fifty miles, plus the distance he had to travel from his ranch to town, was a long ride to make in one day.

"Bring your horse over here. You can bed down with us," Zeke said.

"I thought I'd bed down next to Anna."

"You can try if you want." Zeke couldn't keep a hint of amusement from his voice.

Ben got to his feet. His muscles had stiffened from sitting so long, and he stumbled before regaining his balance. "She's going to be my wife. She ought to want me to sleep next to her."

"You think she's going to let him?" Hawk asked after Ben had started toward the campsite.

"Don't know," Zeke said. "I never have understood women."

"Hasn't stopped you from admiring Josie."

Zeke directed a hard look at his friend. "I'll be the first man to admit Josie is a beautiful woman, but I'll also be the first one to tell you she's as hard as nails. I feel perfectly safe admiring her beauty because I know she wants nothing to do with me."

"How about you? You want something to do with her?"

Zeke wasn't sure how to answer that question. It was useless to deny that he was attracted to her. Any man would be. What disturbed him was the fear that this might be more than simple physical attraction. From the moment he'd set eyes on her, he'd had the disquieting feeling that Josie was someone special in a way that had nothing to do with her beauty. It made absolutely no sense. They were about as close to opposites as two people could be.

"It wouldn't matter if I did." Zeke felt like a fool admitting even that much to Hawk, but they'd been closer than most real brothers for too long to start withholding confidences now, especially about something like this. "You saw what she's like, the way she dresses. You also saw the way she reacted to me."

"She could be very different once you get to know her."

Too restless to remain still, Zeke got to his feet. It angered him that he could be so agitated over any woman, but especially a woman like Josie. Everything about her—her clothes, the face paint she used, the way she looked at him, the way she talked—all of it practically shouted that she found everything about the kind of life Zeke lived distasteful. The way she acted toward him—moving away when he approached, glaring at him, resenting his help and trying to refuse it—said that she disliked him in particular. He kicked the sand, but the futile gesture only made him more disgusted with himself.

"She's not going to be any different," he said, turning back to Hawk. "The trouble is, I want her to be."

Zeke forced himself to stop pacing and sit back down. If he kept this up, he'd make the horses restless. Besides, stewing over the situation wasn't doing him any good. He had to accept the fact there were some things even his iron will couldn't control. His best course of action would be to relax and let the situation take care of itself. He and Hawk would leave tomorrow. As soon as they reached their ranch, he'd have too much to do to worry about a woman he'd never see again.

But what if she got that job in Tombstone? It wasn't so far from their ranch that he couldn't ride over once in a while. Hell! She couldn't stay in Tombstone. Besides, the town was dying now the mines were flooded. Maybe she'd go to Bisbee. Even better, maybe Zac Randolph could get her a job at his old saloon in San Francisco. That was far enough to guarantee he'd never see her again.

"Just how different do you want her to be?" Hawk asked.

"You know what I want," Zeke said, his voice devoid of anger, even lacking energy. "You want the same thing, but we both know we're not going to get it." He sighed. Dammit. All his brothers had managed to find women who could love them. What was so different about him and Hawk? He knew the answer to that question. He also knew that saying it wasn't fair wouldn't change anything. "This thing with Josie probably won't last more than a couple of days. It's probably the shock of finding such a beautiful woman out here."

"A beautiful black woman?"

"That, too. What about Suzette? She spent nearly an hour with you."

45

"She spent it with the horses. I just happened to be there."

Zeke looked at Hawk from under his hat. "You like her?"

"I don't let myself think about that anymore."

"I wish you could tell me how you do it."

Hawk removed his dusty hat and slapped it against his jeans. "I guess it's because I know nothing will ever change. Dusky Lady is as close as I'm going to come to finding a female to love me."

"I wouldn't advise you to get between her and that stud when she comes into heat."

They were both laughing when Ben returned, leading his horse and looking glum. "Josie said it was bad luck for the groom to be with the bride on the night before the wedding."

"Pull up a chunk of ground and make yourself comfortable," Zeke said. "But if you snore, you'll have to bed down across the creek."

Despite the late hour, Suzette didn't feel sleepy. She supposed it was the excitement of Anna's marriage. She was sorry that she wouldn't be with Anna when she stood up with Ben before the justice of the peace, but she was glad she wasn't going back to Globe. And to be frank, she was relieved she wouldn't be forced to witness another woman's happiness. If Josie hadn't been adamant, Anna would have spent the night by Ben's side. She hadn't looked any happier than Ben when Josie made him leave. She'd climbed inside the wagon with a muttered good night.

Suzette stirred the coals of the dying fire with a cottonwood limb, mulling over whether to put on any more wood. The temperature had dropped at least twenty degrees since the sun went down. If she stayed up, she'd need something warm to put on. She looked in the direction of the men's camp. She wondered if they were still talking or if they'd gone to sleep, if Dusky Lady was still grazing, or if she'd lain down to rest. Did horses in the wild actually lie down when they could sleep standing up? Wasn't it too dangerous if wolves or cougars were around? Hawk would know. Maybe she'd ask him tomorrow before he and Zeke left.

She poked at the fire some more, causing sparks to rise in the air. She stopped. Was it possible for sparks to start a fire in the desert? Hawk would know that, too. She wondered what he was sleeping on. She couldn't remember whether she'd seen a bedroll tied to his saddle, but surely he had one. The desert floor was covered with too many tiny thorny plants to sleep on the bare ground. She wondered if he slept in his clothes or without them.

Suzette tossed her stick into the fire and gripped her hands across her chest as a slight shiver shook her body. The last thing she needed was to be thinking of Hawk's unclothed body. She'd sung and danced in front of hundreds of men, maybe thousands, since her husband had died, but she couldn't recall a single one who had engendered such a strong physical response in her. It was almost as if there was something connecting her to Hawk that allowed his energy to flow into her body, that caused her to be acutely aware of his physical presence. She had been married for a year, so the source of that attraction was no mystery to her. It was sexual, and it was very strong.

Another shiver shook her body. She couldn't decide whether it was from the cold or the sexual need that was burning a hole in her insides, but she was reluctant to disturb the other women to get a cloak from the wagon. She'd never loved her husband—he'd been chosen for her—but she'd developed a keen appreciation for their physical relationship. In the five years since his death, she'd had a difficult time sublimating her need for a man. Most of the time, she simply concentrated on her work, or on the fact that she wouldn't have gone to bed with any of the men she knew even if her body had been on fire.

She didn't feel that way about Hawk. The fact that the horses trusted him, that Dusky Lady would walk up to him to take sugar from his hand, proved he was reliable as well as kind. You could tell a lot about a man from the animals in his care. Hawk might be just as attractive on the inside as he was on the outside.

Which was exactly what Suzette was afraid of, especially now, when Anna's impending marriage was causing her to feel so needy. She hated feeling vulnerable, unable to cope with the challenges before her. She knew she *could* cope with them, and had been doing so for years. What was it about Hawk that unsettled her so? She couldn't have fallen in love with him so quickly; it was probably pure lust. Yet it would be impossible to satisfy even that simple physical need, because they were going their separate ways in the morning.

"If you're planning to stay up all night, you need something to keep you warm."

Josie's voice jerked Suzette out of her reverie. "I didn't know anybody else was awake."

"I couldn't sleep, either. Anna is still whimpering, and Laurie's breathing has gotten noisier."

"You think she's worse?"

"I don't know. She's been blubbering all night, saying she's so happy for Anna she can't stop crying. I'm glad we're close to her parents' place."

"I think I'll sleep outside tonight," Suzette said. She didn't want to be kept awake. What she needed was oblivion until tomorrow solved her problem by taking Hawk away.

Josie knelt by the fire, poured herself some coffee, and sipped the bitter brew. She didn't like coffee, but she needed something to wake her up. She hadn't slept well because Laurie had gotten worse during the night. She and Suzette had done all they could, but nothing helped. Curious about why they were up, Hawk had come to see if they needed anything. After talking with Laurie, he'd gotten his saddlebags, put some herbs in water, and brewed a tea that lowered Laurie's temperature and eased her breathing so she could sleep. Hawk and Suzette were with her now, discussing what they ought to do.

"I feel bad leaving you when Laurie's so sick," Anna said.

Ben stood next to Anna, a troubled look on his face. Josie knew he was worried that Anna might refuse to leave.

"There's nothing you can do," Josie said. "Hawk says he has enough herbs to take care of her until we reach her parents' place. Suzette and I will keep an eye on her. There's no need for you to stay."

49

"I know, but I still feel guilty."

"No point if there's nothing you can do," Ben said.

Josie had to give him credit. He was trying not to show how impatient he was to leave. His arm around Anna's shoulder tightened. He was visibly staking his claim to her. Josie resented his possessiveness. It was just like a man to think a woman belonged to him once she agreed to be his wife.

"We need to be going if we're going to get married today," Ben said to Anna. "And we gotta get married today," he said when Anna seemed to hesitate. "I don't think I can stand being separated from you for another night."

"Oh, Ben, I'm sorry. It's just that I'm so worried about Laurie."

"You don't need to worry," Josie said.

Ben took Anna's elbow and tried to steer her toward his horse. "Come on, honey, let's go."

Anna held her ground. "Are you sure?" she asked Josie.

"Positive. Now get out of here and be happy."

Anna threw her arms around Josie. "I wish you were going back with us."

"We'll find better jobs in Tombstone."

Anna released Josie and turned as Suzette climbed out of the wagon. "Promise you'll write."

"You'll have to write, too," Suzette replied. "If your first child is a girl, you can name her after me."

"I'll have three girls so I can name one after each of you."

Ben smiled down at her. "We can have as many as you want."

"I've got to say good-bye to Laurie, and then I'll be ready to go," Anna said to Ben.

"You take good care of her," Josie said to Ben after Anna disappeared inside the wagon. "If you don't, I'll come after you."

"I'm crazy about that woman." Ben's eyes were on the back of the wagon where Anna had disappeared. "I'll do everything I can to make sure she's happy."

"I'll hold you to that promise," Josie said. "Now put her on that horse and get going. We need to get started ourselves."

Anna emerged from the wagon with tears running down her cheeks. She cried some more as she hugged Suzette and Josie good-bye once again.

"Go," Josie said, pushing her toward Ben. "Your future husband is about to bust open with impatience to have you to himself."

Ben lifted Anna into the saddle, then climbed up behind her. Anna kept looking over her shoulder, waving to them, until she was out of sight. Her disappearance left Josie feeling empty. They'd been friends for more than two years, but she knew that part of the reason she was feeling so low was that Anna had found a man who made her very happy. Anna's happiness reinforced Josie's own sense of loneliness.

"I guess I'll have to drive now that Anna's gone," Suzette said.

"Why? Do you think I can't handle a pair of mules?" Josie asked.

"You can take care of Laurie and figure out what you're going to fix for dinner."

"You're better at sitting with sick people than I am."

Josie felt guilty about not wanting to sit with Laurie, but being strong and self-reliant, she didn't understand someone like Laurie. She tended to grow impatient with Laurie's dependence on other people.

"You can both sit with her," Zeke said.

Josie hadn't heard him come up. "And how can we do that?" she snapped.

"I'll be driving. Hawk and I are going with you."

The words popped out of Josie's mouth before she realized what she was saying. "Then I'm staying here."

Chapter Four

Zeke had been counting on leaving at dawn, but Hawk had decided they should stay close to Laurie until they could turn her over to her parents. She hadn't gotten any worse, but she hadn't gotten better either, and traveling would be hard on her. Zeke never argued with Hawk about anything medical.

"Do you have everything you'll need?" Zeke asked.

"What are you talking about?" Josie snapped.

"Food, something to heat water in, and enough clothes to keep warm at night."

"Josie's not going anywhere by herself," Suzette said, her attitude a mixture of frustration, irritation, and amusement.

"She said she was."

"Josie's got a real problem with men, especially with men telling her what to do. Sometimes it makes her say things she doesn't mean. And even when she does mean what she says," Suzette continued when Josie tried to interrupt, "she can't always do it. Hitch up the mules. We'll be ready when you are."

Disgusted with himself for feeling relieved, Zeke headed off to get the mules, grinning at the lecture Suzette was giving Josie. Suzette was making no attempt to keep her voice down, and Josie made even less. Zeke found himself thinking that being paired off with Josie would be like being penned up with a bobcat. She'd be untamable, and he'd be clawed to death. What was it that caused some men to fall for the one woman who was the worst possible choice for them?

"Come on," he said to the mules as he pulled up their pickets. "Time for all of us to get to work." The animals looked healthy and reasonably good-tempered. Someone had known enough to buy a big, strong pair for the difficult journey. The mules were reluctant to stop grazing but didn't balk when he led them to the river. They waded in until they were fetlock-deep and sank their muzzles into the cold, clear water.

"Don't drink too much," Zeke said, pulling the mules from the river before they'd drunk their fill. "I don't want you to founder."

When he reached the wagon, Suzette was putting away everything they'd used to fix breakfast. Josie was out of sight. "You two got everything straight?" Zeke asked.

"I wish you'd stop trying to rub Josie the wrong way." Suzette paused in what she was doing and looked up at Zeke with eyes that showed as much compassion as impatience. "You must know she has a temper."

"I hadn't noticed," Zeke said with only mild sarcasm.

Suzette's lips twisted in a grin, but the look in her eyes didn't change. "We're all upset about being driven out of town. It's not pleasant being portrayed as immoral women, especially when the *really* immoral women are still there. They couldn't get rid of the women they wanted to drive out of town—the men wouldn't let them—so they settled for us as substitutes."

"Are you surprised by that kind of hypocrisy?"

"No, but it doesn't make it any easier to stomach. I imagine you know something about that."

"A little."

Zeke backed the mules into position so he could begin harnessing them to the wagon. He didn't want to talk about himself. He'd learned through bitter experience that some things couldn't be changed. You either learned to put up with them, you got out of the way, or you drove yourself crazy trying to fight battles that couldn't be won. He and Hawk had decided to get out of the way.

He fitted the collars around the mules, then threw the harness over their backs.

"Do you need some help?"

Zeke looked up, surprised to see Josie. He stifled his initial impulse to tell her he could handle the job on his own. Considering what she'd said a few minutes ago, this seemed like an attempt to apologize.

"You can hold their heads while I hook everything up," he said. "They don't seem especially anxious to go to work this morning."

Zeke took his time. He made sure the harness was in good shape and nothing was loose or worn, that the

55

collars were riding properly on the mules' shoulders and not rubbing any places raw. Despite his deliberate slowness, it seemed Josie wasn't going to say anything. He picked up the reins and tied them to the brake. "Is everybody ready?"

"I'll see."

Josie left without a backward glance. What was wrong with this woman? Did she think apologizing would show a fatal weakness?

Josie returned moments later. "I don't see Suzette."

"She offered to help Hawk with the horses. She's riding my horse since I'll be driving the wagon."

It was clear from Josie's expression that Suzette hadn't told her of this change in plans. It was equally clear that she didn't like it.

"You might as well get it off your chest," Zeke said. "You look like you're about to bust."

Much to his surprise, his words appeared to defuse her anger. "I thought you were staying with us so Hawk could take care of Laurie."

"We are, but Hawk's better with horses and I'm better with wagons. We're depending on you to keep an eye on Laurie and let us know if she starts getting worse."

"Suzette knows more about nursing than I do."

"She also knows more about horses, and Hawk could use some help. Anything else you need to know before we can get started?"

Zeke only realized how rude he sounded when surprise flashed across Josie's face before being replaced by anger.

"I didn't mean that the way it sounded," Zeke said.

"I guess Suzette should have told you she was riding with Hawk."

"It's okay," Josie said, making an obvious effort to rein in her temper. But even after she'd schooled her expression into a rigid smile, her eyes remained stormy.

"You need a hand up?" Zeke asked.

"No. I can do it myself."

He didn't argue. Once she was in, he closed up the back, went around, climbed into the driver's seat, and untied the reins. "Ready?" he called out.

"Ready."

"Giddyaup!" Zeke called as he snapped the reins. The mules leaned into their collars, and the wagon bumped and lurched as it began the day's journey.

Hawk wasn't used to being around attractive women. He was even less used to being alone with one for the better part of a day. Being forced to watch Suzette in the saddle ahead of him had caused him to feel completely off balance all morning. Not to mention being so worked up, he was uncomfortable. He'd hoped that growing older would make his monklike existence easier. Apparently all he needed was a woman like Suzette to stoke the coals until they were red hot once more.

Since horses could travel over rough terrain more easily than a wagon, he hadn't pushed the mares. Yet even at their leisurely pace, they'd outstripped Zeke and the wagon. Much to his surprise, Suzette had been very good at finding the best path for the horses to follow. Only once had they had to backtrack.

"Hold up," he called to Suzette. "Pull over to that

cottonwood," he told her when she stopped and turned in the saddle toward him. "It's time to let the wagon catch up."

Once Hawk staked Dusky Lady, the mares started to graze. Suzette had already dismounted by the time he reached the shade of the ancient cottonwood. Its trunk was about five feet in diameter, its branches reaching more than fifty feet to the river's edge. He judged it to be at least two hundred years old. It was incredible that the tree had managed to survive so many years of flash floods capable of carrying large boulders downstream. He brought his horse to a stop under the tree, grateful to be out of the glare of the intense Arizona sun.

His aroused condition made him so self-conscious, he was undecided whether to stay in the saddle or dismount. He realized it was ridiculous to consider staying in the saddle. His horse needed the break even if he didn't. Suzette must have seen a lot of lovesick men, but being on a stage in a crowded saloon was very different from being alone with one in the middle of the desert. It made things much more personal. Accepting the inevitable, Hawk slid from the saddle. He untied the canteen from his saddle, uncapped it, and held it out to her.

"You thirsty?" he asked.

"Isn't the river water safe to drink?"

"Yes, but I boiled some water last night. It's always better to be on the safe side."

It was difficult to interpret the look in her eyes. His gut instinct told him she was just as attracted to him as he was to her, but he didn't trust his own inflamed emotions. She could merely be surprised at his generosity or his being so careful. She could be thankful he considered her safety as important as his own. It could simply be the way she looked at everybody. They'd known each other for less than a day. Why should she feel any different about him than she would any other stranger?

And what accounted for his attraction to her? Was it that faint accent that sounded intriguingly foreign, the hair so blond it looked silver in the moonlight, or those eyes so blue they reminded him of the Texas sky on a spring day? Such a woman ought to be the creation of some artist, his version of the perfect woman, captured on a canvas and hung in a museum for everyone to admire. But Suzette was flesh and blood, warm and smiling, and she was here—alone with him.

His mind went blank.

He watched, fascinated, as she raised the canteen, opened her mouth, and lifted it to her lips. He could feel the breath catch in his throat when her lips closed around the mouth of the canteen. They were so warm, so full, so moist, he could practically feel them on his own mouth. He took a deep breath, moistened his lips with his tongue. He watched the motion of her throat as she swallowed, entranced by the delicate movement of muscles beneath the pale, flawless skin. A drop of water escaped at the corner of her mouth. Mesmerized, Hawk watched it run down her chin, hang there for a moment before running down her neck and onto the top of her breast.

"Thank you."

Hawk's body jerked slightly as he came out of his dream state. Suzette held the canteen out to him as she wiped her mouth with the back of her hand, then ran her fingers over the top of her breast in search of the errant drop of water. Hawk felt a burning desire so intense he had to turn and focus his attention on the distant horizon to keep from taking her in his arms. "I need to check the horses' hooves to make sure they haven't picked up any stones."

"I can help."

"Stay here. No reason for both of us to get a heat stroke."

He headed toward the nearest horse without waiting for her to respond. He practically walked into a creosote bush before he could get his mind to focus. He had to start paying attention. If he blundered into a cholla cactus, the thorns could give him a serious infection.

The mare, a sorrel, didn't object when he lifted her foot. He forced himself to examine the hoof rim for wear, the hoof walls for gouges, the frog for possible bruises. He even felt the muscles in her legs to make sure they weren't overheated. By the time he'd finished with the third mare, the pressure in his body had eased enough for him to take a deep breath. He didn't know what he was going to do if they didn't reach Laurie's home tonight. He wasn't sure he could stand another day of this. Hell, he hadn't even survived the morning yet.

The sun beat down on his back as he bent to check the hooves of the next mare, a dun with a black mane and tail. She preferred to be left alone while she searched for graze.

"I'll hold her head."

Hawk decided he was getting old when Suzette

could walk up behind him without his noticing. "She's a bit cantankerous. This is her first foal."

"I'd be nervous, too, if I was having my first child."

Hawk busied himself with the mare's feet. He didn't want to think about Suzette having a baby.

"Have you found a stone?" Suzette asked.

"No. You've done a good job finding easy trails this morning."

"It wasn't hard. I just followed the ones the wild animals have already made."

"They're not always easy to see. You have a good eye."

He wondered how she could have grown so comfortable with travel in the desert. Her background—growing up privileged, then working in a saloon—wasn't exactly the best training ground for survival in the wild. He moved to the next mare, an Appaloosa. She was as sweet-tempered as she was beautiful. Suzette patted her neck while he checked her hooves.

"Why are you trying to avoid me?"

The question caught Hawk by surprise. He held the mare's right front hoof without seeing it. It was a difficult decision: lie and have her know he was lying, or tell the truth and make her aware of the effect she was having on him. He released the mare's leg and stood. "Because being alone with you is driving me crazy. It's causing me to . . . well . . ."

It shocked Hawk to see a slow smile curve Suzette's lips. He'd expected her to be embarrassed at the least, to launch into a noisy tirade at the worst.

"What makes you think you're the only one who can

feel a strong physical attraction? I'm sure there have been lots of women who didn't hesitate to let you know you're a very handsome man."

Hawk was glad he had his hand on the Appaloosa's withers. Suzette's words had rocked him so badly he needed the solidness of the mare's body to steady himself. He'd never met a woman who was so willing to speak of her physical desires for a man or who appeared so unembarrassed by them.

"Don't look so stunned," Suzette said. "I've been married. It wasn't a good marriage, but it was good enough to teach me that men and women can take great pleasure in their physical relationship. My husband has been dead for five years, but I haven't forgotten what it was like to sleep with a man."

Try as he might, Hawk couldn't find his tongue. Nor could he form a coherent thought.

"I didn't want to offend you," he finally managed to say. "Besides, I'm sure that on some occasions you've had reason to be afraid of a man who—"

"Yes, but I'm not afraid of you."

She continued to pat the mare's neck, but when the mare moved away to look for more grass, they were left standing alone facing each other. Hawk didn't know what she meant by her statement. More important, he didn't know what she wanted him to do about it—*if* she wanted him to do anything about it. She couldn't mean what was running through his mind— not when Zeke could show up with the wagon at any minute—but what *did* she mean? It was obvious from the way she was looking at him, steady, her gaze open and trusting, that she meant *something*.

"Which mare do you want to check next?" Suzette asked.

At least he was sure of one thing. She *wasn't* talking about checking horses' hooves. "The paint," he said and followed Suzette as she walked to where the small, short-coupled mare was quickly decimating a patch of grama grass. They finished checking the rest of the horses without returning to the subject that was burning a hole in Hawk's mind. He had used the time to sort through his thoughts, catalog the possible meanings of her words, and decide on the most tactful way to find out what he wanted to know. But his plan had to be postponed when the wagon lumbered into sight.

"You'd better check on Laurie," Josie called out before the wagon came to a stop. "I think her temperature is going up."

Hawk had expected that. The rising temperature inside the wagon as the sun neared its zenith, in addition to the irritation of being tossed around, would inevitably make Laurie hotter. It was probably best that he hadn't gotten a chance to tell Suzette the things he'd been thinking of. She couldn't have meant what he'd thought. Spending time with Laurie would give him a chance to bring his own temperature down. Maybe then he could think clearly. If not, he was in for a rough night.

"Of course you'll stay the night with us," Laurie's father said to Hawk and Zeke. "Put your horses in the corral. I'd offer you a place to sleep in the house, but Laurie's friends are taking our only spare room."

63

"Thank you, but that's not necessary," Zeke said.

"If I let you leave now, my wife would never let me hear the end of it, not after you brought our Laurie home and took such good care of her."

"We didn't do anything," Hawk said. "We just traveled along with the women."

The last hours of the trip had been tense. The heat and the discomfort of traveling over rough ground in a wagon with nothing to absorb the shock had worn Laurie down until Hawk had begun to worry if she'd make it home. He'd considered stopping to give her a chance to rest, but she had begged him to get her home as quickly as possible. Now that she was home again, she already looked better.

"That's not what my daughter told me," Mr. Pettinger said. "She said she would probably have died without your medicine."

Zeke didn't want to spend the night on Mr. Pettinger's farm any more than Hawk did, but there seemed little sense in refusing his invitation, especially since it was too late to travel more than a few miles before they'd have to make camp. Besides, he looked forward to eating a meal that hadn't been cooked over a campfire.

"You sure you won't stay longer?" Mrs. Pettinger asked Suzette.

"Thank you, ma'am, but we need to be on our way."

Suzette experienced a pang of regret at having to leave the Pettingers' place. It had been a comfort to spend an evening in a genuinely loving home, a real delight to eat good food and enjoy convivial company, a great comfort to go to bed and fall asleep without the shouts of drunks or the smells of alcohol and tobacco. The visit reminded her so much of when her mother was alive that she felt her death more keenly than she had in a long time. And the absence of her sister, whom she hadn't seen since her own marriage six years ago.

"My husband and I feel we ought to do something to show our appreciation to you for bringing Laurie home to us," Mrs. Pettinger said.

"Giving us a bed for the night and doubling our supplies is more than enough reward," Josie said.

Neither Suzette's nor Josie's protests had been enough to stop Laurie's parents from loading them down with food, an extra quilt in case it got colder, and home remedies to ward off sickness. Even now, as they waited for Zeke to arrive with the mules, they suspected Mrs. Pettinger would try to put something else in their wagon if they turned their backs.

"I feel like I ought to do more," Mrs. Pettinger said. "Our daughter could have died."

"Then thank Hawk," Suzette said. "He's the one who knew what to do to bring down her temperature and what herbs would make her feel better."

She was disturbed by Mrs. Pettinger's attitude toward Hawk. Her discomfort when he was present the evening before had been impossible to miss. No white man could have been more polite or more cordial, but Mrs. Pettinger's relief when Hawk and Zeke left had been so obvious, Suzette had been hard-pressed not to ask if she was afraid Hawk might scalp them in their sleep.

"Please thank him for me," Mrs. Pettinger said, her gaze swinging toward the path Zeke would use to bring the mules. "I must tell you I don't feel easy knowing you will be alone on the trail with those men."

"Your daughter wouldn't be with you now if it weren't for *those men*," Suzette said, trying hard to keep her voice level, her expression neutral. "It they hadn't fixed our wagon, we'd still be at the creek."

"But Anna's young man would have helped you when he arrived," Mrs. Pettinger said.

"We'll be quite safe with Hawk and Zeke." Tension had been gathering in Suzette all morning, first from having to stave off the Pettingers' excessive largesse, and now from trying to hold her tongue in the face of Mrs. Pettinger's groundless prejudice. "In fact, I wish they were going to travel with us the rest of the way to Tombstone."

She hadn't meant to say that—had only said it, she was sure, because Mrs. Pettinger had angered her— but she knew it was true the moment the words were out of her mouth. Aside from her physical attraction to Hawk, she'd started to like him. He wasn't very talkative and had yet to tell her much about himself, but she'd never met a man as kind and thoughtful. It must have annoyed him to have to prolong his own journey to stay with the wagon and take care of Laurie, but never once had he made her feel she was imposing on him. And though it was obvious to Suzette that he desired *her*, he'd never done anything to make her uncomfortable or fearful.

"It's very brave of you to travel such a long distance on your own," Mrs. Pettinger said. "I would have expected you to hire a guide."

"I hadn't thought of that," Suzette said to Josie. "Do you think Hawk and Zeke would be our guides?"

"I didn't mean *them*," Mrs. Pettinger hastened to say.

Suzette realized Mrs. Pettinger's fears were based upon the very real fact that some Indians *had* committed atrocities. What was unfair was that white men who'd committed equally vile acts were treated as heroes. She was relieved to see Zeke coming with the mules. "Josie, why don't you help Zeke with the mules while I go inside to say good-bye to Laurie?" As much as she appreciated the Pettingers' hospitality, she couldn't wait to leave. The strength of her anger at Mrs. Pettinger's attitude toward Hawk surprised her. She hadn't realized she'd come to like him so much. It was probably a good thing they were going to go their separate ways for the rest of the journey. Hawk had no place in her plans for the future.

"Are you going to ask Hawk and Zeke to travel with you?" Laurie asked when Suzette entered her room. She was still sick, but she already looked better for being home and in her own bed.

"Why would we do that?" Suzette asked.

"Because it's dangerous for two women to travel alone. They'd take good care of you."

"Your mother doesn't think so."

"Mother will never stop being afraid of Indians and distrustful of black men, but that's no reason I have to feel the same way, especially after Hawk took such good care of me."

"We can't ask them to slow down enough to stay with us," Suzette said. "We've already held them up long enough."

"I bet they'd do it if you asked."

"Well, I'm not going to ask, and you can be sure Josie won't." Suzette needlessly rearranged the quilt over Laurie, plumped a pillow, and positioned the water pitcher a few inches closer to her. "I don't think he likes Josie any more than she likes him."

Laurie was pale with dark circles under her eyes. "Of course he likes Josie. How can a man not like a woman that beautiful?"

"When that woman makes it plain she doesn't like him and wants nothing to do with him."

"She's only doing that because he doesn't make a fool of himself over her like other men. Regardless of what Josie says, she wants men to make a fuss over her."

"Of course she does. It's the way she judges her appeal to an audience. When they stop making a fuss over us, we'll have to find another way to make a living."

"Josie may not like Zeke yet, but she's intrigued by him. Just like you're intrigued by Hawk."

Averting her gaze, Suzette started to fuss with the quilt again. "I don't know if you're right about Josie, but you're right about me. However, it doesn't matter. We'll never see those men after today."

Laurie grabbed Suzette's hand to keep her from fussing. "You could change that."

Suzette pulled away. "You know why I can't."

"Are you sure?"

"Yes."

Suzette didn't like the look Laurie gave her. It clearly said she thought Suzette was making a mistake, but Suzette didn't have time for a romantic interlude with Hawk. She already had a pressing job—to make sure her sister didn't suffer the way she had. Besides, even though she liked men, she didn't trust them. None of them appeared able or willing to live up to their commitments. And a man who'd reached Hawk's age without getting married was clearly a man who didn't *want* commitments.

"Don't worry about me and Josie," Suzette said. "Stay here with your parents, get well, and meet some nice farmer boy."

"I think I'll do that," Laurie said with a weak smile. "I used to think my life was unbearably boring, and I couldn't wait to get away. But almost from the time I got to Globe, all I wanted was to come home. I can't thank you enough for bringing me here."

"We couldn't think of leaving you. Now give me one last hug. I've been expecting Josie to drag me out of here for the last five minutes."

She hugged Laurie, only slightly jealous that she wasn't the one to sleep in a soft bed under a handmade quilt, to live in a snug house, to know that her future was safe and secure. Yet as she stepped through the door, she realized she would have felt confined by the life Laurie would lead.

Outside, Suzette saw that Zeke had brought up the mules, but nothing, had been done to harness them to the wagon. Instead, Josie and Zeke were squared off against one another like two young roosters. If Suzette didn't do something in a hurry, the fur would begin to fly.

Chapter Five

Suzette didn't know whether to intervene or let them battle it out. Those two had been spoiling for a fight from the moment they'd met, each encounter ratcheting up the tension another notch. Now they were so wrapped up in their confrontation, they appeared to have forgotten they were supposed to be harnessing the mules. Hands clenched at his sides, Zeke was glaring at Josie dangerously.

"I have no doubt men whose jobs keep them from seeing many women gape at you like starving kids at a table loaded with food, but I'm not starved for a woman."

"Is that why you can't keep your hands off me? Or your eyes?"

"I look at you because you get in my way," Zeke snapped. "Only a woman who thinks every man finds her irresistible would interpret every accidental contact while harnessing a couple of mules as an inability to keep his hands off her."

"So you didn't touch me?"

"It certainly wasn't intentional." Zeke walked around Josie, picked up a collar and lifted it over the head of one of the mules. Josie followed suit with the other.

"So it was an accident that your arms just happened to be around me."

Zeke turned, his hold on his temper tenuous. "Since you don't know enough about harnessing mules to know when to move out of the way, I had to reach around you."

The way they were arguing, they'd soon be saying things they couldn't forgive. Suzette forced her way between them. "Are the mules harnessed and ready to go?"

"Done," Zeke barked.

"Thank you. Why don't you climb in the back, Josie? I'll drive for the first hour."

"You'd better drive all the time," Zeke said. "She seems to have difficulty staying in touch with reality."

"And you have difficulty staying in touch with the truth," Josie said.

Zeke leveled a look at Josie that should have pushed her back several feet, but she held her ground. "I don't know anything about the truth of your reality, but I want nothing to do with it," he said.

"Good," Josie said when Zeke turned and strode away. She continued to glare after him, but he didn't turn around or show that he'd heard her.

"What was that all about?" Suzette asked.

"That is the most infuriating man who ever lived,"

Josie said. She was so worked up, Suzette could almost see fire coming out of her nostrils. "He practically holds me in an embrace, then denies he even touched me."

Suzette thought it was a good thing Zeke and Josie would be going their separate ways. If they were together much longer, there'd be a terrible explosion.

"Come on," Suzette said, "get in. Let's go before Mrs. Pettinger tries to give us anything else."

But Josie continued to stand staring at the spot where Zeke had stalked off, a look of mingled fury and chagrin on her face. It appeared to Suzette that Josie didn't know how to react, and that was unlike her. She always knew what she wanted to do, didn't hesitate to say what was on her mind, and could take command of any situation. Suzette had her own ideas about what might be throwing Josie off stride. Zeke was a man who might turn any woman's head, but Suzette had no intention of letting Josie guess what she was thinking. If she was wrong, Josie would be furious with her. If she was right, Josie would be more angry still.

Suzette pulled herself up into the driver's seat and untied the reins from the brakes. "Are you coming?" she asked when Josie still hadn't moved.

Josie stalled a moment longer before turning and climbing into the wagon without a word. Suzette slapped the reins and called, "Giddyaup!" She smiled to herself when she remembered that Zeke and Hawk's ranch wasn't far from Tombstone. She had a feeling Josie had finally met a man who could get past her formidable defenses. Suddenly she was more eager than ever to reach Tombstone.

* * *

"Are you done complaining?" Hawk asked Zeke. They were seated on the ground under the shade of a sycamore tree, leaning against the trunk. Hawk gazed up at the light filtering through the canopy overhead, watching the five-pointed leaves as they rustled in the barely perceptible breeze, occasionally allowing a shaft of sunlight to reach the ground. They had paused to allow the horses to drink and graze a few minutes. Zeke had taken the opportunity to fill Hawk's ear about Josie.

"I haven't complained all that much," Zeke protested.

It amused Hawk to see his cynical brother so worked up over a woman, but it worried him as well. Zeke pretended to have a thick hide and not care about anything, but Hawk knew he cared about some people very deeply. He hoped Josie wasn't going to be one of those people. "Every time you open your mouth you talk about Josie. Even the horses are probably tired of hearing her name by now. I don't see why she bothers you so much if you dislike her."

"It's her ingrained belief that no man can ignore her, that every man who sees her can't keep his hands off her."

Hawk shrugged. "All beautiful women are like that, especially the ones who make a living being attractive to men."

"She's not that beautiful."

Hawk wasn't about to let Zeke get by with that piece of fiction. "Don't be stupid. She is, and you know it."

Hawk had to admit it was a pleasure to look at a woman as beautiful as Josie, but he'd felt much more comfortable around Suzette. She wasn't so beautiful or so perfect that she couldn't be touched. Besides, there was something about Suzette that said she wanted to be touched, that she wanted to be close to him, that she was as aware of his physical presence as he was of hers, and she wasn't afraid to admit it.

Zeke got up and moved away from Hawk. Hawk was sure the only reason Zeke had walked away was that Hawk had forced him to admit Josie was beautiful. He was unable to be still, unable to keep his mind on anything except Josie for more than a few minutes.

"I don't know why she gets under my skin," Zeke said, "but everything about her irritates me. I tell myself it doesn't matter, that I'll never see her again, but it doesn't make any difference."

"I don't know why you're getting so upset. It's not the first time you've been attracted to a woman. Or have you forgotten Rosie? I think the other one was called Tess."

"This is different," Zeke said as he paced back and forth among the trees. Occasionally he would bend over to pick up a dead branch, then break it into tiny pieces before tossing it away. "They actually liked me. Josie can't stand the sight of me."

Hawk wondered if his feelings for Suzette were any clearer. And how did she really feel about him? Lots of women had flirted with him. Sometimes they thought it was exciting to be with an Indian—maybe it was their expectation of danger. Their interest seemed to be mostly because he was a novelty. No woman had ever been interested in him as a man. Certainly none had ever helped him with his horses. There was nothing flashy about Suzette. She was quiet, steady, genuine.

"I can't understand why she works in a saloon if she hates men so much," Zeke said.

"What else could she do? You certainly can't believe she'd work as a maid or a dressmaker. Can you see Josie putting up with some demanding rich man's wife?"

Zeke chuckled. "She'd probably throw the woman out of the shop."

"Not the way to build a successful business. Now let's get our horses back on the trail. That ranch isn't getting any closer with us sitting on our butts."

Hawk got to his feet, brushed the debris from the seat of his pants, and ambled toward his mount, which was cropping grass in the bright sunlight. He caught up the reins and led the horse to the river for a drink. As the animal sank its muzzle into the clear water, Hawk wondered where Suzette and Josie were now, if they were making good time, if they were close behind, if they were safe. In his own way, he was just as bad as Zeke. He'd had a couple of relationships with women in the past, but no woman had affected him the way Suzette had.

Unfortunately, the timing was all wrong for him and Zeke. They'd decided they were too old to get married. They knew they were too different to fit into normal society, so they'd bought a ranch a good distance from any town, where they could live alone and raise their horses. They had a good plan, and the first phase would be complete when they got these mares to their ranch. Now was not the time to start thinking about a serious relationship, certainly not with a woman who made her living as a singer and dancer. Their brother Sean had been lucky when he married a woman who

75

owned her own saloon, but Hawk couldn't expect the same thing to happen twice within the same family.

"You ready, or are you going to stare into space all day?"

The sharp edge of Zeke's voice brought Hawk's thoughts back to the task at hand, getting the mares to their ranch before they started dropping their foals. A gentle tug on the reins and his mount raised his dripping muzzle from the water. Hawk led him out of the riverbed and up a sandy bank. "Want to trade places? You've been eating dust all morning."

"Nah. If it weren't for the dust, I'd be thinking about Josie all the time."

"Forget about Josie, and concentrate on the changes we need to make to the ranch house. I hope you remember all those carpenter skills you said you learned when you were a slave."

"I haven't forgotten *anything* about being a slave."

"Just be grateful Isabelle adopted you. None of us had much to live for before she found us," Hawk said.

Thinking of how Isabelle had changed his life forever caused Hawk's thoughts to wander back to the years he had spent growing up as part of that cobbled-together family of orphaned misfits. Despite their differences and the inevitable fights with his adopted brothers, it was the only time in his life he felt like he really belonged. "Do you ever think of going back to Texas?"

"Sometimes. How about you?"

Hawk gripped the saddle horn but didn't raise himself into the saddle. "Sometimes. I miss that bunch."

But things had changed in the years since they all worked with Jake and Isabelle on the ranch. Practically everybody was married. The Hill Country was overrun with children who called Jake and Isabelle their grandparents. Now Zeke and Hawk had virtually nothing in common with their brothers and sisters. Whenever the family got together, everyone was talking about children inside of five minutes.

"Me, too," Zeke said. "But I don't miss Isabelle telling me I ought to get married before I'm so old nobody will have me. I love that woman, but I can't take her looking at me with those sad eyes."

Hawk swung into the saddle. "Did Jake tell you he's saving some land for us?"

"Yeah, but I told him we'd already bought a ranch."

"Isabelle's never going to be happy until she's got us all within shouting distance."

Zeke swung into the saddle, guided his mount toward Hawk. "The last thing she needs is two crusty, cranky bachelors in the middle of all that connubial bliss."

"I tried to make her understand we'd be happier by ourselves."

Together, they rode toward their small herd. "Did she believe you?"

"Isabelle never believes anything she doesn't like."

Zeke chuckled again, but Hawk heard the same softness in his voice that all the orphans had when they talked about the determined, vibrant woman who'd changed their lives.

"That's how she gets everybody to do what she wants," Zeke said.

Hawk's sharp whistle brought the mares' heads up from where they were grazing. Within moments they had formed a line behind Dusky Lady. A second whistle started them moving down the trail toward the ranch. Isabelle wouldn't get what she wanted this time, because neither Zeke nor Hawk was the marrying kind.

Thoroughly tired of her own company, Josie climbed onto the wagon seat next to Suzette. The desert landscape was monotonous, but it was better than her own thoughts. Occasionally they came to a tree-lined trickle of water that emptied into the San Pedro River, but mostly they crossed dry washes bordered by sagebrush, mesquite, ironwood, several kinds of cactus, and an occasional cottonwood. The slopes rising to the mountains on both sides of the river were covered in juniper. Pine, fir, and spruce farther up teased her with promises of cool temperatures and deep shade, but they passed each mountain without pausing. Tombstone lay to the south.

"You've been in a strange mood all day," Suzette said to Josie. "Want to tell me what's bothering you?"

"Pay no attention to me. You know I get out of sorts when I can't have a hot bath. And I can just feel my skin drying out in this sun."

Josie had spent most of the morning inside the wagon trying to sleep. She hadn't been tired, just trying to escape thoughts that kept nagging at her. She couldn't decide whether thinking about Zeke or the rocking of the wagon had been responsible for her being unable to doze, but the result was that she was in an even worse mood than when Zeke had stalked off earlier that morning.

"I've known you too long not to sense your moods.

You've been thinking about your attraction to Zeke," Suzette said.

"Then you know I don't want to talk about it."

"It might be better if you did. At least it'll stop festering inside."

Josie didn't want to tell anybody what was bothering her. She couldn't believe it was Zeke, just about the last man on earth she'd ever expected to think about for more than five minutes. What was worse, she couldn't even figure out what it was that made her think about him. He was rude and bossy. He didn't give her credit for being able to do anything by herself. And when she got angry at him, he got just as angry at her. He'd even walked away and left her standing.

"I know it's Zeke," Suzette said. "What I don't understand is why."

"Do you think I do?" Josie snapped, angry that Suzette knew and had forced her to face the truth.

"He's a nice man. Attractive, too."

"I don't agree, but that's not the point."

"I know how your father treated you and your mother, but you shouldn't let that turn you against all men. A couple of men who came to the saloon were really interested in you."

"I wasn't interested in them."

"Maybe not, but what if you fall in love with Zeke?"

"I'm not insane," Josie exclaimed. "I'll never fall in love with any man, but certainly not a man like Zeke."

"I like him."

The wheel bounced over a stone causing Josie to grab on to the seat to keep from tumbling out of the wagon. "Then *you* fall in love with him."

Josie didn't like all this talk about falling in love. She wasn't sure anybody ever really did fall in love. A man wanted a woman to cook, take care of his house, his physical needs, and have his children. No love there. A woman wanted a husband to provide for her, protect her, and father her children. No love there either, just two people depending on each other for their own benefit. Mother Nature had planned it so it was practically impossible for men and women not to marry. And to make sure it happened, she'd created this illusion called love, a kind of mental breakdown that removed common sense and replaced it with a belief that a woman *wanted* to belong to a man, *wanted* to be his virtual slave.

"I thought you didn't believe in love," Suzette said.

"I don't."

"Then how do you account for your interest in Zeke?"

"I can't, and that's what's making me so angry."

Josie moved her leg to keep it from being brushed by the thorny arm of a catclaw bush. She couldn't imagine why any man would want to live in a desert, especially when it was covered in cactus and thorny bushes. To say nothing of the dirt, the snakes, and the killing heat. Drops of perspiration rolled down her back.

"I think it's because he doesn't treat you like some delicate piece of porcelain or worship your beauty."

"I'd be in a fine fix if men didn't appreciate my looks. How would I earn a living?"

"I don't know. But I still don't believe you like them falling all over you."

"You're my best friend. You're supposed to believe

what I say." Josie hated it when she sounded sulky. It made her feel like a child.

"I'm also supposed to tell you when you're fooling yourself, and you're doing that now if you don't believe you like it that Zeke can keep his head while he's looking at you."

Josie looked at the various cactuses they were passing and tried to interest herself in identifying each kind, but how was it possible to care if one cactus was called a prickly pear and another a cholla when they were all covered with thorns and all you wanted to do was stay away from them? Men were a lot like a cactus. Some were round barrel cactuses, some prissy pin cushions, some wiry ocotillo, and some majestic saguaro. But all were thorny, stiff, unbending. "I know I like it when men look at me on stage. But maybe you're right—I *don't* like it any other time."

"You can't have it both ways."

"Our act has never caused me any trouble I can't handle."

"I'm not talking about our act. I'm talking about you not being able to stop thinking about Zeke, any more than I wager he can stop thinking about you."

"You mean wanting to wring my neck."

"Probably, but that still means he's thinking about you."

"I'd rather not have a man think about me if he's going to contemplate my murder."

Suzette laughed.

Josie didn't like it when anyone laughed at her. In her experience, laughter was never about fun unless people were drunk. "Why are you laughing?"

Suzette shook her head, continued to smile. "It must be worse than I thought. I've never heard such foolishness come out of your mouth before."

"I'm just tired." Josie didn't try to hide her irritation. "It's been a long day."

"Do you want to stop?"

"No. Let's keep going as long as possible. I don't want to spend one night more than necessary in this desert." She let her gaze roam over the forbidding landscape. "I can't imagine why we ever decided to travel on our own."

"Because *you* didn't want a man telling you what to do even if we'd hired him to do exactly that."

Josie decided she needed to get down from the wagon, but even though they were within sight of the river, she didn't see a good place to camp for the night. Thickets of acacia, sagebrush, ironwood, creosote bush, and mesquite choked the bank of the river. Damp mud—evidence of recent rain—covered the only open area. The desert was so choked with thorny plants it would have been nearly impossible to spend as much as an hour here without getting at least one thorn buried deep in their flesh. Josie had seen what cactus thorns could do, and she was determined it wasn't going to happen to her.

"I'll drive if your shoulders are too tired." Josie reached for the reins. "You can lie down until I find a good place to stop."

Suzette held the reins away from Josie, a motion that caused the mules to throw up their heads and snort in protest before lowering their heads and continuing as though nothing had happened. "I'll drive, you look."

Moments later they reached a spot where the river divided into two channels. The low banks on each side were relatively clear of vegetation and rocks. "This looks like a great spot to stop for the night."

Suzette turned the mules off the trail, and the wagon bounced over a rock-filled streambed until they reached a wide, sandy area. Relieved when the wheels didn't sink deeper than two inches, Suzette pulled the wagon to a stop and put on the brake. She tied the reins to the brake, arched her back, and hunched her shoulders.

"It feels good to stop."

Josie climbed down from the driver's seat. "I'll take care of the mules."

"*I'll* take care of the mules," Suzette said. "You start the fire."

"What makes you think I can start a fire?" Josie knew she sounded petulant, but she was tired of people assuming that just because she cared about her appearance and her comfort, she couldn't do anything practical. The fact that she wanted to forget every minute she'd spent on that farm growing up didn't mean she'd actually forgotten everything she'd learned.

"You can do anything you want," Suzette said. "I just want to take care of the mules because I like animals. Hawk is great with them. You ought to see him."

Josie had started to climb into the wagon to get the things they needed to prepare supper, but she backed down and walked around the end of the wagon so she could see Suzette. "Let's agree not to mention Zeke or Hawk ever again," she said.

"Ever?"

"Okay, just for tonight, then. We've got to fix supper, eat, clean up, and get to bed. It's been a long day and we need a good night's sleep." Josie pulled out the bag of provisions, then set about gathering wood. The river had washed plenty of debris up on the sandbar, but she was looking for mesquite and ironwood. Mesquite burned fast and hot, while ironwood coals would still be glowing in the morning. She didn't find any ironwood, but she found plenty of cottonwood, mesquite, and some juniper that had been washed down from the slopes. She had the fire started by the time Suzette finished unharnessing and picketing the mules.

"Since we're not thinking about the men," Suzette said when she returned, "we should think about making some changes in our act."

"Why? It's good like it is, and nobody in Tombstone has ever seen it." They had used the same five songs with their accompanying dances for two years. Though she and Suzette could do the act in their sleep, the men never seemed to tire of it. "Will you get the water?"

Suzette reached for the bucket hanging on the side of the wagon. "Our act needs to be great, not just good. You know I don't want to spend the rest of my life going from one mining town to another. I need to make a lot of money if I'm going to go back to Quebec to help my sister make a good marriage."

"Don't worry. You'll make plenty of money. Now go get the water. I've been thinking about that ham Mrs. Pettinger gave us ever since noon."

Suzette went off to get the water, but Josie's thoughts weren't on a new act or a new town. She was wondering where Zeke and Hawk were, if they'd stopped for the night or if they were pushing on, trying to get as close to their ranch as possible.

And as far away from her and Suzette as they could.

Dammit! What was it about that man she couldn't forget?

Suzette gave up trying to go back to sleep, but she didn't get up. It wouldn't be dawn for another half hour or so. For the rest of last evening, they hadn't mentioned either of the men who'd invaded their thoughts, but both knew they were thinking about them. Suzette turned on her side in an effort to get more comfortable, but not even a thick quilt could soften the impact of the ground on her body. The sand had proved hard and uncomfortable. Suzette wondered how Hawk could sleep on the ground night after night and not seem to mind it. She would be glad to reach Tombstone and sleep in a bed again.

She wondered how often Hawk came into Tombstone. The two men couldn't stay on that ranch all the time. Even if they didn't want to see other people, they needed supplies. She wondered if they ever went to saloons, if they enjoyed watching the dancers and singers, how often they sought the company of women. They weren't as young and randy as many of the miners who had come to the saloon in Globe, but it only took one look to see that Hawk was still in the prime of his life, physically active and brimming with good health.

Thinking of Hawk, visualizing his body—the way he sat tall in the saddle, the grace with which he moved around camp—ignited a small flame of need in her belly. The longer she lay there picturing Hawk in her mind, imagining what it would be like to touch him, to feel his powerful muscles move under her fingertips, to experience the warmth of his skin against her own, the more the flame grew, until she was unable to lie still. She felt too hot to remain under her covers, yet shivers sent chills through her body. She didn't want to admit it, but she could no more put Hawk out of her mind than Josie could banish Zeke from hers. Her attraction was physical, while Josie's was psychological, but she wasn't sure that made any practical difference.

Unable to remain still any longer, Suzette threw back the covers and sat up. Her shoulders were stiff from holding the reins the day before. She rotated them, almost enjoying the ache of her stiff muscles. Next she rolled her neck from side to side.

"You look like you're drunk."

Suzette looked up to see Josie climbing down from the wagon. "My whole body is stiff. How about you?"

"I tossed and turned too much to get stiff. Just sore."

Suzette bent forward from the waist, feeling the ache as her muscles stretched. "I don't know what it is about holding reins and sleeping on the ground that's so different from dancing for several hours, but I've never felt this stiff in the morning."

"It's the cold air," Josie said, pulling her shawl more tightly around her shoulders. "I need some coffee to warm up. Are there any coals left?"

"I haven't looked." There would have been if Hawk or Zeke had made the fire. They seemed to know everything without having to think about it.

"I'll look for some wood. We'll need it regardless."

"Don't go too far, and be careful not to pick up anything with thorns. I'm not as good as Hawk when it comes to medicine."

"I know more than I want to know about cactus and the wounds they make," Josie said. "You keep forgetting that I grew up on a farm. Come to think of it, why don't I start the fire and you look for firewood? You can bring the mules in at the same time."

"I'll be glad to." Suzette put on her boots, threw a blanket over her shoulders, and headed off.

Digging among the ashes, Josie located one coal that burned red when she blew on it. She shredded some leaves, sprinkled them on the coal, then blew on it until the leaves burst into flame. To this she added twigs, choosing larger and larger ones until she had built up a steady blaze. Being careful to avoid the thorns, she laid a couple of dry mesquite branches across the fire and kept adding kindling until the branches caught. Confident the fire wouldn't go out, she grabbed a bucket and walked down to the river to get water. When she returned, she poured some into a pot, then put it on the fire to boil for coffee. She was about to take out the bacon to slice when Suzette returned, her arms full of wood but her expression worried.

"I can't find the mules," she said. "They must have wandered off during the night."

Chapter Six

"Maybe we should just point the mules in their direction," Zeke said to Hawk as he led their saddled horses into the campsite. "They won't be happy when they find out we know how inept they are."

The sun had just peeped over the horizon, its warm rays quickly dispelling the chill of the night. Birds and small animals scratched among dry leaves looking for something to eat before taking refuge during the heat of the day. Zeke and Hawk had finished their breakfast, but finding the mules with their horses had forced them to postpone their departure.

"They'll be too glad we found the mules to be angry with us," Hawk said.

Zeke kicked more sand on the campfire to make sure it was out. "That may be true of Suzette," he said, "but Josie won't be happy to see my face."

"Then I'll take the mules myself."

"That's because you want to see Suzette."

"So what if I do?"

A small vessel in Hawk's temple began to throb, an infallible sign he was getting angry. Zeke directed his gaze to the job of rolling up his bedroll. "You can't go getting interested in a female now. Think about the ranch."

Hawk snatched up his saddlebags and tied them to his saddle. "And I suppose you're not *interested* in Josie."

Zeke tied his bedroll with two strips of rawhide. "It wouldn't matter if I were."

Zeke didn't want to go within a hundred yards of Josie, yet neither would he let Hawk take the mules to the women by himself. He *hated* it when part of him wanted to do one thing and the rest of him wanted to do just the opposite. And all because of a woman who couldn't stand him. What was wrong with him? He'd never done anything like this before. He might have liked a woman who didn't return his interest, but he'd always been able to shrug his infatuation off and turn his attention elsewhere. Why couldn't he do that with Josie? Hell, he'd only been around her three days. How could a woman get her hooks in a man that quickly? He packed the rest of the supplies in his saddlebags and stood. "Let's finish packing up, and we'll both take the mules over."

They didn't speak, but their abrupt motions spoke eloquently of the tension between them. Five minutes later they were headed to where the women had camped, each leading a mule. Angry at the whole situation, Zeke charged into the lead. He dodged a cholla cactus only to nearly fall into a prickly pear.

"Watch where you're going," Hawk said. "We can't afford to have you laid up with a dozen poison thorns in your hide."

The mule Zeke was leading looked nearly as disgusted as Hawk sounded. "I was thinking," he said.

"I could tell. You've got that *Josie* look about you."

Zeke ground a small barrel cactus beneath his boot, then spun around to face Hawk. "What the hell is a *Josie* look?" He was tempted to knock the smile off Hawk's face.

"It's this vacant look," Hawk said, "like you aren't aware of anything around you."

Zeke turned and plunged ahead. "I was aware of you the whole time. It's hard not to be when you insist upon wearing that damned feather."

Zeke had done his best to convince Hawk that wearing rawhide leggings was okay as long as he wore a normal shirt. He could even wear moccasins if he wanted. But a single feather, even one discreetly hanging down from the back of his headband, would bring out the worst in people who feared or hated Indians. Zeke wasn't sure Hawk actually *wanted* to wear the feather. He thought it was Hawk's way of forcing people to recognize he was different and accept him anyway.

"You weren't aware of that cactus," Hawk said.

Zeke swung his arm in an arc that encompassed half the Arizona Territory. "There are cactus all around us. It's impossible to be aware of all of them." A hundred yards from the river, the landscape was virtually bare of anything except cactus until they encountered the beginning of the junipers and pinyon pine on the lower flanks of the Santa Catalina Mountains to the west and the Galiuro Mountains to the east.

"How many times have you walked into a cholla?"

"Never. The damned things are poisonous."

"Exactly."

Zeke made a point to give the next cholla a wide berth, but that just made Hawk chuckle. Zeke's fist clenched around the lead rope. He wasn't about to let Hawk get to him. If he did, Hawk would tease him unmercifully. Neither one of them would hesitate to give his life for the other, but they were also each other's severest critic. Outside of Isabelle, that is. She was *everybody's* severest critic.

"Let's just deliver the mules and leave," Zeke said.

"We will as soon as they're ready to travel."

Zeke swerved to give a wide berth to a large jumping cholla. "Why should that make any difference to when we get started?"

"Because we have to make sure they get to Tombstone."

"And how are we supposed to do that when they can't even keep track of their mule team?"

"We take them with us."

Suzette hadn't been aware of the ball of tension until it started to unravel when she saw Hawk and Zeke each leading a mule toward her. She hadn't been terribly worried about finding the mules. She'd been following their hoofprints, confident the mules hadn't gone very far during the night. If she hadn't been able to find them, it wouldn't have been too difficult to return to the Pettingers' farm. So what was the reason for the knot in her stomach?

Hawk. As he drew closer, she felt her whole body relax, and a lazy smile begin to curve her lips. She couldn't put it into words, but there was something about that man's presence that made everything better. Maybe it was the confidence with which he walked, the easy strength of his body, the steadfastness of his gaze. It could be something else entirely, but right now she wasn't especially concerned about discovering the source. He was here. That was enough for now.

"You're probably thinking me a great idiot." She spoke directly to Hawk, only vaguely aware she'd walked past Zeke to do so.

"No, but I'll teach you how to put a stake in the ground so it won't come up."

"My only experience was with horses who spent their nights in a comfortable stall."

"If you're not sure, you could tie them to a tree."

"How will they be able to graze at night?"

"Maybe I ought to teach you how to hobble them instead."

"Is Josie looking for the mules, too?" Zeke asked.

Suzette turned to Zeke, embarrassed to have ignored him. "She stayed in camp to fix breakfast." She pointed in the direction of the river at a narrow tendril of smoke rising in the brisk morning air. "I'm the one who lost the mules, so I insisted I should be the one to look for them. Besides, I'm better with animals than she is."

Zeke hoped Josie hadn't burned the coffee. He could use a cup right now.

"Zeke and I have been thinking," Hawk said. "Since we're all going in the same direction, it seems only logical that we travel together."

Zeke hadn't been thinking any such thing. It certainly wasn't logical in his mind, but he'd do just about anything to be close to Josie. He didn't want to get *next* to her. That would be too close for either of them. Just close enough to keep her in sight, close enough to figure out what she was like, close enough to figure out the hold she had on him.

Close enough to break it.

"You don't have to do that," Suzette said. "We'll slow you down."

"Not much," Hawk said.

"Thank you, but we'll be fine."

"Don't you trust us?" Zeke asked.

Nobody trusted a black man and a half-breed Indian, Zeke knew, especially when they rode together. They might as well have *thief* written across their foreheads. Women would yank small children out of their path, merchants dog their every step, men avoid them in saloons, and rowdy boys shout insults at them.

Suzette looked surprised. "Of course I trust you. What makes you think I wouldn't?"

Zeke didn't tell her he had a lifetime of reasons. "You don't seem to want us around."

"I didn't think you wanted *us* around."

Zeke couldn't miss the fact that Suzette appeared to be asking that question of Hawk. He wondered if she was as interested in Hawk as Hawk was in her.

"It's not a matter of wanting or not wanting to be around you," Hawk said. "It's just logical that people traveling in the same direction would be safer together."

Well, that wasn't true, either. Two women traveling through the desert were bound to attract the attention of any men in the vicinity. And the last thing he and

93

Hawk needed was for greedy men to know they were traveling with a herd of blooded mares, all carrying foals nearly as valuable as their mothers. They'd already had one brush with horse thieves. Traveling with these women would make them more vulnerable.

"You're not going to Tombstone," Suzette said.

"Our ranch is close enough," Hawk said.

Zeke wasn't sure which was a more dangerous cargo, a herd of valuable horses or two beautiful women. It was certain that neither his nor Hawk's mind would be entirely on the horses. They didn't need the distraction, but he didn't open his mouth to withdraw Hawk's invitation.

Suzette turned to Zeke. "I didn't think you liked Josie."

"I think it's more accurate to say she doesn't like me, but we don't have to be friends to travel together. She'll be in the wagon, and I'll be with the horses, so we won't get in each other's way."

Suzette looked from Hawk to Zeke, then back to Hawk. "Are you sure about this?"

"It would have been stupid to offer if I hadn't been," Hawk said.

Not that Zeke wanted him to be a smooth talker just now, but Hawk needed to learn how to talk to women if he ever hoped to keep one interested in him for anything but the money he was willing to spend on her. Suzette didn't seem to be offended by his offhand manner, but Zeke could just imagine how Josie would have reacted to a statement like that.

"Well, we'd better hurry back to camp to tell Josie the good news."

Zeke didn't trust Suzette's grin. There was something about it that said she knew something he didn't and found it amusing. Zeke couldn't remember a single instance when someone being amused at his expense had been a good thing, and he was certain this instance was not about to reverse the trend. He fell in behind Hawk and Suzette, who walked side by side in silence. That was something else about Hawk. Women didn't like silence. It drove them crazy. He was going to have to learn to talk or give up being interested in women altogether.

But as far as he could see, Suzette didn't seem to mind. She was speaking softly now, in a slow, easy manner, not bothering to wait for Hawk to answer or comment. Zeke was used to Hawk's silences, but he'd never expected a woman to accept them. Zeke had been putting up with those silences for twenty-five years. He could remember some days when he felt he was living with a figment of his imagination.

When the wagon came into view, Zeke couldn't decide whether he wanted to pull to the side so Josie could see him or hide behind Hawk until the last minute. Never one to hide behind anybody else, or put off the inevitable, Zeke pulled over to the side and moved up alongside Hawk.

"I see you've decided it's better to put on a brave front."

There were times when Zeke wished Hawk didn't understand him so well. "No point in avoiding the inevitable."

But that wasn't the only reason he had refused to hide behind Hawk. Though he would have denied it to everybody in the world, including Isabelle, he was anxious for his first sight of Josie. Yes, she was a beautiful woman. Yes, it annoyed him that she disliked him so. Yes, she was so feminine it made his body ache with desire. But none of that explained why this woman had him by the jugular. He was helpless to break the hold she had on him, a hold she didn't appear to want any more than he did. So yes, he was anxious to see her. He couldn't wait to be close to her again. He hadn't wanted this, but it had been forced on him by something deep inside. They were going to tangle until he figured out what she'd done to him. He had no idea what the outcome would be, but the battle was inevitable.

Josie sliced the bacon with quick, skilled movements and tossed the pieces into the hot pan with practiced precision. When the water came to a boil, she knew exactly how many scoops of grounds to use to make the right amount of coffee at the right strength. Though it had been years since she'd done anything like this, she hadn't forgotten the skills she'd acquired nearly as soon as she was able to reach her mother's stove top.

She hated anything to do with cooking. The sound of the bacon frying in the pan, of grease popping into the crisp morning air, fueled her agitation. It reminded her of the way her father treated her and her mother like virtual slaves. It didn't matter that her white father had loved his slave enough to take her west after the war and marry her. It didn't matter that her mother loved her father enough to do whatever he wished. It mattered to Josie that her father treated them both as though they had no purpose in life other than to satisfy his every wish. When she tried to rebel, she felt the lash of his tongue or the back of his hand. Later, her mother would spend hours trying to convince Josie that her father was the most wonderful man on earth. Josie had finally learned to keep her opinions to herself, her gaze lowered so her father couldn't see the fury in her eyes, and to find something that needed doing as far from her father's presence as possible.

She wasn't in a receptive frame of mind when she looked up and saw Suzette and the mules approaching, accompanied by Zeke and Hawk. She slammed down her knife and wrapped up the bacon. She hoped they'd already eaten, because if they hadn't, they'd go hungry before she cooked for them. She hadn't fixed enough coffee, and it wasn't nearly strong enough for Zeke's taste. She didn't understand how he could drink the stuff he liked. It looked like the tar she used to collect from an oil seep on their farm in Wyoming. They'd used it to start fires.

She could imagine the superior smile on Zeke's face right now, the smirk that said he knew she couldn't make it to Tombstone without his help. Knowing he was right made that truth even harder to swallow. She stopped pacing, turned in their direction, placed her hands on her hips, and tried to think of some withering remark that would tell Zeke in a single sentence exactly how she felt about his presence.

"They found our mules," Suzette said.

The obvious statement threw Josie off stride, but not nearly so much as Zeke's expression. He looked like he was braced for an attack. He came to a stop with his legs apart, arms held slightly out from his sides, his body balanced on the balls of his feet. His gaze was fixed on her, but his jaw was clenched and his lips were compressed until they formed a tight circle. The hand still holding the rope attached to the mule's bridle was clenched into a tight fist.

It shocked Josie to realize that his reaction was entirely due to his expectation of what she would say and do. She'd never thought her behavior was so terrible, her words so ill-natured. She just didn't mind telling people who bothered her that she didn't want them hanging around. Zeke's reaction made it plain he saw her as some kind of hellcat. If not a hellcat, at least a very nasty woman. But she wasn't like that. All she wanted was to be left alone.

"Thank you."

The words surprised Josie as much as they appeared to surprise Zeke and the others. She wanted to retract them the moment they left her lips, yet she didn't want Zeke to go on thinking she was some kind of raving, irrational, ungrateful woman. She wasn't. Really. But life had taught her some particularly painful lessons, and she had no intention of allowing herself to be in a position to experience any of them again. She moved her hands from her hips, gripped them together in front of her, a gesture she realized was totally out of character.

"I'm afraid I haven't made enough breakfast for everybody," she said. "If you want something to eat, there's plenty more—"

"We've already eaten," Zeke said.

Thank goodness Zeke interrupted her. She was about to say she could cut some more bacon, make some more coffee. She was about to act just like her father had expected her to act. Knowing that clarified some of the confusion in her mind. She didn't intend to cook for Zeke and Hawk. But she also didn't want Zeke to continue thinking of her as some kind of hate-filled woman. She didn't hate him. She even thought he was attractive, probably nice as well, but she knew what she wanted out of life. More importantly, she knew what she *didn't* want, and she didn't want anybody to be in doubt about that.

"Would you like some coffee?" Suzette asked.

"I'd love some," Zeke said.

Josie grabbed the pot. "It's not strong enough for you."

"I don't care," Zeke replied.

"It won't take long to make some more," Suzette offered. "I'll just have to heat some more water."

"You know you can't make decent coffee," Josie said to Suzette.

It had always seemed ironic to Josie that Suzette didn't mind living in the West but knew so little about how to take care of herself, while Josie hated it but could survive quite nicely on her own. The difference hadn't mattered in Globe, because they lived in a rooming house where they had their meals prepared for them, their washing sent out, their rooms cleaned, even their beds made. Now Suzette's lack of knowledge manifested itself constantly, especially when she offered to do things she couldn't.

"It doesn't matter. I can drink the coffee you already have," Zeke said.

"There won't be enough for all of us," Josie pointed out.

Josie realized she was sending mixed messages, neither of which was what she wanted to say. She was merely pointing out the obvious, but Suzette looked embarrassed, and Zeke looked like he'd rather be any-where than where he was. Hawk looked from one to the other with no identifiable expression.

"It won't take but a few minutes to make some more," Josie said.

Again, she'd said something she hadn't meant to say, but she couldn't back down now. To cover her confusion, she turned away and walked to the wagon to get some more coffee beans. Once she was out of sight of the others, her body sagged against the wagon. She didn't know what was wrong with her. Her brain and her tongue didn't seem to be connected. Either that, or her brain had divided into halves, with each sending different messages. Whatever the problem, it was Zeke's fault.

"I'll take the mules for a drink before we harness them," Hawk said.

"I'll go with you," Suzette offered.

Josie grabbed the coffee beans and scooted around the corner of the wagon, protests against being left alone with Zeke teetering on the end of her tongue, but Suzette and Hawk had already turned toward the river. To call them back now would be to offer an even bigger insult. As much as she didn't want to be left alone with Zeke, he didn't deserve that.

"You want me to leave, don't you?" Zeke asked.

"No." That wasn't exactly a lie. She'd rather he were not here, but her real objection was to being left alone with him. His knowing smile made her squirm.

"I never pictured you as one to lie, even about little things."

"I didn't lie. I don't want you to leave."

"Okay, but you don't want me to be here either."

She nodded.

"Because you don't like me."

"I don't dislike you."

Josie didn't understand why it should be so important to her that Zeke believe she didn't dislike him. Maybe she just didn't want him to have the wrong impression about her. After all, she wasn't cruel. She simply didn't want a relationship with a man, and Zeke seemed exactly the kind of man she *most* wanted to avoid. If she lacked any other reason—and she had plenty—the fact that he confused her was enough.

"Why don't you fix your own coffee?" she said, holding the coffee beans out to him. "You know better than I how you like it."

Zeke took the coffee from her with a disbelieving grimace. "You just can't bring yourself to do anything for me, can you? I wish you'd tell me what I did to make you dislike me so much."

"I don't dislike you."

"Yeah, and the look you're giving me isn't saying *I wish you were dead*." He strode to the back of the wagon. "Where do you keep your extra pots? Never mind. I found one." He filled it with water and settled it on the coals. "Hawk and Suzette have decided that since we're going the same way, we ought to travel together," he said, looking up at her from where he was squatting by the fire. "We need to get a few things straight between us if that's going to work."

Josie's confusion of the last several minutes was nothing compared to the chaos Zeke's announcement created among her thoughts. She was furious at Hawk and Suzette for making such a decision without consulting her, surprised Zeke would even consider it, and petrified that she might actually be feeling relieved. "What do you think?"

Zeke's gaze narrowed. "That depends on you."

His gaze was so piercing, she had to stop herself from stepping back. "How do you mean?"

Zeke's gaze didn't waver. "I'd prefer to get our horses to the ranch as quickly as possible. That would be easier without a wagon, and traveling alone, we'd be better able to avoid trouble with horse thieves."

"How many times has somebody tried to steal your horses?"

"Just once, but we got away without too much trouble. The mares can run faster than a horse carrying a man. Your mules couldn't, even if they weren't dragging a wagon."

She faced him squarely. "Then leave us."

"We couldn't do that."

"Why not? You're more concerned about your horses than you are about us."

Was that one of the reasons she was so irritated with him? She hoped she hadn't become so pathetic she could be jealous of a bunch of pregnant mares.

"If we decide to take you with us, we'll be just as responsible for you and Suzette as for the horses."

"I thought it was already decided."

He gave her a questioning look. "It won't be if you or I don't go along with it."

"And whether you agree depends on me."

Zeke poured a healthy amount of coffee into the boiling water. "Look, we both know you practically get hives when you see me. I'm not about to spend the rest of this trip having to watch my back."

"You think I might try to hurt you?" Surely he couldn't believe she was violent. "Look, I've had some bad experiences with men."

"Then you shouldn't hang around with men who're drunk and starved for the sight of a woman. It's a bad combination."

Josie's body stiffened at the implied insult. "I entertain men. I don't *hang around* with them."

"What do you call working in a saloon?"

"A job."

"If you lie down with dogs, you're bound to get up with fleas."

Rage consumed Josie so completely, she picked up the pot of brewing coffee and hurled it at Zeke before she realized what she was doing. When he yelled and threw himself to one side, escaping the boiling water, she went after him, the pot raised over her head. One minute she was chasing him. The next he had her firmly in his grip, her body pressed tightly against him. He applied pressure to her wrist until her grip relaxed and the pot slid from her grasp.

"What in hell is wrong with you?" Zeke demanded.

"I won't let anybody call me a whore." She struggled to break away, but Zeke's grip was like iron. She tried to kick him, but he pinned her legs between his.

"I never said anything like that," Zeke protested. "I wouldn't even if I'd thought it."

"You accused me of lying down with dogs."

"That's just an expression. It means if you hang around dangerous people, you can expect dangerous things to happen to you."

The fight went out of Josie, but she didn't stop

103

struggling. She didn't want Zeke to know how relieved she was he didn't think she was a whore. "I don't believe you."

"So what else is new?"

The feeling coursing through her body was new. Now that the blinding rage had receded, she was aware her body was in intimate contact with Zeke's. Her back was pressed against his chest, his arms across her chest resting against her breasts as he held her hands in his unbreakable grip. But it was the power of his thighs holding her lower body motionless that was gradually draining the strength from her muscles, making it impossible for her to struggle against him.

Even though she tried to tell herself she didn't want him to touch her, that she didn't even want him close to her, her body was ignoring her brain and sending its own messages, forcing her to acknowledge them in spite of herself. She didn't want to feel pleasure at a man's touch. She didn't want to feel excitement at his closeness. Most of all, she didn't want to feel desire for a man, *need* for one. That need had made a slave of her mother even after the law had declared she was free.

"Let me go," Josie said.

"Not until I'm sure you won't throw anything else at me."

"I won't."

"How do I know you're telling the truth?"

She couldn't tell him she wanted him to let her go because she was afraid she would start to like being held in his arms. She certainly wouldn't tell him the feel of his body against her own was making her so warm she was having trouble thinking clearly. She absolutely wouldn't tell him that she was ·beginning to wonder if he might be different from all the other men in her life.

Despite the fact that he was attracted to her—she'd seen evidence of that on at least two occasions—he didn't lose control. She felt something perilously akin to regret. She took pride in her ability to control her feelings for men. Consequently, it embarrassed her to be unable to control her feelings for Zeke. In the same vein, she prided herself in her ability to make any man want her. It hurt her vanity—and threatened her security—to discover that Zeke could control his feelings for her more effectively than she could control her feelings for him.

"You don't, but you can dunk me in the river if I make any attempt to attack you again."

"Well, well." Suzette's voice came from behind them. "And I thought you two didn't like each other."

Chapter Seven

Zeke released Josie and stepped back. It would be impossible to explain the circumstances. He could tell from the expressions on Suzette's and Hawk's faces that they weren't going to believe anything he said.

"We've decided to become best friends," Josie said, sarcasm vying with embarrassment for prominence in her voice. "That was just our way of sealing the agreement."

The satisfied look disappeared from Suzette's face. Hawk's expression barely changed. It was his eyes that told Zeke he didn't believe a word. He looked for the coffeepot and found it only a couple feet away. He poured more water in it and set it back on the coals.

"I thought the water would have been hot by now," Hawk said.

"We had an accident," Zeke said.

"It was no accident." From her stormy expression, it

was clear that Josie didn't mean to hide behind Zeke's excuse. "Zeke is just trying to protect me. I misunderstood something he said and threw the coffee at him." Her cheeks aflame, she faced Hawk and Suzette as though daring either of them to say anything. "I missed. He very wisely grabbed hold of me to prevent me from throwing anything else. I should apologize. He's never done anything to make me think he would make a rude remark."

Leaving three people staring at her in disbelief, Josie walked away and disappeared along the path to the river. Zeke was surprised that Josie had taken responsibility for the misunderstanding. It was even harder to believe that she'd apologized.

"What did you say to her?" Even Hawk, usually indifferent to people's behavior, was curious about what could have caused such a change in Josie.

His words hadn't seemed ugly when he'd said them, but now Zeke felt slightly embarrassed. "If you lie down with dogs, you have to expect to get up with fleas."

"That doesn't sound so terrible," Suzette said.

Zeke ducked his head. "It's what I said earlier that made it sound bad."

Hawk chuckled softly. "And you're supposed to be the one who's good at talking to women."

Zeke looked up, shrugged, and reached for the coffee beans. "All bets are off when it comes to Josie."

Suzette moved closer to Zeke. "It's not your fault. She's had some bad experiences with men."

"I'm not asking her to fall in love with me." Zeke was unable to keep the frustration out of his voice. "But I don't see how traveling together will work if she's going to take everything I say the wrong way."

Leigh Greenwood

"Are you saying you won't let us travel with you?" Suzette asked.

Suzette's dismay was obvious. Zeke measured out the coffee with great care to give himself a moment to think. He moved the pan with the cooked bacon to the edge of the coals and put the coffeepot in the center. It wasn't any better for Hawk to become emotionally entangled with Suzette than it was for him to become entangled with Josie. Would he be doing Hawk a favor by forcing him and Suzette apart before they could become seriously interested in each other? Did he have the *right* to decide something like this for Hawk?

"No, I'm not," he said. "But you'd better talk to Josie before we decide."

He and Hawk had each been interested in several women over the past twenty years, but this was the first time Zeke thought Hawk might be on the verge of developing a serious relationship. He didn't know why he should think that—Hawk and Suzette barely knew each other—but there seemed to be something between them he'd never seen in any of Hawk's previous affairs.

"I should go talk to Josie," Suzette said.

"Good idea. Would you like me to make some biscuits?" What the hell was he doing, trying to bribe Josie with his cooking? So far his competence had done nothing but irritate her. He wondered if she'd like him better if he was so helpless she had to do everything for him. Some women liked it when they believed a man couldn't survive without them.

"Can you really make biscuits?" Suzette asked.

"Sure. Hawk and I learned to cook for ourselves

108

long ago. If we hadn't, our choice would have been to starve or eat bad food."

"I'll be back soon."

"Take your time. It'll be better for everybody if Josie is sure about what she wants to do." His expression turned stony. "You can also tell her we reserve the right to reconsider this arrangement at any time."

Suzette's eyes widened in surprise. She turned to Hawk. "Do you agree with that?"

Hawk stared at Zeke for a moment before swinging his gaze to Suzette. "Yes."

Suzette looked disappointed. She appeared to want to say something. Instead, she shrugged her shoulders, turned, and started down the path Josie had taken.

"Are you sure you want to do this?" Hawk asked.

Zeke poked needlessly at the coals and reconsidered his offer to make biscuits. He and Hawk had already eaten. Why had he offered to cook for the women? Making biscuits wasn't going to make Josie like him any better, and it would make them even later getting on the trail. He got to his feet with a frustrated grunt. He might as well stop debating and get the makings from the wagon. For reasons he couldn't identify, he had to make biscuits.

"I'd rather wrestle a grown steer," he said to Hawk as he gathered flour and hog fat from the wagon, "but you know as well as I do this woman is under my skin. I've got to get her out before she drives me crazy."

"We could just leave."

"What about Suzette?"

Hawk's expression didn't change. Only his eyes indicated that Zeke had touched a nerve. "What about her?"

"You like her. I think she likes you."

"We're attracted to each other, but it's something either of us can walk away from. It's not like that with you and Josie."

Zeke wasn't sure Hawk was right, but he was too confused about his own feelings to think he knew what was going on with Hawk. He dumped some flour on a board and began mixing it with lard until the mixture was crumbly. It felt good to have something to do with his hands, something he knew he could accomplish. "Whatever is between me and Josie isn't going anywhere, but that's not true of you and Suzette. It could develop into something serious."

Hawk's gaze seemed to bore into Zeke. "If it did, would you mind?"

Zeke opened the can of milk the Pettingers had insisted on giving the women. He grinned when he saw globs of butter floating on top. The action of the wagon had churned the cream until it separated into butter. He poured out some milk for the biscuits. He'd fish out the butter later. It would taste great on hot biscuits.

"I'd hate it, but I'd also be happy for you," Zeke said as he poured milk into his batter. "I've gotten so used to the two of us working together, it would feel strange to be alone."

"I'll stake the mules so they can graze some more," Hawk said. "Then I'll get the mares and bring them back here."

"You think Josie is going to agree to travel with us?"

"She won't want to, but she will. I'll be back in half

an hour. Save me a couple of biscuits." He took the mules and went off to look for a place to graze them.

Great, Zeke thought as he drove his fist into the dough. After being talked into doing something against her will, Josie would be in a fine mood. He retrieved a Dutch oven from the wagon, formed the biscuits, put them inside, and put the cover on tight to keep out dust and ashes. After digging a shallow hole, he set the oven in it, then began heaping coals on top. The biscuits ought to be ready in less than twenty minutes.

Zeke looked down the path that led to the river, but he saw no sign of Josie or Suzette. Muttering an oath, he pulled out his tin cup and poured himself some coffee. It was strong, black, and hot, just the way he liked it, but it didn't improve his mood.

He'd never thought he and Hawk might separate, might go their different ways. As the only two orphans who weren't white, they'd gravitated toward each other while growing up. They'd never questioned that they would leave the ranch together, that they would work together. They were outsiders who didn't belong anywhere. Despite forming several attachments with women over the years, none of their relationships had lasted. After twenty-five years, they'd come to think of themselves as permanent partners. That's what the ranch was all about.

Zeke turned his gaze toward the river, but the path was still empty. Uttering another oath, he started down the path, only to stop before he'd gone a dozen steps. This was something Josie had to decide for herself. Putting pressure on her wouldn't work. He turned around, but rather than go back to the wagon, he started off on a path parallel to the river. He had some decisions of his own to make. If they traveled to Tombstone with these women, life as he'd known it for the last twenty years could very well come to an end. If that happened, what was he going to do?

"We don't have to do this," Suzette said to Josie. "We can get to Tombstone by ourselves."

"It makes sense to travel together." It was hard for Josie to say or do anything that implied she needed to depend on a man to help her, but she was also too smart to deny the truth. "They know the way better than we do; they know more about traveling through the desert; they can offer us protection; they can even help us if we get into trouble."

"It's not all good. Those horses may attract thieves, men willing to kill to get what they want."

"Would they be any more dangerous than men looking for women and willing to use them for their pleasure?"

Josie was sitting on a bank cut by the river when it had run several feet higher. She had dug her heels into the sand repeatedly until she had made a rut about six inches deep. It wasn't the only outward sign of her inner turmoil. Several times she'd found herself gripping the fingers of one hand with the other until she'd popped her knuckles twice.

Her gaze settled on the river as it raced over rocks in a shallow crossing. The crystal-clear water was barely six inches deep, but the sound of it tumbling over and around multicolor stones created a murmur soothing to her raw nerves. It was a calm, serene scene, the river against a backdrop of trees on the far side, the sun coming over the horizon creating bursts of brilliant color, the wide expanse of the desert spreading out behind her. She could almost believe she would never have to work in another saloon, never have to sing and dance for men who wanted her for only one purpose. Out here, in the quiet isolation of the morning, all that seemed very far away.

"I'll ride with Zeke," Suzette offered. "You can ride with Hawk."

"Don't be ridiculous," Josie snapped. "You like Hawk, you like to ride, and you adore horses. You should ride with him."

"But that leaves you with Zeke."

"I've been left with worse men before." She was immediately sorry for her words. Her feelings about Zeke were contradictory and chaotic, but he'd done nothing to warrant a statement like that. "I shouldn't have said that. Zeke seems to be a good man."

"What is it about him that you don't like?"

"All I have to do is close my eyes and I can see my father."

"Zeke can't help that."

"He doesn't want to. He likes being more powerful than a woman, thinking he knows more than a woman, that a woman ought to listen to what he says because he says it. All men are like that."

"Hawk isn't."

"Sure, he is. You just haven't disagreed with him yet." Josie dug her feet deeper in the sand until water began to seep into the bottom of the hole.

"I expect I'll have plenty of opportunity to judge for myself before we reach Tombstone. Are you ready to go back?"

Josie began pushing the sand back into the hole.

"Give me a minute. I'm still embarrassed about throwing that coffee at Zeke."

Suzette's brow creased with worry. "What made you do something like that?"

Josie shrugged. "I don't know. Something about Zeke brings out the worst in me."

"Well, he's making biscuits. That ought to raise him a little in your estimation."

Josie grudgingly laughed at the thought of Zeke cooking. "Maybe, if they're edible."

Suzette rose from her position next to Josie and brushed the sand and bits of debris off her skirt. "Don't wait too long. They'd like to be on the trail as soon as possible."

But Josie wasn't concerned just now about getting on the trail. Her mind was focused on her situation. She'd finally figured out what was causing her to act like an irritable wildcat half the time. Her experience had proved to her that she couldn't trust men to protect her or do anything else they'd promised. Her personal life had been immeasurably better since she'd made up her mind to have nothing to do with them.

Then Zeke came along and upset everything.

Somewhere inside was a part of her that liked everything about Zeke. Before she knew what was happening, she was at war with herself. And she was miserable. Part of her wanted to believe in Zeke, to trust him, to open up to him. The other part of her was petrified of what would happen if she did.

But circumstances had stepped in and made it difficult to refuse Zeke and Hawk's offer to escort them to Tombstone. Her agony of indecision would have no easy resolution.

* * *

By the time the stranger rode up to their wagon, Zeke was ready to welcome any interruption to the uneasy silence that existed between him and Josie. He'd tried to talk to her on a variety of subjects but gotten only reluctant responses for his efforts. When he asked about her past, she said she'd rather not talk about it. When he asked about her hopes for the future, she said that depended on luck. When he asked what she wanted, she said she didn't know yet. When he asked if she was sleepy and wanted him to shut up and leave her alone, she said she was never sleepy during the day. Besides, she couldn't sleep with the wagon lurching over the uneven ground. Zeke replied that he'd once read about a magic carpet that could provide a smooth ride over even the roughest landscape, but he'd never been able to afford one.

After that they didn't talk at all. She had retreated into the wagon, leaving him alone on the bench.

"Mind if I join you for a spell?" the stranger asked. "We seem to be headed in the same direction."

"Not at all," Zeke said. "Where are you headed?"

"Tombstone. Then to Bisbee. I have some business interests there. My name's Solomon Gardner. You might have heard of my father, David Gardner. He established our ranch in Gardner Canyon."

David Gardner had come to Arizona after the Civil War to fight Indians. Later he established one of the most successful cattle ranches in the San Pedro Valley, which now belonged to his only son. David had also been one of the first men to invest in mines in the valley, which now made Solomon one of the richest men in Arizona. His reputation with the ladies was rapidly becoming legendary. Considering that his biblical namesake had a harem of more than five thousand women, maybe that was only to be expected.

"I didn't expect to see a man driving a wagon through the desert. Wouldn't your horse have been faster?" Gardner asked.

There were lots of reasons why Zeke didn't want Gardner to know he was traveling with a woman, not the least being that he would assume Josie was Zeke's woman—in the biblical sense. Josie emerged from the wagon before he could decide how to answer.

"He's tied to a wagon because he and his partner came across two women foolish enough to think they could travel from Globe to Tombstone on their own."

It didn't bother Zeke that Gardner's eyes grew wide at the sight of Josie. Even rich men didn't come across a woman like Josie more than once or twice in a lifetime. What *did* bother him was the lust he saw flame up immediately in their depths. Gardner recovered his tongue quickly.

"If your friend is only half as beautiful as you, I'm surprised the good citizens of Globe didn't come up with a *petition* to beg you to stay."

"Actually their wives *petitioned* for us to leave."

Zeke didn't like the way Josie was looking at Gardner. Her gaze covered him in one thorough, analytical sweep. She took in the quality of his mount, the silver work on his saddle and bridle, the heavy saddlebags, and the quality of his clothes. Nor, Zeke was certain, did she overlook his handsome face or impressive physique.

"I can sympathize with the wives, but I feel sorry for

their husbands," Gardner said. "Where are you headed?"

"To Tombstone," Josie said. "We hope to find jobs there."

Gardner's eyes lit up, and he smiled so broadly Zeke ached to knock the grin off his face. Gardner was rich and Josie was out of a job. It would be easy for a man of his resources to see that Josie landed in a comfortable position when she reached Tombstone, but Zeke was certain that position would have little or nothing to do with singing and dancing. His fingers closed around the reins in his hands until his fingernails dug into his palms.

"I'm sure in your case that won't be a problem." Gardner continued to eye Josie in a manner that made Zeke itch to knock him off his fancy bay horse. The animal looked like it had thoroughbred blood and hadn't been gelded. Only vanity would cause a man to choose a high-strung stud horse as a mount for a trip of more than a hundred miles through the desert. Zeke almost wished the mares were in season. Then he would have had a legitimate reason for telling Gardner to get lost quickly.

"Do you know a lot about the saloons and theaters in Tombstone?" Josie asked Gardner.

Zeke wondered why Josie hadn't asked him or Hawk that question. They'd been to Tombstone at least a dozen times over the last ten years.

"I own part of the Birdcage, the best theater in the Arizona Territory," Gardner said. "A word from me would guarantee you a job. What do you do?"

"My partner and I sing and dance."

117

"You could make a lot more money serving drinks and getting friendly with the customers."

"I know, but I discovered most men don't agree with my definition of *friendly*. They seem to think it gives them the right to take certain liberties."

Zeke couldn't quite figure out Josie's intent. Even though the meaning of her words was clear, her tone implied just the opposite. He'd run across more than one honey-voiced female in his lifetime, but Josie was the best yet. A man could just about drown in her velvety voice. Zeke was ashamed to admit it, but he wouldn't have cared what she said to him as long as she sounded like that when she said it.

To look at her, you'd think she was flirting with Gardner. She was smiling, dipping her chin and turning her head to the side like she was shy, maybe even embarrassed by Gardner's open admiration. Since Zeke was positive that Josie didn't have a shy bone in her body, he had to assume she was putting on an act to see what she could get out of Gardner. It was probably the way women in her profession did business, but it made Zeke so angry he wanted to shout at her to stop acting like a strumpet.

"You can't blame the men. They must think they're seeing a vision from heaven when they see you," Gardner said.

Zeke was sure he was going to puke. This guy was rich. He didn't have to talk like an idiot to get women. "Only if they're too drunk to remember their feet are on the ground," he growled before Gardner could say something else nauseating.

"They'd probably feel that way even sober. I thought I might be suffering from a heat stroke."

Zeke hoped Josie didn't believe anything this man said.

"Do you think you could help me find a job?" Josie asked.

"Sure. Do you mind if I camp with you tonight? I'd need to meet your partner before I could make any promises. Then we'd need to talk about a few things, like exactly what kind of act you do, what kind of music you need, how much you'll expect to get paid, where to find accommodations, that sort of thing."

Josie turned to Zeke. "I'm sure Hawk won't mind if you don't. This could be the perfect situation for Suzette and me. She really needs money for her sister."

This was the first Zeke had heard about Suzette having a sister, but he had no doubt that Suzette would be just as anxious as Josie to talk with Gardner. If he really was part owner of the Birdcage—and Zeke had no reason to doubt him—meeting him on the trail was an incredible stroke of good fortune, but Zeke was worried just the same. Men like Gardner never gave something without expecting even more in return.

"I've got my own supplies," Gardner said.

"That's not a problem." Zeke was aware that his voice showed no enthusiasm. "We have more than enough."

"I'm glad I ran into you. I wasn't looking forward to making this journey alone."

"Weren't you planning to spend the night at various ranches along the way?" Zeke asked. "You must know all the owners." Ranchers always stuck together to protect themselves against rustlers. The threat from the Apaches was gone, but there were more than enough renegade Indians, Mexican bandits, and American outlaws and freebooters willing to take up where Geronimo's braves had left off.

"I enjoy sleeping out. It reminds me of going on cattle drives when I was a boy." Gardner shaded his eyes and looked at the sun, which was sinking over the Santa Catalina Mountains to the southwest. "When do you think you'll be making camp?"

"My partner is probably doing that right now," Zeke admitted reluctantly. "We're taking a few mares to our ranch. We like to give them time to graze before it gets dark."

"You're a rancher? I've never heard of you."

He hadn't heard because he hadn't had the courtesy to ask Zeke's name. Zeke would have taken offense at Gardner's surprise if he hadn't become inured to white men thinking it impossible that a black man could earn enough money to buy a ranch.

"We have a small ranch on the Babocamari River just outside of Fairbank."

"I didn't catch your name," Gardner said.

"It's Zeke Maxwell. My partner is my brother. His name's Hawk."

"I look forward to meeting him, and your partner," Gardner said to Josie.

The trail passed through a spot where the cactus grew so close that Gardner had to drop back. Even the mules moved a bit closer together. Zeke could hear the spines of the cholla scratch their way along the canvas wagon cover as it passed. He hoped they didn't cause any rips.

"Why don't you want Mr. Gardner to camp with us?" Josie asked.

"I never said I didn't want him to come along."

"You didn't have to. One look, and it was obvious you wanted to hit him. Do you dislike every man except Hawk, or are you afraid you can't measure up because you're black?"

Chapter Eight

Zeke turned away from Josie to stare at the trail ahead. Her question reached down deep into the core of him, to a place where even Hawk was seldom allowed to go.

He'd spent the first fourteen years of his life as a slave, ripped from his mother and sold to a woman who beat him, starved him, berated him, told him he was stupid and not worth the hundred dollars she'd paid for him. His home had been her attic, his bed the bare floorboards, his food the scraps from her table. His work had been whatever menial chore she assigned him, his reward constant complaints that he couldn't do even the simplest job right. She had threatened to shoot him, sell him, give him to the Indians. In the end she'd sold him to some farmers who'd nearly killed him with overwork. It wasn't until Jake and Isabelle adopted him that people stopped treating him as the lowest form of life.

Years later he finally realized he'd survived those first fourteen years only because he hated that woman for making him feel unworthy. He'd fought his adopted family at first because he didn't believe anyone could like him. He'd gravitated to Hawk because the two of them were the only nonwhite kids among the eleven orphans Jake and Isabelle had adopted, not because he thought Hawk liked or trusted him any more than he liked or trusted Hawk. He'd only begun to change when he realized that regardless of the stupid or mean things he did, Jake and Isabelle weren't going to throw him out. He found that hard to believe, but it was even harder to believe they wanted him to stay because they loved him.

He'd only begun to believe it might be possible, to *hope* it was possible, when he and Hawk had come home after being away for nearly a year and Isabelle had greeted him by throwing her arms around him. Her tears had practically soaked the front of his shirt. Then, after making sure both he and Hawk were healthy and unharmed, she'd given them a first-class dressing down for being gone so long without writing. She'd ended up saying that if they ever did that again, she'd come after them herself. She'd then punched each of them in the chest before breaking into tears and telling them to get out of her sight until dinner was ready. Naturally she'd fixed their favorite foods.

He'd been so caught up in his thoughts, he hadn't realized the mules had slowed down to sample the leaves of a stand of young willows. A sharp crack of a whip over their heads got them started again.

But while he'd finally come to believe that Jake and Isabelle thought he was just as good as any other human who'd ever been born, the rest of the world hadn't agreed. He and Hawk had been hired by some of the most important people and some of the biggest businesses in the Southwest. Most men he'd worked with respected his judgment and character, but as soon as he and Hawk finished their work, they wanted them out of sight. Preferably, out of town. He told himself he was as good as anybody else. He believed it when Isabelle treated him exactly as she treated her other sons, but did he believe it when the rest of the world didn't? He turned to Josie.

"I'm not afraid to measure myself against any man in the world. Somebody will prove to be better than I am at everything I can do, but that doesn't make me less of a man. Do you feel like you're less respectable because your mother was a slave?" They had avoided the issue of the color of their skin, but now they were in it up to their knees. Josie acted as if he'd stuck her with a pin.

Unfortunately, the trail had widened and Gardner pulled even with them again. "I hate these damned cactuses," he said. "I had a man who nearly lost a finger before my mother could get the thorn out."

It was all Zeke could do to keep from telling Gardner to get back behind the wagon. By the time he managed to control his anger enough to be sure he wouldn't say anything stupid, he realized it was probably better that he and Josie had been interrupted. They'd never been able to have a discussion without it turning into an argument. But the issue Josie had brought up went way beyond any differences between them. It reached all the way down to a level where they were the same, a place he was sure Josie didn't want to go any more than he did.

"We always try to camp next to the river," Zeke told Gardner. "That gives us easy access to water, and means we aren't as likely to wake up with thorns in our behinds."

Gardner's gaze moved past him to Josie. "It would be a great shame to ruin such perfection."

Zeke wondered if the man was taught to talk like that or if it came naturally.

"You don't have to worry about me," Josie said to Gardner. "I sleep in the wagon."

"And I sleep next to it," Zeke added. "But I don't sleep very well. The slightest noise tends to wake me up."

Gardner flashed another one of those smiles Zeke wanted to knock off his face. "What a coincidence. I don't sleep well, either. I often have to get up and move around for a while before I can fall back to sleep."

"Then you'd better be careful," Zeke said. "I'd hate for my brother to shoot you, thinking you were out to steal our horses."

"Hawk's an odd name for a black man."

"He's not black. His mother was a white woman. His father was a mean-tempered Comanche."

"Then he's not really your brother."

"We were adopted along with a bunch of white boys. I've got *lots* of brothers."

It pleased Zeke to see Gardner's confusion. He was certain the man was trying to come up with a reason why any white couple would adopt a black kid and a half-breed. Before Gardner could ask any questions, Suzette appeared on the trail ahead of them. If she was surprised at seeing Gardner, she didn't show it.

"Hawk has made camp," she called out to them. "It's just a short way ahead."

It had been a long time since Josie had endured a more uncomfortable meal, and it was all Zeke's fault. She didn't know why he had to try to act like her body-guard. It wasn't as if she was in any danger from Gardner. The man was so rich he probably thought he was entitled to anything he wanted, but Josie was fully capable of explaining, if necessary, that he wasn't entitled to her. And to be fair to him, the worst thing he'd done was act as if he should be the center of attention. He hadn't stopped talking since they'd made camp. And asking questions.

"Are you sure you don't want anything else to eat?" Suzette asked Gardner. "If we don't eat it now, we'll have it for breakfast."

"I couldn't eat another bite." Gardner stood and stretched his legs. "I need to settle my dinner before I bed down for the night. If you have no objection," he said, turning to Hawk, "I'll go with you to check on the horses."

"Sure," Hawk said with a decided lack of enthusiasm.

Hawk had started out the day in jeans and a check shirt, but sometime after stopping for the night he'd found time to change into buckskins and exchange his boots for moccasins. The feather was back on his head, too. Josie didn't understand the significance of the change, but she'd noticed two sharply whispered exchanges between Hawk and Zeke.

"Zeke tells me you have a mare with Morgan blood," Gardner said to Hawk. "I've been looking for a mare like that myself. If I like her, would you consider selling her?"

Hawk handed his bowl to Suzette. "None of our horses are for sale. Come on if you're coming."

"I can pay top price," Gardner said as he followed Hawk out of camp.

"We don't need your money." Josie barely caught Hawk's reply before he and Gardner were swallowed up by the night.

"I don't trust that man," Zeke said.

"You don't have to trust him," Josie said, impatient with Zeke's dislike of Gardner. "He's not offering you a job."

"You don't know that he has any jobs to offer."

Zeke gathered up the bowls. Josie wondered if he'd leave Gardner's, but he finally picked it up.

"If he can't give us the jobs he promised, we'll find someone who can. Now if you want me to help you clean up, let's go."

"I don't understand it," Zeke said, disgusted, as he followed Josie toward the river. "A man just has to be rich and good-looking and women believe everything he says."

"We like them tall with broad shoulders." Josie knew she shouldn't intentionally annoy Zeke, but his dislike of Gardner was getting on her nerves. "It's even better when they're single." She glanced back at Zeke. "Everybody knows that single men never lie to women." She nearly laughed aloud at his outraged expression.

"I know what I'm talking about. I've seen too many men like Gardner," he said.

127

"I've probably seen more men than you'll see in your lifetime." Josie reached the edge of the river and squatted down to rub sand in her bowl and the pot they'd used to cook the stew. "There's nothing you can tell me about men I don't already know."

"You've only seen them from the stage or in a protected situation," Zeke said as he knelt down beside her. "I've ridden with them in cattle drives, worked with them on nearly every kind of job a man can do, worked *for* them when they thought they were too good to do the work themselves. I know what they're *really* like, not what they want you to think when they've had a bath and changed their clothes."

"Are you going to clean those bowls, or are you going to keep trying to convince me that Gardner is too dangerous to talk to?"

Zeke tossed a handful of wet sand in each of three bowls. "Dammit, Josie, I don't care if you sit up all night talking to Gardner. I just don't want you to trust him."

"I trust you."

"No, you don't." Zeke looked across the river to where stars were beginning to show in the sky above the Galiuro Mountains. "You wouldn't be here if Suzette hadn't twisted your arm."

Josie didn't know whether Zeke's feelings had been hurt by her reluctance or whether he was jealous. "Look, I don't understand why you're so upset about Gardner, but it's not like I'm running off with him. It's not even a question of whether I like him. The man has said he can give me a job."

"I know, but—"

"If he can give me a job, fine. If he can't, that's fine,

128

too. Any relationship between us will be strictly a business arrangement."

"For men like Gardner, there's no such thing as a *strictly business arrangement* when it comes to women. He'll expect you to be properly appreciative."

Josie rose to her feet with an irritated grunt and walked to the edge of the river to wash the sand out of the pot. "I've always wondered what it would be like to have a protective older brother. Now I know."

She knew from the silence behind her that she'd said something wrong. She turned to see Zeke staring at her with the saddest eyes she'd ever seen. Much to her surprise, her irritation faded. She didn't mean to argue with him all the time. She didn't like to keep pushing him away so that he thought she hated him. He was bossy and had a touchy temper, but she was no angel herself. He and Hawk had changed their plans to make sure she and Suzette reached Tombstone safely. Unlike nearly every other man she knew, he expected to help with the cooking and the cleaning up. He was really a rather nice man. She wouldn't mind having him around if he didn't upset her so much.

"Suzette has had even more experience than I have," she said when Zeke continued to stare at her, "and she doesn't see anything wrong with Gardner."

Zeke moved to the edge of the river to wash the sand from the bowls. She was prepared for him to argue, to tell her she didn't know what she was talking about, even to say no woman could take care of herself. She wasn't prepared for silence. Hawk was the silent one. Zeke could carry on a conversation with a cactus.

129

"Are you so angry at me you can't even talk to me?"

"No." He spoke without looking up from the muddied water. "I just don't have anything else to say." He stepped farther into the river and rinsed the bowls and the pot in clear water. Zeke kept rinsing the bowls again and again until there couldn't possibly be a grain of sand or a speck of food adhering to them. She found his silence almost as upsetting as his constant irritability.

"Okay, what do you want me to do?" she asked, her voice rising in frustration.

"Just be careful," he replied in an uncharacteristically quiet voice. "You ready to go back?"

She wanted to take a long walk to get away from the most confusing and frustrating man she'd ever met, but that wasn't a wise choice, so she settled for going back to camp. "Suzette's probably wondering whether I've fallen into the river and been swept away."

"No, she's not. She knows your big brother is here to protect you."

It hit her like a smack in the face. Josie didn't believe for one minute Zeke was in love with her—or even liked her very much—but no man wanted to feel like a woman's brother. He wanted to believe she thought he was strong, virile, exciting, possibly even a little dangerous. Saying he was like a brother practically emasculated him.

But having hurt his feelings, she didn't know how to go about apologizing without making it worse. She'd never been around a man like Zeke. She didn't really know what went on inside his head. At first she'd thought he was just a big showoff. But even though she'd only known him for a few days, she'd discovered there was much more to him than she had guessed. She had to find a way to let him know she hadn't meant to hurt him.

"Suzette and I trust you and Hawk to make sure nothing happens to us. I don't know why you decided to let us travel with you, but I know it's not what you wanted to do."

Zeke walked out of the river. But instead of heading back to the camp, he stopped in front of her. "Hawk was convinced you'd never make it to Tombstone without running into trouble."

"Do you always go along with what Hawk wants?"

At first he seemed angry at what she implied, but that faded quickly to be replaced by something like sadness.

"Hawk and I are brothers, and not just because we were adopted together. I do things because he wants, and he does things because I want. I know people don't like or trust us because we're different. But no matter what happens, no matter how great the danger, I know I can count on him to cover my back. We've been each other's best friend for twenty-three years. Yes, I'd do anything for Hawk just because he wanted it."

Josie didn't know what to say. She'd never met two people who'd developed such a close, trusting, and giving relationship. She had thought it was impossible. Yet as hard as it was for her to understand, she believed Zeke. He had spoken easily and directly—from the heart.

"I wish I had somebody I felt that way about," Josie said.

"You won't as long as you fight with people who try to help you."

The truth of Zeke's words was like a stab of pain. Josie was embarrassed by her behavior, frightened by how close Zeke had come to the truth. She *had* been afraid to trust people, so she'd used them, making her almost as bad as her father. But she'd had no other choice. She did it to survive. She spun on her heel and headed back to camp. She probably ought to ask Gardner to accompany them to Tombstone so Zeke and Hawk could go straight to their ranch.

But she wouldn't do that. Despite their inability to be together without fighting, she trusted Zeke. She didn't trust Gardner's silver tongue, but that didn't mean she wouldn't use his interest in her to get a job. Life wasn't easy for women who entertained miners.

"Where's Zeke?" Suzette asked when Josie returned to the campsite alone.

"Probably trying to forget he ever met me."

Suzette was seated close to the fire, her knees drawn up under her chin, her arms wrapped around her legs. "Is it possible for you two not to fight for the rest of this trip? Hawk says we ought to reach Benson in four days. From there we could make it to Tombstone by ourselves."

Josie strode around the fire, her skirt swishing angrily around her legs. "I'm sure Zeke wouldn't fight if I didn't drive him to it."

Suzette's gaze narrowed. "I've never seen you act like this."

Josie stopped in her tracks. "You make it sound like a lovers' quarrel."

Suzette's smile was wry. "I certainly hope this isn't how you'll act when you fall in love."

"I'm *never* going to fall in love." She started circling

the fire again. "I thought Hawk and Gardner would be back by now."

"You know what men are like when they start talking about horses."

"No, I don't. How are they?"

Suzette shrugged, but Josie thought she saw the suggestion of a smile.

"They get so involved they can't stop. Sometimes I think it's their substitute for talking about women. There are lots of things they can't say about a woman, even to another man, but there's nothing you can't say about a horse. I've seen men go glassy-eyed talking about a mare's limbs, her shoulder, her rump, her breeding potential. And the whole time they're running their hands all over the poor horse."

Josie looked at her friend in dismay, only to realize Suzette's eyes were twinkling with merriment. "You awful woman. You were kidding me the whole time, making me think terrible things."

"I would never do such a thing." But Suzette could barely manage to protest without laughing.

"I never knew you were such a dishonest woman." But Josie's accusation lacked conviction. She wasn't immune to the laughter in Suzette's eyes. Giving in to the impulse, she dropped down next to her friend. "What prompted you to say something like that?"

Suzette leaned toward Josie until their shoulders touched. "It stopped you from thinking about Zeke, didn't it?"

Josie sobered. "For a few seconds."

"Well, don't start again. Put your mind to work figuring out how we're going to get the best possible deal from Mr. Gardner."

"Do you think he really owns part of the Birdcage?" Suzette turned to Josie. "Don't you?"

"I don't know what reason he would have to lie about something so easily disproved, but Zeke keeps telling me not to trust him."

"Zeke is jealous."

"No, he's not!"

"I'm not saying he's in love with you, but no man likes to have another man show up and monopolize the attention of a woman he previously had all to himself."

"Considering what he thinks of me, I'm surprised he wasn't delighted."

Josie didn't believe she could have been so wrong about a man's feelings for her. She prided herself on knowing exactly the effect she was having on a man, or men in general. It was what made her successful. If she'd misjudged Zeke, then it was possible she'd misjudged other men in the past.

Zeke's return kept Josie from asking Suzette why she thought Zeke liked her, but she made a mental note to ask her as soon as they were alone. The possibility that she'd made a mistake in judgment bothered her almost as much as this inexplicable attraction she had for Zeke.

"Hawk and Gardner not back yet?" Zeke asked Josie.

"Nope. You ready to go to sleep?"

"No. Just wondering what they could be talking about for so long."

Almost as if they knew they were being talked about, Hawk appeared out of the night, followed closely by Gardner.

"That's a fine group of mares you boys have," Gardner said to Zeke. "I'm surprised you managed to find them, much less talk their owners into selling."

"A lot of people owe us favors," Zeke said. "And when that fails, there's always cash."

Gardner laughed easily. "I expect you had to hand over quite a bit of that."

"No more than we had," Zeke replied.

Josie thought Gardner's questions were getting a bit too personal, but she was relieved Zeke didn't appear to be upset. It certainly would be a relief if he could be so reasonable for the rest of the trip.

Hawk poured coffee into his cup, swallowed the hot liquid without waiting for it to cool, then hung his cup on a mesquite branch. "The horses are quiet, but I don't like to leave them alone. I'll see you in the morning."

"Aren't you going with him?" Gardner asked Zeke.

"I sleep next to the wagon."

"I thought since I'm here you wouldn't have to stay."

"Hawk doesn't need my help. And if he does, he'll call. Now, I'm bedding down between the fire and the wagon. You got the rest of the ground to choose from."

"I guess that means I don't get to sleep in the wagon?"

It was obvious Gardner was trying to make a joke, but Zeke set about laying out his bedroll as though he hadn't spoken. Tired of the tension between the two men, Josie turned to Suzette. "I'm worn out."

Suzette got to her feet. "Me, too. I'd forgotten how tiring it can be to ride all day."

Josie didn't think it could be as tiring as being caught between Zeke and Gardner. She was looking forward to a full night without having to deal with any man. The only problem was that she couldn't stop thinking about Zeke. Last night he'd even invaded her dreams. No man was that important to her. She simply wouldn't allow it.

Suzette waited outside the wagon until Josie got settled. There wasn't a lot of room inside, so it was easier if both of them weren't trying to move around at the same time. She didn't mind, because the wait gave her a few moments to think back over the day.

She recalled how all during breakfast that morning Zeke had practically walked on eggshells to keep from upsetting Josie. He hadn't complained when Suzette wordlessly helped him clean up, and just as silently helped him harness the mules to the wagon. He kept up a steady conversation, answering his own questions when necessary. If there hadn't been so much tension in the atmosphere, it would have been funny.

Suzette had looked back at the wagon several times during the day, but all her hopes of seeing Zeke and Josie talking together in a relaxed and pleasant way came to nothing.

"Zeke did all the cooking," Josie had announced after breakfast. "He said I wasn't used to cooking over a fire yet, that I didn't know how to keep grit or ash from getting into the food."

Josie appeared to be taking the criticism in stride, but Suzette had never known Josie to take *any* criticism well. She just hoped the two of them could get along a little better from now on. The sexual tension between them at breakfast had given her a knot in her stomach. There would be no living with Josie until she figured out her feelings for Zeke.

But most of her thoughts were about Hawk. The longer she was around him, the more she saw of him, the stronger her attraction to him became. In almost no time at all it was threatening to become an obsession. She had felt a strong physical desire for several men since her husband's death, but she'd been able to handle it without any undue strain. Why was it so different with Hawk?

During the day they'd been separated by the mares, but once they stopped, there was no distance separating them. She could see him when she looked up, stand close to him, even bump into him. Sometimes, when their eyes met, he would smile at her. Whenever that happened, something inside her would turn over and she'd feel almost light-headed. At the same time, she could feel heat stir in her belly. Once that morning, her limbs felt so weak she'd grabbed the saddle horn to steady herself. Though she relished the time they spent looking for good graze, and picketing and hobbling the horses for the night, she had been relieved when they went to the wagon for supper.

"You can climb in now," Josie called. "I'm all settled."

It was so dark inside the wagon, Suzette had to feel around with her hands to find the small trunk that contained most of her clothes. She had to choose the items she wanted by texture. Experience had taught her to separate her clothes into piles in the morning when she got dressed, but tonight she wasn't looking for her nightgown. Instead, she searched for and found the quilt Laurie's mother had given them. Next she took the two blankets Josie wasn't using. "I'm going to sleep out tonight," she said.

Josie sat up. "Why? There's plenty of room in the wagon."

They were friends and partners, but Suzette wasn't ready to discuss her real reasons. "I feel guilty letting the men sleep on the ground while we sleep on a soft bed in the wagon."

"They *want* us to sleep in the wagon because it's safer."

"Maybe, but my mind's made up." She was relieved it was impossible to see Josie's expression in the darkness. Or for Josie to see her expression. She was certain the truth was written all over her face.

"You won't be able to sleep on the ground. It's too hard."

"I'll have to learn." She felt around until she found a small canvas tarp to put under her to keep moisture from seeping into her bedding. "If I get too miserable, I can always come back."

"Are you sure about this?" Only one question was asked, but many were implied.

"Yes." She wasn't, but she'd made her decision.

"Come back if you change your mind."

But as Suzette walked through the darkness, she knew she wouldn't come back. Each step she took away from the wagon made her less sure she was making the right decision, but this was something she had to do. She had mapped out the course of her life several years ago, and there was no place in it for a man like Hawk. Her commitment was firm, her vision unclouded, yet she couldn't make herself turn around and return to the safety of the wagon. She knew what she had to do, and once she reached Tombstone she would do it. But this trip had given her a window of time when, for a few days, she was outside the world she occupied, when the plan for her life could be set aside. Maybe, for the next little while, she could have what life had denied her.

"What are you doing here?" Hawk asked when Suzette reached the spot where he'd laid out his bedroll.

"I've come to spend the night with you," she said, then dropped her bedding next to his.

Chapter Nine

There was enough light for Suzette to see Hawk's expression . . . or lack of one. He rarely showed emotion, but now his face seemed frozen, a locked door that concealed and protected his thoughts. Suzette hadn't minded this barrier before, but now she wanted to know what was behind it. She'd walked out on a limb, and she wanted some warning if it was going to break beneath her.

Seated on his bedroll, Hawk hadn't moved; he just looked up at Suzette. "Are you sure you don't want to sleep in the wagon with Josie?"

She thought he must know the answer to that question. There was only one reason why she would be here.

She'd studied her decision from every angle, but she hadn't thought about it from his perspective. Was he interested in a temporary relationship? If so, would he want one with her, especially under these conditions?

Regardless of the answers to those questions, she'd come too far to back down now.

"Once I reach Tombstone, I'll spend the rest of my life sleeping inside a building on a soft bed. While I've got you and the horses to protect me, I want to sleep under the stars. I want to know what it's like to feel absolutely free."

"Sleeping under the stars won't make you free."

"I know that, but it's so different from anything I've ever done in my life that it will make me feel like a different person. And that will make me feel free."

He hadn't moved; his expression hadn't changed. Maybe he was afraid to move until he was sure of her decision. "Do you want to escape who you are that badly?"

She hadn't thought of it as an escape. She knew that wasn't possible. She had responsibilities that had to be honored regardless of the cost to herself. She knew that and accepted it, but circumstance had offered her a chance to do something for herself, and she meant to take advantage of it. She wanted to close the distance between them. She sank down onto her bedding. Now their bodies were only inches apart.

"Escape is the wrong word. Let's say I want to step outside my life for a few days. I'll go back when I reach Tombstone."

"This might make it harder."

She couldn't tell whether he was asking these questions for her or for himself. Surely he had to feel just as trapped by the circumstances life had imposed on him as she did. He couldn't *want* to be an outcast, to feel he had to live on the fringes of society.

"I'll take that chance." She waited uneasily for his

response, but she knew his reluctance to ask her to stay didn't stem from a lack of desire for her. He, too, had to decide if stepping outside the limits he'd set for himself would make it impossible to step back when they reached Tombstone. "If you want me to go back to the wagon, just say so."

"I don't want you to go back." A note of longing throbbed in Hawk's voice. "I haven't wanted you to go back since that first night."

"Why didn't you say something?"

"Why didn't you?"

She didn't think it would be fair to burden him with her story. He couldn't change what had happened in the past, and he would have no part in what would happen in the future. She looked into his eyes. They were large and black with moonlight reflecting in them. She wanted to tell him everything, to reach out for the strength she knew would be hers for the asking, to shelter in his protection, but she pulled back. She didn't want to tear down any barriers she'd have to rebuild later. It would be too painful.

"Maybe I didn't say anything because I thought it would make you think badly of me," she said.

"That's not possible."

"Sure it is. Men make assumptions about women all the time."

He was silent for a moment. "People are always making assumptions about me. I know what it's like."

Why did she keep forgetting that? Why was it that she saw a man when others saw an Indian? "Then you know how lonely it can become."

"And you think spending the night with me will make a difference?"

She thought of several responses, some flippant, some racy, but her answer was a single word. "Yes."

Hawk reached out and cupped her cheek with his hand. "I never expected anything like this."

"You thought about it?"

"Yes."

"A lot?"

"Too much."

She wondered if he'd thought about it as much as she had. Maybe he had insisted she ride ahead of the horses so she wouldn't see his reaction to her. Maybe she was kidding herself that she was so attractive Hawk couldn't control himself. Nothing about the man indicated that he moved so much as a muscle without intending to. "I thought about it, too. At first, I thought it was impossible."

"What changed your mind?" he asked.

"You."

"How?"

She wasn't sure she could answer that question. It was instinct more than knowledge that told her she could trust him. It was something physical—equally instinctive—that ignited the attraction she felt toward him. But to say the attraction was based only on that would strip their relationship of anything personal, of anything warm and positive, of anything wonderful and affirming.

"You've gone out of your way to help us even though it would be better for you if you'd left us far behind."

"Any man would have done the same."

"Maybe, but it wouldn't have been the same."

She had to find the words to explain how he was dif-

Leigh Greenwood

ferent from every other man she'd known. Her father, stepfather, and husband had been thoughtless, selfish, even cruel. They had never considered her wishes or her welfare, only their own comfort. The men she worked for were the same. The men she danced for were even worse. She'd only known men with huge appetites which they were determined to satisfy regardless of the cost to others. She reached up and covered Hawk's hand with her own.

"It's not what you did, but the kindness that motivated you. No one has ever been so nice to me without expecting something in return. And after the way Josie acted with Zeke, I wouldn't have been surprised if you'd left us that first day." She pulled his hand down to her lap, clasped it between both of her palms. "Why didn't you?"

"I didn't want to."

His answer was more than she'd hoped for. She reminded herself this could only last until Tombstone. "You don't know me at all."

"I know as much about you as you know about me."

That couldn't be true. His history was in the color of his skin, in the shape of the bones of his face, in the single feather he sometimes wore. It didn't matter that he was one of the most attractive men she'd ever met. She was certain his handsomeness made his life all the more difficult. How many women had yearned for what they knew they shouldn't want, couldn't have, and had taken out their frustration on him? How many men, knowing how their wives, daughters, even mothers felt, had intentionally made everything harder for him?

"Then you know this must end when we reach Tombstone?" she asked.

He was silent for a long time, his body motionless, but his eyes bored into hers as though trying to peel back the layers of her mind. "Why must it end?"

He didn't sound angry. Not even upset. Just curious. She had to tell him. She knew now it would only work if she was completely honest with him.

"My mother was a beautiful woman," she began. "When my father died, a rich man from a proud and titled family wanted to marry her. Because my mother was not from a noble family, he moved to Quebec to spare himself embarrassment. Unfortunately, my mother died shortly after we arrived in Canada, and my stepfather found himself with two unwanted daughters."

"I didn't know you had a sister."

"I was sixteen, my sister just seven, when my stepfather married again to a woman of his own class. She didn't want anything to do with us, so he married me off to the first man who would have me. My husband used my dowry to go to Colorado to look for gold, but it was much easier to spend my money than to dig in the dirt. After the money was gone, he did go to the gold fields, but he got into a fight and was killed. When I returned to Quebec, I found my stepfather was sending my sister out to do housework. Much of my father's money had been used to support us after he died. My stepfather took the rest. I was forced to take a job to support myself and educate my sister. My father had been a wealthy man, and I had been reared as the daughter of a gentleman. I was taught all the things young ladies were expected to learn, among them how to sing and dance. So that's what I did."

"You couldn't get any of your money?"

"I tried, but I didn't have the money for lawyers. Nor could I afford to stay in Quebec for the length of time it would have taken to pursue such litigation. I had to get my sister in a proper school and earn the money to pay for it. So I went back to Colorado and kept working. Later I met Josie, and we built an act together."

"So what are you trying to tell me?"

His unwavering gaze comforted her. Somehow it calmed her, helped her believe he was willing to hear anything she told him without judging her. She hoped that was true, because what she had to tell him now was worse than the rest. "I must have money for my sister, lots of money. I'm determined she'll never be treated the way I have been. She's going to be educated as a young lady so she can meet a nice young man who will give her her proper place in society."

"And how do you plan to get that much money?"

"Work for it. Marry for it, if I have to." There, she'd said it. Now that he knew the worst, he had more than enough reason to turn her away if that was what he wanted.

"Somebody like Gardner?"

"Maybe."

Why was that so hard to confess? It wasn't that she disliked Gardner or had any reason to believe he was anything but what he said he was. Hundreds of women would jump at the chance to marry a man like Gardner, so why did saying that make her feel so awful? If she did marry, she'd do her best to be a good wife.

"Do you plan to go back to Quebec?"

Even if she'd wanted to go back, that life was closed to her now. Her presence would be an embarrassment to her sister and her future husband. "I show my legs to men for a living. I don't want my sister ever to know what I do."

"Where does she think you get the money to keep her in school?"

"I told her my husband found gold and I bought a ranch. She wants to visit, but I've always found a reason why she can't."

"Why are you sacrificing your life for your sister?"

"I'm not sacrificing. I like what I do, and I'm good at it. Besides, I wouldn't marry a man just to get his money. If you think I'm that conniving, I'm surprised you didn't leave me in the desert to fend for myself."

Hawk withdrew his hand from her grasp, then took both her hands in his. "I don't think you're conniving. I think you're a wonderful woman who's sacrificing her life because of a misguided sense of duty."

"It's not misguided. My sister is too young to take care of herself."

"She should be grown up by now."

"She's not like me. She doesn't understand how the world works. I think Mother knew she'd made a mistake in marrying my stepfather. Before she died, she made me promise to take care of Cecily. I can't go back on that promise now."

"I never expected you would."

"Then why—"

Hawk put his fingers to her lips. "You don't have to explain anything to me. We all have to do what we think is right."

"Then you're not upset with me?"

"No. I have my own reasons for doing things with my life that you might think are senseless. I respect your decisions because I want you to respect mine."

She started to feel a little uneasy. "How can I do that when I don't know what they are?"

"You don't want to know."

She laughed though she didn't feel like it. "You realize, don't you, that you've done a very cruel thing? You've told me you have a secret, then refused to give me even a hint as to what it might be. That's torture for a woman."

"My secrets will never hurt you."

She had never believed they would, but she had a gut feeling his decisions had hurt Hawk, and would keep hurting him. She wanted to do something about that, but she had no right to interfere when they were going to be together for such a short time.

"I've known from the first you wouldn't hurt me." She held his face between her hands. "You're probably the kindest man I've ever met."

"And you're one of the most beautiful women."

"How can you say that when you see Josie every day?"

"We all have a different idea of what we find beautiful. You're my idea of perfection."

Suzette knew that couldn't be true, but she loved him for saying it. Not once had he mentioned a part of her body, or made her feel uncomfortable with his stares. She was so used to being seen as a pair of legs, a pair of breasts, a pretty face, that she'd almost come to think of herself in those terms. It was wonderful that Hawk could look past all that and see the woman she was. Why did she have to find a man like this when she knew she couldn't have him?

"People admire perfection, but they don't want to live with it," she said sadly.

Hawk's smile vanished. "That wouldn't be true for me."

The knot in Suzette's stomach tightened. She didn't want to know this. She simply wanted to enjoy his nearness for the next few days. "I thought you'd already figured out I'm far from perfect. I can't cook as well as Zeke, and I can't take care of the horses as well as you. I barely remember how to ride properly."

Hawk took her hands in his once again. "I wasn't talking about things like that. I was talking about what's inside you."

"You haven't known me long enough to know what I'm really like."

"I can see it in your eyes, your smile, the way you worry about Josie and Zeke even when you know there's nothing either of us can do about their situation."

Suzette was afraid she was going to cry, which was far from what she wanted. Maybe she ought to go back to the wagon. She'd thought they could enjoy each other for the next few days with no strings attached, but now she was afraid she'd made a mistake. It was impossible not to feel something special for a man who felt about her as Hawk did. It was just as difficult not to want him to think she was special.

"For a man of few words, you certainly know how to choose the right ones."

"It would be impossible to choose the wrong ones for you."

Okay, she was going to cry so she might as well do it now and get it over with. If she was quick about it, maybe she wouldn't scare Hawk off. She felt the tears well in her eyes before they rolled down her cheeks. She hoped he would miss them in the dark but feared they would glisten in the moonlight.

"Why are you crying?" Hawk's fingertips touched her cheeks and gently brushed the tears away.

"It's a problem a lot of women have. You can beat us, berate us, even treat us like a slave, and we'll just grow stronger. Say something sweet and kind, and we become as fragile as butterfly wings."

"You're as beautiful as the butterflies that fly down to Mexico every winter, then head back north in clouds of wings in the spring."

"If you don't stop, I'll have to go back to the wagon."

Hawk stiffened. "Did I say the wrong thing?"

She shook her head, and teardrops splashed down on her hands. "What you said was very beautiful."

"Then why . . ." He let the sentence die away.

"Because you've made me very happy."

"Isabelle used to say that, but I never understood."

Giving in to an impulse, she kissed him on the cheek. "Don't try."

Hawk reacted so strongly she was afraid she'd done something wrong.

"Why did you kiss me?" he asked.

The answer to that question was so complex she couldn't begin to sort it out, even for herself. Hawk's words had touched her in places she didn't know she had, had uncovered pools of emotions she'd thought were dried up. Most devastating, he'd reminded her of things she'd long ago decided were impossible. "You said something sweet, and I wanted to thank you."

"Don't ever do that again!" He drew back as if she'd insulted him. She could see a flash of anger in his eyes, feel it in the coldness of his withdrawal.

"Why not? What's wrong?"

"I don't want you to kiss me because I said something nice. I want you to kiss me because you care for me."

Despite Hawk's deepening scowl, Suzette felt herself begin to smile as understanding dawned. Hawk wasn't any different from her. He didn't want bribes or reasons. He just wanted her to feel that nothing would make her happier than kissing him. He wanted to know she wasn't looking for any reward beyond the kiss itself and the way it made them feel to share it with each other.

Resting her weight on her hands, she leaned forward until her lips touched Hawk's. His lips were dry but soft, his mouth hard and unrelenting. She kissed him and felt a slight relaxing of the muscles around his mouth. She shifted her weight, lifted her right arm, slipped her hand around his neck, and pulled him toward her. He resisted only a moment before practically overwhelming her with his response.

Almost before she knew it, she was lying on her back and he was kissing her with a passion that seemed to have been heated white hot for being restrained so long. For a moment she was too overwhelmed to respond. It was one thing to say pretty words. They were nice, but they lacked the impact of physical contact. Kissing Hawk was like being caught up in a flash flood, unexpected and overpowering.

Hawk's sudden withdrawal was unwelcome. He

151

pushed himself up and pulled back from her. "I'm sorry. I shouldn't have done that."

Suzette reached out to keep him from pulling farther away. "You startled me. You've always been so quiet, so reserved, I was unprepared."

"You're not angry?"

She was ecstatic. Jubilant. Exultant. Hawk wanted her as much as she wanted him. She had to calm down before she did something to drive him away. "I came here tonight hoping you liked me well enough to let me stay. I never dreamed you liked me that much." She was petrified she wouldn't be able to control her feelings for him, but was determined not to let this opportunity to experience something close to love slip from her grasp.

"I never dreamed you'd want to stay with me," Hawk said.

"I can't imagine why any woman wouldn't want to spend the night in your arms."

"I've never wanted just any woman."

But he wanted her. She could see it in his eyes and hear it in his voice. She could practically feel his heat despite the cooling of the night air around her. The scents of the river and sagebrush weren't nearly as strong as the scent of a man burning up with his need for a woman. She reached out to touch his arm. The hair on his arm was fine and soft. Hawk trailed his fingertips over her throat, the column of her neck.

"You're so soft," he murmured.

She squeezed his arm, enjoying the strength of the muscles that had lifted the wagon wheel effortlessly. "You're not."

His response was a ragged breath. She realized immediately what she'd said and felt heat flood her cheeks. She didn't want him to think she was a blushing maiden, but she didn't want him to think she was a brazen hussy, either. She hadn't been with any man since her husband. She caressed his cheek with her hand. "I've never seen a man without facial hair. Your skin is incredibly smooth."

"It's not just my Comanche heritage. My mother said her father had very little beard."

She wondered if he'd ever felt inferior because he didn't have facial hair. So many men judged each other by foolish standards—how tall they were, how broad their shoulders, how big their muscles, how much whiskey they could drink before passing out, how well they could fight, how many women they could seduce, some even by the amount of hair covering their body. Some women admired those things, but most wanted something very different in a man. They wanted a man like Hawk.

"I like it," she said, "just as I like your gleaming black eyes and thick black hair."

"How about my dark skin?" She could feel the muscles in his shoulder tighten.

"You're the shade of a farmer who's spent the summer toiling in his fields. That's the color of honest labor and well-earned sweat. I can't think of any coloring that's more admirable." She didn't know if he believed her, but was relieved to feel some of the tension leave his body. He lay down next to her, and she rolled on her side to face him.

"Do you mean that?"

"Why shouldn't I?"

"You know why."

"Your being part Indian is what makes you who you are. It gives you the width of your brow and the strength of your jaw. Your upbringing has also made you prone to long periods of silence. No woman will ever have cause to say you talk too much to hear what she's trying to tell you."

"I don't talk much to women. I don't do it well."

She let her fingers roam over his whole face. She couldn't seem to get enough of touching him. It was like she was discovering him all over again. "I think you do it remarkably well, better than any man I've ever met."

"That's only because I'm talking to you."

Who could possibly have made this man think he didn't know how to talk to women? His words made her feel she was about to melt. She lay on her back, and he lifted himself on his elbow to look down at her.

"You're lovely," he whispered. "Your skin is the color of moonlight on the water and soft as the muzzle of a newborn foal."

His kiss was gentle yet firm, inviting her to join him, yet willing to take the lead. His touch released in her a hunger she'd tried to ignore. Its escape was so explosive it caused her whole body to shake.

"Are you cold?" he asked.

"No."

The word had barely escaped her lips before she pulled him into a kiss so fierce she was sure it would bruise her mouth. Her need was so sudden, so desperate, it scared her, but she couldn't hold back. She felt as if her soul was being nurtured for the first time in her life. It was impossible to describe the feeling of holding this man in her arms, of being held by him.

She didn't know how it was possible, but it was as if she was experiencing a man's embrace for the first time, as if everything that had gone before had ceased to exist, and her life was starting anew. She knew that was foolish, that it was wishful thinking, but it was such a wonderful dream, she didn't want to relinquish it, couldn't let it go.

"Are you sure you're not cold?" Hawk asked again.

"No one has touched me since my husband died," she said, her voice shaking from the force of the impact his touch had on her. "But those memories can't compare to the way I feel now."

Hawk gently rubbed her lips with his thumb. "I hope that's good."

"It's better than that." She unbuttoned his shirt and slipped her hand inside. "It's better than I ever imagined." She let her hand roam over his chest. She explored the planes and contours that had been hidden from her sight by his shirt. She smiled when she brushed a nipple and he flinched. "You're so warm."

"I'm so hot I'm burning up," Hawk whispered in her ear.

She smiled more broadly and continued her exploration. Her touch caused the muscles to quiver under his skin. "I don't understand how you can feel so hard and soft at the same time."

The tip of his tongue traced the outline of her ear, causing her body to shiver with pleasure from head to foot. She slid her hand over his rib cage, across his side, and onto his back. Yielding to her pressure, he rolled toward her until his body was pressed against her. Suzette was certain that she, too, was burning up. Her clothes felt hot and confining. She was unable to remain still. Her body moved against Hawk, her hand roamed his back, and she covered his face with kisses.

Hawk slipped his hand between them to cover her breast. Suzette's body shuddered, and she moaned into his mouth. The heat that had centered in her belly began to spread to the rest of her body like the slow but relentless spilling of molten lava from the mouth of a volcano. Her body became so rigid she felt like she was in a splint. She moved her shoulders and arched her back to release some of the tension in her muscles, but the feel of Hawk's hand on her breast continued to wind her tight until she thought she would break.

Hawk's hand on her breast stilled. His breathing seemed to stop. "Are you sure you want to do this?"

Chapter Ten

For a moment, fear paralyzed Suzette. Her hand had closed around the back of his neck before she realized he was worried he'd somehow scared her. Gradually she relaxed her hold on him. "I've never been more sure of anything in my life."

One by one Hawk undid the buttons from the top of her shirtwaist to the bottom. Suzette shivered slightly as the cool air touched the bare skin of her shoulders and penetrated the thin fabric of her muslin chemise. But that was nothing compared to the feel of Hawk's lips on her skin when he kissed her bare shoulder. She felt as though she would jump out of her skin; at the same time she was certain her bones would melt if he continued to touch her.

But she wanted him to touch her. Every part of her begged for it, rejoiced in it. It was all she could do to keep from throwing her arms around him and smothering him with her need of his touch, his closeness, his caring. Except for her sister, she hadn't felt cared for since her mother died. Her stepfather's shame and her husband's indifference had left her feeling alone, divorced emotionally from the two men who should have been closest to her.

Hawk's gentle touch and sweet kisses melted away her belief that all men were hard creatures with no thought for anything but their own pleasure. The warmth of his body and the strength of his arms formed a protective shield that invited her trust, gave assurance that he cared for her. His touch stoked the fire that spiraled its way through her limbs with the sensuousness of silk being drawn across her body. The faint sound of his kisses and his soft groans of pleasure gradually closed out the world around her, reducing her consciousness to a small sphere that contained only their two bodies.

Suzette had anticipated this moment in her dreams the last two nights, but when Hawk slipped her chemise off her shoulders and she felt his tongue lave one hard nipple, she cried out so loudly she disturbed the birds asleep in nearby trees. It was at once the most wonderful, the most electrifying, feeling she'd ever experienced. He seemed to understand that for her, making love was more than a quick satisfaction of physical needs, that it was more an emotional experience than a physical one. He also had a genuine appreciation for her body and the pleasure he could give her through it. The lovemaking she'd shared with her husband had been nothing like this. Hawk had not only aroused her physical needs, he was embracing the needs of her soul and spirit as well. He'd stepped in to fill an emptiness that had been a quiet ache for as long as she could remember.

She wanted to touch him, to give him even a fraction of the pleasure he was giving her, but her muscles had lost their strength. She felt barely able to move her hand, much less lift her whole arm. The feel of Hawk's lips and hands on her breasts made her feel exquisitely helpless. She hadn't the force of will to think about anything except the stockpiling of sensations that was rocking her body from end to end. She wasn't even aware that Hawk had undone the belt that held her skirt in place until he slipped the garment under her hips and off her body. It was a simple matter to slip off the moccasins she wore in camp, and then she was naked except for her chemise.

"Take off your shirt." She couldn't summon the energy to do it herself, but she wanted to feel his naked skin against her own. She wanted to explore every contour, to slide her fingers over every rib, to glory in the softness that covered such great strength. She wanted to find out if she could give him even a small portion of the pleasure he was giving her. Being with Hawk had given her hope that lovemaking could be something more than a quick physical gratification, that he could enjoy nearness and touching as much as she could. She wanted to know if it was possible to *share* the experience rather than be the object of it.

She felt the loss of his heat when he sat up to remove his shirt.

Hawk couldn't have looked more beautiful in the full glare of day than he did at this moment in moonlight. His skin glowed like rich honey. She was sure that one taste would render her a helpless addict. She couldn't resist resting her hand on his back, marveling at the play of muscles across his shoulders as he worked to remove his boots. He was like a large cat, sleek, powerful, and hot to the touch. Drawn irresistibly to his warmth, she slipped her arms around his waist and leaned against his back. He was so hot it was like snuggling up to a stove. Tossing aside his second boot, Hawk turned to her, but she said, "Your pants, too." He must not stop now. She had to have all of him.

"I don't wear anything under them."

She wasn't sure she was ready to have him next to her completely naked. Up to this moment, they'd shared this experience. She was afraid that nakedness would make his physical need impossible to postpone, but she wanted to be rid of the barrier his buckskins put between them. "That's okay."

"I'll trade you, pants for chemise."

All of a sudden things were moving too fast. She thought he'd understood that for her the most important part of making love came before the ultimate consummation—their closeness, the touches, the shared warmth, the feeling that *she* mattered to him, not just her body.

"We don't have to do anything that makes you uncomfortable." With surprising gentleness, Hawk took her face in his hands and kissed her. "We can just lie next to each other if that's what you want."

The relief and happiness that flooded through Suzette was followed almost immediately by a churning physical need to have more of Hawk than just his kisses and embraces.

"I want that very much, but I want more. Much more."

Hawk's kisses were so sweet, so loving, she nearly dissolved right there in his arms. She wasn't aware that he had deftly slipped the chemise over her shoulders and down to her waist until the cool air on the heated skin of her abdomen caused her to shiver. So slowly that she felt she was sinking into a cloud, Hawk leaned her back until she was resting on the bedroll. He trailed kisses across her stomach, causing her body to shake with anticipation. She had never known that every part of her could be so sensitive. Maybe it was Hawk's touch that had awakened a sensitivity she didn't know she possessed. Maybe it was his making love to her whole body, to her whole being, that had penetrated an inner core she'd always kept protected until now. Whatever it was, his magical touch was communicating with her body in a language all its own. He didn't have to tell her to raise her body. His hands moving along the outside of her hips was all the encouragement her muscles needed to rise until she was free of the chemise. She shivered in anticipation.

"You're so beautiful," Hawk whispered into the hollow of her shoulder.

She didn't realize until the air in her lungs escaped her body in a shuddering breath that she had been so tense, that she had been afraid that in some way she'd fall short of his expectations. Knowing she hadn't gave her courage to say, "I want to see you." The words tried to stick in her throat, but she forced them out.

Using only one hand so he wouldn't have to break contact with her, Hawk slipped out of his pants and tossed them aside. Without giving Suzette a chance to look at him as he had looked at her, he put his arms around her and pulled her against him. The feel of his arousal against her thigh ignited a fire that threatened to consume her in a conflagration of desire and need. She tried to tell him that she wanted to explore his body as he'd explored hers, but once again her desire was swept away by her own need to be consumed by him. She wanted him to touch her everywhere. She *needed* him to want her as much as she wanted him.

Her arms encircled Hawk's neck to pull him down so she could kiss him, hold him close, glory in the feel of his body next to hers, in the knowledge that his heat flowed into her as hers flowed into him. She couldn't explain why this closeness was so important to her. She wanted to bind him to her, absorb him. She kept being distracted by his hand as it trailed down her side, swept across her belly, and moved down the outside of her hip and thigh. His touch was so feathery it raised goose bumps on her skin. She didn't understand how she could feel so hot and cold at the same time. When Hawk's lips found her breast once again, the heat that surged through her body banished all traces of cold. The beginnings of a wildfire lurked just under her skin.

Hawk teased her breasts with his tongue and teeth. Her nipples were sensitive and swollen from his earlier attention, but her body arched against him. She wanted to press hard until their bodies merged, until she felt like she was part of him. His hand cupped her behind and pulled her hard against his arousal. A soft moan escaped him. He took her earlobe between his teeth and bit down until she couldn't stand it any longer. In desperation to experience him before she lost control completely, Suzette moved her hand down his back, across his thigh, and between them until she touched him.

"Don't!"

His body flinched, and she snatched her hand back. His protest had been so sharp she feared she'd hurt him, but the need to touch him was nearly uncontrollable. "I want to hold you."

Speaking through clenched teeth, he said, "Take it easy, or I'll explode."

Loath to move quickly, Suzette ran her hand over the small of Hawk's back before moving down to encounter the swell of his buttocks. Excitement bloomed within her as she slowly moved her hand over his posterior. Hawk's muscles clenched at her touch, turning the soft flesh into mounds of hard sinew. The sensation nearly left her breathless. She moved her hand farther down to explore the powerful thighs that gripped his horse's sides for hours every day. Once again the feeling of great power flowed from him.

Suzette's breath paused when she moved her hand over Hawk's hip and found her way between their bodies. As she gradually folded her fingers around him, she felt that she was holding a column of fire. He was incredibly hard, but his skin was soft and warm. She wanted to caress him, fondle him, even kiss him there, but his body was so rigid, his breathing so labored, she was afraid it would drive him over the edge. It seemed unfair that she shouldn't have as much freedom to explore his body as he had to explore hers.

His hands roaming over her back and buttocks only made her uncomfortably warm. He slid his hands between her legs, but she didn't explode. He touched her at her entrance, and she tensed only slightly. But when he found and massaged a small, incredibly sensitive nub, she felt she would explode.

"What did you do?" she gasped once she'd recovered her breath. She must have cried out, because the birds were fluttering in the trees again.

"What you did to me."

That was impossible. It couldn't be the same, or he wouldn't have been able to endure it in silence. But she was completely uninterested in weighing the intensity of their separate experiences. Hawk had now entered her with his fingers, and he was driving her crazy, making it impossible for her to care about anything except what he was doing to her. The molten heat that had centered in her belly was now spreading to the rest of her body at an alarming rate. Before long she would be so consumed by it, she wouldn't be able to think of anything else.

But she didn't *want* to think of anything else. Nothing else was important. She wanted to pull away from him, yet she pushed herself against him, trying to drive him deeper inside. As the spirals of pleasure wound tighter and tighter around her body, she grew more frantic until her breath was coming in gasps. "What are you doing?" She had thought she knew what being with a man was like, but she'd never experienced anything like this.

"Giving you pleasure."

His hand plunged deeper inside her while his mouth tortured her breasts until she was sure she would lose control. She tried to speak, but couldn't. She tried to move her body, but her muscles wouldn't respond. She tried to think, but gradually abandoned the effort. It was all she could do to exist, to endure Hawk's exquisite torture. But as he continued to make love to her body, that became harder and harder. She wanted to cry out, but his kisses swallowed her protests. She attempted to pull away, but his arms held her in a firm embrace. Finally, when she was certain she couldn't stand it any longer, something inside her seemed to burst and flow from her like liquid heat.

Gasping, Suzette surrendered to waves of pleasure such as she'd never experienced before. She wanted to ask Hawk what he'd done to her. She wondered if it was possible to do it again, but even if she'd been capable of speech at that moment, she would have been afraid to ask. The experience had been so overwhelming, so shattering, she didn't know if she could survive it again. Yet even as that thought crossed her mind, it was shoved aside by the sure knowledge that she wanted it to happen again, that she *needed* it to happen again.

Her breathing hadn't yet become regular when, without warning, Hawk rose above her and slowly entered her until she was certain she could stretch no more. In seconds the tension in her body was back, the coils of desire wrapping around her with suffocating strength. She tried to speak, to gesture, to communicate, but she was incapable of doing anything but reacting to the excitement thrumming through her body. It seemed to be the same with Hawk. As he moved inside her, he fell farther and farther under the sway of his own need. The expression on his face gradually changed from one of concentration to one approaching a kind of mindless ecstasy. His eyes gradually closed and his mouth fell open. His breath became as ragged as her own. Suzette wanted to give him the same pleasure he was giving her, but everything became so blurred she was conscious only of them moving together toward ecstasy. Her gaze became unfocused and she gave herself up completely to the pleasure that welled up from her core and spread to every part of her body.

Suddenly Hawk's body became rigid, his moans turned to grunts, and she felt him explode within her. That set off an answering explosion inside her, and she slowly slid down the other side of consciousness.

Suzette was incapable of response when Hawk pulled away and lay down next to her. She didn't know how long she lay without moving. Hawk's breath gradually slowed and his body became motionless, and still she couldn't move. Even when he fell asleep, she continued to lie there gradually absorbing what had happened to her. It wasn't what she had expected. It wasn't exactly the same as being created all over again, yet she couldn't help believing that practically everything in her world had changed. Or maybe just the way she looked at things had changed.

She might not know what it was for days, maybe even weeks, but something was different. She wasn't the same person she'd been when she'd left the wagon to spend the night with Hawk. She didn't know how this was going to affect her future, but the fact that it *would* affect it scared her. She'd figured everything out long ago. She knew what she had to do and how to do it. Nothing could change what she owed her sister.

Yet tonight had added something new to the

equation—something that threw everything out of balance. She had no doubt that the something was Hawk.

She turned and burrowed next to him. He reached out in his sleep and pulled her closer. Even as she melted into his embrace, she knew she'd made a mistake in not sleeping in the wagon. She also knew the cost of that mistake was going to be high.

Hawk lay on his back and stared at the stars in the cloudless sky. Suzette's head rested on his shoulder. The cold had awakened him and he'd gotten up to dress and find a blanket to throw over her. But even as the warmth returned to his body, he was unable to fall asleep. He didn't want to miss the feeling of her sleeping in his arms. It felt natural to have her there, to feel her warmth, the weight of her body against him, to hear her breathing, to sense her body's expansion and contraction against him with each breath. Even the smell of her hair seemed familiar and comforting.

He should feel crowded, uncomfortable, anxious to get away and return to the comfort of his solitude, his companionship with Zeke. That's the way it had worked for two decades, and that's the way it ought to be working now.

He'd been with several women. Some he'd liked enough to continue the relationship for more than a week, even more than a month. Some he'd thought he could marry. Some had wanted to marry him, but it had never worked out. Either they didn't like Zeke or they wanted Hawk to settle down and take a job in an office. He'd finally come to the realization that *he* was the reason those relationships didn't work out. After that, he'd stayed away from women.

So what was different now? He knew the answer—at least, he knew the superficial answer. Suzette. It was the *why* that baffled him. From the first, she'd acted as if they'd known each other long enough to be comfortable riding together, taking care of the horses, or sitting around the campfire. But it was a mystery to him how that could have happened so quickly with a total stranger.

Okay, he wasn't totally mystified. He'd felt a special attraction to Suzette from the beginning. She wasn't the most beautiful woman he'd ever seen, but he'd never been as attracted to a woman as he was to Suzette. He could remember a couple of times he'd lost his head, but it was different this time. The strength of attraction was there without the feeling of insanity, the feeling he was losing control, the feeling he was falling and there was nothing to catch him.

He wondered if he should try to dress her. He'd managed to wake her long enough to put her chemise on, but he hadn't objected when it was clear she'd much rather be warmed by him than her clothes. He pulled her closer and tucked the blanket more closely around her.

As he began to drift back to sleep, he reminded himself that this was a short-term relationship. It was important that he not construe anything that happened in the next few days to mean they could have more than these few days together. He didn't have the kind of money Suzette needed for her sister. And even if he had, it wouldn't have made any difference. She wanted her sister to have a place in society. That was so important to Suzette, she was willing to remain separated from her only living relative for the rest of her life to make it happen. It was so important, she was willing to pretend to be somebody she wasn't.

That was something Hawk would never do. Any woman who wanted to be his wife would have to be proud of him, willing to consider his differences a strength rather than something to be ashamed of. If Suzette couldn't admit that she sang and danced for a living, how could she possibly take pride in being married to a half-breed?

She couldn't, so that was the end of it. He ought to take what he had and be grateful for it without asking for the impossible. But just before he slipped over the edge into sleep, Hawk admitted he could never give up hope that someday he'd find a woman who could love him just as he was.

Zeke didn't know what woke him, but he came wide awake with the feeling that something was terribly wrong. He sat up and looked around the camp, but nothing seemed out of place. Gardner had spread out his bedroll on the other side of the wagon. Zeke could just barely make out the dark shape against the ground, but he didn't see any movement. He listened carefully, but nothing came to his ear beyond the usual sounds of the night. For a moment he thought he might look inside the wagon to make sure Josie was okay, but he changed his mind quickly. All she needed was to see him attempting to crawl into the wagon in the middle of the night to convince her that her worst fears were true.

It would have been different if Suzette slept in the

wagon, too, but she'd gone to bed down with Hawk. Zeke hadn't liked that one bit. Zeke and Hawk had been with several women during their years together, but none of those relationships had ever affected their feeling of being brothers. There had been times when Zeke thought Hawk might have found someone to marry, and there'd been one time when Zeke thought he'd found the woman of his dreams, but the relationship between the two men hadn't changed.

Zeke wasn't sure that would be true with Suzette. He didn't know why he felt this way, but he got the feeling she was the kind of woman who would claim a man's first loyalty. He liked Suzette. She seemed immune to the kind of temper that plagued Josie. Still, she would be the type of woman who could come between even the closest of brothers.

Zeke didn't remember what he'd been dreaming before he woke up, but it must have been really depressing to leave him in such a rotten mood. Or maybe he should blame his bad mood on his irrational attraction for Josie, or her refusal to listen to his warning about Gardner. Not that Josie couldn't take care of herself under normal circumstances, but running into a man like Gardner wasn't a normal circumstance. Not when he was a rich theater owner and Josie was in need of a job. Josie might think she could take care of herself in any situation, but Zeke had lived long enough to know that a woman who didn't have a man she could depend on was vulnerable.

But that wasn't his worry. Even if he'd wanted it to be, Josie wouldn't allow it. He listened intently, but heard nothing to alarm him. He lay back down. It took a few seconds to get comfortable again, but the moment he stopped moving, he heard a sound in the brush surrounding the wagon. There was no way he could go back to sleep until he found out what it was.

Chapter Eleven

The sound of Dusky Lady blowing through her nostrils woke Hawk. Even though he heard nothing to alarm him, he rose to his knees and immediately reached for his rifle. Dusky Lady was hobbled. If a cougar or something else was stalking the mares, she was the one least able to defend herself.

"What is it?" Suzette asked, her voice husky with sleep.

"Something has disturbed the horses," Hawk said as he slipped his feet into a pair of moccasins. "I'm going to see what's wrong. Stay here and keep warm."

"Wait. I'll come with you."

She started to throw aside the blanket, but he stopped her. "You're not dressed." He reached for the extra rifle next to his saddle. "Keep this beside you until I get back."

"I want to help."

"You can help by staying out of danger."

Being careful to avoid patches of dried leaves, Hawk melted into the brush, moving through the thickets of tamarisk and willow and avoiding the thorns of mesquite and prickly-pear cactus until he could see the horses silhouetted against the horizon in the moonlight. The mules grazed on, seemingly impervious to any potential danger, but the mares and the saddle horses were on their feet and alert, their heads turned away from the river. Hawk saw nothing, but he heard something moving toward them from the direction of the mountains. No cougar or other predator would make so much noise.

It could only be somebody attempting to steal the mares.

Moving quickly and staying close to the ground, Hawk ran to Dusky Lady.

"Easy, girl," Hawk said softly. "As soon as I get rid of these hobbles, I want you to hightail it up the trail. I'm gonna draw those low-down, horse-thieving scalawags out in the open where I can get a shot at them. We'll catch up with you in the morning."

With deft fingers, Hawk removed the mare's hobbles. He still saw no sign of intruders, but the horses hadn't returned to their grazing. Whatever had spooked them was still out there. Hawk gave Dusky Lady a slap on her haunch. "Get going."

The mare whinnied, shook her head up and down, then started down the trail at a trot. The mules continued to graze, but one after another the mares turned and followed Dusky Lady. Almost immediately Hawk heard a shout and saw a man burst from a juniper thicket and run out into the open yelling at someone still concealed to get moving before the horses got away. Hawk sank to his knee, took careful aim, and fired. The man threw up his arms and fell to the ground.

Immediately the quiet of the night was shattered by a fusillade of rifle shots.

Hawk dived behind a low bank amid bullets hitting the ground all around him. Once over the bank, he crawled quickly on knees and elbows until he was about twenty yards from where he'd fired the first shot. Working his way through the underbrush on his belly, he lay perfectly still until he saw three men moving toward the river. Incredibly, the mules had gone back to grazing as soon as the echoes of the rifle shots died away. At least he wouldn't have to worry about them going berserk.

Hawk knew Zeke was out there somewhere, probably with Gardner right behind him. If these three men were the only thieves, they shouldn't have any problem driving them off. Taking time to make sure his aim was perfect, Hawk fired at the closest thief. Then he backed up until he was over the bank once again, but this time he sprinted toward a large cottonwood on the edge of the river. From that vantage point he could see that the man he'd shot was down on the ground, groaning and holding his leg. Hawk didn't want to kill the man, but he did want to make sure he never tried to steal any more horses.

The sound of a rifle shot brought Zeke bolt upright. The burst of gunfire that followed had him on his feet and reaching for his rifle. Hawk had gotten him into the habit of wearing moccasins to bed so he wouldn't have to stop to put on his boots. He crossed immediately to the wagon.

"Somebody's after the horses." He hoped Josie was awake enough to hear and understand him. "Stay here until I get back."

Josie stuck her head from between the canvas flaps. "What about Suzette?"

"Hawk will take care of her. Gardner can stay with you." Since the man hadn't awakened, he probably wouldn't be any good in a fight. But when Zeke rounded the wagon, he saw that Gardner's bedroll was empty. "Gardner's not here. He may have gone to see what the shooting's about, but I don't trust him."

He didn't want to leave Josie, but she knew how to handle a rifle. Since Hawk had bedded down close to the river, Zeke decided to circle around the other way and try to catch the horse thieves in a crossfire. He didn't like the ominous quiet that had fallen after the initial burst of gunfire, but he knew Hawk wouldn't make himself a target. There probably weren't five white men in the Arizona Territory who could find Hawk when he didn't want to be found, and Zeke had the advantage of being difficult to see in the dark.

Before long, Zeke caught the sound of whispered conversation on the light breeze blowing from the south. The sound of boots on rocks and clothes brushing against branches and thorns told him the thieves weren't used to walking quietly through the desert landscape. He'd moved into position to the east of the thieves when Hawk's rifle shot had broken the stillness. The moans of the wounded man were momentarily drowned out by return gunfire. They sounded unnaturally loud in the stillness that followed.

"I think my leg's broken," the man said.

"Dammit, this was supposed to be easy. We come in while they're sleeping and run off the horses before anybody wakes up."

"How bad is Munson hurt?"

"Bad enough he ain't breathing."

"Where the hell is that guy with the rifle?" a third voice asked.

"I don't know, but I'm getting the hell out of here. If Gardner wants them horses, he can get them himself."

Anger boiled up from Zeke's stomach. Why hadn't he paid attention to his instincts instead of putting his uneasiness down to jealousy over Gardner's attention to Josie? That woman was messing up every part of his life. The sooner he could be rid of her, the better. Pushing his anger aside for the moment, he worked his way through a tangle of plants until he was directly behind the thieves. The mules were grazing on the far side of an open area, but Zeke didn't see any sign of the mares or the riding horses. He was tempted to put bullets into the two men still on their feet, but Hawk was obviously hidden across the clearing. There was virtually no chance he'd miss at such close range, but Hawk might not know it was Zeke shooting and might return fire.

"I've got both of you in my rifle sights," Zeke said, speaking from his place of concealment in a mesquite thicket. "Drop your rifles."

The men turned and fired blindly into the thicket, but Zeke dove behind a large rock.

"That wasn't very smart. Drop your rifles, or I'll start shooting. And I won't miss." To emphasize his point, Zeke fired at the rifle held by one of the men. When the bullet shattered the stock, the man yelled and threw the rifle to the ground. The other man dropped his rifle and raised his hands.

"Hawk, you over there?" Zeke shouted.

"Yeah," came the answer. "Want me to plug them from here?"

The two men whirled to face the second voice coming at them from the darkness.

"No. I say we tie them to their horses and drop them off at Redington. Let the Redfields and the Sozas take care of them. They're not especially fond of horse thieves."

"We didn't steal any horses," a man with dirty blond hair said. "We was just riding through minding our own business when whoever's hiding in those trees by the river shot Munson."

"Tell it to the Redfields," Zeke said.

"Where the hell are you?" the blond demanded.

"Where I can keep an eye on you. Come on out, Hawk," Zeke called.

Hawk emerged from the trees along the river, his rifle leveled at the two men left standing. Zeke kept his eye on the man with the broken leg just in case he went for his gun. Zeke was not happy to see Suzette step out of the trees not far from where Hawk had emerged. In a situation like this, a woman was a complication they didn't need. She carried a rifle, but did she know how to use it? He thought of Josie back in the wagon and hoped she had stayed put.

Zeke emerged from hiding. "Where are the horses?" he asked Hawk.

"I sent them off with Dusky Lady. We'll pick them up in the morning." Hawk turned to the thieves. "Where's your boss?" he asked.

A warning look passed between the two men before the blond answered, "We ain't got no boss."

"I heard you say Gardner was the one who wanted these horses."

"I don't know no Gardner," the blond said.

Zeke wasn't going to waste time arguing. "Now put your hands behind your backs while my partner ties you up."

The blond looked apprehensively at Hawk. "He ain't going to scalp me, is he?"

"Not unless you try to get away."

Zeke waited impatiently while Hawk tied the hands of first one man and then the other. "What are you going to do with *him*?" he said pointing at the man with the broken leg.

"Leave him there. I expect the coyotes will soon make sure there's nothing left to find."

"You gotta take me to Redington," the man pleaded. His hat had fallen off, revealing a head of thick, curly black hair.

"Why? They'd only hang you as a horse thief."

"We didn't steal no horses," the blond said again.

Zeke was about to ask Hawk what he wanted to do with the thieves until morning when he heard the sound of a woman's voice raised in protest. Josie! Hawk jerked his head in the direction of the wagon. Zeke was already moving. Where minutes before he'd moved with stealth, now he barreled his way through the brush, using his rifle to push aside thorn-laden branches that snagged at his clothes and skin from all sides. Why had he left Josie? What man would worry his head about horses when there was a woman like Josie around?

The sounds of the struggle grew louder when he rounded a tamarisk thicket. He burst through the underbrush to find Josie fighting off Gardner.

The moment Gardner saw Zeke, he swung Josie in front of him. "Stay back." His pistol was pointed directly at Zeke.

Zeke skidded to a halt. "Don't be a fool. We caught your men, so there's no way you can get away with Josie." Zeke moved back and forth, zigzagging, constantly in motion so Gardner was forced to keep twisting to hold his gun on Zeke.

"Close your eyes, Josie." Zeke hoped Josie could figure out his message before Gardner did. "I don't want them open when I blind Gardner."

"What the hell are you talking about?" Gardner demanded.

The words had hardly escaped Gardner's mouth when Josie closed her eyes, threw her weight to one side, and jabbed Gardner in the ribs with her elbow. She succeeded in distracting him long enough for Zeke to grab a handful of dirt and toss it into Gardner's face. Coughing and clutching at his eyes with one hand, he fired wildly with the other, but Zeke was able to knock the gun out of his hand. A second fist sent Gardner to the ground. A third and fourth guaranteed he would stay there. Several more would probably have followed if Josie hadn't pulled Zeke back.

"You'll get in trouble if you hurt him real bad," Josie said.

"I ought to kill him."

"I agree, but there's no point in your getting hanged."

Zeke got to his feet, brushed the dirt off his pants. "Do you have some rope I can use to tie him up?"

"You can't do that to me," Gardner protested, still attempting to get the dirt out of his eyes. "I didn't do anything wrong."

"What do you call trying to carry off a woman against her will?"

"I was just trying to protect her, and she misunderstood."

"I've never misunderstood a man like you." Josie handed Zeke a rope she'd gotten out of the wagon.

"A man in my position doesn't have to *carry off* women," Gardner shouted when Zeke jerked him to his feet and yanked his arms behind his back. "I can have almost any woman I want."

"Josie doesn't qualify as *almost any woman*," Zeke growled as he bound the rope around Gardner's wrists.

"You'll regret this," Gardner said. "I'll put a reward on your head."

Zeke sat Gardner down on the ground and began to tie his feet. "Make it a big one. I don't want to mess around with boys looking for just enough money for a night on the town." Zeke dragged him over to the wagon and began tying him to the wheel.

"I've got a dozen men on my ranch that can take you any time I want."

"Tell them to look for me in Tombstone after Hawk and I drop off these ladies. Now I'm going to see if Hawk needs any help with your horse thieves."

"I've got nothing to do with any horse thieves," Gardner protested.

"Don't let him out of your sight," Zeke said, turning to Josie. "If he tries to get away, put a bullet in him somewhere."

"Will you be gone long?" Josie asked.

Zeke had gone through at least a dozen emotions during the last several minutes, all of them negative in nature, but he thought he just might have to thank Gardner before they hanged him. For the first time since they'd met, Josie didn't look or sound like she was angry at him. She actually sounded as though she would be anxious for him to come back as soon as possible.

Fortunately, a lifetime of caution came to his aid before he did or said anything stupid. "It shouldn't take long. Hawk had them at gunpoint before I left."

"So Suzette is okay?" Josie looked relieved.

"More than okay. She looked delighted to be holding a rifle on Gardner's thugs."

"*They're not my thugs!*" Gardner practically shouted.

"They're certainly not very good," Zeke said. "If you were going to be alive long enough, I'd suggest you fire them."

As Zeke hurried back through the brush, he couldn't decide which part of the situation they were in bothered him most. They were behind schedule returning to their ranch. If they delayed much longer, they faced the possibility that at least one of the mares would drop her foal. That would slow them down even more. He hoped the mares hadn't run far. Horses wandering unattended, even for a short time, were an open invitation to trouble. It would be better for Hawk to find them and bring them back tonight.

He was also concerned about the difficulty of getting the thieves to Redington. It wasn't going to be easy to escort five men, even if one of them was dead, while they also had to keep a lookout for the mares and protect the women. He and Hawk were good, but that was stretching things. His biggest worry was that some more of Gardner's men might come looking for their boss. It seemed unlikely that five men on a ranch would know about a plan to steal valuable mares without someone else knowing about it, too. When the boss didn't return as expected, the natural thing for his hands would be to go looking for him. Nearly as unsettling was the possibility that tonight's gunfire would attract the attention of other men just as willing to try to steal the mares.

Then there were the women. But he didn't want to think about that. At the moment, it was simply more than he could handle.

About the last thing he expected to see when he emerged from the brush was Suzette standing watch over three men bound hand and foot and tied together. "Where's Hawk?" he asked, looking around for his partner.

Suzette didn't take her eyes off the men. "Gone to find their horses."

"He shouldn't have left you alone with these men." Zeke didn't bother to check the ropes. No man had ever escaped after Hawk had tied him up.

"They're tied up, and I have a rifle."

"Do you know how to use it?"

"Of course."

"Would you?"

Suzette gave the blond man a particularly angry look. "I wouldn't hesitate."

"Are you sure you don't mind being by yourself?" he asked Suzette.

She nodded her head.

"Then I'll go after the mares."

* * *

"Okay, it's settled," Hawk said to Zeke. "Josie and I will take the men on to Redington, and you and Suzette will follow with the wagon and horses."

Suzette was not happy about the arrangements. Not that she minded being with Zeke or that Josie would be with Hawk. She minded because Josie's experience growing up on a farm and knowing how to ride and handle a rifle made her more suited to help Hawk get the prisoners to Redington. She acknowledged the value of Josie's experience, yet still felt it somehow devalued her. Her reaction wasn't logical, but that didn't change how she felt.

"Are you sure you're comfortable riding ahead of me by yourself?" Zeke asked Suzette when he'd finished harnessing the mules to the wagon.

"Why shouldn't I be?" She didn't mean to sound argumentative, but being judged insufficiently experienced to help Hawk had hurt.

Zeke met her gaze. "Knowing how to find your way through the desert isn't exactly the same as singing and dancing—even though it might be less hazardous."

She couldn't take out her frustration on Zeke. "It won't take any skill to follow the trail left by seven horses."

"You'll be by yourself."

"You'll be right behind me."

"But you'll *feel* alone."

Suzette decided right then that Zeke was a dangerous man. He saw too much, understood too much. Maybe that was why Josie was so afraid of letting him get close. Josie had secrets she didn't want to share, and a man like Zeke had a way of seeing into all the dark corners.

"I'll be okay." Suzette swung into the saddle and prodded Zeke's horse into a trot until she reached the clearing where the mares waited. As soon as Zeke brought the wagon up, Hawk waved good-bye and he, Josie, and the prisoners disappeared around one of the many bends in the river. "Come on, girl," she said to Dusky Lady. "It's time to hit the trail."

In less than five minutes, the mares were strung out behind her in a line reaching back to Zeke and the wagon. They moved out of the trees on the open valley floor, which allowed her to see Hawk riding not far ahead, and all her feelings of hurt came rushing back. She did feel alone. She did feel rejected. She did feel she wasn't good enough, and telling herself it was all nonsense didn't change a thing. She'd thought the night spent in Hawk's arms had meant something. Yet after seeing him ride off as though nothing had happened between them, she couldn't help wondering.

Fortunately for her, her horse didn't need her guidance to weave among the cactus, catclaw, acacias, and mesquite, avoiding sharp needles and hooked thorns from protruding limbs. The strip of green that bordered the river was beautiful, but she couldn't imagine why anyone would want to live in this desert. It was hot, dry, empty, and unfriendly.

She was feeling out of sorts with the whole world, but that was her fault. She'd made it clear she wasn't looking for an emotional relationship. She'd said she wanted to enjoy the next few days, then go her own way with no hard feelings, so what did she expect Hawk to do? Hell, he was a man. Everybody knew men had no trouble falling into and out of temporary relationships. A man who'd reached Hawk's age without being married had to be an expert at it. Which was one of the reasons she'd had the courage to sleep with him. Now that the game had started, she was wanting to change the rules.

That wasn't true. She didn't *want* to change the rules. Rather, the game was changing *her*.

She didn't want it to be a game. She wanted it to mean something. But how could it mean anything of importance if they could walk away from each other without a backward glance? Did she want it to mean something to Hawk but not to her? Did she need to feel that he didn't want to let her go, but would because that was what she wanted?

She wasn't sure what she wanted or why, but she was certain she was being unfair to Hawk. Yet knowing that and admitting it didn't keep her from being piqued that he'd gone off and left her. She'd never felt like this about a man, but apparently this feeling— whatever it was—didn't allow for logic. She couldn't want their time to be meaningful if she was prepared to turn her back on it in less than a week. She had to stick with her original plan or give up sleeping with Hawk.

But that was the trouble. She didn't think she could.

Josie looked at Gardner's back as he swayed on the horse to which he was tied. "Do you think he really owns part of the Birdcage?" she asked Hawk.

"Can't say."

"Is he really rich?"

"Must be. He controls most of the land along Aravaipa and Copper Creeks."

"Is that a lot?"

"More than you can ride over in a couple of days."

Charging one of the owners of the Birdcage with trying to steal horses pretty much eliminated any chance they had of getting a job in any business he owned, and that dimmed their prospects of finding decent employment in Tombstone. She wasn't afraid she'd be unable to find a job. She knew enough about men to know they'd challenge the devil himself for a chance to get close to an attractive woman, but she wasn't willing to work in a place where the men had actual contact with her. She'd been through that before, and once was enough. It was like being embraced by a centipede with a hundred hands instead of legs.

"What do you think will happen to Gardner and his men?" They were approaching Redington.

"They don't have any judge here. The trial will have to be in Tucson," Hawk said.

"Will we have to testify against them?"

"Can't say."

She didn't know how Suzette could stand riding with Hawk all day. She'd only been with him for one morning, and he'd talked more in the last five minutes than in the previous five hours. She'd tried to get him to talk about Zeke, but he'd said if she wanted to know anything about Zeke, she'd have to ask him. Only a man would say something as stupid as that. Any woman knew if you wanted to know something about a man, the last person you'd ask would be the man himself. As far as she knew, there wasn't a man in the world who knew the truth about himself.

Which brought her back to Zeke. It seemed nearly everything did. She'd met the man less than a week ago, and already her life seemed to be divided into two pieces, before and after. She wondered if all women felt this way when they met a man they couldn't forget, much less ignore. No man should be that important to a woman. They were too undependable, too selfish, too . . . male.

So why was she still thinking about Zeke? He had been a bachelor for so long, he wouldn't know how to settle down if he wanted to. Wandering all over the West shooting it out with outlaws was no way to prepare for being a father, much less a dependable husband. And what was she doing thinking about husbands and fathers in the first place? She didn't want a husband. And since she couldn't have children without one, she'd made up her mind to do without them, too.

She was relieved to see they were coming to Redington. She was tired of her thoughts and the endless circles they made in her head.

"Is this all there is to the town?" She counted less than a dozen buildings.

"It's easier for the ranchers to send a supply wagon to Tucson for what they need than to open up stores here."

"Who's going to take these men?"

"Just about anybody will see they get to Tucson."

"Is there a jail here?"

"Nope."

She could see people staring at them through windows as they passed. Most of the buildings seemed to be saloons, and everybody was male. No one appeared pleased to see them. "Do you know anybody here?"

"Nobody that matters."

Did that mean he only knew a stable hand or a clerk? She didn't feel any better when the men watching them with unfriendly eyes began to come out of the various buildings. Their beards were unkempt, their clothes looked as though they could stand up on their own, and not a single pair of boots had seen polish since they went on their owner's feet. She didn't know whether to be relieved or worried when Hawk brought their little group to a stop in front of the only dry-goods store in town. Her throat felt dry when a man came out holding a shotgun.

"That's my cousin you got tied across that saddle. I want to know who killed him and why."

Chapter Twelve

Zeke could feel trouble in the air before he reached the single street that ran through Redington. Maybe it was the sixth sense he'd developed over the years. Maybe it was the fact that he and Hawk were strangers in a part of the Arizona Territory dominated by powerful ranchers like the Redfields, the Sozas, and the Gardners. They wouldn't take kindly to an ex-slave and a half-breed Comanche accusing one of their own of being a horse thief. They'd be even less pleased to see the men brought into town tied to their horses like common criminals. He wanted to ride ahead and see what was going on, but he couldn't leave Suzette. Neither did he want to take the mares into town and expose them to still more men who might want to steal them.

"Let's change places," he called out to Suzette.

She stopped and turned in the saddle. "Why?" The mares bunched up as they stopped behind her.

Leigh Greenwood

"There could be trouble. You'll be safer in the wagon."

Suzette cast a worried gaze toward the town before turning back to Zeke. "Do you think they'd hurt Hawk?"

"They'd have to be pretty stupid to try, but someone might risk it if they think he's by himself."

Suzette rode back to the wagon and dismounted immediately. "Tell me what you want me to do."

"Act like nothing's wrong, but keep your rifle handy." He jumped down from the wagon and helped Suzette up. "No matter what happens, don't get down until Hawk or I tell you it's safe."

"Why did Hawk bring those men here if it's not safe?"

"I don't know anything's wrong. I just like to be on the safe side."

Zeke mounted up and headed toward the town. The mares gradually swung into line behind him. He looked back to make sure Suzette was okay, but she appeared to have the mules well under control. He urged his mount into a trot but dropped back to a fast walk when the mares refused to keep up. He kept telling himself Hawk could handle any situation, but Hawk had never been saddled with Josie as well as five rustlers. He didn't feel any happier when he spotted knots of men gathered in the street up ahead. That was never a good sign. Time for a distraction.

He rode back to the wagon. "I'm going to take the mares in at a canter."

"Why?"

"To give everybody something else to think about."

He whipped his horse around and let out two sharp

whistles that rent the air like a lightning strike. Using his hat, he urged the mares into a trot and then a canter. He rode down the middle of the street yelling like a cowhand trying to herd wild horses. The men in the street backed away to let the mares through, but they stopped when the mares slowed to a trot, then a walk as Zeke stopped yelling. Dusky Lady came to a halt when she reached the flank of Hawk's mount.

The men moved back into the street.

"You with that Injun?" a man asked.

Zeke nodded.

"These the horses those fellas tried to steal?" another man asked. His expression darkened as he looked from Zeke to Suzette and back again.

"Yes," Zeke replied. "What's going on?"

"Darcy Brigham talked that Injun into letting him have his cousin to bury."

Zeke didn't know why that should have taken any persuasion. Hawk would have been glad to leave the man's burial to his family.

"What are you going to do with the others?" The man followed Zeke as he rode toward Hawk and Josie.

"Leave them here."

"We don't have no jail and no judge."

"Then somebody can take them to Tucson to stand trial."

"You going to Tucson to testify against them?"

"No."

"Won't do no good, then. Where're you going?"

Zeke didn't like discussing his business with strangers, but he couldn't see any reason to make a secret of where he was going. "We're escorting these ladies to Tombstone."

Zeke was feeling increasingly uneasy. The transfer of the dead horse thief's body didn't appear to have improved the mood of the crowd.

"Them's some fine-looking mares you got there," the man said. "They yours?"

"Yes."

The man turned in the direction of the thieves. "Did they really try to steal 'em?"

"We wouldn't have brought them here otherwise."

"Well, if you want to get to Tombstone with your horses and your hides in one piece, you'd better get going now and take those men with you."

Zeke jerked his attention from the group of men gathered about the body that was now laid out on the boardwalk. "Why's that?"

"Because Harvey Redfield is due to come through here sometime this evening. I don't know that anything will come of it, but one of his girls is sweet on that Gardner fella you've got tied up."

"He's a horse thief."

"Seems to me *you've* got the horses, not him."

Zeke could see the way this was going, and he didn't like it. "Are you saying nobody's going to believe us?"

The man didn't blink. "You ain't white and you ain't rich. If that Injun didn't have that woman with him, there might have been trouble already. As it is, she's so pretty nobody's been able to think of much else."

Zeke didn't need things spelled out for him. "I'm obliged for the advice."

"Don't like to see trouble," the man said.

Zeke didn't like to see trouble, either, but it seemed that trouble couldn't resist him and Hawk. How else could you explain running into four women and a rich horse thief in one of the most isolated parts of the Territory? He rode up to where Josie sat her horse. "Come with me," he said softly. "I don't have time to explain, just act like nothing's wrong." He turned and rode back to the wagon and Suzette. Mercifully, Josie followed without any argument. "You and Suzette take the mares and head out of town right now."

Suzette glanced back at the men gathered around the prisoners. "What about Hawk?"

"Hawk and I can take care of ourselves better if we don't have you and the horses to worry about."

Josie looked ready to argue, but Suzette said, "Start the mares moving, Josie. I'll be right behind you. *Now*," she said when Josie hesitated.

Zeke was thankful for Suzette's willingness to do what he asked without hesitation, especially since he knew she was worried about Hawk. "Take hold of Dusky Lady's halter," Zeke said to Josie. "Put them into a canter once you clear town."

"Are you sure this is the best way?" Josie asked. "I know how to handle a rifle."

"Most of the men will be watching you and Suzette. Some will be looking at the mares. That'll leave just a couple still thinking about Hawk and me."

"Are you ever afraid of anything?"

The question caught him by surprise. Josie had never seemed impressed by anything he did. Even the *possibility* that she might have a bit of respect for him was a shock. Of course, she could think he was too stupid or too blind to be frightened. "There are some things that scare me to death, but this isn't one of them."

He sat astride his mount in the middle of the street

as first Josie and then the mares moved past him. He was grimly pleased that most of the men were more interested in Josie and Suzette than in the prisoners, but he knew that would change once the women were out of sight. He looked for the man who'd advised him to leave town quickly, but he'd disappeared. He and Hawk were on their own.

The prisoners hadn't moved since they'd reached town. Their horses had been tied together to prevent them from trying to run off. The two unwounded thieves looked about as happy as a heifer caught in a bog. Since Gardner had already said he knew nothing about the two men, they knew they weren't going to get any help from that quarter. Their best bet was to convince a judge they weren't horse thieves because they were never actually in possession of any horses. Zeke knew that in a case of our-word-against-theirs, the men had a good chance of getting off. Not many men put any credence in the word of a black man or a half-breed.

Gardner, on the other hand, looked quite content. Zeke didn't know whether he expected someone in Redington to come to his aid or whether he expected a judge would believe he was too rich to stoop to rustling. Just knowing he was certain he would get off made Zeke angry. He rode up to Hawk's side.

"I'm told you don't have a jail in town," Zeke said to the assembled group, "so we've decided to take the men to Benson." When he grabbed hold of the nearest bridle and turned the horse around to follow the women and the mares, Gardner's complacency vanished.

"I demand that you leave me here."

"I'll take him to Tucson," one of the men volunteered.

"It's easier for us to take them to Benson than for you to take them to Tucson," Hawk said. Without questioning Zeke, he'd taken hold of the bridle of Gardner's horse and was forcing him to follow the others despite Gardner's efforts to stop him.

"Harvey Redfield will be coming into town sometime soon," someone said. "You can let him decide."

"Nobody can question anything Harvey decides," Gardner said.

"Mr. Redfield is a busy man." Hawk had gotten Gardner clear of the men in the street. "I'm sure he has enough to do already."

"You can't let them take me!" Gardner shouted over his shoulder. "They'll probably kill us in our sleep."

The men in the street started to grumble.

"If we'd wanted to do that," Hawk said, "we'd have killed them where we found them and let the wild animals take care of the evidence."

"You can't let me be hauled off by a black man and a half-breed," Gardner shouted. "They're savages. You don't know what they'll do."

"We'll let you know when the trial is set," Hawk said to the group. "You can come see for yourself that they get a fair hearing."

Zeke breathed a sigh of relief once they'd cleared the buildings of Redington. He knew it was possible for the men to follow them, but he also knew it wasn't likely.

"You won't get away with this," Gardner shouted at both of them. "Redfield will come looking for me."

"You'll be in Benson by then," Zeke called back to him. "You'll be easy to find in jail."

Gardner continued to shout at them, but his threats lacked conviction as they got farther from the town without anyone following. Once the last building disappeared around a bend in the river, Hawk rode up to Zeke.

"Are you going to tell me what that was all about?"

"We need to talk," Zeke said to Josie. "Why are you still being so difficult?"

Once they were safely away from Redington and were sure they weren't being followed, Suzette had exchanged places with Josie. Suzette now led the way, followed by the prisoners. Hawk rode behind Gardner, with the mares following. Zeke and Josie brought up the rear with the wagon. It was nearly time to make camp for the night, and Josie had barely spoken a half-dozen sentences to Zeke. It wasn't the silence that bothered him. It was the tension, the unspoken words between them, that wouldn't allow him to relax.

"I'm not trying to be difficult."

Josie had spent most of the afternoon riding inside the wagon. She said it was to protect her complexion from the sunlight. Zeke was certain it was really to keep from having to talk to him, but he'd decided this state of affairs couldn't continue. He had to know what made her so sullen around him. Maybe he couldn't do anything about it, but he certainly couldn't if he didn't know what the problem was.

"Then why do you act the way you do? I'm fed up with feeling like you can't stand to be around me."

"I told you. I don't like men."

"Maybe not, but I don't think that's why you're so anxious to stay as far away from me as you can."

"I'm not trying to stay away from you. I told you, I was protecting my complexion."

"Well, the sun is behind us now, so you can sit up front with me without endangering your complexion." Her silence didn't encourage him to think she was going to move. "It won't hurt for us to get to know each other a little better."

"Why? We'll never see each other again after we reach Tombstone."

"I've known a lot of women in my life, some of whom weren't all that fond of me, but they didn't hide whenever I was around."

He heard Josie stirring inside the wagon, then a moment later she climbed up on the seat next to him. "Are you satisfied now?" she asked, giving him an angry look.

"I won't be satisfied until I know what's wrong. Isabelle taught me to be polite to a woman, never take advantage of her, and never assume anything until I was sure of my facts. I haven't had a problem doing that until now."

"Sounds like you think a lot of Isabelle."

"If it hadn't been for her, I'd be dead. Hawk, too. I'd kill anybody who laid a finger on her."

"I never had anybody good like that in my life."

"What did you have?"

Josie turned away from him, but he knew she wasn't interested in the vista of the distant Galiuro Mountains set against a backdrop of a deep blue, cloudless sky, or the taller Rincon Mountains with the orange-yellow rays of the setting sun shimmering around their tree-covered peaks. A pair of gray hawks circled lazily overhead, while somewhere along the river a woodpecker banged out a staccato rhythm on a hollow trunk. Bees buzzed around a paloverde tree covered with bright yellow blossoms, while an oriole watched their passage from his perch atop a fragile-looking ocotillo branch.

Josie sighed, and Zeke waited expectantly for her explanation, but she remained silent, the stillness of the desert broken by the grinding sound of the wagon wheels, the thud of dozens of hooves hitting the ground, and the occasional clink of harness chains striking each other. She sighed again.

"If it's that much trouble, don't bother. I can last a few more days."

Josie cast him an exasperated look, but there was no anger in it. "My father was a white man," she said, resignation in her voice, "my mother his slave. After the war, my father married her and brought her out West."

"That wasn't good?"

"My mother worshiped him, but he still treated her like a slave. She cooked and cleaned for him, took care of the garden, and worked with him when he needed help. I don't know why he treated her so badly unless it was that I wasn't a boy and she couldn't have any more children. She trained me to cater to his every whim. When I was slow or questioned him, he'd slap me. The two times I tried to defy him, he beat me."

Zeke tried to imagine what it would have been like to have a mother and father, regardless of what they were like. He'd been sold as a baby. He'd always wondered who his parents were, but the woman who owned him would only say she'd bought him from another plantation owner. When the war came too close to her home, she sold him to farmers, who nearly killed him. He'd tried to find his owner again after he grew up, hoping she'd finally tell him something about his parents, but she'd died. He knew he had been incredibly lucky to end up with Jake and Isabelle, but the ache of never knowing his family had never gone away.

"My mother died when I was fifteen," Josie continued. "I missed her terribly and cried myself to sleep for nearly a month, but my father missed her more. He was always in a bad mood, would get drunk, couldn't sleep, would often stay away from home all night. Then after about six months, he seemed to recover all at once. He sobered up, stayed home, and started attending to the farm. He even started being nice to me. I didn't know what was happening, but I was glad because he was finally treating me like his daughter rather than his slave, like he might even love me."

"So what went wrong?"

"Sometimes I'd catch him staring at me like I was the only thing in the room. At first I thought I reminded him so much of my mother that watching me was making him sad. Most of the time he'd get up, go outside, and not come back in for a while. The one time I tried to ask him what was wrong, he yelled at me to go back inside and leave him alone. I did until he tried to get in my bed."

Zeke had sensed what was coming, had made sure he wasn't looking at Josie when she finally put it into words. He could only guess how difficult it was for her to tell him about this. He didn't want to make it worse by looking at her with an expression she would probably interpret as shock or pity.

"The first night he stared at me from the doorway without saying a word. The second time he sat on the edge of the bed, telling me how much he loved me and appreciated how hard I'd worked since my mother died. I was so happy that when he told me he wanted to love me the way he'd loved my mother, I didn't understand at first. But when he touched me, I did."

"Did he . . ." Zeke couldn't put his fears into words.

"No. He left when I pushed his hand away, but I was frightened of him after that. His eyes followed me with that look all the time. And he would touch me. Not in the wrong places, but it felt wrong because I knew what he wanted to do."

Zeke felt cold anger well up in his belly. He couldn't understand how a father could do something like that to his own child. It made him feel sick to his stomach.

"When he started to drink again, I was so frightened I locked my bedroom door. Many a night I heard him try the lock before stumbling off to bed. One night I didn't lock the door properly—I don't know whether I didn't check it or if he jammed the lock—and he came into my room after I was asleep. I woke with him kissing my arms and neck. I pushed him away and yelled at him to go back to his own room or I'd tell the sheriff."

Zeke didn't realize how tense he had become until the mules started tossing their heads. Fear of what Josie's father might have done had caused him to clench his fingers around the reins and pull them too tight. He forced himself to relax and let the reins drop.

"Next morning, my father told me he'd decided to sell the farm and was sending me to live with my uncle. I hadn't been there a week before my uncle told me he'd been disgusted when my father married my mother, that the only way he was going to let me stay was if I did all the housework. One night he didn't like what I cooked for dinner and he took a stick to me. He'd have beat me real bad if one of his boys hadn't stopped him. I ran away that night."

"Where did you go? How did you take care of yourself?"

"I went to the nearest town and took any job I could get. None of them lasted very long, because the husband, son, or boyfriend would become interested in me, and I'd be dismissed."

Zeke couldn't imagine how any man could look at Josie and not want her. It was easy to understand why a woman wouldn't be anxious to have her in her home.

"I soon discovered I could make more money in a saloon than working in private homes. The men still wanted me. I had to endure being touched, but they couldn't do anything more in public. Then one night I got to sing and dance in place of a woman who got sick. I was such a big success, men started promising me anything I wanted if I would let them in my bed. One man swore he'd marry me, that he couldn't live without me. He even set the date for our wedding. Only problem was, he was engaged to a woman in another town."

The mules were tossing their heads again. Zeke had to ease up on the reins.

"It would have been better if my father had been black," Josie said. "Nobody wants a mixed breed. White women think I'm after their husbands, and white men hope I am. Black people don't trust me, because they believe I think I'm better than they are."

Leigh Greenwood

Zeke had no problem understanding that. That was how Hawk had felt all his life.

"Every man I've known has tried to use me for his own pleasure, has lied to me at every turn. Men don't care what they say or do as long as they get what they want. If I gave in, lost my reputation, and fell upon hard times, people would say it was my own fault, that I deserved what had happened to me."

Zeke had no trouble believing that, either.

"So I made up my mind to avoid men completely," Josie said. "I work hard, save my money, and keep to myself. When I get enough money, I'm going to retire and open a boardinghouse for women." For the first time since she'd started talking, Josie looked at Zeke. "Now you understand."

"Then why did you flirt with Gardner?"

"I've had to learn to use my skills as a woman to survive with men like Gardner."

"But you didn't use them on me."

Josie's smile was faint, unsure. "I didn't need to."

"I still don't understand. Why are you so angry with me? Not all men are like the ones who've misused you," Zeke said. "I'm not."

Josie looked away. "That's what worries me."

"How are we going to work this?" Josie asked when they made camp for the evening.

"If you and Zeke will see to the cooking," Suzette said, "Hawk and I will look after the horses and the prisoners."

Josie turned to Gardner, who had lapsed into sullen silence most of the afternoon but had recovered his temper once they stopped for the night. "I need to use your supplies," she said. "We didn't plan on having three extra people to feed."

"If your friends had left us in Redington, you wouldn't have to worry about us."

Josie wished they had left the prisoners in Redington. She didn't think there was much chance Gardner would be convicted, but she wasn't going to oppose Zeke any longer. He'd kept Gardner from kidnapping her. The idiot had tried to coax her into running away with him with promises of beautiful dresses, fabulous jewels, and life in a luxury hotel. Did he think she was a fool who didn't know what he was really after? The dresses would be flashy but cheap, the jewels would be fake, and she would live in a hotel until he got tired of her or found someone he liked better. Zeke had made sure that wouldn't happen.

"If I had my way, you wouldn't get anything to eat until Benson," Josie said, "but Zeke doesn't want you to have an excuse to tell anyone you've been treated badly."

"You don't think being tied to the back of a horse and paraded through Redington as a horse thief is being treated badly?"

"Maybe that'll remind you, next time you take a fancy to a horse, to offer to pay for it."

Suzette returned with an armload of wood. "If you'll start the fire, I'll get the water."

"Where are Hawk and Zeke?"

"Hawk's taking care of the horses. Zeke is taking the men, one at a time, to answer nature's call."

"When can I go?" Gardner asked. "I've been miserable for the last hour."

They'd had to stop during the afternoon for him, so Josie had no sympathy for his alleged discomfort. She'd long ago decided he had no thought of anyone's comfort but his own. "You've been once. The other men go first."

Gardner continued to fuss about being bound hand and foot, tied to the wagon wheel, treated like a common criminal. Josie ignored him and concentrated on building her fire. With plenty of twigs, dry leaves, and Zeke's sulfur matches, she had a blaze going before Suzette returned with the water. "If you'll bring me the coffee beans, I'll put the water on to boil," Josie said to Suzette. She had decided to fix a stew made of jerked beef and dried vegetables. If Zeke was in a good mood, maybe she could talk him into making biscuits. She was a capable cook, but she had to admit Zeke's biscuits were better than any she could make.

She got a large pot from the wagon and filled it half full of water. Using rocks to keep it off the coals, she placed it in the center of the fire. She shoved some mesquite and ironwood branches under the pot. Opening the several saddlebags Zeke had left her, she began to assemble the ingredients for her stew.

"Do you know how to cook?" Gardner asked.

"I've been cooking since I was tall enough to reach the stove."

"You two women are too beautiful to be traveling in a wagon through the desert and cooking over a campfire. There are trains in the Territory now. And hotels that will serve you fabulous meals."

"There's no train from Globe to Tombstone," Josie said, wishing Gardner would be quiet so she could concentrate on how much of each ingredient she needed to feed seven people. "Do we have enough bowls?" she asked Suzette.

"Hawk said we should feed the prisoners first and get them settled."

"Stop calling me a prisoner!" Gardner shouted. "This whole thing is a mistake. I didn't hire those men to steal your horses, and I wasn't trying to kidnap Josie. Why would I do that when I'd already offered to give you jobs in my theater?"

"*If* you have a theater." Suzette was setting out cups for coffee.

"You'll find out when you reach Tombstone."

"But you won't give us jobs now, will you?" Josie said.

Zeke returned with the other three horse thieves. "It's about time," Gardner growled at Zeke. "I've been dying over here."

"Too bad you didn't," Josie said. "It would be a lot quieter around here."

She was certain she heard Zeke chuckle, but she didn't look up from her work until Zeke and Gardner had disappeared through the thick brush that grew on either side of the river. "Do you want coffee?" Josie asked the three men.

They nodded their heads.

"You'll have to wait until Zeke or Hawk returns," Suzette said. "We aren't allowed to untie your hands unless one of them is here."

Josie poured the coffee beans into the boiling water. Ironic that she, who refused to cook for any man, was now cooking for horse thieves. And what surprised her almost as much was that she was only mildly irritated by it. She would have to spend some time tonight trying to figure that out. Along with a long list of—

A rifle shot followed by a yell snapped her train of thought.

Chapter Thirteen

"You'd better pull your pants up," Zeke said to Gardner. "I expect both women to come bursting through that thicket in about twenty seconds."

"You shot me!" Gardner shouted.

"Just the heel of your boot."

"You're crazy," Gardner said as he clutched at his pants.

"*You're* crazy if you thought I'd fall for that trick of telling me you couldn't take care of your business with me watching."

"A man deserves privacy when—"

"When you attacked Josie and tried to steal our horses, you forfeited all rights to privacy." Zeke didn't know what it was about rich men that made them think they were the only ones with any brains.

"I wouldn't—"

The sound of someone stumbling through the brush

caused Gardner to abandon his argument and pay attention to his pants. He was still pulling them up when Josie and Suzette burst into view.

"What happened?" Josie asked, looking from Zeke to Gardner.

"Gardner thought he could make a break for it, so I shot the heel off his boot to slow him down."

"You can shoot that well?" Suzette exclaimed.

Josie seemed more interested, and amused, that Gardner was struggling to get dressed and, in his hurry, bungling it.

"That's the only way to stay alive when you do the kind of work we've done most of our lives," Zeke said.

"Where's Hawk?" Suzette looked around as though she expected him to be just out of sight.

"With the horses. He knows I can handle my own trouble."

Suzette looked disappointed. "You helped him in Redington."

"He was facing a whole town. I had just one man, and he had his pants around his ankles."

Embarrassed, Gardner plunged into a tamarisk thicket.

"Can he run with his pants like that?"

"Not well."

Suzette tried to smother her laughter but failed. Zeke grinned when Josie, equally unable to stifle her amusement, ducked her head and started back to camp. Suzette followed quickly, the sound of their laughter hanging in the night air to taunt Gardner.

His clothes finally in place and limping because of his heelless boot, Gardner emerged from the tamarisk thicket. "I'll kill you for that."

Zeke shrugged. "Forget it. Everybody gets caught with their pants down sooner or later. Now, unless you want me to shoot off the other heel, you'll head back to camp without any funny business."

"At least I wouldn't have to limp."

The sound of the rifle exploding less than six feet behind him caused Gardner to yell and throw himself into the clutches of a mesquite bush. Eyes wide with shock and tinged with fear, he stared down at his other boot—now missing a heel—then back at Zeke.

Zeke kept his expression bland. "You said you didn't like to limp."

Grimacing from pain at the scratches down his arms, over his shoulders, and across his back, Gardner jerked several thorns loose from his clothes. "I hope those women know they've hooked up with a crazy man."

"All they care about is getting to Tombstone. Now if you want any supper, you'd better get moving."

Gardner looked around for the boot heel, which had landed several feet away.

"With all your money, it'll be easier to buy some new boots—if you think you'll live long enough to need them."

"Do you really think any judge is going to hang me?"

"I'm counting on it."

Gardner glared at Zeke, hate luminous in his eyes, but he got to his feet without further comment.

Once in camp, Zeke seated the prisoners in a row, bound their feet, then tied the four of them together. "Now you can have your coffee. If you behave yourselves, I'll leave your wrists untied until it's time to go to bed."

"I can't sleep tied up," Gardner said.

"Then you can keep watch for wild animals," Zeke said. "We get wood rats and kangaroo rats at night looking for crumbs, but watch out for raccoons and coyotes. They'll try to get into the saddlebags or carry them off."

"I'm not looking out for anything," Gardner snapped.

"You'd better hurry with his coffee," Zeke said to Josie. "He's definitely out of sorts."

"If you'd ever been tied up like I am, you'd know why."

Before he knew what he was doing, Zeke had Gardner by the throat. "You can't begin to know what it's like to *really* be out of sorts. I was worked from dawn until dark, beaten when I was too weak from hunger and exhaustion to stand on my feet, then chained up at night and forced to sleep in my own filth. And that was *after* the liberation of the slaves."

Gardner had turned blue and was making gobbling noises. Disgusted with himself for losing control, Zeke tossed Gardner from him, then thrust his rifle in Josie's hands. "Keep an eye on them."

Then he stalked out of camp into the comfort of the enveloping darkness.

It seemed to Josie that Zeke had been gone for hours. Everybody had finished eating, and Hawk had taken the prisoners for their last trip into the bushes for the night. She and Suzette had washed and put away the cups and bowls. A single pot containing Zeke's supper remained on the glowing embers of the fire. Josie had added water three times to keep the stew from burning. For the last several minutes, Hawk and Suzette had talked quietly, so intent on each other, Josie was sure they'd forgotten her presence. Finally unable to stand the suspense any longer, she asked Hawk, "When is Zeke coming back?"

"He said he'd whistle when he was ready for me to relieve him," Hawk answered.

"Aren't you worried?"

"No."

She couldn't understand the relationship between the two men. Zeke said they were closer than brothers, practically like twins, yet they never seemed to worry about each other. No woman could stand seeing her sister or best friend as upset as Zeke had been and not try to do something about it. He had to feel abandoned. She marched over to the wagon and pulled out a bowl and a spoon. "I'm taking his supper to him."

"He's not hungry," Hawk said.

"How do you know?" she asked, unable to contain her impatience. "You haven't set eyes on him in more than two hours."

"I saw all I needed to see."

She took the pot of stew off the fire. "Well, I haven't seen all *I* need to see."

She turned away, irritated by Hawk's look of sympathy. How could he possibly think she needed sympathy? Zeke was the one who'd been forced to remember a horrendous time in his life. He was the one who had to feel that no one understood, cared, or could be bothered to share his pain. It was impossible for anyone to have endured what he had endured and not be permanently scarred by it.

She picked her way through the barrier of dense,

tangled growth. Less than a hundred feet from the river, the cottonwoods and willows abruptly gave way to scattered mesquite and ironwood interspersed with cactus and barely enough grass to supply the horses and mules for the night. Moonlight reflecting off the tawny rocks and dun-colored soil enabled her to see the livestock, but not Zeke. She knew he must be close by. He wouldn't leave the mares unattended.

"Zeke."

The huge emptiness of the desert swallowed the sound of her voice. Not even the sounds of the horses cropping grass could erase the feeling that she was alone in the night. The canopy of stars taunted her with their tiny pinpricks of light. Even the moon seemed cold and unwelcoming. She shivered, unsure whether it was from cold or apprehension. She felt stupid standing there, a pot of rapidly cooling stew in one hand and a bowl and spoon in the other.

"Zeke, where are you? I've brought your supper."

Silence. Stillness. Emptiness. She was starting to feel embarrassed, like she was standing there naked for the whole world to see. If he didn't want her around, the least he could do was tell her so. She turned in a complete circle without seeing him. She was about to go back to camp when she saw a shadow unfold from the larger shadow of a boulder.

"I'm not hungry."

She didn't recognize his voice. It was a pale, listless imitation of the vibrant man she had come to know. He walked toward her with slow, deliberate steps, like a man going to his own execution. His attitude surprised her; it frightened her, too.

"You need to eat." She tried to sound optimistic,

even cheerful. "I didn't break down and cook just to feed horse thieves." Even in the moonlight, it was hard to see his expression, hard to tell what he was thinking, what he was really feeling. He was close now. She could feel the energy pouring from him, could almost feel his presence touching her. She nearly sighed with relief. He'd lost none of his strength, none of the vibrant energy that made him seem so alive.

"I'm glad you brought a bowl." He made a feeble attempt to smile. "Isabelle would wake out of a dead sleep if I so much as ate a spoonful from the pot."

She would have to meet Isabelle someday. It was hard to believe that anyone could have had such a powerful influence on this man.

"Is there someplace we can sit without getting thorns in our bottoms?"

Zeke pointed toward the spot where he'd been sitting in the shadow of the boulder. "I can watch the horses from there."

Josie followed him, not knowing what to do, much less what to say. When they reached the rocks, she set the bowl down, poured the stew into it, and handed it to Zeke. "I didn't bring any coffee." Why was she apologizing? She'd already done more for him than she'd done for any man since her father.

"That's okay. I can always get a drink out of the river."

He tasted the stew. "It's really good." She suspected he would say that, no matter what it tasted like, but he ate with gusto. She lost her appetite when she was unhappy. Most of the women she knew did, too, but not the men. They could be in the middle of a life-altering tragedy and they'd still want their three meals a day.

She sat in silence while he ate. She didn't move except to serve up the rest of the stew when he'd finished the first bowl. She tried to concentrate on the sounds of the night—the horses, the murmur of the river, the rustling of small creatures among dry leaves—but she heard only the sound of Zeke chewing and swallowing. She tried to survey the sights of the night—the looming black shapes of cactus, boulders, the horses, even the towering cottonwoods that lined the bank of the river—but all she could see was the outline of Zeke's powerful body as he sat next to her, the movement of his mouth and jaw as he chewed his food.

He finished and placed the spoon in the bowl. Then the hand holding the bowl sank to his lap, and he remained motionless for several minutes. "Thank you," he said. "It was kind of you to bring me my supper."

His response was polite, reserved, completely unlike the Zeke she'd come to know, the man she'd come to believe was impervious to hurt of any kind. They hadn't always had a good relationship, but it upset her to see him so obviously wounded.

"It must have been really bad." She didn't know whether she should bring up what he'd said, but it stood between them like a barrier and she was tired of barriers.

"Even after Jake and Isabelle adopted me and I knew I was safe, I still had nightmares."

"Do you want to talk about it?"

"No."

But she could tell he did. No matter how painful, no matter how the memories haunted him, the past was part of who he was. Just as her past would forever bedevil her.

"It's all in the past," Zeke said. "It's not important anymore."

"It's important because it happened to you. And nothing important is ever all in the past."

He didn't respond, just set the bowl down, got up, and walked a few steps away. When he stopped with his back to her, she could see the tension cause his shoulders to rise until the muscles fanning out from his neck formed a ridge. His head rolled back until he was looking at the heavens. It was like watching him wrestle with himself; she wondered which side of him would win. She longed to know what was hurting him so much, but she knew she had to wait for him to speak.

"I was sold as a baby." He didn't turn around, just spoke into the emptiness of the night. "I never knew my mother or father. I don't know if I have brothers and sisters, aunts, uncles, or cousins. I simply existed alone in the universe."

She found it impossible to conceive of the loneliness of such a life. Even when things were at their worst for her, she knew who she was, where she came from, knew her mother loved her. She had roots that helped to ground her.

"My owner said she bought me because I was a handsome baby. She brought me up in the house because she wanted me where she could watch me all the time. That didn't mean she treated me any better than the other slaves. She just wanted to watch me. It made all the other slaves jealous. They thought I was getting something they weren't. They were right, but I'd have traded places with any boy who had to bed down on a hard floor in a cold cabin at night. At least I could have slept through the night without being awakened by nightmares of what could happen—of what *did* happen."

A chill of apprehension raced down Josie's spine. Could he be talking about what she was thinking? Did women do the same thing to boys that men did to girls?

"She made me sleep in a small room in the attic of the big house. Some nights I'd wake up to find her staring at me. In the beginning she never did or said anything, just stood there with this strange smile on her face."

"When I got older, she used to run her hands over my arms and chest. Even my legs. She would tell me how proud she was of the muscles I was developing, how handsome I looked, what a nice-looking man I would become someday. Then she'd tell me about the work she planned to give me so I could grow bigger and stronger. Some days I was so tired I could hardly eat my supper, but she'd make me sit at the table until I finished every mouthful. She said I needed to eat to grow big and strong."

Zeke bent down and picked up a rock, which he tossed from one hand to the other. Suddenly he reared back and threw it as hard as he could. She heard it rip through the leaves of the trees bordering the river. He bent down and picked up another rock, but a moment later he dropped it. He turned, walked back, and picked up the pot and bowl. "I'll wash these."

"I'll go with you." She knew there was more to his story. He wasn't ready to talk about it yet, but he needed to get it all out now. "What about the horses?"

"Dusky Lady is better than any watchdog. She'll let me know if anything is around."

Josie followed in his wake until they reached a narrow sandy patch of riverbank. Zeke worked in silence with quick efficiency. She'd hardly knelt down beside him before he handed her the pot and bowl, both scrubbed clean with sand and rinsed with water that sparkled beneath the shafts of moonlight filtering through the trees.

"You should go back," he said.

"Not yet."

He paused. Was he testing her, questioning in his mind whether she was strong enough to hear the rest of what had happened to him? She had known for most of her life that she had to be strong for herself, but this was the first time she wanted to be strong for anyone since her mother. It was a mystery to her how a man could be so strong he could overcome anything that happened to him, yet could still need the strength of a woman.

They walked back side by side.

When they cleared the trees, Zeke walked over to a pinto mare. She raised her head when he approached and moved away. He stood still and held out his hand. She hesitated, her large brown eyes watching him closely before she took slow steps toward him. She pushed her head against his chest, and he wrapped his arm around her neck and buried his face in her mane. It shocked Josie to realize she was jealous of the mare, that she wished she were the one giving Zeke comfort, the one offering him the consolation of her warmth, her presence. She tried to tell herself she was a fool,

217

but it didn't work this time. Here was a man who'd taken on the burden of making sure she got to Tombstone even though it endangered his goal of getting his mares safely to his ranch. In addition, he'd risked his life to rescue her from Gardner. Of course, she wanted to give him something in return. But how did you offer comfort to a man who wouldn't accept it?

"Are you going to tell me what happened after that?"

He didn't move from the mare, who kept nuzzling him. "I don't want to."

"You need to."

Why did she think she knew enough about any man to know what he needed? She'd done her best to avoid having anything to do with men. Their wants and needs didn't concern her. She didn't care. But that wasn't true with Zeke. It might not concern her, but she did care.

"She was delighted with my physical growth." Zeke spoke into the mare's mane. "She even kept a chart of how much I grew each year, how much weight I gained, the size of my chest. She did the same thing with the horses she raised. I started to feel like a prized piece of livestock. The other slaves said she was raising me to sell, that planters on the Mississippi delta would pay up to two thousand dollars for a healthy adult male slave."

He straightened up, patted the mare's neck, then walked toward a sorrel. The mare trotted away from him and started to graze again after she'd gone about thirty yards. When Zeke approached her a second time, she didn't run, just kept grazing while his hand rested on her withers.

"Things got worse when my voice dropped and I started to grow a beard. She made me go to bed without any clothes. Even when it got so cold I shivered, she'd run her hands all over me. If I begged her to stop, she'd get angry and beat me. She wouldn't stop until I'd made a mess of myself. Then she'd pretend to be angry, tell me I was a wicked boy, and order me to wash myself under the pump behind the house. I don't know what she'd have done if the war hadn't started. When Union soldiers landed in Texas, she sold me to some farmers. I never saw her again."

Zeke turned to face Josie for the first time since he'd started his recital. She supposed it was too difficult for him to look at her when telling of things that must have scarred his young soul, but she would never look down on him, never blame him for what had happened, because she knew it wasn't his fault any more than what had happened to her had been her fault. But it had been worse for him, because he'd been a child. She'd been old enough to defend herself. She stepped forward and took his hand. "Tell me about the farmers."

He hesitated briefly before his fingers closed around her hand. She could feel some of the tension leave him, heard him exhale. Had he been holding that breath, waiting to see how she would react to what he'd said?

"They didn't care about anything but getting as much work out of me as possible. They adopted boys without families, then treated them like slaves. They worked us until we were too exhausted to move, fed us little better than their pigs, and chained us up at night. After one boy died, another boy, Buck, ran away. If he hadn't come back for me after Isabelle found him, I'd probably be dead."

"I'd like to meet Isabelle someday," Josie said.

Zeke chuckled, and Josie felt herself begin to relax. "Everybody loves Isabelle, but if you don't watch out, she'll run right over you."

"Then why do you love her so much?"

"Because her love is so fierce, you can't help loving her, even when she's trying to talk you into doing something you don't want to do."

"Does she do that a lot?"

"Sure. Isabelle thinks she knows what's best for everybody."

"Does she?"

"Not everybody has the courage to reach for the best. Sometimes, second best is all a person can handle."

That was one of the most enigmatic statements Josie had ever heard, but she couldn't escape the suspicion that Isabelle would have said that she—Josie—had settled for second best. She didn't like the feeling, but her conscience wouldn't let her ignore it.

"It's time for you to go to bed," Zeke said. "You have four extra mouths to feed tomorrow."

"If it wasn't too much trouble, I'd make them cook their own breakfast."

"It's only three more days. We should reach Benson by then."

She should have been pleased as well as relieved, but a vague sense of dissatisfaction wouldn't go away. As much as she'd complained about Zeke, she'd found she enjoyed being treated as a person rather than a body and a face. She had become accustomed to men's adulation, had managed to convince herself she wanted it because it meant she would be successful, but she had stepped out of the role with unexpected ease. Still more unanticipated was her reluctance to take it up again. Even cooking breakfast didn't seem too high a price for the freedom from being stared at, grabbed at, hollered at, even having money waved at her. She liked what she did, but she nearly always came off stage with a bad taste in her mouth.

"You should check on jobs in Benson," Zeke said. "Tombstone won't last much longer. Everything is moving south to Bisbee."

"How can you think about a job for me after what you've just told me?"

"Those people can't hurt me. As for the rest, my adopted family has made me believe I'm as worthy of love and respect as anybody else. As long as I have them, I don't need anything else."

Josie wasn't so sure about that.

Suzette lay next to Hawk, listening to the soft sound of his breathing as he slept. She resisted a strong impulse to wrap her arms around him and hold him close. Their time together was coming to an end. Tomorrow they'd reach Benson. Both Hawk and Zeke agreed she and Josie ought to look for jobs there before going on to Tombstone. If they didn't find anything in Benson, they could always go to Tombstone or even Bisbee. It was a very sensible plan, but Suzette was feeling rebellious. And angry.

In a few short days she'd become convinced that the only man she could ever love, the only man she would consider spending her life with, slept beside her. And he was the one man with whom such a life was impos-

Leigh Greenwood

sible. He didn't have the money she needed to finish her sister's education and support her properly until she married. He was not the kind of husband she could take back to Canada. One look at him, and Quebec society would close its doors against her and her sister forever.

She was afraid her will was failing. It had wavered a few times in the past, but reminding herself of what happened when her mother died, when her husband died and left her stranded in the gold fields, renewed her determination that nothing like that would ever happen to her sister. She planned to return to Quebec as a wealthy widow with enough money to see her sister properly married. After that, she would disappear. She didn't know what she'd do, but she wouldn't come back to the Arizona Territory.

Hawk wouldn't be waiting for her.

She'd been staring at his face for the last hour as if that would somehow prolong their time together. She wanted to memorize his face, touch him, caress his cheek, brush her fingertips across his lips, but she knew the slightest movement would cause him to wake up. It was torture to have him so close yet to know he'd always be out of reach. She was a fool to have slept with him in the first place, but she wouldn't give up this time in his arms despite all the pain she knew it would cause her in the future. This was something she'd done for herself, even though she knew it was unwise. Falling in love with Hawk was a completely unexpected complication.

She'd probably fallen in love with him the day he let her go with him to take care of the horses, but she'd only figured it out tonight as she lay next to him with nothing to do but think about a future without him. The realization seeped into her gradually, like the cold from the ground seeped into her bones during the night, until she felt it with her whole being. It filled her with the warmth of passion and the chill of knowing it was the biggest mistake she'd ever made, but it was impossible to deny that she loved him.

Hawk lay on his side facing her, one arm curled under him and the other resting on his side. His shoulders were so wide, his chest so broad, she felt he was shielding her from the dangers of the night. He slept just as he was when they finished making love. The stars above looked down on the swell of his buttocks, the power of his thighs, the bulge of his muscled calves. In the milky-white light of the moon, his eyebrows looked like inky smudges, his lashes ebony lines, drawn on the pale mahogany of his skin. His wonderful lips that did such incredible things to her body were ever so slightly parted. Unable to stand it any longer, she reached out.

He spoke even before she touched him. "Can't you sleep?"

Her hand came to rest on the inside of the arm curled under him. "I just wanted to look at you."

He looked at her through half-open eyelids. "Not much to see."

He couldn't have been more wrong. There was so much to see, she didn't know where to begin. There was a whole universe of undiscovered riches inside him, riches that would remain unexplored once he isolated himself on his ranch. She wanted to tell him that, to make him believe in himself, but she was leaving. Only a woman who meant to stay had a right to do that. "There's a lot more than you think."

"Not enough to keep you awake. You'd better get some sleep. Tomorrow could be an important day."

The most important of her life—the day she walked away from everything she'd ever wanted.

"That's Benson," Zeke said to Josie when the outlying buildings of the town came into view. "In a few hours we'll be rid of the thieves and we can see about finding you a job."

Not wanting to attract the attention of strangers, he and Hawk had decided to leave the horses outside of town. They'd found a rancher more than willing to accept a gold coin in exchange for holding the mares overnight.

Hawk and Suzette rode in front of the prisoners. Josie followed behind with the wagon, Zeke riding alongside.

Several times during the last two days Zeke had started to ask Hawk to change places with him. It was odd that, now Josie was being nice to him, he felt uncomfortable around her. Considering how much he was attracted to her, his reaction didn't make sense, but there was no use denying the fact. He'd wracked his brain trying to figure out why he'd told her about having been a slave. He hadn't talked about that in twenty years. Only Hawk knew all that had happened to him.

And now Josie.

He'd never been tempted to mention his owner or the farmers to any woman before, so why should he go and spill his guts to Josie? He wasn't feeling sorry for himself. He'd stopped doing that years ago. What had happened was terrible, but it had toughened him up, taught him he could survive anything. It had made it possible for him to live the life he and Hawk had lived for the past twenty years—ranch hand, hired escort, guard for shipments of valuable properties, from women and children to gold and silver. They'd transported prisoners and hunted down criminals, scouted for the army and carried messages through battle lines. He'd worn his accomplishments like a shield, like an accolade, but telling Josie about his past had stripped him of all that, leaving him feeling naked and exposed.

"How long are you and Hawk going to stay in Benson?" Josie asked.

"I'm not sure. It's less than twenty miles to our ranch."

"Do you come to town often?"

"No more than we have to. Once we get ahead enough to hire someone to work for us, we probably won't come in at all."

That was the whole point of buying a ranch in a part of the country so sparsely settled it was still a Territory. He and Hawk had decided they were tired of putting up with the insults and slights they encountered every time they entered a town. And if Josie got a job in Benson, that would be still another reason to stay away. He hadn't liked it when Josie couldn't stand to be around him, and he didn't like it any better now that he could see sympathy in her eyes every time she looked at him. He didn't need sympathy, and he didn't want it. Knowing that was the way she now felt about him angered him. He couldn't explain it, but he felt diminished by her sympathy.

Up front, Hawk brought his horse to a stop.

"What's wrong?" Josie asked.

A group of horsemen had ridden out of town and were coming toward them. Zeke had no reason to expect they had any interest in him, the women, or the prisoners, but his instincts kicked in the moment he realized the riders were approaching abreast of each other. That made it impossible for anyone to ride past them without leaving the road.

"Get behind me," he said.

"Why?"

"Because I don't want you to get shot."

Chapter Fourteen

"Are those men coming to meet us?" Suzette asked Hawk.

"Looks like it." He'd been worried something like this might happen ever since they had to leave Redington without dropping off their prisoners. It would have been very easy for anyone wanting to cause trouble to get here ahead of them and spread whatever story they wanted. If that person had been Harvey Redfield, or anyone sent on his behalf, the situation could get a little ticklish.

"What are you going to do?"

"See what they have to say."

They were a motley collection of men, no two appearing to represent the same stratum of Benson society. A badge identified one as the sheriff. Next to him rode the town banker or leading merchant. Dark suit, white shirt, and shoes rather than boots gave him away. The man in the checkered vest and pencil-thin mustache had *gambler* written all over him. Then there was the cowhand identified by his worn, dusty boots, battered hat, and chaps. But what surprised Hawk was the discovery that the fifth man wasn't a man at all, but a mannish woman riding astride. It was only a guess, but he supposed she was the daughter of Harvey Redfield who was supposed to be sweet on Gardner. The grin he saw on Gardner's face seemed to confirm his suspicion. Hawk pulled his mount to a stop. "We'll wait for them to reach us," he said to Suzette. He knew Zeke would guard their rear.

"I got word you were bringing me some prisoners," the sheriff said when his group stopped a few yards away.

"Do you usually come out to meet prisoners?" Hawk asked.

"No, but I'm told you have a very special prisoner."

"I have *four* special prisoners. Maybe the most special is the one with the bullet hole in his leg. It's clear of infection, but he probably needs to see a doctor."

"What are your prisoners charged with?"

"Trying to steal our horses."

"Why would they try to steal a few riding horses and a couple of mules? It doesn't seem worth the risk."

"They were trying to steal nine blooded mares."

"How do I know you have any mares if I can't see them?"

"You can ask either one of these ladies. They were coming south to look for jobs when we met up on the trail."

The sheriff looked from Suzette to Josie. Hawk could practically see what he was thinking, but there was no law against a man thinking, not even when it was something he shouldn't. "I suppose you ladies saw the mares?"

"I helped take care of them," Suzette said.

"What kind of jobs are you ladies looking for?" the sheriff asked.

"My friend and I sing and dance. We were hoping you had a theater in town."

Gardner had nudged his horse forward until he was abreast of Zeke and Suzette. "I offered them jobs at the Birdcage."

"You ladies don't want to work at the Birdcage?" the sheriff asked. "It's the best theater in the Territory."

"We weren't sure he had a theater," Josie said. "When a man tries to kidnap you, you naturally assume he's not the truthful kind."

"I didn't try to kidnap you," Gardner said. "I've explained that a dozen times."

"You didn't believe him?" the sheriff asked Hawk.

"I wasn't there," Hawk replied.

"I was," Zeke said. "He pulled a gun on me when I told him to let her go."

"I was just defending myself," Gardner said. "I thought he was going to attack me."

Hawk knew how this was going to end and didn't see any point in prolonging the inevitable. "Since you're here, why don't we turn the prisoners over to you? We've got business to attend to."

The sheriff looked surprised. Apparently, he'd been prepared to *persuade* them to hand over the prisoners. "Sure. You coming by to file a written complaint?"

"Why? You already know what they did."

"How about you?" the sheriff asked Josie.

"I do intend to file a written complaint." She directed a definitely unfriendly glance at Gardner. "I'll be by sometime today."

Handing over the prisoners took only a few minutes. Rather than follow immediately, Hawk decided it might be better to wait a little while before they headed into town.

"Why did they come out to meet us?" Josie asked.

"How did they know we were coming?" Suzette wanted to know.

"The woman was Harvey Redfield's daughter," Hawk said.

"What woman?" Josie asked.

"The person on the far right was a woman," Zeke said.

Hawk smiled. A woman couldn't come within a hundred feet of Zeke without his sensing it. "Zeke said a man in Redington told him she was sweet on Gardner. I expect she wanted to make sure we didn't hurt him." Hawk saw comprehension dawn in the eyes of both women.

"The sheriff is going to let them go, isn't he?" Josie asked.

"I expect so."

She looked as angry as Suzette was unemotional. "That's the way it is in Quebec if you have money and a position in society," Suzette said.

"We're a black man and a half-breed traveling with women of dubious reputation," Zeke said. "You didn't really think they'd believe us, did you?"

It was clear from Josie's expression that she had. Then her temper snapped and she let loose with a tirade that covered virtually every sin men had committed since the Garden of Eden. Hawk had to smile at the expansiveness of her vocabulary and the imagination she employed to evoke visual images of some of the punishments she thought particularly suitable for men like the sheriff. Before she ran down, women like Redfield's daughter came in for their share of attention.

"Both of you knew this, didn't you?" Josie's gaze switched from Hawk to Zeke.

"I suspected as much when the man in Redington told me to get out of town quickly," Zeke said.

"But we couldn't be sure until we saw the woman and I saw Gardner grin," Hawk added.

"And I'm supposed to meet him on the street and not claw his eyes out?"

"He expects you not to worry about what you can't change," Suzette said.

Picking up on Josie's agitation, the mules shook their heads up and down, stamped their feet, even attempted to start forward before being abruptly halted.

"Let's head into town." Hawk waited for Suzette to fall in beside him. "We need to find a place for you to stay. Then you can begin to look for work."

"What are you going to do?" Suzette asked.

"We're leaving," Hawk said. "You don't need us anymore."

Even though only a few feet separated Josie from Zeke as he rode beside the wagon, she fell silent. The muted clip-clop of horses' hooves over the rough trail and the occasional squeak of a saddle provided a quiet backdrop to her gloomy thoughts. She knew she'd overreacted when Hawk said he expected Gardner to be let off without anything happening to him. It wasn't fair that a man could do virtually anything he wanted and get away with it just because he had money—or because the woman he'd assaulted worked in theaters and saloons. Getting drunk and staring at women's legs and breasts didn't automatically make men morally corrupt. Why should singing and dancing for their entertainment brand her as a woman of no virtue?

She knew she was wasting her energy, but it was impossible for her to accept the inevitable as calmly as Suzette. She had to fret and fume and concoct terrible revenge before she finally ran out of steam, gave a fatalistic sigh, and moved on. That process usually took several days, during which time she was liable to lose her temper for any reason at all.

Though she didn't like to admit it, she would miss Zeke. It had taken her a while to believe he wasn't like every other man she'd met, but now that she realized he was someone special, he was going to bury himself on a ranch miles away from anything and anybody. She didn't know how he could stand it. She'd been dying to get away from their farm almost from the time she realized there was a world beyond the limits of her father's acres.

It wasn't that she was entranced by the world of bright lights, rich ranchers, or rowdy men. She simply didn't want a life filled with the drudgery of cleaning, cooking, taking care of babies, and submitting her will to that of a husband. Though if she were honest with herself, she didn't really like the life of a singer/dancer. She played to the audience because she knew that was what she had to do to make the money necessary to retire before her looks faded and her legs gave out, but she didn't like it. In a way, she envied Zeke. His might be a boring life filled with hard work and empty nights, but at least he would be living his life the way he wanted, with no pretense and no being treated as an object.

"You've been silent for a long time," Zeke said. He had glanced over at her several times in the last few minutes but hadn't spoken.

"I thought it was probably better I didn't say anything until I calmed down."

Maybe she ought to tell him some of what she'd been thinking, but she couldn't summon the courage. She'd never trusted a man enough to reveal her true feelings. She knew the revelation would change their relationship, but she didn't know in what way, and that scared her. She thought of Zeke as a friend, but it didn't take a genius to know he was looking for much more.

"Did you know Gardner was going to go free?" she asked.

"No, but it didn't surprise me. I've seen it too often."

"Doesn't it make you angry?"

"It used to, but I decided my life was too important to squander getting angry about people like Gardner." His sudden grin surprised her. "It's easier to outsmart him."

Josie fell silent. She was too busy trying to absorb the fact that Zeke's grin had made her stomach flip violently. She'd thought he was physically impressive the first time she saw him. She'd even admitted he was handsome, but never in her life had she felt devastated by a smile. She understood being attracted to a man. She understood liking a man. She even understood being physically attracted to a man she didn't like, but none of that explained the weird things going on with her stomach. Or the faint dizziness she felt.

It had to be the hot days followed by cool nights, a perfect formula for getting a cold or influenza. Once she got settled in a hotel, she'd make a tea of vervain flavored with honey. She didn't especially like the bitter taste, but she couldn't afford to get sick and be unable to work.

Yet she didn't feel confident she had the answer to why she was feeling so peculiar. She remembered more than one of the women she'd worked with describing how they felt when a particularly handsome cowboy or miner started to show an interest in them. The description of their feelings sounded much too close to what she was feeling right now for her comfort. She wasn't in love with Zeke, nor was she in any danger of falling in love with him, but she did like him and didn't want him to disappear from her life.

Maybe he wouldn't leave, not entirely. Surely Zeke and Hawk would have to come to Benson on business. There was no reason they couldn't stop by to see her and Suzette. She started to feel a little better. That would be the perfect way to keep up their friendship.

"Are you going to stop talking to me altogether?" Zeke's words jerked her out of her abstraction.

"Sorry. I'm always a little nervous when I come to a new town."

"You have nothing to worry about. I haven't seen your act, but there aren't any women in Benson half as pretty as the two of you. Men will be fighting over seats. Ask the manager to charge extra and give you a percentage."

He couldn't know it was the men in the first row she disliked most. They were the ones who shouted lewd comments so loud they could be heard over the music. They were the ones who tried to touch her. She'd once suffered a bad fall when a man grabbed her ankle. She'd been unable to dance for a week.

"Will you come see our show?" She shouldn't have asked. She shouldn't have cared, but she did.

Zeke's expression clouded. "I don't expect we'll get into town very often. With just the two of us, the horses will keep us mighty busy."

"Is Tombstone closer to your ranch?"

His gaze seemed to be locked between his horse's ears. "Yes, but it's not a question of distance. We can't leave the horses unattended."

And he couldn't spend his time on a woman who offered only friendship. Her father had once said men and women couldn't be friends. Up until now she had agreed, but she hoped he was wrong. Zeke's friendship had become very important to her.

Suzette couldn't work up any enthusiasm for the owner's description of his theater or his promise it would be filled with men anxious to see Josie and her perform.

"You'll play to a full house every night. The railroad has made us the most important town in this area. Silver and copper are sent here for smelting and shipment. You won't just be performing for miners and cowboys," the man said when she didn't respond to his enthusiasm. "We have a higher class of customer. You'll have businessmen and tradesmen coming to see you."

Suzette couldn't tell him it wouldn't matter because none of them would be Hawk. She couldn't even say that to Josie, who, fortunately, was paying careful attention to everything the man said. She'd questioned him on the details of the musicians, the dressing rooms, even the number and placement of the lamps used to light the theater. Both had worked in a theater that burned down when some lamps were turned over by overenthusiastic customers.

"We've never had a fire," the manager had said. "Our customers are very well behaved."

Men who hadn't seen a woman in several days, sometimes weeks or months, were never well behaved. For those men, women belonged to two distinctly different and separate groups. *Nice* women were usually left back home. The nice ones who came west almost invariably avoided any contact with strangers, never set foot in saloons or theaters, and kept their daughters safe at home at night. Women who worked in saloons and theaters were considered only a small step above soiled doves, and all were fair game. Suzette had never liked that attitude, but she'd accepted it as part of the job.

"Can you start tonight?" the manager asked.

"We just got into town," Josie said. "We don't even have a place to live yet."

"That's no problem. I know a real nice widow who's looking to rent some rooms. Her husband was killed in an accident at the railroad, and she's got five kids to feed."

Suzette wasn't sure she could live in such a house. It would remind her too much of her own mother after her father died.

"I don't know," Josie said. "We haven't had a chance to practice since we left Globe. After riding in a wagon for a week, I doubt I can do a high kick."

The manager's eyes grew about as big as a full moon in the night sky. "I'll give you all the proceeds of the front row," he said.

Josie turned to Suzette. "What do you think?"

Suzette wanted to turn on her heel, walk out of this place, and never look back, but she'd laid out a careful plan for her life years before. It was too late to change it now. Hawk had no room in his life for a woman, and she couldn't afford to make room in her life for a man like him. It was time she stopped thinking about the impossible and started concentrating on the necessary. Pure chance had brought her together with Hawk, but the natural course of their lives would keep them separated.

"I suppose we could do it," Suzette said, "if we can find a place to stay and run through a couple of numbers with the pianist before tonight."

"Are you sure?" Josie asked, looking at Suzette more closely. "You don't look like yourself. Are you sure you're not too tired?"

Suzette knew that what ailed her had nothing to do with being tired. She also knew it wouldn't be cured by inactivity. She needed to focus her attention on her work. If she had to think about a man, she ought to look around for a nice, wealthy mine owner or merchant who was in the market for a wife. Her being a dancer was a drawback, but being attractive was in her favor.

It was time to stop kidding herself. A month ago she might have been able to marry a man she didn't love, but that was impossible now. She would have to earn all the money her sister needed, so she couldn't afford to be sick or to sit around feeling sorry for herself. Hawk was gone. She had to get on with the rest of her life.

"I'll be fine." Suzette forced herself to smile at the theater owner. "All I need is to hear the sound of ap-

237

plause and see a theater full of eager faces. You know how performers are."

The look Josie gave Suzette said she didn't believe a word she was saying, but they made the final arrangements with the owner and then headed out of the theater with the address of the needy widow in their hands.

"Once we get settled in our rooms, we're going to sit down, and you're going to tell me exactly what's bothering you," Josie said.

Suzette stood looking down the street in one direction and then the other. This was a different town in a different area full of different people, but it looked exactly the same as all the others. It could have been any one of a dozen towns she'd been in. As far as she was concerned, they consisted only of saloons, hotels and restaurants, and were filled almost entirely with men anxious to make a fortune and go back to the world they had left behind. Even for them, living here was only a temporary existence.

But places like this *were* her life. She was locked in with no escape. Even after her sister got married, she'd have to go on living in a town like this. She wouldn't be welcome anywhere else.

"There's nothing to talk about," Suzette said. "I admit I'm feeling a little down. It always takes a while for me to start feeling at ease in a new town."

Josie turned to the left. "Jerome Street is supposed to be two streets over." They started walking in that direction. "Don't think we're through talking." Josie looked down an alley to make sure no one was coming through. "Something's wrong, and I mean to find out what it is."

Suzette came to a dead stop. "If you must know, I miss Hawk. It was stupid to allow myself to care so much, but I couldn't help it. It just happened." She started walking again. "I can't fit into his world and he can't fit into mine, so that's the end of it. It'll take me a while to get all that straight, but I will. The sign on the side of that building says Jerome Street, so we're almost there." She stopped in her tracks and turned to face Josie. "Let's make a pact. No more talking or thinking about Zeke and Hawk."

"I'm not thinking about Zeke."

"You can save yourself the trouble of telling me lies. I know better." She grabbed Josie's hand. "We've got to do this."

"I don't see how just mentioning their names—"

"Promise me."

"What if they come into town?"

"They won't. Tombstone's much closer to their ranch."

"How do you know?"

"I asked. Don't tell me how desperate that sounds. I had to know. Now promise me. I don't think I can make it alone."

Suzette didn't like the hesitation she saw in Josie's eyes. She'd been depending on Josie's strength of will to sustain her until she got her emotional feet back under her. But if she was any judge, Josie was having trouble accepting that Zeke had walked out of her life just as abruptly as he'd walked into it.

Josie squeezed Suzette's hand. "I could use a bit of help myself. Think we can do this together?"

"What other choice do we have?"

"We got no business coming into town." Zeke had to walk fast to keep up with Hawk. "We ought to be at

239

the ranch getting ready to ride out first thing in the morning."

Hawk didn't turn around or slow down to answer. "We can still do that."

"Not if we spend half the night getting drunk."

"You know I don't drink."

"You don't need to. You're already drunk on Suzette. You stay around her much longer, and you're liable to pass out."

Hawk kept right on walking. "I told you I wanted to make sure they had a good place to stay and the job was working out."

"If that widow woman was any more respectable, she'd have to take up living in the church."

They hadn't had to ask where Suzette and Josie were staying. That was all everybody was talking about. Half the men in Benson must have seen the two women on their way to the Widow Jameson's house. The other half had seen them make their way to the theater. Both halves were planning to be at the theater tonight. Zeke thought it was good everybody was so excited about their appearance. The sooner they earned a lot of money, the sooner they could stop dancing. Hawk didn't take any comfort in their apparent good fortune. In fact, he seemed downright upset by it. Zeke knew Hawk was sweet on Suzette, but he hadn't realized it had gone this far.

"I'm not worried about their landlady." Hawk slowed down as they approached the theater. There was a line in front to purchase tickets.

When a few of the men started pushing and shoving, Zeke got a bad feeling in the pit of his stomach. Even though this was a theater instead of a saloon, beer and whiskey were on sale for anyone with the price of a drink.

"What are you doing here?" one of the men demanded of Zeke.

"We want to see the show."

"We don't want no blacks in our theater. No Injuns, either," he said, eyeing Hawk.

They'd encountered this kind of prejudice most of their lives. Even though it still made them angry, they'd learned the only way to handle it was to ignore it or pretend indifference.

"There's no law against it," Zeke said.

"There ought to be."

Hawk ignored the man, and Zeke didn't answer. They reached the front of the line.

"I want a seat in the front row," Hawk said to the man in the ticket window.

"They're all gone."

"How about the second?"

"I've got two left, but it'll cost you double."

Hawk reached in his vest pocket and pulled out a gold coin. "Give me both of them."

The man at the ticket window gave him his change and the tickets. "They've got numbers on them," he said. "You gotta take the seats with the right numbers."

The lobby was packed with men drinking or men trying to get to the bar to order something to drink. Already the heat of so many people in the confined space had caused the smell of liquor and unwashed bodies to reach an unpleasant level.

"Let's go to our seats," Hawk said.

They worked their way to the front of the theater. It was surprisingly large and decorated in white and silver. The stage curtain was deep blue with silver fringe. Some kind of blue material was looped over the balcony railing. Already the balcony seats were filled with men crowded too close together. Zeke and Hawk had to climb over eight people to get to their seats. The seats were covered in what looked like red velvet, but they were so hard, Zeke figured there was no padding underneath. They got angry looks from several men, but that changed as soon as a man sat down at the piano and started to play. As best Zeke could tell over the noise of men rushing to their seats, he was playing a collection of Stephen Foster melodies. Zeke wondered if any in the audience knew those songs had been made popular by black-face minstrel shows back East.

The first act was a juggler. He wasn't bad, but the audience was more interested in his pretty assistant, who posed first on one side of the stage and then the other. The juggler didn't seem to mind that he was largely ignored. He obviously knew what made his act popular.

The juggler was followed by a comedy skit. The jokes were poor, the set worse than nothing, and the actors clearly scraped from the bottom of the barrel. Still, they got a round of applause when they finished.

Several more variety acts followed: a singer, a dog act, a magician, a strong man, even a dramatic reading by a woman whose voice was well past its prime. All through these acts, the audience grew more and more restive. They knew the best act always came at the end of the first half. The audience grew silent when the owner came out in front of the curtain.

"We have a special treat this evening," he announced. "Straight from Globe, let's welcome Miss Josie and Miss Suzette."

The piano started playing a spirited tune Zeke didn't recognize, and the curtain opened on a set that looked like the inside of a saloon. For a moment nothing happened; then just as the audience started to squirm, two women appeared, one from each side of the stage. Zeke was sure he'd never seen either of them before.

Both women wore elaborate wigs decorated with ribbons and feathers. They wore bright red lipstick and rouge, but it was the costumes that caused the audience to catch its collective breath. Both dresses were bright red and tantalizingly brief. The women wore long red gloves, but their arms and shoulders were bare. A tiny skirt kept the costume from being indecent while covering only a small portion of long, shapely legs encased in black net stockings. The heels of their shoes were so high, Zeke expected the women to tumble forward any moment.

When the women came to the front of the stage and began their number, the audience made so much noise, Zeke couldn't hear a note of their song. But that didn't matter. He sat there in a state of shock, marveling how the two women he'd traveled with for over a week could have transformed themselves into performers he barely recognized. He'd become so engrossed in studying what they'd done to themselves, he was slow to realize some of the men were standing up and calling out invitations of every description. He didn't like their reaction, but he could understand it. Suzette and Josie were beautiful women, but the two women on stage were exotic beyond a man's wildest imagination. Now he understood why they were so popular.

Chapter Fifteen

Suzette nearly forgot her words and steps when she saw Hawk. So many questions flooded her mind, she couldn't focus on any one of them. The only thought that was clear, the only one that mattered, was that Hawk hadn't left, that he was here. She glanced over at Josie to see if she'd noticed that Zeke was sitting next to Hawk, but Josie was performing to the audience in the balcony. She said performing to the men in the front row would encourage them to get too friendly.

They were performing as close to the footlights as possible. Josie said it was good to get close to the audience while still keeping a barrier up. Josie knew all kinds of tricks when it came to putting over an act, but Suzette forgot all of them now. She kept her eyes on Hawk. When she realized he was looking directly up at her, she nearly forgot to execute a flurry of quick steps intended to carry her and Josie to opposite sides of the stage. They circled to the back, then came together as they danced toward the front and center.

"Did you see Hawk?" Josie asked surreptitiously while continuing to smile broadly at the audience.

"Zeke's here, too," Suzette whispered back.

They reached the front of the stage and separated. Suzette didn't know why Hawk was in the audience, but she told herself he was just making sure she and Josie had a job before they left for their ranch. That seemed reasonable. After all, the men had escorted them to Benson just to make sure they were safe.

She saw a man in the front row stand up. She tried not to grin when Hawk jerked him back into his seat. The two men exchanged some hot words, but men were always doing that. Some men were far too intense, especially when they'd been drinking. The man jumped up out of his seat again and reached for Josie, but she had no trouble evading him. Suzette expected him to reach for her, was ready for it, but wasn't prepared for him to practically throw himself on the stage. He got his fingers around her ankle, but she was able to break loose without missing a step.

The next pattern in their performance required them to turn their backs to the audience and walk upstage, making sure to wiggle their bottoms. This usually evoked a loud reaction, so she wasn't surprised when a roar went up from the audience. She was stunned when she turned around to see every man in the front half of the theater on his feet and engaged in a melee that promised to send dozens of men home with black eyes, contusions, torn clothing, and possibly a few broken arms.

"What happened?" Suzette asked. The dance routine had her turning her back to the audience a couple of steps after Josie.

"Hawk picked up the man who grabbed your ankle and tossed him halfway to the back of the theater," Josie said.

All her happiness and relief at Hawk's presence changed into fear. If Hawk was responsible for starting the fight, the other men in the audience would take their anger out on him and Zeke. With a couple hundred men occupying seats in the lower level of the theater, they would be beaten unmercifully.

"We've got to help them get away," Suzette said.

"How?" Josie asked, not missing a step.

"The exit the owner showed us in case of fire."

"There are at least a dozen men between them and us."

"They'll move for us." Suzette abandoned the routine, stepped between two footlights, and dropped from the stage to the theater floor. Josie was right behind her.

Suzette started pushing her way between knots of fighters. She got jostled, elbowed in the ribs, even almost knocked to the floor, but the man who did it apologized even as he smashed his fist into the face of another man. Back up on stage, the pianist kept right on playing. Suzette pushed her way through until she came up behind Hawk. When she tried to grab his arm, he whirled, fist drawn back, ready to strike. The shock of recognition paralyzed him momentarily, long enough for a man to hit him upside the head. Hawk turned and hit the man so hard he slumped to the floor.

"Get back on the stage before you get hurt," Hawk

said, pushing away a man who stumbled in between them.

"You've got to get out of here," Suzette said. "They'll kill you if you don't."

Hawk ducked two men who were coming at him from opposite directions. They collided with looks of stunned surprise. "I can't leave Zeke."

"Josie's getting him. Come on. I know a way out the back."

By now the fight had become so general, no one seemed to care who had started it. Even the men in the balcony were fighting. Hawk was reluctant to follow Suzette, but she had a firm grip on his sleeve. He had to fight his way to the edge of the melee, but she escaped with only a few more bumps. She'd have sore ribs tomorrow.

"I'm not leaving without Zeke," Hawk said when Suzette tried to pull him through the door leading to the back of the stage and the rear exit.

It took only a few seconds for Suzette to find Zeke and Josie in the brawl. Without a word, Hawk fought his way through the tangle of bodies and pulled Zeke and Josie free.

"Go!" Josie pushed both Zeke and Hawk toward the door.

"We can't leave you," Zeke said.

"Nobody's going to hurt us."

Josie and Suzette pushed both men through the door and along the passage toward the rear of the building. On stage, the pianist continued to play a sprightly dance tune, providing an incongruous backdrop to the fight. The men balked at the rear door.

"I've never run from a fight in my life," Zeke said.

"With the odds at least a hundred to one, this is a good time to start," Josie said, her tone stinging. "What possessed you to throw that man into the middle of the audience?" she asked Hawk.

"He grabbed Suzette."

"Men do that all the time. We can take care of ourselves."

Suzette could tell that Josie was worked up, but she didn't know exactly why. She couldn't be upset that a fight had broken out at their first performance. Now people would be willing to pay even more to see what all the fuss was about. Maybe she was upset that their performance had been stopped. Josie complained all the time about having to dance for a living, but she took great pride in her work. If their routine wasn't better than everybody else's, she wouldn't rest until it was. She might be afraid there'd be so much damage to the theater, the owner would be afraid to hire them, but Suzette discounted that, too. She was certain Josie's present mood stemmed from a quite different reason.

She was upset because Zeke had been in danger.

"Get your mares and head out for your ranch," Josie said. "When those men sober up, they'll remember who started the fight and come looking for you."

Hawk looked reluctant, but Zeke turned him around and pushed him through the rear door. "Come on. I told you it was a mistake to come back."

Hawk spun away from Zeke and turned. "Are you sure you'll be okay?" He glanced at both women, but his gaze settled on Suzette.

"We will if you two disappear before anybody knows we helped you escape," Josie snapped.

"We're fine." Suzette hoped Hawk believed her. After being so happy that he'd come back, she was now weighed down with guilt for having put him in danger. "Josie and I are going inside and closing this door. There's no reason for you to stay here one more minute. Get your horses and leave tonight."

Stepping back through the door and closing it on Hawk and Zeke was just about the hardest thing she'd ever done. It was like closing the door on the best part of her life—again. It was getting harder each time.

"Do you think they'll leave for their ranch tonight?" Josie didn't look any happier than Suzette felt.

"Did you ever know a man to take advice from a woman?"

"You got any cuts that need tending to?"

They hadn't spoken during the ride back to the ranch where they'd left the mares, but Zeke wasn't about to let Hawk go to sleep before they had a good talk. He had to know what had prompted Hawk's action.

"I don't guess so. Nothing's bleeding."

They had unsaddled the horses and turned them into the corral with the mares. The darkness under the trees as they walked along a creek prevented Zeke from seeing Hawk's expression, but he didn't need to see it. After twenty years, he knew exactly how he looked: as if nothing had happened.

Zeke had seen the cuts and bruises, but he wasn't going to force Hawk to let him clean them or put salve on them. If he wanted weeping wounds that would attract flies, that was his problem. Zeke had washed his head in the creek. "What about heading for the ranch tonight?"

They had dumped all their gear under some cotton-woods that bordered the tiny creek that emptied into the San Pedro River a few hundred yards away. Most years it would have been dry until the monsoon rains of summer, but the wet winter had provided additional runoff. Zeke didn't particularly like the idea of travel-ing at night, but he didn't like the possibility of being confronted by an angry vigilante committee the next day either.

"We've got plenty of time to make it tomorrow." Having reached the spot where they'd dropped their gear, Hawk knelt down to untie his bedroll and spread it out on the soft ground next to the creek. "I'm tired."

Zeke stopped, undecided whether to lay out his bedroll or try to convince Hawk to leave tonight. "You lie down now and you'll be stiff in the morning."

Hawk sat down on his bedroll and started to pull off his boots. "I'm always stiff when I sleep on damp ground. Maybe you haven't noticed, but we're not in our twenties anymore."

"Then you ought to know enough not to start fights."

Hawk hunched his shoulders.

Deciding it was useless to try to convince Hawk to leave tonight, Zeke reached for his bedroll. "You can't start a fight every time someone tries to grab her. If you do, you might as well reserve a jail cell. Better yet, buy a plot for yourself in Boot Hill and save us all a lot of trouble."

Hawk reached for his saddlebags to use as a pillow. "Go to sleep."

Zeke sat down to remove his own boots. "Not until you tell me why we were at that theater tonight."

"I told you."

"I want the real reason. And don't think you can go silent on me. I'm going to keep after you until I get the truth. All of it."

Zeke wiggled his toes. It felt good to have them out of his boots. It would be nice to reach the ranch and take a bath in the Babocomari River, which ran alongside their property. It had been a long time since he'd had a real bath in a real bathtub, but that would have to wait until they went into Tombstone or Bisbee for supplies. Hawk had fixed it so they couldn't go back to Benson. "You ready to talk?"

Hawk lay down on his bedroll but didn't cover himself. They had climbed in altitude as they traveled up the river, but the spring day had been so warm, the night hadn't cooled the air yet. Hawk turned on his side to face Zeke. "No, but you're going to plague me until I do."

"You're damned right." Zeke went on when Hawk fell silent again. "Look, I know you're hung up on Suzette. What I want to know is what that means."

"I don't know."

"Great. That helps a lot."

"I can't tell you what I don't know."

"You could if you stopped lying to yourself."

"What about you?"

"I was the one who wanted to push on to the ranch, remember. I was the one who *didn't* throw a drunk fool into the middle of the audience."

"He shouldn't have tried to touch Suzette."

It was worse than Zeke had thought. He wouldn't be surprised if Hawk went back to Benson to make sure Suzette was all right. "Okay, I'll make it easy for you. Just answer one question. Are you going to be able to leave Suzette, or do I have to look for another partner for the ranch?"

"Would you do that?"

How could Hawk ask a question like that? The two of them had been partners for more than twenty years. "What choice would I have?"

"You didn't answer my question."

"You didn't answer mine."

This was stupid. They were acting like kids. They'd been together too long for it to end like this. "I don't think I could work with anyone else," Zeke said. "If I couldn't run the place by myself, I'd have to do something else, but I don't know what that would be."

"You could go back home."

There were times when Zeke thought he'd give anything to do just that, but going home would be admitting defeat. Jake and Isabelle would swear he was finally coming to his senses, but you go home when you have a choice. Otherwise, you're just retreating from life. "I can't go home any more than you can, so don't ask that again."

Hawk sighed deeply, something he never did. "I'm going to the ranch. I still want us to be partners, but I might not leave here tomorrow morning. I've got to make sure Suzette is really okay."

"You sure you're not hoping for more than that?"

"She has a sister she has to educate and support until the girl marries. There's no place in her plan for me."

"What happens after she's done that?"

"It doesn't matter. Her sister's going to have a place in society. She can't have a half-breed for a brother-in-law."

If Hawk had been thinking about marriage, things were a lot more serious than Zeke had suspected. Hawk had to be hurting bad. Zeke wished there was something he could do, something he could say, but Hawk hated sympathy. If he thought Zeke was feeling sorry for him, he'd get angry.

"Why don't I take the horses and head for the ranch?" Zeke suggested. "You can follow when you're ready."

"We're going together."

The words sounded like they came from between clenched teeth. Not a good sign. "I think I ought to go on ahead," Zeke insisted. "Dusky Lady has been showing signs of getting ready to foal."

"She'll hold off for a few more days."

"Maybe, but I'll feel a lot safer with her at the ranch."

Hawk sighed again. "I'll go into town in the morning and get back in time to leave by noon. That will put us at the ranch the next day."

It wasn't really the delay in reaching the ranch that bothered Zeke, or even Dusky Lady's impending foaling. He was worried about Hawk. He'd never seen him act this way about a woman. It was obvious he'd fallen in love with Suzette, and having to leave her was tearing him up.

Why wasn't leaving Josie tearing *him* apart? Zeke wondered. Because there had never been a question of love between them. Josie had been friendly the last couple of days, but only because he'd protected her from Gardner. She'd never given him room for even the slightest hope there could be anything more between them. Maybe his heart could have been engaged

253

by Josie if she'd spent the last week making love to him, but she hadn't. Leaving wasn't tearing him up, because there was nothing to leave.

That was what was nearly tearing him up.

Much to Josie's surprise, the brawl had stopped almost as quickly as it began. The audience had poured out into the lobby to get drinks, and the owner had managed to get the theater cleaned up enough for the second half of the evening's entertainment to begin only an hour late. Instead of being upset, the owner seemed delighted. The men in the audience had drunk up every ounce of beer and whiskey even though he doubled the prices. Afterwards, the audience was in such a good mood, they loved everything. Even a midget act. Suzette and Josie had to do their number three times before the audience finally agreed to leave the theater.

"The place will be packed again tomorrow," the owner said, almost dancing with excitement. "I'm doubling the prices."

"I hope that means you're doubling our share." The men weren't coming back to see the dogs or the midgets.

"Of course," the owner agreed immediately.

"We want a share of tonight's bar taking," Josie said. The owner didn't look too happy about that.

"The men spent the hour waiting so they could see us," Josie said before he could protest. "I know you doubled the prices. We want half."

The owner got a stubborn look on his face. Josie hadn't dealt with sleazy men for years without knowing what he was going to do next.

"Before you start making threats, let me tell *you* a few things," Josie said. "If you don't pay us, we won't come back tomorrow. Before we leave, we'll make sure everybody knows you refused to pay us. That ought to make you about as popular as a cholera epidemic."

The owner turned to Suzette, but she said, "Josie speaks for me."

"We'll take our earnings now," Josie said before he could decide they needed to help pay for the damage to his theater.

There was a good bit of haggling about how much money had been made selling spirits, but that was settled when Suzette went to the bar manager, dazzled him with her smile, and got him to tell her exactly how much money he'd taken in. The owner threatened to fire the bar manager, said Josie and Suzette were no better than robbers, and threatened to tell the sheriff they'd organized the fight just to squeeze extra money out of him, but in the end he paid up. They left his office with a very satisfying weight of gold in their purses.

"If things keep up like this, we can retire early," Josie said to Suzette as they crossed the theater lobby and headed for the front doors. "You'll be able to go back to Quebec in style."

"I don't want to go back to Quebec. I hate the city and the people in it."

The passion and anger in Suzette's voice surprised Josie.

"But you said—" Josie broke off when she stepped through the theater door to see Gardner waiting for them. "What are you doing here?" Even though she knew what kind of man he was, she had to admit his smile was disarming. No wonder the Redfield girl was willing to do anything for him.

"The sheriff couldn't believe that a man of my reputation would attempt to kidnap a woman. He found it completely believable that I was protecting you from that black man. After all, that's what a man of my wealth and reputation would naturally do."

"Even when the woman you were trying to protect was black?" she demanded. "What about your men?"

His grin grew still broader. "They weren't my men. But even if they were, they didn't have any stolen horses, so they couldn't possibly be horse thieves."

"In other words," Josie said, "the sheriff wasn't about to believe accusations made against white men by a black man and a half-breed."

"What about our word?" Suzette asked.

"Don't be ridiculous," Josie snapped, barely able to keep her temper in check. "Any man's word will be taken over a woman's."

"Women don't understand the West and what it takes to survive out here." Gardner's smile was so self-satisfied, Josie longed to slap it off his face. "Things aren't like they were back East."

Josie didn't bother to tell him she'd never lived *back East*, that she'd spent her whole life in the West and knew as well as any man what it took to survive. "We're tired and need to get some rest. Good night." They'd turned before Gardner spoke again.

"You helped them get away."

Suzette turned back. "Who are you talking about?"

"Hawk and Zeke. They started the fight."

"The man who grabbed me started the trouble."

Gardner's chuckle was so jovial it was unnerving. "He was a harmless drunk. Your Injun friend started the fight."

"It was the least we could do after all they did for us," Suzette said.

"You mean like accusing me of trying to kidnap Josie? Or did you have something else in mind?"

Josie could guess what Gardner was thinking. Men like him always assumed the worst about women, hoping it was true.

"She means fixing our wagon wheel when it was broken and taking care of our sick friend until we could get her to her parents' farm," Josie said.

"And finding our mules when I didn't tether them properly," Suzette added.

"You make them sound like regular good Samaritans."

"We'd have had a very difficult time making the journey without their help."

"The sheriff doesn't have the same high opinion of them."

Josie thought Gardner had waited for them just to gloat, but she should have realized he didn't really care about their opinion. His real animosity was directed toward Zeke and Hawk. Josie's stomach tightened. She wondered what Gardner was up to.

"What do you mean?" Suzette asked.

"The sheriff doesn't believe a black man and an Injun could have come by mares of that quality honestly. Where would men like that get that much money?"

Josie had no idea how Zeke and Hawk made their money, but she was confident they'd paid for the mares with money they had earned. "We just met them a few days ago, but I'm certain they're honest men."

"I hope you're right," Gardner said, his smile growing bigger still, "but don't be surprised if the sheriff holds the mares until they can produce a bill of sale."

Josie saw Suzette tense, start to say something. She reached out, took her hand, and squeezed. Suzette looked puzzled but remained silent.

"You might want to reconsider my offer to have you perform at the Birdcage," Gardner said when neither woman responded to his taunt.

"We're being paid very well here," Josie said. "You'd have to come up with a really good offer to get us to leave. I hear Tombstone is dying fast."

Gardner's smile shrank a little. "You can't believe everything you hear."

"Like the fact that you own part of the Birdcage?"

His smile withered a little more. "I own seventy-five percent. The place is a virtual gold mine."

"Well, you think about how much you can pay us," Josie said, "and we'll think about how much it'll take to lure us away."

"Your Injun won't be able to start a fight for you every night."

"Our success doesn't depend on cheap thrills," Josie fired back.

"In a few days, the novelty will wear off."

"Talk to us then. Good night."

"My offer might not be as good later," Gardner called after them.

"We'll take that chance," Josie replied and walked faster.

"Why are you in such a hurry?" Suzette asked when they were out of hearing range.

"We have to warn Zeke and Hawk that the sheriff means to steal their mares."

"Wouldn't it be easier if just one of us rode out to warn them?"Josie asked.

That had been the original plan, but the more Josie talked about what she believed the sheriff *really* intended to do, the more certain Suzette became that it wouldn't be safe for either of them to remain in Benson.

"Gardner will know we warned them," Suzette said.

She opened the livery door slowly and looked out. The street was empty, but she stood quietly for a moment to make sure no one was moving about nearby. After discussing every possibility for more than an hour, they'd finally decided to load everything back into the wagon and sneak out of town after everyone had gone to sleep. They'd been concerned about the watchman at the livery stable, but there had been no one there when they'd arrived. It hadn't taken long to harness the mules. Now they had to try to get away without being seen.

There were sounds of music and laughter from the main street, but all the buildings and houses near the livery stable were dark. Suzette led the mules from the stable, then went back to close the door so no one would have a reason to look inside until morning. Still leading the mules, her hand over the muzzle of one to keep him from making any noise, she led them toward a belt of trees that bordered the town on the north side. Once there, Josie stopped the wagon, and Suzette climbed up beside her. "Do you know a good place to cross the river?"

"I thought I could remember where we crossed yesterday, but everything looks different in the dark."

Suzette wasn't particularly worried. The water was no more than a couple of feet deep in any place. "I guess one spot is as good as another."

But she wasn't thinking about crossing the river. She was thinking about Hawk. She hadn't been able to stop thinking about him since she'd seen him in the audience earlier that night. He hadn't left town. He had come to see her. He'd started a fight to protect her. No man would do that for a woman he didn't care about. She knew all the reasons why she couldn't have what she wanted, but she couldn't make herself give up the opportunity to see him again. She wasn't certain whether she and Josie would really be in danger once Gardner found out what they had done. It was simply an excuse to see Hawk again, and she'd reached for it.

She promised herself she wouldn't let her emotions get out of control. She had to warn him and thank him for what he'd done. Maybe they'd spend a couple more days together before she and Josie decided whether to move on to Tombstone or Bisbee, but right now all she could think about was seeing Hawk again. She remembered every detail about him. She wrapped herself in the memory of the happiest times of her life, the nights she'd spent in his arms. She could practically feel the texture of his skin under her fingertips, sense the warmth of his body, taste the sweetness of his kisses. She could hear the sound of the river as it murmured nearby, remember the smell of moist earth. She was so wrapped up in her memories, she wasn't aware they'd entered the river until the wagon stopped moving.

"We're stuck," Josie said.

Suzette jerked her mind back to the present just in time to see two drunk cowboys on horseback gaping at them from the opposite bank.

Chapter Sixteen

"You're the ladies who danced in the theater tonight," one cowboy said.

"What are you doing here?" the other asked, suspicion evident in his expression despite the numbing effect of too much whiskey.

Neither cowboy seemed sober enough to understand an answer, but Josie didn't want them telling everybody the dancing ladies were running away. "It's so noisy in town we were unable to sleep. We're going to stay at a ranch a little way from here." It was still possible to hear the sounds of revelry coming from town. "I grew up on a farm," Josie explained when the cowboy seemed to have trouble processing what she'd said. "I can't sleep unless it's completely quiet."

"I hate quiet," the first cowboy said. "It feels lonely."

"What are you doing out so late?" Josie asked.

"Heading back to the ranch where we work."

"Where's that?"

"A little way up Tres Alamos Wash."

Josie felt some of the tension in her shoulders relax. If the cowboys were leaving town, they wouldn't be able to tell anybody they'd seen her and Suzette. "Our wagon is stuck. Could you give us a hand?"

Despite being drunk, they understood they were expected to help ladies in distress. They slid off their horses and walked straight into the river without checking how deep it was. One stumbled and went down to his knees, but he got back up and kept walking as if nothing had happened. Josie was sure his boots were full of water. Each man put his shoulder to a rear wheel.

"When I give a yell, lay into those mules," one called to Josie on the bench.

The words were hardly out of his mouth before he let loose a yell Josie was sure would have half the people in Benson racing down to the river to see who was being murdered. She cracked the whip over the mules' heads, and they leaned into their collars. For a moment the wagon didn't move. Then it lurched free of the mud so abruptly, Suzette nearly lost her balance. Josie didn't let the mules stop until she was safely on the opposite bank. The two cowboys sloshed out of the water grinning like little boys.

"I can't thank you enough," Josie said. "Can I offer to pay you?"

She didn't expect the boys to accept, but she hadn't meant to offend them, either. "We don't accept nothing for helping ladies," one said.

Josie suspected they were so drunk they wouldn't remember any of this in the morning. She hoped they wouldn't. "Well, we have to be on our way if we're going to get any sleep tonight. Thanks again."

"You ladies going to be at the theater when we come back to town?"

"The owner wants us there every night," Josie said. That was true enough.

The cowboys let loose with another yell, mounted up, and rode off acting like two kids trying to pull each other out of the saddle.

"Get us to the ranch before anybody else sees us." Suzette's voice sounded thin from worry. "We can't expect that everybody we meet will be drunk and harmless."

It was only a short drive to the trail leading to the ranch where they'd left the mares. Being very careful to make as little noise as possible, Josie pulled the wagon around the side of the corral farthest from the house. The corral was empty. Maybe the sheriff had stolen the mares already.

"What happened to the horses?" Suzette asked.

"Zeke and Hawk could have moved them. There's not enough grass in that corral. Maybe they've left already. Zeke wanted to get to the ranch before Dusky Lady foaled."

That seemed like the most logical explanation. If somebody had tried to steal the mares, Zeke and Hawk would have put up a fight that would have been heard all the way into town.

It was too quiet. Josie had lived on a farm long enough to know the night was never completely silent unless someone or something dangerous was present. Normally, crickets chirped, frogs croaked, and nocturnal animals moved around searching for food. Tonight even the creek seemed to have fallen silent. Moonlight made it easy to see the farmhouse, but it was impossible to penetrate the inky shadows under the trees that bordered the small stream. Their out-flung branches reached for the sky like the arms of so many skeletons. A feeling of dread seeped into her body through the bottoms of her feet, but she had to know what had happened to Zeke. "Stay here," she said to Suzette. "I'm going to check under those trees."

"It's too dark to see. Besides, if they're gone, you won't find anything."

"I have to know." Josie didn't like the idea of wandering around a strange ranch in the dead of night. Even less did she like approaching dark woods at any time. The clatter of her shoes on the rocky ground sounded unnaturally loud in the silence. She approached the edge of the trees and peered into the darkness, but couldn't see anything.

"Zeke."

She didn't dare call loudly. Rather than enter the darkness, she walked along the edge of the trees, calling softly as she went. The farther she went without getting a response, the more nervous she got. If the men were here, why didn't they answer? Suzette said Hawk would wake up if she breathed too loudly. Zeke didn't sleep soundly either. Why hadn't one of them heard her? Deciding she'd gone far enough from the comparative safety of the wagon, she stopped and tried to peer into the darkness, only to have the silence mock her fear. Feeling more uneasy than ever, she turned to find Zeke standing only inches away. She was barely able to stifle a scream.

"What are you doing here?" he demanded.

Josie's heart thumped so hard it was painful. It took her several moments to recover her breath. The shock of Zeke materializing out of nowhere when her nerves were already wound tight caused a sudden weakness in her limbs. She swayed and reached out to him for support.

"Are you okay? Are you sick?"

She forced herself to concentrate, to *will* her limbs to regain their strength. "I'm fine. You just surprised me." And stunned her as well. It was stupid to believe she could walk away and forget Zeke any more than Suzette could forget Hawk. She wasn't in love with him, but she could be if she let herself. "Where are the mares?"

"We heard you approaching from the road. It sounded like your wagon, but we figured someone might be using it to lure us out into the open, so we hid the horses. Why are you here?"

No matter what happened, Zeke and Hawk always seemed to be a step ahead, but they couldn't know what the sheriff planned to do. "Gardner said the sheriff means to impound your mares until you can produce proof you own them. He said he didn't think you and Hawk could have earned the money to buy such quality animals."

"We have the bills of sale."

"From the way Gardner enjoyed telling us about it, I don't think that's going to be enough."

"You mean he's going to say they're forged and take the mares anyway?"

"I don't know what he's going to do, but I think you ought to leave tonight."

She'd been so caught up in her worries, the sound of

wheels on rocky ground hadn't registered until now. She turned to see Hawk and Suzette approaching with the wagon. Suzette held the reins, but her gaze kept returning to Hawk. One glance, and Josie knew Suzette had reached the point of no return. Heartbreak was inevitable.

Why hadn't Zeke and Hawk kept going after they fixed the wheel? Why hadn't Hawk refused to let Suzette spend the nights with him? Why did Zeke have to be so nice even when Josie did her best to drive him off? She and Suzette had their lives carefully planned. They knew what they wanted to do, how to do it, and how to keep from getting hurt in the process.

But Zeke and Hawk had ruined all that.

"Suzette's not going back."

Suzette and Josie had already decided that, but Hawk said it as if something had changed.

"Neither am I," Josie told him. "We're going to Tombstone."

Zeke's expression hardened. "After this, you're going to work for Gardner?"

"There have to be other places where we can work."

"Tombstone is too small to have more than one theater that can pay you the kind of money you got in Benson."

Josie hadn't expected that, but she was certain they could find a well-paying job. Their act was too popular to believe otherwise. "We'll find something even if we have to go to Bisbee."

"Gardner's going to know you helped us," Hawk said to Suzette. "He might pursue you there."

"Stop worrying about us!" Josie's patience was running out. She wanted the men to get started toward their ranch so she and Suzette could head toward Tombstone. Or Bisbee. Anyplace but with Zeke and Hawk.

"We know this man who had a gambling hall in San Francisco," Hawk said. "I think we could get him to give you a job."

Josie didn't let herself think about San Francisco. After New York, that was the ultimate dream of every entertainer. "Who is he? How do you know him?"

"He's Zac Randolph. Jake served with his brother during the war. Zac used to own a place called the Little Corner of Heaven. His old partner runs it now."

Josie had heard of the Little Corner of Heaven. She had no doubt Hawk had been there, but she considered it unlikely he knew Zac Randolph well enough to get jobs for two women he'd never seen. "Fine. Send him a telegram, but you've got to leave tonight. I don't trust Gardner not to do something underhanded."

"I'm just waiting for you to get in the wagon," Zeke said. "Hawk and I are ready to go."

Though she'd never done it before, Josie let Zeke help her climb up on the wagon seat next to Suzette. Something about his touch, his mere presence, made her fears seem less pressing. As absurd as it sounded, she felt as if nothing really terrible could happen to her when Zeke was around. But that was stupid. The worst thing possible had already happened.

Zeke and Hawk led the mules into the woods, through the creek, and into the open area on the other side where the mares grazed hungrily on grass that grew with surprising abundance among the cactus and mesquite. The horses the men rode stood, saddled and ready, under a sycamore. The two men walked toward their horses, but instead of mounting immediately, they stood talking for so long Josie started to get worried. "What are they talking about?" she asked Suzette.

"Hawk told me they had been talking about not following the river. Now that they know what the sheriff intends to do, I expect they're deciding what route to take."

Josie looked to the south. About ten miles away the Whetstone Mountains reared up against the night sky. She was sure that going around them was certain to add at least two days to the trip, but she wouldn't have to worry about that. Once the men got under way, she and Suzette would head for Tombstone.

Why hadn't they left already?

She didn't know how it had happened, but she felt a deep personal connection with Zeke. She wasn't in love with him, but the connection was strong nonetheless. She liked and admired him. She enjoyed being with him. She had a feeling she'd only scratched the surface when it came to getting to know the *real* man, the one he kept hidden from everyone but Hawk and the members of his adopted family. Knowing she was left out of that charmed circle made her feel jealous and a little sad.

"What can they be talking about?" Suzette had clasped her hands in her lap so tightly her knuckles cracked.

"Us." Anyone who'd been around the two men for as much as a day knew they thought virtually with a single mind. They were so used to working together, they could probably defend themselves in their sleep. It was the presence of two women that had put a knot in their thinking.

"What will they make us do?"

Josie had never seen Suzette look so despondent. The moonlight gave her drawn face a bleached-out quality. She was so white she looked like a ghost.

"They won't make us do anything we don't want to do," Josie said.

"That's not what I meant to ask. Do you think they'll let us go with them?"

The desperation in Suzette's voice cut through Josie's tangled thoughts like a hot knife. Suzette was in love with Hawk and wanted to be with him.

"What do you mean by *go with them?* Are you saying you love Hawk and want to live with him?"

Suzette stared at Hawk in the distance. "Yes."

"What about your sister? What about our act?"

Suzette's gaze didn't waver from Hawk. "I don't know."

"Does he know?"

"No."

"Is he in love with you?"

"I don't know."

Josie had been aware of pressure building inside her, but now it increased until she felt as if she'd swallowed a ball of fire that was threatening to consume her. Ever since those housewives in Globe started their crusade against loose women, her life had come apart faster than a rockslide down a mountainside. They'd lost good jobs in a prosperous town and had been forced to travel through the desert in the company of two of the most self-sufficient men in the world.

They'd gotten involved with a rich horse thief, and had to leave another good job. Now their unwanted attraction to these two men was threatening to destroy their act and the rest of their lives.

"Maybe we ought to turn around and go back to Benson. If we're lucky, nobody will know we left. Gardner can't prove we warned Zeke and Hawk."

"I'm not going back."

"We can head for Tombstone."

Suzette turned to face Josie. There was no hesitation in her eyes. "I'm not going to Tombstone or Bisbee."

"Ever?"

Suzette's gaze swung back to Hawk. "I don't know."

Josie wanted to shout at Suzette for threatening their futures, but she didn't, because she knew her friend was suffering. It must be agonizing to love someone without knowing if he loved you in return.

"Have you ever known you had to do something even though it could ruin your whole life?" Suzette asked.

"Only when I ran away."

Josie would never forget the fear that had encased her from head to foot, making it hard for her to move one foot in front of the other, but each step forward had made the next one easier. The whole time she'd believed she was protecting herself, that she could take care of herself. But falling in love meant losing control, something Josie could never do. Just the thought of it threw her into a panic.

"Running away would be easier," Suzette said.

"You're not talking about running away from somebody else. You're talking about running away from yourself. That's impossible."

"No, it's not. You've been doing it for years."

An unnamed fear emerged from its hiding place and began circling just out of reach in the back of Josie's mind. The feeling of foreboding was so strong, she could barely resist the impulse to look over her shoulder. "What do you mean?"

"You're so afraid that some man will hurt you, you've closed down inside. You think you don't have any feelings for Zeke, but that's because you won't let yourself look."

"That's not true," Josie said, feeling unfairly maligned. "I like Zeke. I even told him so. I know he'd never hurt me."

"If you gave yourself half a chance, you'd fall in love with him." Suzette searched Josie's face. "You might be already."

The circling fear leapt out of the darkness with a suddenness that caused Josie to start visibly. The dream she'd kept at bay for years burst its bonds and exploded in her mind—the nightmare that she was in the power of a man who was about to rape her. Icy chills caused her to shake uncontrollably. Fear, an emotion she'd steadfastly denied, ran rampant. To be in love was to lose control. Loss of control meant danger. Danger meant she must run before she was lost.

It took a tremendous amount of willpower, but Josie refused to let herself panic. "I don't want to love any man," she said as calmly as she could. "I don't want to be in any man's control, and I'm not in love with Zeke. I respect and admire him, I appreciate what he did for us, but that's all." The sound of her own words made her feel stronger, more resolute, able to withstand Suzette's scrutiny without flinching.

Suzette studied her for a long time in silence. One of the mules stamped his foot and blew through his mouth, probably from impatience at being kept standing so long.

"You may be right," Suzette said finally. "But if so, it's because you won't let yourself feel."

"Why should I want to feel? Being in love with Hawk is making you miserable. You don't know whether he loves you. And if he does, you don't know whether he wants to marry you. That man has suffered from prejudice all his life. You know he's not going to marry anyone who can't be proud of him. And how would your sister feel if you married a half-breed? You know no man in Quebec society wants a half-breed for a brother-in-law."

Suzette seemed to shrink into herself a little more with each word out of Josie's mouth. Josie hated to do this to her friend, but Suzette had to know what she was facing.

"I don't have the answer to any of your questions," Suzette said. "I can only take things one step at a time."

Suzette's dilemma wrung Josie's heart, but she wasn't about to let her get away with fooling herself. "It's not that simple. You'll have to choose between Hawk and what you want for your sister. You can't have both."

A single tear welled up in Suzette's eye, spilled over her eyelid, and rolled slowly down her cheek leaving a narrow trail of moisture glistening in the moonlight. The second, which followed quickly after the first, just made Josie feel worse. She leaned forward and put her arms around Suzette. "I'm sorry. I shouldn't have said that."

"It's true."

That just made it all the harder to hear. They sat with their arms around each other until the sound of footsteps on dry leaves warned them that Zeke and Hawk had finished talking.

"You cold?" Hawk asked.

"A little," Suzette said, not showing her face.

"What have you decided to do?" Josie asked to deflect Hawk's attention until Suzette had a chance to get her emotions under control.

"We're going to head for the mountains. There are plenty of places to hold the mares until the sheriff and Gardner get tired of looking for us. Then we can head for the ranch."

Josie held her breath. Her nails dug into the palms of her hands as she waited for Hawk to say what he wanted them to do.

"We can't take the wagon through the mountains." Suzette was asking whether Hawk would take her with him. Josie could tell from the deadness of Suzette's voice that she believed Hawk was going to send them away.

"We'll leave the wagon here," Zeke said to Suzette. "We can leave the rancher a note, telling him we'll come back for it. You and Josie can ride our horses. Hawk and I will ride the mules."

"But you don't have any saddles." Josie didn't know why she was pointing out the obvious unless she was so overcome with relief for Suzette that her brain wasn't working.

"Comanches never use saddles," Hawk said.

"And slaves weren't allowed to ride anything but mules," Zeke added.

"All of our costumes are in this wagon," Suzette said. "Everything we own."

It was clear to Josie that Suzette wasn't stating this as an objection. Leaving her costumes behind meant something very specific and important. She wanted Hawk to tell her what it meant to him, but Josie wasn't sure she wanted Hawk to do that yet. Whatever happened, she wanted both of them to have more time to think about it. She liked Hawk, but she loved Suzette. She didn't want to see her ruin her life.

"We can come back for the wagon once they give up trying to take the mares." Josie turned from Suzette to Zeke. "How long do you think that'll take?"

"I can't say. We're going to try to make the sheriff think we disappeared. We don't want to get in a fight with a lawman. Since people pay him to uphold the law, it would be hard to convince them he's in the wrong."

Josie knew he meant that nobody would believe a black man and a half-breed they didn't know instead of the sheriff they did know. Once more she felt guilty for having caused them trouble.

"We're ready," she said. "Tell us what to do."

It took only a few minutes to put the wagon under a shed behind the ranch house. Zeke woke up the owner to tell them what they were doing, while Hawk un-hitched the mules and led them back to the clearing where Suzette and Josie waited. There was some awkwardness about the women mounting up. Their long skirts made it virtually impossible to mount without displaying an indecent amount of leg. Suzette didn't seem to care, but Josie made Zeke turn his back while she climbed into the saddle and adjusted her skirts.

Just one more reason why no sane woman would have anything to do with a ranch.

"Where are we going?" Josie asked once they were under way. As usual, Hawk and Suzette were in the front while Josie and Zeke brought up the rear.

"Up into those trees," Zeke said, pointing at the tree-covered slopes to the south.

The mountain appeared to rise straight up out of the surrounding desert. This route would make it harder for the sheriff to find them, but she had never ridden a horse into the mountains. The slopes ahead looked too steep to climb.

For the next two hours the land rose so gradually, Josie wouldn't have been aware of the rise if it hadn't been for the appearance of juniper and pinyon pine among the cactus, mesquite, and ironwood. The ground became more uneven, and loose rocks made it harder for the horses to find secure footing. Josie worried that the noise of so many shod hooves on the rocks could be heard for miles.

"The rocks will make it harder for anyone to follow our trail," Zeke said, apparently understanding her worry. "Once we reach the pine and fir forest, the needles will muffle the sounds."

Josie looked up at the tall trees that clung to the seemingly vertical sides of the mountain. "How can we get up there?"

"Game trails."

"Can't the sheriff find the same trails?"

"Maybe, but that would bring him directly into our line of fire."

"What do you think he'll do?"

"I don't know. I never expected he would try to take

our horses. I'm sure Gardner's behind that. Since I don't know his relationship with the sheriff, I don't know how much influence he has over him. When he finds us gone, I'm hoping he'll think we're too far from Benson for him to follow."

Josie was unprepared for the change in temperature when they reached the slopes of the mountains and started to climb. The drafts of cool, moist air that flowed down the slopes raised goose bumps on her arms. She was relieved to see the first shafts of sunlight begin to peep over the Dragoon Mountains on the far side of the San Pedro River Valley. Her mind told her it was easier to hide in the deep shadows of the night, but the rest of her preferred the warmth of sunlight. Somehow things never seemed quite so terrible in the daylight.

They reached the first of the ponderosa pines just before the sunlight could have spotlighted them against the mountainside. It took Josie's eyes a few moments to adjust to the dark under the canopy, which grew thicker and more lush as they climbed. Before long, she felt like she was back in the forest of Colorado. In front the mares bunched up.

"What's wrong?" she asked Zeke.

"The trail is so steep Hawk has to take the mares up one at a time."

Josie watched with increasing uneasiness as each mare struggled to climb the loose shale on the slope.

"It's easy for a hundred-and-fifty-pound deer to climb the trail, but it's not the same for a thousand-pound horse," Zeke explained when it came time for her to climb the slope. "I'm going to lead you up."

"Can you stand up on that stuff?"

"We'll see."

"Isn't there another way up?"

"Probably, but that would mean going back down again."

"Why can't we do that?"

"Because the sheriff is down below."

Chapter Seventeen

"Can they see us?" Hiding from the sheriff and Gardner brought back memories of the way Josie had felt years ago when she was hiding from her father. She'd hated the feeling then and she hated it now. And she hated Gardner for making her feel this way.

"We'll be better concealed once we get up this slope." Zeke took hold of Josie's mount's bridle. "Let go of the reins and hold on to the pommel. Grip with your knees as tight as you can, but take your feet out of the stirrups."

"Why?"

"If the horse falls, you'll be able to throw yourself clear."

The horse didn't want to climb the shale-covered slope. He snorted and tried to back up, but Zeke didn't release his hold on the bridle even when the horse shook his head.

"Maybe I ought to walk up."

"He'll be okay in a minute. He just has to convince himself it's all right to try."

Josie had come to have considerable faith in Zeke, but this time the horse agreed with her. Still, she wasn't going to let Zeke see her fear. From the beginning, she'd insisted she didn't need his help. Shaking in fear because she had to climb a steep slope covered with loose rocks wasn't the way to convince him she was right. She gripped the saddle horn, tightened her knees, and waited.

The horse placed a foot on the bottom of the slope. When it held, he placed a second. Moments later he was slowly climbing, despite sliding back at least one foot for every eighteen inches forward. Josie told herself she ought to look at Zeke, the sky, even the mountain above, but she couldn't take her gaze off the loose rocks under the horse's hooves. She held her breath each time he took a tentative step until he found his footing. Glancing ahead at the distance to go and the few feet they'd come, she figured it would be noon before they reached Suzette and Hawk.

"You okay?" Zeke asked.

"Yes."

She wasn't, but she couldn't say so when she was safely in the saddle and he was stumbling and sliding alongside the horse. Thinking of that brought the guilt back with a rush. If he and Hawk hadn't insisted upon helping her and Suzette, they'd be safely on their ranch by now with no threat from Gardner or the sheriff.

"I'm sorry."

A look of confusion crossed Zeke's face before his

foot went out from under him and he turned his attention back to climbing the slope. "About what?"

She'd never told anybody she was sorry and hadn't intended to start now, but the words just popped out of her mouth. Once said, they couldn't be retracted. She realized she didn't want to. "Helping us got you in a lot of trouble."

Zeke's broad smile was a complete surprise. "You call this trouble? I remember a time we were cornered against a sheer cliff by nearly a dozen men. We ran out of food the third day and water on the fifth. It was two more days before we drove them off. We only had one round of ammunition left at the end. We had to stay awake the whole week to keep from being buried by snow."

"What were you trying to do?"

"Catch a gang of smugglers."

"How did you escape?"

He looked offended that she would ask such a question. "We didn't. We captured what was left of the gang."

"How?"

"We knew we couldn't hold out any longer, so the last night we built a huge fire. It was snowing so hard, we knew they'd be more concerned about keeping warm than watching us. We built the fire up until it was so high it blinded them to everything else. Using the snow as a cover, we managed to work our way off the cliff. Once we did that, getting behind the smugglers was easy. We had to shoot a couple to convince them it was time to give up, but we managed to deliver them to the marshal two days later."

Josie was surprised to find she'd been so enthralled

by Zeke's story, they'd climbed halfway up the slope without her noticing. She wondered if he'd made up the story to distract her, but decided it was probably true. Zeke told it like he thought it wasn't anything out of the ordinary.

"Have you and Hawk always done things like that?"

The horse stumbled badly, and Josie pitched forward over his withers. If she hadn't been holding on to the saddle horn, she'd probably have been thrown over his neck. Zeke steadied the horse with one hand and helped Josie regain her balance with the other.

"We've pretty much hired out for anyone who needed some kind of protection." He started forward again, helping the horse to its feet and at the same time keeping Josie from falling. "Nobody really trusts us, so they pay us well to do the job and then disappear. That's how we got the money for the ranch and these mares."

"Why did you decide to take up ranching?"

"We got tired of dodging other people's bullets."

Zeke hadn't answered until he'd gotten them over a treacherous part of the slope, but Josie had the feeling something else had been responsible for his delay. She'd sensed that her question had caused Zeke to withdraw. There was something more to the answer, something he wasn't willing to share with her.

She hadn't expected his reluctance to bother her, but it did. She had to remind herself she knew only a few important facts about him, some of the events that had shaped his life, but she didn't really know anything about his ideals, his hopes, his frustrations, the things that made him happy or angry. Except for the ranch, she didn't know what he wanted out of life. What could have driven a man who had been adopted and loved by a large, wealthy family to hire himself out as a gunman for twenty years? What was he trying to prove, and to whom?

"There's a bad spot coming up." Zeke pointed to a place where the trail turned sharply to the right. "Be ready to throw yourself free if the horse falls. If he falls on your leg, it'll probably break."

That would be the end of her career as a dancer. "Can't I walk?"

"You'd never make it on foot."

It looked like none of them would make it. The passage of the other animals had churned up the rocks until they were like quicksand, constantly shifting and giving way under the horse's hooves and Zeke's boots. For each foot forward they advanced, they slipped back a foot. Without warning, the horse gathered himself and jumped forward. Zeke scrambled to keep up, and Josie struggled to keep from falling. The horse was frantic now, leaping and falling to his knees and getting up and trying again.

"Hold on!" Zeke yelled.

Josie's hands were already frozen to the saddle horn, but her body was being whipped around so hard she was afraid her shoulders would be ripped out of their sockets. The horse righted himself and gathered his muscles for another leap. Instead, his hind legs went out from under him and he fell. Josie threw herself from the saddle and landed on Zeke. Both of them went down.

The horse scrambled to his feet and raced to the top of the slope, leaping and bucking like a mustang. Hawk caught him before he could run away.

"Are you hurt?" Zeke asked Josie.

"Only my pride. How about you?"

"Pretty much the same. Are you ready?"

She was more than ready, but she didn't know how they were going to make it without a horse.

"I'm going to stand up," Zeke said. "Once my feet are securely under me, I'll help you up. Then we'll make our way to the top holding on to each other. We'll go as slowly as you want."

She didn't want to go slowly. She wanted to be at the top immediately. She watched as Zeke got to his feet, then held out his hand to her. When she reached up and took it, she felt the strength to make it to the top of the slope. She couldn't understand what it was about his hand that made her feel so strong, but she was renewed and refueled physically and emotionally. The climb didn't intimidate her. The fear of stumbling on the rocks and hurting herself faded away. Against all reason and the evidence of the last few minutes, she felt able to accomplish anything.

When the ground gave way under her as she got to her feet, her confidence was shaken but not destroyed. She held on to Zeke and forced her legs to support her. Then, taking measured steps, she started to climb.

She slipped and slid. She sank to her knees twice, but she made steady progress. The closer she got to the top, the less worried Suzette looked. Then when she was almost there, she hit a patch that defied her best efforts to find footing.

"Let me carry you."

Josie's heart jumped in her throat. She was afraid of not being able to reach the top of the slope, but she was terrified of being in Zeke's arms. She'd never allowed any man to carry her. "You won't be able to stand up holding me."

"The extra weight will help," Zeke insisted.

She didn't know why—probably the perversity of Fate—but Zeke had no trouble getting his feet firmly planted. He held out his arms, inviting her to walk into them, but she couldn't force herself to move. If holding Zeke's hand could practically raise her off the ground, what would being in his arms do?

"I've got a good foothold," Zeke said, still holding his arms out to her. "It'll be easier if you come to me."

Not if her body refused to move. Despite her fears, she couldn't remain on this slope. With her luck, the rocks would slip out from under her, and she'd slide the whole way back down. Then she'd have to do this all over again. She took a big breath and launched herself at Zeke. Somehow he caught her without losing his balance.

"When I pick you up, put your arms around my neck," Zeke said. "Once I get you settled, don't move a muscle until I reach the top."

That would be easy. She was practically paralyzed already.

"Put your arm over my shoulder." The moment she reached over his shoulder, he put one arm behind her back, the other under her legs, and lifted her off the ground.

Her heart practically stopped beating. Her body was as rigid as a starched collar.

"Relax. I'm not going to drop you."

Falling would have been easier on her. At least she would have been able to breathe.

"Now remember, don't move even if I stumble. I won't drop you."

Steadying himself and shifting her weight for better

balance, Zeke took a step forward. His boots slipped, then took hold. Shifting his weight, Zeke swung his other foot forward. Again his boot slipped several times before he was able to secure a firm footing. Unable to contain her breath any longer, Josie let it out in a noisy whoosh.

"Are you afraid?"

"Of course not. I try to fall down a mountainside at least once a week."

She felt Zeke's body shake slightly. He was laughing at her.

"If you dare laugh at me, I'll never speak to you again."

"Some men would consider that a fair exchange."

"Not you. You can't stop talking and asking questions. Sometimes I think the reason Hawk is so quiet is that you never give him a chance to get in a word edgewise."

He was laughing again. She was going to have to hurt him.

"You'll never learn if you don't ask questions," Zeke said.

"Some questions don't need to be answered."

She didn't know why she was chattering like an idiot, or why he was encouraging her, but talking kept her from thinking about his arms around her or the muscled chest pressed against her. It served to distract her attention from the powerful attraction that seemed to be winding its coils around the two of them until it would be impossible to tear themselves apart.

"Some answers are never found until the question is asked," Zeke said.

Either he was trying to confuse her with riddles or

he was making fun of her. Either way, she didn't like it. But he'd distracted her so successfully, she was caught by surprise when he set her on her feet on firm ground.

"That wasn't hard," he said with one of those grins that made it impossible to stay angry at him. "Just get you mad, and you forget everything else, even the danger of falling down a mountain."

So he'd said all those things just to upset her. Well, he hadn't actually said anything of importance, but it felt like he had. And it had all been fake. That was worse than his laughing at her. She struggled to keep from showing the pain that suddenly was almost more than she could bear. "How long do we have to stay up here? We can't find a job by hiding in the woods."

Hawk moved through the trees with quick, silent steps. After Zeke and Josie had safely climbed the slope, he'd doubled back down the mountain to get close enough to hear some of what Gardner and the sheriff were saying. He had to know their plans before he and Zeke could make theirs. Because of the steepness of the mountainside, it was possible to get close and still be above them. Taking advantage of the pine needles to absorb the sound of his moccasins, he slipped from behind a ridge of rock and crawled on his belly until he reached the edge of a drop-off. He could make out at least six men through the trees. He recognized the sheriff, Gardner, and the two men who'd tried to steal their horses earlier. He assumed the sheriff had deputized the others to make the seizure seem legal.

"I tell you he couldn't have come this way," the sheriff was saying. "It's impossible to climb that slope. I know men who've tried."

"What about the hoofprints?" Gardner asked.

"There weren't no footprints," the sheriff said, "just disturbed rocks. Probably wild burros. We've got plenty in this area."

"I still say he's up there," Gardner insisted.

"Fine. You go after him, but don't expect me to cover you. Those men aren't stupid. They had enough sense to come back from the theater and take off. I bet they were twenty miles away before dawn."

"Not with those dancing girls."

"There's no sign of that wagon. Since you offered them jobs at the Birdcage, I expect they've gone on to Tombstone. The Birdcage is a whole lot more famous than our little theater."

They argued a bit more, but Hawk didn't stay to listen. He'd heard all he needed. He and Zeke were free to head to their ranch. The question now was what to do about Suzette and Josie.

"You're sure you don't mind going to our ranch?" Hawk asked Suzette. "Tombstone is only a short distance away. It wouldn't be any problem to take you there."

"We can't perform until we get the wagon back."

"You could still wait in Tombstone."

"I'd like to see your ranch. Josie would, too."

Hawk wasn't at all sure Suzette was reading her friend right. From the moment Zeke had set Josie on her feet at the top of that slope, she'd looked as nervous as a young cougar surrounded by a pack of hounds. If anybody had asked him, he'd have said she couldn't wait to get to Tombstone. The signals Suzette was sending out were exactly the opposite, and that was what made Hawk confused . . . and hopeful. He wasn't good at reading women, but he was certain Suzette was in love with him.

He was a fool to have let Suzette sleep with him. He'd known from the beginning he was attracted to her. That should have been warning enough, but she'd explained her plans to him. That should have been plenty to caution even the most stupid man to back off. He supposed the problem was that he'd underestimated the strength of his attraction to her. He'd been certain he could control his feelings.

He'd been wrong.

He *was* in love with her. He'd been telling himself it was only sexual attraction, but he should have known it was a lot more when he threw that drunk into the audience. He'd never let a woman cause him to do things he knew he'd regret. He'd never met a woman he couldn't leave when the time came. So what the hell did he do now? It didn't matter how they felt about each other. Their lives could never fit together.

"It's just a ranch," Hawk said. "Out here that means little more than a house, maybe a bunkhouse, and a few corrals." He couldn't imagine a woman who'd been reared in wealthy society wanting to spend more than five minutes at their place.

"There have been a couple of times when I'd have been thankful for a roof over my head that didn't leak."

"That won't be a problem in Arizona. It hardly rains except in winter and late summer."

They had rested in the pine and fir forest until afternoon to make sure Gardner and the sheriff had gone. Using a trail to the south, they were able to get down the mountain with little difficulty. The temperature had jumped abruptly when they left the forest. The juniper and pinyon pine slopes gradually gave way to broad areas of mesquite, ironwood, and sacaton, bunchgrass that grew up to four feet in places. Towering saguaro topped with white flowers and staghorn cholla with deep red blooms contrasted with the yellow of brittlebush, prickly-pear cactus, creosote bush, and paper flowers. Bees buzzed industriously, while tiny hummingbirds flitted from flower to flower with dazzling displays of speed. White-tailed deer feeding on the abundant grass watched the passing group with wary eyes, while hawks hovered overhead looking for unwary mice.

It was hard to believe there could be any serious conflict in such a pastoral setting, but Hawk knew the calm was as superficial as the tranquillity of Suzette's smile.

"Tell me about your ranch," Suzette said. "I've never seen one before."

"There's nothing to tell," Hawk said, wondering what she could expect. "It's just a house in the middle of land like this."

Suzette looked around, and a smile curved her lips. "I can't think of a more beautiful place to have a house."

How could a woman who grew up in a house with servants even begin to understand what it was like to live in the desert? She hadn't seen the snakes or scorpions. She certainly hadn't listened to coyotes howl outside her window, or watched a cougar stalk her milk cow. And that didn't take into account the heat, the dust, and the loneliness. Add to that the backbreaking work necessary to care for livestock and put food on the table. It was virtually impossible to keep anything clean, including oneself.

"It's not as easy as it looks."

"Nothing ever is." But she didn't seem discouraged.

"I thought the desert was empty and so hot it would kill you in a few hours." She flung out her arm to take in the entire vista. "This is beautiful. There are flowers everywhere."

"Only for a short time. Everything dries up or dies until the monsoon rains in late summer."

"You have forested mountains, tree-covered streams, and grassy plains. What more could you want?"

Hawk had never made a list of requirements for an ideal world. He accepted things the way they were. He couldn't recall ever thinking any place was beautiful. All that mattered was whether it was easy or hard to live there. "I doubt anybody in Quebec would think it's beautiful."

He regretted the words as soon as they were out of his mouth. Suzette turned away from him, but not before her smile faded and was replaced by an expression so bleak he wouldn't have been surprised to see tears fill her eyes. "I think it's beautiful," she said softly. "It would be wonderful to live here and never again have to fulfill someone else's expectations."

Hawk knew there was virtually no place where that was possible, but he didn't say so because he'd already ruined her sunny mood. Not that *his* mood was any better. And all because both of them had chosen to set aside reality for a few nights to take refuge in a fantasy that had become a dream they couldn't forget.

"You'd miss the excitement of living in a town, of entertaining, of—"

"Have you ever performed before a theater full of men?" She pulled her horse alongside his, locked her gaze on his. "Nobody sees me as a person. I don't have likes and dislikes, hopes and dreams, fears or

worries. I'm just a female with a set of body parts.
The men may enjoy my singing and dancing, but it's
really only an excuse to look at me, to fantasize about
me, to turn me into the kind of woman who'll satisfy
their sexual urges. They don't want to touch me because they care for me, only to undress me. They
don't want to make love to me, only to relieve their
sexual tension."

"I didn't mean—"

"You may think what I do is harmless, but I know
what those men are thinking, and a little piece of me
dies every time I get on stage."

"I thought you liked it." It was a feeble response, but
it was the truth.

"I dance because it's the only way I can earn the
money to support my sister."

Suzette pulled back on the reins and her horse
dropped back behind Hawk's. That left him feeling
like a heel. It also left him wanting more than ever to
protect her, to give her the kind of life she deserved.
But it was impossible for a half-breed Comanche to do
anything to help a woman whose values had been set
by Quebec society.

"I suppose living on a ranch for a while might be a
nice change," Hawk said, choosing his words carefully.
"It'll take a couple of days to get your wagon to Tombstone. That'll give you a chance to see if you think
ranch life is better than what you have."

"And if I think it is?"

He was glad she was behind him and couldn't see
his face. He was certain it betrayed what he was thinking. "Then we'll have to see what we can come up

with." He didn't dare be more specific, because he knew there was no way they could be together.

"Is that your ranch?" Josie asked.

After what seemed like an endless ride through belly-high grass, they had come to a modest house set in the midst of a grove of towering sycamores that leaned inward as if to protect the house from the glare of the sun. Not far away was a small garden where peas, beans, and potatoes in desperate need of watering grew in crooked rows of different lengths. Two dozen hens surrounded by what seemed like a sea of chicks scratched for food in every corner of the yard. Josie didn't see her, but she was certain a milk cow lurked in the vicinity. All they needed was a pig pen to make the picture complete.

"That's the house," Zeke said. "The ranch is two thousand acres in a rough arc between the San Pedro and Babocamari Rivers."

"It must have cost a lot of money to buy so much land."

"Everybody in the area was much more interested in mining than ranching. Besides, the last few years have been dry, and some ranchers had to sell up. Cows are hard on the range. The owner of this place was glad to get his hands on some cash."

Josie wasn't looking for a lecture on ranching. She was just trying to make conversation. Anything to keep her mind off the fact that she'd been riding next to Zeke for more than twelve hours. She was so tense she thought she'd jump out of her skin. She hadn't been able to think of anything except being held in his

293

arms. It horrified her. It terrified her, and she couldn't wait for it to happen again.

She'd already decided she was insane. What other possible explanation could there be for her attraction to a man who would clearly expect his wife to live in this remote corner of the desert and like hard work as much as he did? There would be no bright lights, no admiring men or extra money. Instead, she'd be expected to cook and clean and like it. She'd be expected to submit to his physical demands and like it. And that didn't take into consideration the children.

Okay, so she wouldn't mind a couple of children. She could grow quite fond of a couple of little boys who looked like Zeke. She didn't mind cooking all that much, but she wasn't too keen on cleaning. With a couple of children and a man around, nothing would stay clean long.

Then there was the part about her husband's physical needs.

Josie admitted she had a problem with the idea of being physically close to a man. How was she supposed to think of sex as an expression of love when nothing in her past had led her to associate it with anything except fear or disgust? She knew what her father had been thinking about her body even though he'd never articulated it. Nobody had to tell her what was in the minds of the men who came to watch her sing and dance. Just in case she hadn't known, the women who did go upstairs with those men had told her far more than she wanted to know.

Why was she thinking this way? She didn't want to get married. She didn't want to live on a ranch. It was too much like a farm, and a farm required hard work from morning to night.

"Doesn't it take a lot of money to start a ranch?" she asked Zeke.

"Hawk and I have been working for twenty years. We haven't had much reason to spend a lot, so we had a bit laid by."

If Gardner was to be believed, it took more than *a bit* to purchase those mares. And that didn't count the horses Zeke and Hawk already had, or the land. Either they had a lot of money or they were virtually broke. From the way they dressed and lived, she'd guess it was broke.

"Who takes care of this place?"

"We do."

"You cook and clean?"

"If it has to be done, we do it."

She'd assumed they'd hired some woman. Wasn't that what every man did? "You've been gone for weeks."

"We hired a couple of men to look after the place while we were gone."

Hawk and Suzette continued on past the ranch house. "Where are they going?" Josie asked.

"To put the mares in one of the corrals until they get accustomed to the range. Come on. I'll show you around."

Chapter Eighteen

As they approached the house, Josie noticed it had a derelict look about it, as if no one lived in it. She hesitated.

"What's wrong?" Zeke asked.

Unable to restrain herself, Josie exclaimed, "This place is a wreck. It looks like squatters live here."

Zeke looked around him. "Hawk and I aren't used to living in a house. It's easier to sleep in the brush."

"Where do you cook?"

Zeke shrugged. "Wherever we sleep."

It was worse than she thought. These men not only didn't know how to take care of a house, they didn't know how to live in one. "Do you have beds inside?"

"I guess so. I mean, yeah. I remember seeing some."

"Do you have a stove?"

"Yes. I definitely remember seeing that."

"Have you ever actually slept in that house?"

Zeke grinned. "No."

She exhaled a noisy breath to show her frustration. "Why not?"

"Because we'd have to clean it up." Zeke looked and sounded like a little boy caught in mischief and forced to explain himself against his will. "Isabelle taught us how to take care of a house, but Hawk and I didn't take too much to housework. Besides, Isabelle did all the cooking, so we didn't learn about stoves."

If two men ever needed taking care of, it was these two. And nobody could convince her there hadn't been quite a few women more than willing to accept the challenge. The West was full of men, but men like Zeke and Hawk were hard to come by anywhere. A woman looking for a husband would be a fool to reject them even if one was black and the other a half-breed. Giving in to the inevitable, Josie threw her leg over the saddle and slid to the ground. "Show me what you've got."

They started with the garden. "You've got to fence it in," she said, "or rabbits will strip the peas and beans, and the deer will eat what's left."

"We don't—"

"And you've got to plant something else besides peas, beans, and potatoes. What kind of diet is that?" She looked at the soil, which was black and loamy despite being rocky. "You ought to order fruit trees. All this water and sunlight would be perfect for peaches, plums, and cherries."

"I don't—"

Josie turned on her heel and walked rapidly to where several hens were scratching in the dirt with their broods in attendance. "You need a fenced-in yard for the chickens, too. That way you can control how many sit their eggs. I'm surprised you haven't lost them all to coyotes."

"We didn't because—"

"Do you have a milk cow?"

"Yes, but—"

"I don't suppose you know how to churn butter or make cheese."

"No, but—"

"I don't know how you expect to survive. Now let's look at the house."

"You sure you're up to it?" Zeke asked, his temper rising. "The shock might be too much for you."

"Is the roof still good?"

"Yes."

"Then I can stand it."

When she walked inside, she wondered if she'd spoken too soon. The floor in what was the parlor or sitting room was covered by at least an inch of dust. "Do you ever come in here?"

"Why would we?"

"Maybe to get out of the rain."

"We were in Texas during the rainy season. After that we went north to buy the mares."

Unable to believe her ears, Josie picked up her skirts and headed to the kitchen. One look told her it would be unusable without a thorough cleaning. With a sinking feeling, she said, "What about the bedrooms?"

There were two at the back of the house. Much to her surprise, they had been swept and were reasonably organized. The beds had mattresses, sheets, and blankets, and appeared to have been slept in.

"This stuff belongs to Adam and Jordy," Zeke said.

"Who are they?"

"Hen Randolph's boys. He's the man who sold us our stud horse."

"Where are they?"

"With the horses."

"I suppose they cook outside, too."

"Looks like it."

Josie didn't understand it. Zeke and Hawk had been meticulous in their care of the mares. Hawk had known what medicine would help Laurie. They kept their equipment in perfect order and cleaned up after every meal. How could they put up with a house in this condition?

The sound of two horses arriving at a canter drew them to the porch. Two young men brought their horses to a stop in front of the house. The shorter man with a stocky build dismounted and walked up to Zeke with a broad smile.

"You sly dog." He gave Zeke a playful punch on the shoulder. "You said you were going to buy some mares. You never said anything about some damned fine-looking women."

"Jordy has no manners," Zeke said to Josie. "Hen found him sleeping in a stable. Apparently, adopting him couldn't take the stable out of him."

Jordy laughed good-naturedly. "I'm Jordy Randolph," he said to Josie. "That young scamp who's too shy to get off his horse is Adam Randolph, Hen's other effort to redeem an orphan."

Adam dismounted and walked up to Josie. "I wasn't an orphan. Hen married my ma."

Josie thought Jordy was a nice-looking young man, but Adam was going to be a heartbreaker in a few

Leigh Greenwood

more years. She wouldn't have been surprised to learn his father had gotten him a job on this remote ranch to protect him from all the women who'd be after him.

"Hawk told us to get our stuff out of the house so you ladies could move in," Adam said.

Josie turned to Zeke. "They don't have to—"

"Do you want to sleep out in the brush?"

Josie swallowed. Sleeping in a wagon in the desert was one thing. Sleeping in the open in the desert would be something very different, she was sure.

"Suzette and I can share a room."

Jordy looked at Adam and grinned. "I'm not sharing a bed with him. He might think I like him too much."

Adam blushed but managed to get in a hit over Jordy's guard. "He's just jealous because I'm taller than he is."

Josie decided the two boys were true friends, but she wouldn't have been surprised if Jordy was a little jealous of Adam's looks.

"Where's that wagon Hawk said we are supposed to get?" Jordy asked Zeke.

While Zeke gave Jordy directions, Josie followed Adam inside. "Have you boys worked here long?" she asked as Adam started gathering his stuff and putting it in his saddlebags.

"Just a couple of months," he replied. "I'm only sixteen. This is the first time Hen has let me take a job away from the ranch."

"Has your father known Zeke and Hawk very long?"

"Forever. The man who adopted them was in the war with Hen's oldest brother. Hen said if I grew up to

300

be half as good as them, he'd stop being sorry he adopted me." He grinned suddenly. "He said nothing could keep him from being sorry he adopted Jordy." He paused in his packing. "You ladies going to stay here?"

Josie didn't know why the question should upset her so much. It had never entered her mind. If it had, seeing the condition of the ranch would have tossed the notion right back out again. "We'll leave as soon as we get our wagon. We're going to try to find jobs in Tombstone or Bisbee."

Some of the brightness went out of Adam's eyes. "Too bad. I've never seen Hawk look at a woman like he looks at Suzette. Or Zeke like he looks at you."

She tried to deny the question the moment it formed in her brain, but the words came out anyway. "How does Zeke look at me?"

"Like there's nobody else around. Ma says that's the way Jordy looks at Hope. He's saving his money so he can ask her to marry him. Do you think Zeke wants to marry you?"

She'd met this innocent-looking sixteen-year-old barely five minutes ago, and already he'd laid bare the question she'd refused to allow even in the back of her mind. She wouldn't deal with it now. She *couldn't*. She wanted to run away, to pretend Adam had never asked that question, but he was waiting for an answer, his gaze wide and innocent. He was far too young to realize the devastating effect his question had had on her.

"I doubt Zeke is the marrying kind," she managed to say.

"Hen said he wasn't the marrying kind until he met Ma." He grinned. "Now he's got four of his own kids in addition to Jordy and me. He keeps telling Ma he needs one more to bring him up to the family standards, but Ma says he's nothing but a big kid so that gives her seven already."

Josie couldn't imagine how a man who thought he was a confirmed bachelor could end up married with six kids and still want more. She wondered if Zeke or Hawk wanted kids. They'd never said anything about it. But then, they hadn't said anything about wanting to get married, either.

She was allowing this boy's appealing picture of his family to cause her imagination to run away with her. She didn't want to get married. She didn't want to live on a ranch. And she certainly didn't want six children. She had a successful career which would soon allow her to retire before she was thirty and open her boardinghouse. That had been her goal ever since she ran away from her uncle. She couldn't start questioning it now.

"How long do you think it will take to get the wagon?" she asked.

"Are you in a real hurry to leave?" Adam had finished packing his saddlebags and turned to his bedroll.

"Zeke and Hawk have a ranch to run. We've already taken up too much of their time."

"They didn't look like they minded."

She had to get away from this boy. Every word out of his mouth created another breach in her defenses. She had to remember Adam was asking these questions, not Zeke. He was saying what he *thought* Zeke might be feeling.

"They've been extremely kind, but we can't impose on them any longer."

Adam stood and hefted his saddlebags over his shoulder. "There ain't a man in the world who minds being imposed on by a beautiful woman." He grinned shyly. "You got any sisters?"

"No, but Suzette has one just your age."

When he flushed crimson, Josie figured the thought of finding himself face to face with a younger version of Suzette had probably unnerved him as much as it had excited him.

"I'd better get going. Hen says I can talk the ear off a donkey."

"You pack my gear?" Jordy asked when they came out of the house.

"Do I look like your ma?" Adam retorted as he jumped off the porch and walked over to his horse.

Jordy looked disgusted. "You don't want me to tell you what you look like." He headed inside the house.

"I see you boys are getting along as well as always," Zeke said with a grin.

"About," Adam replied with his boyish grin.

"Have any trouble while we were gone?"

"Cougars get one whiff of a dog and go someplace else, but those damned coyotes just don't care. You ought to pen up the chickens."

Zeke turned to Josie. "So I've been told."

"And you'd better water that garden soon," Adam said to Zeke.

"Why don't you do it?"

"I hired on for a riding job. I'm no farmer." Adam looked so affronted it was all Josie could do to keep from laughing.

"Did Hawk say when he was coming to the house?" Zeke asked.

Adam finished fastening his saddlebags to the saddle and reached down for his bedroll. "He said he wanted to make sure the mares were settled first. He seems to think that bay with the Morgan blood is about to foal. I think he means to bring her up to the house so he can watch her."

Josie hoped Dusky Lady would foal before she and Suzette left. She knew Suzette had come to think of each of the mares as a friend. It would be hard for her to leave them behind.

Jordy came barreling out of the house. "I got my stuff," he said as he threw his saddlebags across his saddle and dropped his bedroll. "I'll be ready to ride out in five minutes."

"You know how to find the ranch where the wagon is?" Adam asked.

"A baby could find it, even without Zeke trying to describe every tree between here and there."

"I hope that means we won't make more than one wrong turn."

"We won't make any." Jordy tightened the buckle on his saddlebags and slapped his bedroll across his horse's haunches.

"We'd still be wandering around the Huachuca Mountains if I'd listened to Jordy," Adam said to Zeke. "If you told him to follow the sun, he'd somehow end up going north."

"Your ma's going to be right upset if you show up with a broken neck." Jordy tightened the strings on his bedroll and swung into the saddle. "Come on before I leave you to find your own way."

"I think I can follow the river without getting lost."

"Won't make any difference if I drown you in it."

"Are they always like that?" Josie asked as they rode off exchanging insults.

"Hen says they were trying to get the better of each other the first time he saw Jordy, and they haven't stopped since."

Josie decided that being orphans adopted into the same family had probably caused them to bond just like Zeke and Hawk. It made her feel sad that Hawk and Zeke felt like outsiders. They were two wonderful men who deserved to feel accepted. Why couldn't they see that they were worthy of the same kind of love and loyalty every person deserved?

Why can't you believe you're worthy of that kind of love and loyalty?

At first Josie couldn't believe she'd asked herself that question. She didn't want love and loyalty. She just wanted to be left alone. But no sooner had that thought crystallized in her mind than she knew she was lying to herself. She'd decided she didn't want love or loyalty because she didn't believe anyone could feel that way about her. Men saw only her face and body, thought only of their physical needs. That knowledge hurt, but she'd finally gotten used to it, accepted it as the way things were.

Then she'd met Zeke and things had changed. It scared her even more to realize she *wanted* things to change. She had to leave soon.

"How long do you think it will take them to return with the wagon?"

Zeke subjected her to a long look before he answered. "They'll be back sometime tomorrow. You can head for Tombstone the next day."

Rather than return Zeke's gaze, she looked up at a

hawk circling overhead. Hens clucked urgently to their chicks. Two days. Surely she could hold out that long. There was nothing about this ranch to make her want to stay.

Except Zeke. And he was the one reason she couldn't stay.

"I'd better get to work if I'm going to have the kitchen fit to cook supper. I have a hankering for food cooked on a stove and served at a table. Do you think you could find me a rooster? I'm in the mood for baked chicken."

"That was a great supper," Hawk said to Suzette and Josie. "You've spoiled us for baked beans and jerky stew cooked over an open fire."

"You could learn to cook with a stove," Josie said.

"Too late," Zeke answered. "I wouldn't know what to do if the heat wasn't burning my face and the wind sending grit into the pot."

"You've got a house now," Suzette said. "You don't have to live outdoors."

The men had insisted on helping clean up. Now there was nothing left to do but go to bed. All evening long they'd avoided talking about the feelings that were boiling just below the surface, feelings that colored every comment anyone made. Suzette had tried to decide how Hawk felt about her leaving—about her being there—about her staying, but his expression was as impenetrable as ever. She would have to ask the questions. He never would answer otherwise.

"Hawk is afraid Dusky Lady might foal at any time, so we're going to sleep outside to watch her," Suzette said.

Everyone acted as though what she'd said was perfectly natural, when they all knew it meant her feelings for Hawk hadn't changed. Further, her decision meant Zeke and Josie would be sleeping in the house alone. That might not be fair to Josie, but Suzette believed Josie was close to falling in love with Zeke. She was certain he was in love with her. If there was no chance that Josie could ever love him, then Josie ought to tell Zeke so he could stop hoping. As for herself, she had her own confession to make.

"You can use my bedroll," Zeke said. Suzette had left all her bedding in the wagon.

Hawk didn't say much as they walked toward the small corral where Dusky Lady would spend the night. The trees along the river formed a black silhouette against the sky that made the moon gleam brighter by comparison. Stones crunched under their feet and cicadas chirped in the salt cedar. One of the dogs ran up to fawn over Hawk, but he sent it back to watch the horses. They didn't have to worry about coyotes getting the chickens. Zeke had rounded them up and put them in the pen they'd escaped from earlier. A bat swooped through the air with its fast but erratic flight. Suzette shivered. She didn't like bats even though Hawk said the insects would be unbearable without them.

Hawk stopped at a spot where the ground had been smoothed out. She suspected the men had spent many nights here. They spread out their bedrolls and settled on to them before Suzette said, "We need to talk."

"I didn't think there was anything to say."

"There's a lot to say. I don't know that it will change anything, but it needs to be said."

"If you can't stay, what's the point of saying anything?"

"Because I can't leave without first telling you what I'm feeling. You may not want to hear it, but I need to say it."

"What makes you think I won't want to hear it?"

"It could hurt you as much as it hurts me."

"I can stand it."

He probably could, but she wasn't sure *she* could. Already the tears were welling up in her eyes. How much longer did she have to go on merely surviving? When was it going to be her turn? Suddenly she felt overwhelmed. Unable to stop herself, she burst into tears. Hawk took her in his arms, which made her cry harder. This was where she wanted to be for the rest of her life. She'd given up so much, endured so much, why couldn't she have just this one thing?

"If it helps you to know this, I love you, too."

Suzette's tears stopped with a hiccup so violent it hurt. Not daring to believe what she'd heard, she pulled herself out of Hawk's embrace and stared at him. "What did you say?"

"I said I love you, too."

She tried very hard to restrain herself, but it was impossible. She threw herself at him and burst into tears again. Hawk loved her. She'd thought knowing he loved her would make things easier, but now it was a thousand times harder. Here was more happiness than she'd dared dream about. All she had to do was reach out and grab it. "Are you sure?" Men never fell in love as quickly as women. They practically had to be hit over the head before they'd admit to such a weakness.

His answer was to take her in his arms and kiss her

with so much fervor she couldn't possibly doubt him. Moments later, she emerged from his embrace breathless and as limp as a rag doll. "Why didn't you tell me?" she asked.

"Why didn't you tell me?"

There were a thousand reasons. She hadn't wanted to admit the truth to herself. If she didn't love him, it wouldn't hurt to leave. If she didn't love him, she could smile as she sang and danced for other men. If she didn't love him, she wouldn't miss being in his arms, seeing his smile, being able to reach out and touch him. If she didn't love him, she wouldn't have to dream about making love to him until her bones melted and her senses became so acutely attuned to his presence, they blocked out the world around them.

"I was afraid it would hurt too much," she admitted.

"I thought women believed happiness was worth the pain."

"Do you believe it's worth it?"

"I don't know. I've never been in love before."

Suzette's heart soared. He didn't say he'd never been in love *like this*. He said he'd never been in love at all. Maybe it was selfish to cherish that confession so much, but she couldn't help herself. She didn't know what tomorrow or the next day would bring, but she had tonight. She would forget Tombstone, forget Quebec, forget—

Dusky Lady blew hard through her nostrils. Then she grunted. Suzette turned to see the mare circling, her movements awkward.

"She's looking for a place to lie down," Hawk said. "She's getting ready to have her foal."

* * *

Josie and Zeke stood in the tiny hallway that led to the two bedrooms, neither willing to go just yet, neither quite meeting the other's gaze. Things had gone so well this evening, Zeke had considered trying to clear the air between them. He wasn't about to confess undying love to Josie, but he was willing to admit a nearly overpowering lust to himself. This woman was just too beautiful for words, but her beauty wasn't what attracted him most. It was her vulnerability. Josie didn't know it and probably wouldn't admit it if she did, but she was a very lonely and unhappy woman. It wasn't simply that she'd closed men out of her life. She'd also closed down her spirit and her heart. Life had cleaved her in two, leaving her perpetually in search of her other half. Only Josie denied that she had another half. Zeke knew she wasn't complete just as she was, but he didn't know if he was the person to tell her so.

"Do you think you can remember how to sleep in a bed?" Josie asked Zeke. "With Hawk and Suzette watching Dusky Lady, you don't have to sleep under the stars."

Zeke had been mulling over ways to tell Josie he was going to sleep outside. Now she'd just punctured his only possible excuse. He resented Josie's implication that something was wrong with him because he didn't share her views about the virtues of spending one's whole life inside some building. It was just that two men found it easier not to mess with all the trouble that came with living in a house. "I haven't always lived like an animal."

"I meant that as a joke," Josie said.

Zeke couldn't picture a Josie who made jokes. In his

mind she was a quick-tempered woman who dis-
trusted men and had no problem letting them know
she wanted nothing to do with them.

"Sorry. I'm not used to sharing a house with an un-
married female."

"I make you nervous?"

She seemed surprised. Where had she been for the
last week? Couldn't she tell she drove him out of his
mind? "Look, let's just go to bed, okay? Every time we
talk, you end up angry at me."

"I'm sorry. I didn't treat you very fairly at first."

He was beginning to wonder if Josie was in her right
mind. The Josie he knew didn't apologize or give a
damn about fairness. She only wanted what she
wanted, and to hell with the rest of the world. "Are
you feeling okay?"

"Why do you ask?"

Hell, she was leaving soon. No point in mincing
words now. "For the first few days I was afraid to turn
my back for fear you might stick a knife in it. Now
you're nice most of the time, but you keep looking at
me like I'm a rattlesnake about to strike. I keep waiting for you to reach for a gun."

Josie dropped her gaze. "I misjudged you. You're a
very nice man who's done nothing to earn my distrust,
and everything to earn my gratitude."

Zeke was certain there was a great big qualification
coming that would rock him off his heels. She actually
looked like she was sorry. He had to get a grip on himself, and quick. A churning in his gut urged him to
take her into his arms and kiss her until they both forgot about that terrible beginning.

"You keep talking like this, and I'm going to think

you actually like me." He didn't know why he said that. It was an open invitation for her to plunge a knife into his heart.

"I do. I like you very much."

This couldn't be happening. Maybe he was just dreaming they were standing in the hall having this absolutely out-of-the-blue conversation.

"I'm sure you know you're a handsome man with impressive strength and skills. I'm not sure you know you're also kind, patient, and thoughtful. It was wrong of me to prejudge you."

Okay, if she didn't stop talking, he was going to kiss her even if it meant she'd shoot him the minute he released her. They hadn't been drinking, and they hadn't eaten any bad meat. This had to be real. "What made you change your mind?" How could he have missed something that important?

"The way you protected me from Gardner when he tried to kidnap me."

"Anybody would have done that."

"He could have shot you."

"Hell, I've been shot so many times I've lost count."

"Nobody's ever tried to protect me before."

He didn't know what kind of men she'd been around all her life.

"Suzette told me I was wrong about you, but I wouldn't believe her. I didn't *want* to believe her."

"Why?" It was crazy to want to believe everybody was out to hurt you. It must have made her very unhappy. She certainly looked miserable now, as if she would rather be anywhere else in the world than here talking to him. Her gaze kept shifting away from him, then coming back, only to shift away again. If he was as kind and thoughtful as she said, he'd let her go to bed. It was obviously torture for her to think of a reply that wouldn't hurt his feelings.

"If I believed her, I'd have to admit I liked you. And if I admitted that, I'd have to admit I liked you far more than I wanted to."

"You like me!"

"I just said I did."

"A lot?" The words came out unbidden. He wasn't sure he had any thoughts in his head, just feelings, desires, and desperate hope.

She dropped her gaze. "Yes."

He thought his heart would stop beating. No, it was beating so fast he felt light-headed. First he couldn't breathe. Then he was breathing so rapidly he could hear it. "I don't believe you."

She looked up at him. "What can I do to prove it?"

He clamped his lips together to keep the answers stacked up like a logjam from pouring out. He reached out and gripped her hands. She resisted at first, then slowly allowed him to draw her closer. "You could let me kiss you. I've been wanting to do that ever since I saw you."

He felt her tense, saw the fear in her eyes, but she didn't pull away. He brought her closer, slipped his arms around her waist. She was nothing like the angry and defiant young woman he'd met days ago. Now she appeared uncertain, vulnerable, frightened. In that moment he knew he could hurt her very much.

"I don't want to do anything to frighten you."

"You're not."

The terror in her eyes showed she didn't believe her own words. She had opened herself to a man for the first time, and she was afraid. Zeke pulled her to him. She stayed rigid for a moment before relaxing and slipping her arms around his waist. He told himself he could be happy if he could just hold her like this for the rest of the night, but he knew this wasn't nearly enough. Having come this far, it was impossible to stop, unthinkable to pull back.

"Look up at me," he said.

She was slow to respond. When she did, he could see the uncertainty in her gaze. "I'm going to kiss you. If you want me to stop, just tell me."

She didn't move; her gaze didn't waver. Taking his courage in his hands, Zeke lowered his head and kissed her. He knew immediately she'd never been kissed before. It seemed incredible, but she didn't know what to do. She simply stood there letting him kiss her, waiting for him to tell her what to do next.

"You have to help," he said softly. "It's not as much fun if I do all the work."

Chapter Nineteen

Josie felt as though her body were frozen, locked in place, unable to move. She didn't know if she wanted Zeke to kiss her, but she hadn't been able to tell him to stop. Fear of what this could lead to stampeded through her brain like a runaway steer. She might have pulled back at the last minute if it hadn't felt so wonderful to be in his arms. That was what had disarmed her, had enabled her to slip past the panic long enough to lean against him and put her arms around him. She'd never touched any man or allowed a man to touch her this way. She'd always been certain she didn't want it, would hate it, that it would lead to pain. Then Zeke kissed her, and it was wonderful.

Josie had never felt like this before. Not that she could have said *how* she felt. It was crazy, as it every part of her was trying to overdose on sensations at once. She was in an uproar, unable to move, to think, to react. She just *was*.

"Sorry. I didn't know you'd dislike it that much."

She could barely think, but she could feel Zeke pull away. "I don't dislike it," she managed to say.

"Why didn't you kiss me back?"

How could she explain that she didn't know what to expect, that her reaction had been so overpowering she'd been unable to do anything but stand like a statue? "I didn't know what to do."

"You've never been kissed before, have you?"

She shook her head.

She didn't understand Zeke's smile.

"How ironic. Average-looking girls get kissed every day. Even the ugly ones manage it from time to time. Yet the most beautiful woman I've ever seen has never once been kissed. Want to try again?"

She nodded. How could he ask that question when she was holding his arms in a viselike grip?

"I'm not going to do all the work."

He didn't understand that she was still so overcome she had virtually no control over her mind or her body. Surely he could tell by the fact that she hadn't let go of him, by the way she looked at him, that she wanted him to kiss her again. When she tightened her grip on his arms and pulled him closer, Zeke bent down and kissed her again.

She could hardly believe this big, rough man's lips could be so soft, his kiss so gentle. She could feel the strength in the arms holding her, the power in the thighs pressed against her, but his kiss was as soft as a spring breeze. There was nothing here to fear, nothing to hurt her. No threat. Only an invitation. She moved her mouth against his lips. The response was so immediate, so powerful, it momentarily frightened her. Then she understood it was a sign he wanted her, not that he intended to force her to do anything against her will.

Her confidence restored and her need of him increasing with dizzying rapidity, she rose on her toes to kiss him harder, to pull him against her. It wasn't something she thought about. It just happened. So did the desire to have him do more than just kiss her lips. She wanted to experience all of him. She wanted to—

The sound of the door opening caused Zeke to break the kiss and step back. She stood there unable to move, feeling as if part of her body had been snatched away. Suzette had entered the house and was looking from Josie to Zeke. Her expression of stunned surprise said she knew what she'd interrupted. Her flushed cheeks said she was embarrassed but glad.

"Dusky Lady is having her foal," Suzette said to Zeke.

"Is she down yet?"

"Yes."

Josie felt she was dreaming or in some sort of trance. One moment she was in Zeke's arms, being kissed, awakening parts of herself she'd closed off and sealed up years ago. The next she was standing here, too stunned to move, while Zeke and Suzette discussed Dusky Lady's foaling. Her world had been shaken up, turned upside down, and spilled out in disorder and confusion, and they were acting as if nothing out of the ordinary had happened.

"Hawk said to bring something to clean the foal," Suzette said.

"Come with us," Zeke said to Josie. It was a request, not a command.

After what she'd just experienced, Josie couldn't imagine anything less appealing than kneeling in the dirt while being confronted with the blood and gore of birth. Yet she didn't hesitate to head to the kitchen and collect several cloths. She was certain she had taken leave of her senses, that her body was being directed by external forces, but it was like being back on the farm again. Patterns of activity learned and established long ago took over.

The mare was on the ground when they arrived. "Her labor has started," Hawk said. "It won't take long."

Zeke moved to the mare's head to calm her while Hawk prepared for the delivery of the foal. Suzette held a lantern aloft, and Josie stood ready with the towels. It was an odd gathering in the open desert under the light of the moon, odd because so many humans had gathered to assist in an event that mares had been handling alone for millions of years. Yet, despite the number of times it had been repeated, the miracle of birth never failed to work its magic, to raise spirits and instill hope.

Josie felt she, too, had been given the promise of new life—but did she have the courage to accept it? For years she'd been mortally afraid of what Zeke offered. She was comfortable in her life. She understood its challenges and its limitations. Did she dare consider exchanging the familiar for something so new and dangerous, something she couldn't yet understand?

"It's coming," Hawk said.

Josie looked down to see two small hooves protruding from the mare. They had torn through a milky-colored sack that was still stuck to the foal's hocks.

The mare's body heaved, and the foal's head appeared between her hooves.

"It's going to be an easy birth," Hawk said.

Josie didn't have the same feeling for the mares the others had, but she instantly bonded with the beautifully delicate head of the foal. Even though she'd seen the birth of new life many times before, it stirred something deep within her.

The mare gave another push, and the foal's shoulders and hips were free of the womb. Taking hold of the foal, Hawk pulled its hind legs free.

"It's a filly," he said.

"She's beautiful," Suzette added, her voice filled with awe.

When Dusky Lady didn't immediately get to her feet, Hawk reached for one of the cloths Josie held.

"I can do it." Josie knelt down by the foal, which stared up at her with huge, trusting brown eyes. After she made sure the foal's nostrils were clear, she began to rub its body to encourage circulation.

"She's perfect, absolutely beautiful," Suzette said, "but she's so small."

"That's because, as you predicted, she's a twin," Hawk said.

"How do you know?" Josie asked.

"From the size of her belly." Hawk rubbed Dusky Lady's distended abdomen. "You can tell she's got one more in there." He picked up the filly and moved her so she wouldn't be in the way of the second birth.

Josie removed all remnants of the birth sack but continued to rub the filly dry with the soft cloth. She was awed by the tiny, delicate bones of her legs, by the beauty of her head, the symmetry of her body, but it was the filly's eyes that mesmerized her. It was almost as though the filly thought Josie was her mother and had immediately bonded with her. Josie felt as if this were her horse, that there was a connection between them.

"The other one is coming," Hawk warned.

The second birth was faster than the first. Hawk had hardly announced that the birth had begun when a second filly, identical to the first, slipped free of her mother's womb. Suzette picked up a cloth and started to clean the foal and rub her dry. As soon as she'd rid herself of the afterbirth, the mare lunged to her feet with a whinny of what was certainly pride as well as triumph. She immediately started licking the second foal.

"We can leave them to their mother now," Hawk said.

The two women turned to him in unison. "They're not even standing yet," Suzette pointed out.

"Can she take care of two foals?" Josie asked.

"She's not a new mother," Hawk said. "Twins are unusual, but a healthy mare can take care of them."

"But they're so small," Suzette said. "We can't leave them out here."

"A coyote might try to kill them." Josie couldn't turn her back on the trust in those big brown eyes.

"Dusky Lady is more than a match for any coyote."

"They hunt in pairs, sometimes in packs," Josie said. "She couldn't defend both fillies if that happened."

Hawk looked at Zeke. "What do you think we ought to do?"

Zeke looked at Josie, who was now sitting on the ground with the foal's head in her lap. "That's up to Josie and Suzette."

"We'll stay until they stand and nurse," Suzette said. "After that, we can decide what to do next."

Josie felt almost jealous when Dusky Lady came to claim the foal in her lap. She knew the mare and foals had to bond, but she felt as if the filly belonged to her. She had to force herself not to shoo the mare away.

The next half hour was one of the most rewarding Josie had ever spent. She and Suzette continued to stimulate the foals by rubbing them gently, while Dusky Lady moved back and forth from one to the other, licking each with her rough, powerful tongue. All too soon, Josie's filly began to struggle to her feet. The first effort ended before she got one leg under her.

"Let her do it by herself," Hawk said when Josie rose to help her. "She won't always have you to do things for her."

Josie hated it when the filly tried to stand and fell. She was certain Suzette felt the same as they watched both fillies get one, two, three, and finally four legs under them. It was fun to watch them stagger about on long, spindly legs that didn't yet have the muscle tone to support their tiny bodies. Yet it was sad, because their success meant they didn't need Josie and Suzette anymore. With a little help from Hawk and Zeke, the two fillies found their mother's teats and began to nurse.

"How will you tell them apart?" Suzette asked. "They're identical."

"We don't have to worry about that."

"Of course you do," Josie said. "I want to know which is my filly."

Her filly was on the mare's right flank. Okay, it was silly to talk about *her* filly, but she had already bonded to the little creature. "I think we ought to mark them."

"How?" Hawk asked.

"I have an idea." Grinning, Zeke took out his pocket

321

knife and opened it. "I'll carve a J in Josie's filly's hoof and an S in Suzette's."

Josie started to object even though she knew it wouldn't hurt. The fillies didn't stop nursing while Zeke carved the initials in their hooves.

"I think we ought to call one Josie and the other Suzette," Zeke said, pleased with his work. "Now you can go to bed."

Both Josie and Suzette looked at him as if he were crazy.

"Then *we'll* go to sleep," Hawk said. "Wake us if you need us."

Then, much to Josie's surprise and consternation, the two men lay down on bedrolls and proceeded to fall asleep almost at once.

"I can't believe they did that," Suzette said, but a dreamy smile lit up her eyes.

"I can," Josie said. "That's men all over. Once they've had their fun, they go to sleep and leave the real work to the women."

But somehow she didn't mind. She had a lot to think about, and maybe talking to Suzette would help her come up with some answers.

Suzette was exhausted. After staying up talking most of the night, she didn't know how Josie had the energy to clean the house from top to bottom. It hadn't been too hard to get rid of the dust and dirt in the three other rooms, but the kitchen had taken the better part of the afternoon. She was so tired she didn't think she could summon the energy to eat, much less cook.

She knew Josie was running on nervous energy that stemmed from not being able to make up her mind about Zeke. An odd light gleamed in Josie's eyes. Suzette decided it was one of Josie's repressed instincts coming to the surface, this one the pride a woman takes in having a well-ordered house. Josie looked about the kitchen with satisfaction.

"Now I won't mind cooking dinner in here."

The walls had been scrubbed free of grease. All the cabinets, shelves, and other surfaces had been cleared of their contents, scrubbed, and everything replaced in order. The stove—the biggest hurdle—had finally been scrubbed clean of grease and soot and cleared of old ashes. The nickel surfaces of knobs and decorations gleamed. The stoneware jug had been filled with fresh water, the basket with kindling, and the coffee can with freshly roasted beans. The churn had been scrubbed and was ready for use as soon as the men found the milk cow.

"It'll probably look like we found it a week after we leave," Josie said.

Suzette didn't comment. She'd finally decided what she wanted to do, but she couldn't say anything until she talked to Hawk. She believed Josie was denying with her mind what her actions indicated she wanted, but she'd said all she intended to say last night. It was up to Josie now.

The loud "hello" from outside sent the two women hurrying from the house in time to see Jordy ride into the yard. Adam followed a little way behind with the wagon.

"Got your stuff," Jordy said. "Do you really wear those things when you dance?"

"You looked inside our trunks?" Josie asked.

"Just curious," Jordy said. "I've never seen what dancers wear."

"That's a bald-faced lie," Adam said as he pulled the wagon to a stop. "You never pass a saloon or a dance hall without a look inside."

"I don't know what such pretty women wear," Jordy protested. "I figured it had to be something different. They got nothing to hide."

"I expect your smooth tongue has gotten you out of a lot of jams," Suzette said. Jordy's cheeky grin made her grin right back.

"Not all the time," Adam said as he climbed down from the wagon. "Hen has had to break his head a couple of times."

"You're no angel," Jordy replied as he dismounted. "You got anything to eat? Neither one of us can cook worth a damn."

"Dinner will be ready in about an hour," Josie said. "In the meantime, you can help find the milk cow."

"You should have asked me," Jordy said. "I know where she is."

Suzette went back inside, picked up a pail, walked back out, and handed it to Jordy. "Find her and fill this."

"I don't milk cows." He looked offended.

"Then I guess you don't eat, either."

"That's blackmail."

"It's called working for your supper."

Suzette didn't know which was funnier, Jordy's disgust or Adam's undisguised amusement. "You," she said, turning to the younger boy, "can bring a couple of trunks inside, then find me a chicken for dinner."

"Want to trade?" Jordy asked.

"Nope," Adam said, heading for the back of the wagon. "You're the one who's supposed to be so good with females."

Suzette decided she was going to miss those two boys.

Hawk had come to a decision. He knew he should have talked to Zeke first, but it was something Hawk had to do. He didn't yet know how, but he'd find a way to make it right with Zeke.

"I feel bad about sending the boys off to watch the horses," Suzette said.

"Why? It's what we hired them to do." He thought they were probably happier by themselves. Besides, he didn't like the way Jordy was looking at Suzette. The women treated the boys like younger brothers, but there was nothing brotherly in the way Jordy looked at them.

"Still, we took their beds."

"They got a good supper in exchange. Judging from the way Jordy ate, I'd say he thinks he got a bargain."

As he laid out his bedroll, Hawk tried not to think that this could be the last night he would spend with Suzette. His proposal would offer a solution to only one problem. The biggest one—himself—would still remain.

In the nearby corral, the sound of Dusky Lady busily cropping grass reminded him that his and Hawk's plans for the ranch were coming to fruition. They had all the mares they needed, a fine stud horse, and enough land to support three times as many horses as they owned. After two decades of roaming the West, they had a place to settle down and a reason to stay. He looked at the two fillies that were sprawled out sleeping. He hoped Zeke wouldn't want to sell them.

"You've been awfully quiet this evening." Rather than sit down next to him, Suzette had settled on the other bedroll, facing him.

"Hard to get a word in edgewise with Jordy around." But that wasn't the reason for his reticence. He'd won a hard battle with his conscience. He was still convinced he was doing a terrible thing to Zeke, but he couldn't do anything else.

"I got the feeling it had nothing to do with Jordy."

Hawk was used to Zeke knowing what was in his mind, but he hadn't expected Suzette to be able to do it, too. "It didn't. It had to do with you."

"I've been thinking about you, too," Suzette said. "I want you to come with me to Quebec."

She couldn't have said anything that would have surprised Hawk more. "I can't do that."

"Of course you can."

"No, I can't. The people there would never accept me."

"I don't care."

"You will. They might not do anything to you, but you can be sure your sister would never make the kind of marriage you want for her."

"If the man really loves her—"

Hawk leaned forward to take Suzette's hands in his. "I love that you're willing to face the world with me as your husband, but it would ruin your plans for your sister. As soon as they know you married a half-breed, folks will turn their backs on both of you."

"That doesn't matter to me."

"It does to me. Just think how our children would be treated." He could tell from her expression that she'd never really believed it would work, but she was willing to risk anything to keep from losing him. That made what he was about to do easier. "I have a better solution."

"What?"

He was sorry he'd said it that way. He could tell she expected more than he was able to offer. "All you really need is the money to support yourself and your sister until she gets married. After that, you can do as you wish."

"I don't have that much money."

"I can give it to you."

The happiness that glowed briefly in her eyes gradually faded. "How can you do that?"

He swallowed. Even after reaching the decision, it was hard to put into words, hard to give up the dream of a lifetime. "I'll sell my share of the horses and the ranch. That will give you—"

"No!"

"But I want to do it for you. After your sister is married, you can—"

Suzette jerked her hands from his grasp. "Do you think I'd take your money and spoil everything you've been working for? What kind of woman do you think I am?"

"It would enable you to—"

"I don't care what it would enable me to do. I love you. You can't think I'd do anything like that."

Hawk had been afraid she'd refuse. In a way, he was relieved he didn't have to betray Zeke, but he couldn't give up Suzette. If he helped her take care of her sister, maybe she'd come back to him. Now it looked like he would lose her altogether. "Then what are you going to do?"

"I'm going to stay here with you."

He couldn't believe his ears. "What about your sister?"

"I've been thinking about Cicely. After the way my stepfather treated us, I'm not sure I want her to marry into society, after all. If you're willing, I thought she could spend the summer with us, get to know what people are like here."

Hawk let out a war whoop that brought the twin fillies scrambling to their feet and Dusky Lady rushing to their defense. He moved next to Suzette, took her face in his hands. "Does that mean you'll marry me?"

"What did you think I meant?"

Suzette's smile was so warm it nearly undid him. "That's what I thought you meant. But I wanted it so much, I was afraid it couldn't be true. I don't even know why you love me, much less why you want to marry me."

"I covet one of Dusky Lady's fillies, and I couldn't think of any other way to get her."

With a shout of laughter, Hawk smothered Suzette in a crushing embrace. As far as he was concerned, she could have all his horses as long as he was part of the bargain.

Here they were again, facing each other in the hall, neither wanting to be the first to go to bed. Zeke didn't know what to say. He was even less sure of what to do now than he had been earlier. Josie had allowed him to kiss her, but since then she'd acted as though nothing had happened. For a woman who'd never been kissed before, she seemed pretty much unaffected by their embrace. Zeke had been rejected lots of times, but no woman had ever been indifferent to him. "That was a good supper you fixed tonight."

"Do you really want to talk about food?" she asked.

Food was the furthest thing from his mind. He'd actually had to think hard to come up with something to say that wouldn't show he had practically tied himself in knots to keep from taking her into his arms and kissing her breathless. He couldn't think about anything but how wonderful it had felt and how he'd give up practically everything he owned to be able to do it again. "Not really, but I didn't want to say anything that would upset you."

"I've been dancing for men since I was sixteen. After seven years of being ravaged by their eyes and despoiled in their minds, there's nothing fragile about me."

It shocked Zeke to realize she knew so little about herself. She'd built a hard shell around herself to survive with her self-respect intact, much the same way he and Hawk had done, but she was far more vulnerable than they ever had been. "If I believed that, I wouldn't be standing here now."

"Why are you standing here?"

Did he dare tell her the truth? She'd been running from her fears her whole life. Was he fooling himself when he believed he could give her reason to stop? She wasn't a woman who liked to admit she'd been wrong. Besides, just because he was ready to give up everything he owned for her, that didn't mean she felt the same way about him. She'd spent seven years having men fawn over her, tell her she was beautiful, offer virtually anything if she'd give herself to them. She'd lived in hotels that catered to her comfort, eaten in fine restaurants, and been paid far better than the men she entertained. Why would she be willing to give that up to live on a dusty ranch where she had to work from morning to night?

Still, he couldn't let her go without telling her the truth. The love he'd searched for all his life was within his reach. It wouldn't be fair to himself to leave unsaid what was in his heart. He didn't know if she wanted love as much as he did, but he knew she had to like him a lot to have allowed him to kiss her. It wouldn't be fair not to let her know that he loved her so much it would be safe for her to risk her heart on him. "I'm standing here because I hope you'll let me kiss you again."

"Is that all you want?"

What was she trying to do, pull his guts out and force him to look at them? She had to know he couldn't be satisfied with a kiss. She wasn't just another woman in a long line of women to occupy his attention and take up his time for a few days or months before he moved on. But maybe she didn't know because he'd never told her. "I'm not sure I should tell you what I want."

"Why?"

"Because it might scare you too much."

"Nothing can scare me," she said.

Only a person who was too petrified to think straight could make a statement like that. He'd faced bloodthirsty killers, rampaging steers, and hungry wild animals with less fear than he felt facing the one woman who had captured his heart. Even if she didn't understand it, he knew both their futures were teetering on the edge.

"I'm scared enough for both of us." Zeke expected

some response. When he got none, he said, "I don't want to say or do the wrong thing."

"Just say it. I told you—you can't hurt me."

"I wish I were half that strong. You can hurt me far more than you know."

"You don't look like a weak man."

Time to stop putting it off. He had to bite the bullet and say his piece. "I'm weak when it comes to you. All you have to do is smile at me, and I can't think of anything else. Hell, I haven't been able to think of much else from the moment I saw you, and you did your best to make it clear you wanted nothing to do with me."

"I said I was wrong, that I was sorry about that."

"That made it worse."

"How?"

"Because now I'm in love with you." Her eyes seemed to grow wider, but nothing else changed. He started to grow desperate. Had he been mistaken about that kiss? He thought she'd finally let down the barrier and allowed him inside. "I know you want nothing to do with a man like me, and you want even less to do with a ranch, but there it is. I love you, and I can't do anything about it." He'd expected some response at last, but she continued to stare at him as if she hadn't understood a word he'd said. Or maybe they weren't words she wanted to hear, and she was trying to think of a way to let him down easy. "I thought you liked it when we kissed, but I guess I was wrong."

"I liked it fine."

"Then what's wrong?"

"I want more."

Chapter Twenty

Josie didn't know how she'd found the courage to utter those words. Every word out of Zeke's mouth, every expression that crossed his face, had convinced her he loved her as she'd never thought possible. Yet, knowing that, she still hadn't been able to dispel the fear that held her in its grasp. Her mother had loved her husband, but that hadn't made him treat her as an equal. Her father had loved her, but that hadn't stopped him from looking at her with lust in his eyes. Maybe men had said they loved her, but none had cared enough to wear down her resistance.

Yet she'd never been able to turn her back on Zeke. Every time she tried, he did something to undermine her resolve. He'd smiled at her after she'd been rude, talked to her when she glared at him in stony silence, made biscuits when she thought men felt they were too good to cook. She still might have been able to hold out if he hadn't kissed her. After that, she was lost. Even if it ended up being the most painful thing she'd ever done, she had to find out what it meant to be loved by a man.

"Are you sure?" Zeke looked stunned. "If you've never been kissed, then you've never . . ." He left the sentence unfinished.

"No, but I want to find out what it's like." She was stunned when Zeke reacted angrily.

"This isn't some experiment to find out if you like it," he said, his voice tight. "This is my heart we're talking about. I'm not some guy who's begging for a quick roll in the hay. I'm in love with you. I'm not spilling my guts only to have you say *Sorry, but I think I'd like to shop around*. Now I know what a horse must feel like when someone tries him out to see if he's got a smooth gait. Wait until you get to Tombstone. You'll have dozens of volunteers."

She was so shocked by his response, she just stood there when he turned, marched into his bedroom, and slammed the door. She'd never had a man turn his back on her. He thought she was prepared to use him for her own needs without any thought for his. Jolted out of her immobility, she crossed the hall and opened the door to his room. He was standing at the window staring out into the night. The moonlight cast his body into silhouette. He hadn't begun to undress.

"What do you want now?" he asked.

"I didn't mean it like it sounded."

He didn't turn around. "How did you mean it?"

How *did* she mean it? Everything had happened so

fast, had been so unexpected, she wasn't sure she could say. She only knew she had to make him understand he was the only one who could help her.

"I've always been afraid to let any man touch me. It wasn't just what my father did. I've known women who've been beaten, even killed, by the men who said they loved them. I've known still more who've told me how painful sex was, how much they disliked it, that they'd do practically anything never to do it again."

Zeke kept his back to her. "Haven't you known anybody who was happy to be with a man?"

"Yes, but that's not why I want to be with you."

Zeke turned to face her but kept the width of the room between them. "What changed your mind?"

"You did. When you kissed me, you were so gentle I wasn't frightened. I liked having your arms around me. I liked having you kiss me. I liked it so much I was almost angry Dusky Lady chose that time to have her foals."

"It still sounds like you're just looking for information."

She'd thought men were inherently incapable of keeping their hands off any willing woman, yet Zeke had not taken a single step toward her.

"Before I met you, I was certain I didn't want anything to do with men. I thought being married was the same as being a slave. I thought men were incapable of anything but lust. I believed children were simply a by-product of that lust, and that men only stayed married because they needed someone to take care of them. I didn't believe in love. I thought it was something women made up to make them feel better about putting up with men."

"What about Anna?"

"She was afraid she'd be left to grow old alone."

"And you aren't?"

"I *wanted* to grow old alone. Then I met you, and you confused me."

Zeke slowly closed the space between them. "How did I do that?"

She wished she could see his eyes, but she'd left the lamp in the hall. "I was mean to you, but you were never mean back. I was ungrateful and kept trying to drive you away, but you kept right on taking care of me. You were kind and gentle. You put what *I* wanted before what *you* wanted."

"Put that in a letter to Isabelle. She'll be pleased to know I really do know how to treat a lady. It's late. You've got a lot to do tomorrow."

"I don't understand. What did I say wrong? Why are you trying to get rid of me?"

"You don't know, do you?"

"No." It sounded like the pitiful wail of a child, but she didn't care. Zeke was the key to a future she'd always thought she didn't want. All that had changed now. She couldn't let this chance slip away. "Please tell me what I did wrong."

"You didn't do anything wrong."

"Then why—"

"*I* did." He stepped closer, reached out and touched her lips with his fingers. "I fell in love with you even though you warned me against it every way you could. It's not just your beauty. I love your strength, your spirit, your intelligence, and your stubbornness. You don't lie and you don't pretend. I want to spend my days working by your side, my nights sleeping with

335

you next to me. I want your face to be the last thing I see before I close my eyes and the first thing I see when I open them. I want to know you're near, because even when I can't see you that makes me happy. I want to teach you to believe in love as much as I do. Isabelle and Jake adopted eleven orphans who hated the world, sometimes hated themselves, and who believed love was a fairy tale. I know that love is real because I saw it transform our lives. It's because I love you, because of what love means to me, that I can't be just an experiment for you."

At last she understood. He was putting everything on the table and offering it all to her. He wouldn't accept anything less from her.

"I'm not sure I can love like that, but I want to try. You're the only one who can help me."

"Are you sure?"

"Yes, but I don't think I've ever been quite this scared in my whole life."

Zeke's palm cupped her cheek. "You know I'd never hurt you."

She was trembling. "Some of the girls told me terrible stories."

"Forget them."

She'd try, but now that she'd committed herself, now that she was convinced Zeke wasn't just trying to use her, all her fears returned. Was she doing the right thing, or was she letting her body control her mind? She was young and healthy. Zeke was big and handsome. Nature had arranged it so they couldn't help being attracted to each other, but lovemaking had to be based on more than animal attraction to make surrender worthwhile.

Zeke pulled her into an embrace. "If you don't like something or don't understand it, just let me know and I'll stop. There's nothing to be afraid of."

He held her against him so close she could feel his heart beating. She was amazed to discover it was beating even faster than hers. He rested his cheek on the top of her head and wrapped his arms around her. She was certain she'd never get enough of this feeling of strength, of being protected from the world. She was more than ready when he put his fingers under her chin, tipped her head back, and kissed her. She'd been thinking of this almost every moment since he'd kissed her. This time she didn't wait. She stood on tiptoes and kissed him back with all the energy she'd been saving up for years and years. It seemed that the longer she kissed him, the more she needed to be kissed.

Josie had always disliked being touched, but now she couldn't get enough of his caresses. Her conscious dislike had obscured an unconscious need that now careened out of control. She wound her arms around Zeke's neck, buried her fingers in his hair, gripped his scalp with both hands, and pulled him into a kiss so fierce it bruised her lips. But she didn't care. She wanted more. She molded her body to his, chest to chest, thigh to thigh, but she wasn't prepared for him to thrust his tongue between her teeth. Surprise caused her body to freeze. Zeke broke the kiss.

"Is something wrong?"

She hardly knew how to answer. Her mind told her one thing, instinct another—but Zeke said he loved her, had refused to touch her again until she said she wanted to learn to love. If he wanted to kiss her like that, it must be all right. "No." He didn't look convinced, but he didn't resist when she renewed their kiss.

Sensations from different parts of her body fought for her attention. His tongue's invasion of her mouth was wildly exciting. It was so unexpected, so deliciously erotic, she could hardly believe it was happening to her. At the same time, her nipples had responded to the pressure of Zeke's chest. They had become hard and extremely sensitive. It was a wonderful ache that caused her to rub against him. Her hands remained locked around his neck, but his hands wandered over her back from her shoulders to the small of her back, to the swell of her hips and buttocks. Taken together, the combination was rapidly reducing her bones to the consistency of wet rawhide.

While on one hand her strength was fading away, Zeke's kisses and the feel of his body against hers had tapped into a new source of energy that caused her to feel she was about to jump out of her skin. Every nerve in her body crackled with tiny bolts of energy. Even her muscles were filled with a pleasant ache. She'd never known her body could feel like this. When Zeke's hand moved to cover her breast, she found there was still more to come.

His fingers teased her swollen nipple, and the layers of clothing seemed to melt away. She felt exposed, wanting to pull away yet unable to move. When his other hand cupped her bottom and pulled her against his erection, she gasped. The reality of what was about to happen burst upon her in one blinding flash. She broke their kiss and pulled back.

"Did I frighten you?"

Yes, but the fact that he had let her pull back banished her fear. Her heartbeat slowed, and some of the tension left her body. She reached out, touched his chest with both hands. "Sometimes you surprise me, and I need a few minutes to get used to what's happening."

His hands had dropped to his sides. She took them and placed them over her breasts. She breathed a little more deeply when he began unbuttoning her dress, but she didn't pull back. The feel of his hands through her clothes had whetted her desire to feel his touch on her bare skin. Each released button caused a little gasp until her body screamed to exhale. When his work-roughened hands touched the tops of her tender breasts, the air left her body all at once.

She hadn't stopped to think that a man who worked with his hands would have such callused skin. Yet his touch was gentle. He teased her nipples until they ached. When he bent down and took one into his mouth, Josie's legs gave out from under her. In one fluid movement, Zeke caught her and laid her on the bed. She had barely recovered her breath before he took her nipple in his mouth once more. While he teased and tortured her to the point she was writhing under him, he let his hand roam over her side, her belly, her hips, her thighs. Before she knew it, her whole body was on fire.

She was incapable of objecting when he deftly removed her dress and shift, but the night air on a body that had never been exposed to a man's view quickly cooled the heat in her belly, and she found herself terribly self-conscious. She had to fight the desire to cover herself. She forgot her own discomfort when Zeke started to undress in front of her without any hesitation. The snug fit of his clothes had made her familiar with the shape of his body, but seeing the details emerge one by one caused the dwindling fire inside her to blaze up once more.

When he sat down on the edge of the bed to remove his boots, she couldn't resist running her hand over his back. She paused when she felt some ridges across his shoulders. "Where did you get these?"

"I'll tell you sometime, but not tonight."

He pulled off his socks and stood to remove his pants. What Josie saw when he turned to her nearly took her breath away. It was impossible. He was too large. She couldn't—

"Move over so I can lie next to you."

Helpless to act counter to instinct, Josie moved over. Zeke lay down and ran his hand up and down her arm. "You don't have to do anything you don't want to do."

Zeke continued to touch her gently. He kissed her forehead, even her nose. Gradually Josie's fears receded enough so she could reach out and touch Zeke. Her whole body was covered with goose bumps, but his skin was hot to the touch. She liked that he had no hair on his chest. The smooth softness was exhilarating. He quivered when she touched his nipple. It surprised and pleased her that she could give him some of the pleasure he'd given her. With a growl, he pounced on her, his tongue and lips hungrily attacking her breast, while his fingertips traced designs on her belly.

At first it was only dimly perceived, but the heat radiating out from her belly gradually made itself known. It was like a small fire that grew in intensity, then began to spread out. She couldn't describe the sensation, but it was as if her body were gradually being absorbed by something new.

Suddenly she realized Zeke's hand was no longer on her stomach. It had moved down her hip and across her thigh to the inside of her leg. Reflex caused her to clamp her knees together.

"Open for me," Zeke whispered. "I won't hurt you."

She knew he wouldn't, but it took all her courage to relax. She forgot everything but that he was approaching the most private part of her body. He stroked the insides of her legs until the last tension was released.

"This will feel strange at first, but it won't hurt."

Her entire body went rigid when his finger moved inside her. She braced herself for the pain she'd heard about, but it didn't come. Instead, tiny waves of pleasure began to emerge like ripples on the surface of a pond. The more Zeke moved inside her, the greater the pleasure, the more she was able to relax until she felt almost limp. Then Zeke touched something that nearly lifted her off the bed. She felt like she'd been struck by lightning. Her whole body was on fire.

"What are you doing?" Her voice was unsteady, her words barely distinguishable between gasping breaths.

"Trying to convince you there's no pain, only pleasure."

The pleasure was so intense it was almost painful. Josie would never have believed anything could feel like this. Zeke moved a second finger inside her, but it only increased the pleasure. The heat in her belly was rapidly spreading throughout her body. The waves of pleasure grew more intense, started coming faster, until Josie's body arched off the bed. She heard herself groan—once she cried out—but she couldn't control anything. She was completely in the grip of what Zeke was doing to her.

She gripped the sheets in her hands. She reached out and tried to pull Zeke to her, but he was immovable. She writhed on the bed, tried to pull away from him, but he wouldn't release her. The aching need grew so intense, she let out a cry. As she did, the tension broke and seemed to flow from her like rushing water.

Josie didn't know what she'd expected, but it was nothing like this. If it felt like this for men, no wonder they couldn't stop thinking about it. The wonderful feeling of well-being fled when Zeke rose above her.

"This won't hurt."

How could it not? This had to be what the women had told her about. She tried not to, but she tensed when he pushed against her entrance. Zeke pulled back and used his fingers. Seeking the pleasure his hand had given her, Josie relaxed and pushed against him. Immediately, Zeke withdrew his hand and entered her. Before she knew it, he had filled her completely. It didn't hurt, only gave her a sensation of fullness. When he began to move inside her, the longed-for feelings of pleasure began to twine their seductive tentacles around her once more. Within moments, she had wrapped her arms and legs around Zeke, trying to pull him deeper inside her.

Through the haze of her pleasure, she gradually became aware of Zeke's quickening breaths, his deep moans, the gradually increasing speed of his lovemaking. She watched the expression on his face change as his pleasure caught up with hers. If she hadn't known better, she'd have thought he was in pain, but she'd just had the same experience moments ago. She knew what he was feeling because she'd felt it herself, was feeling it again. Yielding to instinct, her body rose to meet him, to take him deeper inside so he could reach the core of her need, which seemed to remain just out of reach.

Just when she felt herself reaching the edge of the precipice, Zeke's body stiffened and his movements lost their smoothness. Then he uttered a guttural cry and she felt him spill himself inside her. That was all it took to send her over the edge as well. Moments later, they collapsed on the bed side by side, their bodies completely wrung out.

Josie had hardly spoken a word since they'd got up that morning. She didn't avoid his gaze, but there was a veil over her eyes. "I expect everyone will be in for breakfast soon," Zeke said when he finished grinding the coffee beans.

"It'll be ready."

She was at the stove, her back to him, as she fried slices off a ham Laurie's parents had given them. As soon as that was done, she'd fry some eggs Adam had found yesterday. Zeke's biscuits were in the oven, and the water was hot for coffee.

"We need to talk."

She turned to him. "I know, but I don't know what I want to do."

The bottom seemed to fall out of his stomach. "I don't understand. Last night you said you loved me." They had lain awake for nearly an hour while she explained to him why she'd been so afraid of men and how making love with him had changed everything.

"I do love you, but I don't know that I can be the wife you want."

Maybe he'd been reading too much into everything she'd said, hearing what he wanted to hear rather than her reservations. "How do you mean?"

She took the ham off the stove, reached for a bowl, and began to crack eggs. "I hated the farm when I was growing up. I hated cooking, cleaning, and looking after livestock. It was a hard life with no excitement, no variety, nothing to make me look forward to the next day."

He wanted to tell her that having a husband and children would change that, but then he realized a family would actually mean more cooking and cleaning. He started to tell her they didn't have to stay on the ranch, that he and Hawk would be making trips to buy and sell horses, but he knew isolation wasn't really the problem. Josie just wasn't able to bring herself to commit to him. She might say it was the ranch, but if she loved him as much as he loved her, she'd agree to live on the moon. "What are you going to do?"

She turned from him to finish cracking the eggs. "I've got to talk to Suzette. I can't just leave her in the lurch. I thought we might go to Tombstone and get a job. I need time to think." She turned back to him. "It's hard for me to be objective with you here."

"It's supposed to be *impossible* for you to be objective with me here," Zeke said, ready to beat his head against the wall. "That's what being in love is all about. You don't count the cost. You just do it."

Rather than encourage Josie, his words had the effect of sucking the energy right out of her. She looked almost frightened. "I can't do that. Does that mean I'm not in love with you?"

"In all likelihood, it does," he said. "It's probably a good idea to go to Tombstone. I'll get Adam to accompany you."

"Don't you need him here?"

No. He needed to be so busy he wouldn't have time to think.

Any further discussion was postponed when Hawk and Suzette came in, closely followed by Adam and Jordy. Breakfast was a noisy affair punctuated by Adam and Jordy's jabs at each other. Neither Hawk nor Suzette said much, but Zeke could tell by Hawk's grin that he was extremely happy about something. From the smile on Suzette's face, he had a good idea what that was. It just made Josie's decision to leave all that much harder to endure.

"We've got an announcement to make," Hawk said when they finally pushed back from the table. He reached for Suzette's hand, which she eagerly joined with his. "Suzette and I are going to get married."

Jordy whistled, jumped up, and pounded Hawk on the back. Adam did the same in a less boisterous fashion. Zeke hoped Suzette and Hawk were too distracted to notice Josie's stunned reaction. Zeke imagined she was feeling abandoned. He was happy for Hawk and Suzette, but he wondered if their marriage would leave him as alone as Josie. After all, Hawk hadn't told him about his plans.

"I'm so happy for you." Josie had pulled herself together enough to be able to face Suzette with a smile. "I knew you were in love with Hawk."

Leigh Greenwood

During the next half hour, Jordy weaseled out of Hawk and Suzette a step-by-step retelling of their courtship. Adam seemed particularly interested when Suzette said she was bringing her sister to stay on the ranch for a while. Zeke could foresee the boy making a lot of trips from his father's ranch on Sonoita Creek.

"I don't want this to change your partnership with Hawk," Suzette said to Zeke. "I want you two to be as close as you've always been."

Zeke appreciated Suzette's thoughtfulness, but things would have to change. It wouldn't be a good marriage otherwise. As the years went by, a man would naturally share more with his wife and less with his brother. That was as it should be, but even so, Zeke felt abandoned.

"I hate to throw a damper on this celebration," Josie said, "but I have to get ready to leave for Tombstone. Do you mind if Adam goes along with me?"

The awkward silence that followed was an insufficient indicator of the drastic change in the atmosphere. It made everything that had gone before seem out of place, even tasteless. Everyone studiously avoided looking at Zeke.

"I'll go hitch up the mules for you," he said.

He knew that everyone would believe he was running away to keep them from seeing the effect Josie's leaving would have on him. And they were right, but he was also leaving because he couldn't stand to watch her collect her things, pack them, and carry them out to the wagon. It would be the same as killing him inch by inch. He would say good-bye in one quick sentence. Then he'd spend the rest of his life trying to figure out how to live without the woman he loved.

* * *

Josie wished she'd asked Jordy to come with her. Adam, who was riding his horse alongside the wagon, was too sensitive to her mood. Jordy would have chattered on, impervious to the fact that she felt as if her life had come to an end. She still couldn't get over Suzette's deciding to marry Hawk without saying a word to her. Suzette had told her she hadn't decided until last night, but that hadn't made Josie feel less abandoned. She thought at first she was upset about the dissolution of their act, but it didn't take long before she admitted she was jealous because Suzette had what Josie wanted but was too afraid to reach for.

Leaving the ranch was like physically removing a part of herself. She could feel the pain as the widening distance caused her sense of contentment to fade. By the time the ranch house was out of sight, she felt drained.

For the short time it took to reach the nearby town of Fairbank, she'd gone back and forth in her mind, first telling herself every reason why she could marry Zeke, then countering with every reason why she shouldn't. She ended up with lots of reason for marrying Zeke, but only one reason why she shouldn't.

Fear.

"I want to stop in Fairbank," she said to Adam.

"Is something wrong?"

"Everything. I just can't figure out what to do about it."

They had reached the river just outside of town. A narrow canopy of towering cottonwoods offered dappled shade from the sun. The noise of the wagon stilled the song of a vermilion flycatcher and caused a pair of green kingfishers to utter piercing cries of protest. Willow saplings, catclaw, mesquite, and hackberry formed a dense underbrush before giving way to grass and cattails at the river's edge. The thin stream of water snaked through a sand-and-gravel riverbed pockmarked with the footprints of deer, coyotes, raccoons, and many smaller mammals. The mules splashed through the shallow water without hesitation. Just up the bank, she pulled the wagon to a stop.

"Why are you stopping here?" Adam asked.

"I want to stretch my legs." That wasn't the real reason, but she couldn't explain her sudden restlessness. She didn't understand it herself. Adam dismounted and helped her down from the wagon.

"You're in love with Zeke and you don't want to leave him. Don't look so surprised," he said when she stiffened. "Everybody knows it."

"Then why can't *everybody* explain to me why I can't make up my mind?"

"You just have to decide what you want the most."

Why was it young people thought answers were so simple? She walked toward the edge of the trees, looked out over the scrub growth between the river and the town. "I know what I want. I just don't see how it can work out."

"Why? Zeke's a great fella."

She turned to Adam, who'd followed her. "It's not Zeke. I hated growing up on a farm. I'm afraid I'll hate living on a ranch, and Zeke doesn't want to live anywhere else."

"Sounds a lot like my parents."

She withdrew to the shade of the cottonwoods.

"Zeke said your parents have been happily married for more than ten years."

"They have, but it almost didn't happen. My father was a gunfighter. When he was killed before I was born, my mother swore she'd have nothing to do with any gunfighter again. Hen was a gunfighter hired to protect Sycamore Flats from my father's kin. He wouldn't consider marriage because he was afraid he'd turned into a killer. My mother left him, just like you left Zeke, before deciding she had to go back."

"What changed her mind?"

"She loved him so much she decided it would be better to try marriage and fail than not try at all." He grinned suddenly. "Besides, I liked him, too."

Another simple answer. He was a sweet boy, but he had no idea of the pain it would cause both her and Zeke if they tried and failed. It was much easier to back away. "You don't think I love Zeke as much as your parents love each other, do you?"

Movement in the distance caused Josie to look past Adam. She got a sick feeling in her stomach when she recognized one of the approaching riders. She reached out and gripped Adam's arm. "Do you see those men who just rode out of town?"

He looked surprised but turned in the direction of Fairbank. Six men were riding toward the river. "Yeah."

"Do you recognize any of them?" She thought she recognized the two leaders, but they were still a long way off.

He stared for a moment, frowning as he concentrated. "I don't know the others, but one is the sheriff of Benson. I wonder what he's doing here."

Chapter Twenty-one

"The man with him is Solomon Gardner. They're going to try to take Zeke and Hawk's horses." Josie turned and ran back to the wagon.

Adam hurried after her. "Why would they do that?"

She told him about the men who'd tried to steal the horses, and about Gardner's attempt to kidnap her. Then she climbed into the wagon, turned the mules, and drove them into the thick undergrowth.

"What are you doing?" Adam asked.

"The sheriff has no authority this far from Benson. I'm sure he's here to make it easier for Gardner to steal the horses." By now the wagon was out of sight of the river crossing. Without waiting for Adam, she jumped down from the wagon and tied the mules to a cottonwood. "Help me up behind you. We've got to warn Zeke. Don't worry," she said when Adam looked too shocked to move. "I started riding astride before I was four."

"What about your wagon? Somebody might take it."

"I can replace the wagon, the mules, and the costumes."

"Hawk and Zeke can buy more mares."

"But their reputations may never recover from being branded thieves. Now stop wasting time and help me up." With Adam's assistance, Josie managed to scramble up behind him. "Now head for the ranch. We have to get there as quickly as possible."

Adam took her seriously when she said they had to ride fast. She had to wrap her arms around his middle and hold on for dear life. His slim torso was in stark contrast to Zeke's powerful chest. She could feel the sinewy strength in the boy's arms and back, but she could also count his ribs. Being this close to Adam made her realize how much she longed for Zeke's solid strength. When she saw him step out of the ranch house at the sound of their approach, she wondered why she'd ever been fool enough to leave him.

"Josie says somebody named Gardner and the sheriff from Benson are coming to take the horses," Adam shouted to Zeke before his horse had come to a halt.

"We saw them leaving Fairbank," Josie said as she slid from the horse into Zeke's arms. "They've got four men with them."

The others had come out of the house in time to hear what had been said. "Suzette and I will take the mares up into the mountains," Hawk said. "Jordy, take the rest of the horses and head toward Hen's ranch."

"Adam, find someplace along the Babocamari River

to hide Dusky Lady and her foals," Zeke said. "Josie and I will stay here and try to hold them off as long as possible."

Suzette and Hawk headed off at a run. Adam and Jordy mounted up and rode out in different directions. Seconds later, Josie was alone with Zeke in the quiet. It happened so quickly she could almost believe she'd imagined the whole thing.

"You ought to keep out of sight," Zeke said. "If Gardner sees you here, it could make the situation worse."

Josie started to object, then realized Zeke knew more than she did about handling people intent on taking what didn't belong to them. "What do you want me to do?"

"They're after the horses, so they have no reason to search the house. Just stay inside. And no matter what they do, *don't come out until I tell you.* All our lives might depend on it." His mood changed, his features softened. "I don't have time now to tell you how much I appreciate your coming to warn us, but—"

"You can tell me later."

Josie hurried into the house. She couldn't understand it, but she was about to cry. How stupid was that when thieves were practically at the front steps? She didn't want to go inside and hide. She wanted to stay and help Zeke. She wasn't used to feeling useless, and she didn't like it. She wanted to stand at the side of the man she loved.

The man she loved.

How stupid she was to think she could go to Tombstone or anywhere else knowing she loved Zeke and wanted to be his wife, knowing she never wanted to sing and dance for strangers again. She wanted only one man looking at her, thinking of her, wanting to make love to her. She started to go outside to tell him, but Gardner and the sheriff were riding into the yard.

Zeke watched from the porch steps as the men walked their horses toward him. He wondered if it was a mistake to have left his rifle inside the house, but he hoped being unarmed would keep the situation from getting out of control. If they were using the pretense of checking to see that he and Hawk legally owned the horses, they'd have no need for guns. Not that he trusted Gardner. He was the kind of man to take unfair advantage of any situation. Zeke wondered if he and Hawk would ever get to the point where they didn't have to keep proving themselves. They were known in five states and three territories. What was it about them that made it impossible for people to believe they were honest, up-standing citizens?

"Howdy," Zeke said when the men pulled up in front of the ranch house. He let his gaze hone in on the sheriff. "You're a long way from home, aren't you? What brings you out this way?"

"I'm here to check on a complaint."

"What kind of complaint?" Zeke shifted his gaze to Gardner. The man looked unduly pleased and confident. The four men with him looked too hard-edged to be regular cowhands. Zeke was beginning to wish he'd strapped on his guns.

"There's some doubt as to whether you and your partner actually own the horses."

"What horses?" Zeke made a show of looking

around the ranch yard. Except for the chickens in their pen, there was no sign of life.

"The mares you had when I hooked up with you on the San Pedro River," Gardner said.

"You mean the ones your men tried to steal?"

"I told you those men didn't work for me."

"Where are the horses?" the sheriff asked.

"I don't know," Zeke said.

"Where's your partner?"

"I don't know that, either, but I can prove we own the horses. I have the bills of sale."

"I'll have to see them," the sheriff said.

"They're inside. I'll get them."

"Hold it!" Gardner ordered. "You can't go inside by yourself."

"Why not?" Zeke tried to appear utterly unfazed, but inside he was boiling mad. It was preposterous that being young, rich, and white could enable this villainous man to do as he pleased.

"You could be lying, saying you've got them inside just so you can get your gun."

"If I'd wanted my gun, I could have gotten it before you arrived."

"He's got a point there, Solomon," the sheriff said reluctantly.

"People like him don't know how to tell the truth," Gardner said as he dismounted. "I'll go inside with him."

"I ought to do that," the sheriff said.

"You stay here with the boys in case that partner of his tries to sneak up on us. Don't forget he's a redskin. He's liable to lift your hair if you don't keep an eye out."

Zeke's fists clenched, but he knew it was useless to

say anything against prejudices that were deep and pervasive. Gardner's swagger was as offensive as it was unnecessary, but Zeke had learned long ago that little men had to do something to make themselves big in their own eyes. And it had been a long time since he'd met a man who was smaller than Solomon Gardner.

"Where do you keep these bills of sale?" Gardner sneered as he walked up the steps. "In a pot under the house?"

"In a lock box with other important papers."

Zeke hoped Josie was already hidden, or he'd have had to knock Gardner down to keep him from entering the house. "In here," Zeke said, indicating the sitting room. "We keep them in a cabinet." Zeke opened the cabinet door, picked up a key inside, and unlocked a drawer.

"Doesn't look secure to me," Gardner said.

"We've never had any trouble with thieves before," Zeke replied. He opened the drawer and took out the papers lying on top.

Gardner stuck out his hand. "Let me see them." He took one quick look, turned, and walked out of the house. "They're fakes," he said to the sheriff.

"They're copies." Zeke had followed close on his heels. "The originals are in a bank in Globe. I can get the bank president to send a telegram attesting to that."

"You're lying," Gardner shouted. "I knew trash like you and that Injun couldn't have come by such horses honestly. Let's go get them. Harvey," he said, pointing to one of the men, "stay and watch him until we get back. If he tries anything, shoot him. Nobody's going to worry about a dead black man."

"Where are you hiding those mares?" the sheriff asked Zeke.

"I don't know. My *Injun* partner has them. You never know what a redskin will do."

The sheriff didn't like Zeke's tone but ignored it. "They won't be far from the river," he said. "That's where there's the best grass. I don't think we ought to leave any of our men here. We can tie this fellow up and leave him until we get back."

Gardner took personal satisfaction in tying Zeke to one of the chairs in the kitchen. The rope was so tight it nearly cut off his circulation. Gardner looked disgruntled when Zeke didn't complain. He gave one last hard jerk on the rope for good measure. "That's just a sample of what's going to happen to you after we get those horses you stole."

"I've run into a lot of cowards like you who hide behind daddy's money and reputation because they're nothing but pale imitations of their old man."

Gardner backhanded Zeke across the mouth. "Shut up, you black bastard. I'll see you hanged as a horse thief yet."

"There never was a rope that could tell a black neck from a white one."

Gardner hit Zeke again, then stormed out of the house. "Let's go," Zeke heard him say to the sheriff. "The sooner we find those horses, the sooner we can string up that black son of a bitch and his Injun friend."

Zeke waited until the sound of their horses' hooves had died away. "You can come out now and untie me," he said to Josie. "We have a lot to do."

* * *

"It's just a small cut," Zeke said as he collected two rifles. "It's more important that we find Hawk and Suzette."

Josie had been horrified when she saw the blood running down Zeke's chin. She felt more guilty than ever for having stayed out of sight in the bedroom. She had taken one of Zeke's pistols with her. It had been almost impossible not to come out and use it on Gardner. "How can we do that? We don't have any horses."

Zeke took the pistol from her and shoved a rifle and a box of shells into her hands. "We always keep two horses hidden down by the river. That's saved our lives a couple of times."

Josie followed Zeke from the house and down to the Babocamari River, which formed the south boundary of their ranch. Cows had been off the land for more than two years now, and the undergrowth had come back thick and lush. Even though the ribbon of trees was narrow, it would have been difficult to find the horses without knowing where to look.

Josie's horse danced nervously when she tried to mount him. Zeke gave her a leg up. "Do you know where Hawk took the mares?" she asked as she adjusted her skirt under her.

"Back to the Whetstone Mountains."

"How can we find them?"

"Hawk will leave a trail."

"Won't Gardner and the sheriff be able to follow it, too?"

"They won't know what to look for. We've developed our own system over the years."

After he mounted, Zeke led the way out of the trees. He paused a moment to look around before pressing his horse into a canter. It took Josie a moment to catch up. "How are we going to get past them without being seen? There's no cover between the river and the mountains."

"I'm more worried that Hawk didn't have enough time to get the horses into the mountains before Gardner caught sight of them. You can't run mares hard when they're so close to foaling."

"What are you going to do?"

"I won't know until I find Hawk or Gardner."

Josie didn't want to find Gardner and the sheriff. She was certain they'd use Zeke's escape as an excuse to kill him. They didn't know she'd been hiding in the bedroom and had heard everything, but she wasn't sure a jury would believe her instead of a sheriff and a wealthy rancher. After all, she was just a woman who sang and danced for any man with the price of admission. Men might say they were mesmerized by her beauty, but only at certain times and under certain conditions. At all others times, she was like every other woman, a second-class citizen. "There are horse tracks everywhere. How can you tell which ones to follow?"

"You look at the ones on top." He pointed to the jumble of prints. "The Appaloosa mare is bringing up the rear."

"How can you tell?" All she could see was a jumble of hoofprints.

"Hawk lived with the Comanches until he was eleven. He taught me how to read a trail. No two horses have exactly the same hoofprint."

She'd have to take his word for it. They all looked the same to her. "How do you know we're on the right trail? These prints might have been made yesterday or the day before."

Zeke pointed to the limb of a mesquite bush. "Hawk bent the end of that branch to point in the right direction."

She couldn't see anything but branches armed with sharp thorns. "Do you think Gardner saw that?"

"With all these fresh hoofprints, he wouldn't need to look."

"That ought to keep them busy for a little while," Hawk said.

"What do we do now?" Suzette asked.

"We wait for Zeke to come up behind them." Hawk and Suzette had managed to get the mares safely into a box canyon, but with so little cover, Hawk had been fairly sure he wouldn't have enough time to elude Gardner and the sheriff. This was going to come down to a fight. He wondered how determined Gardner was to take their horses.

"What do you think they did to Zeke?" Suzette had hunkered down next to Hawk, feeling uncomfortable with a rifle in her hands.

"They probably tied him up so he couldn't warn me."

"What about Josie?"

"I'm sure Zeke told her to hide." He just hoped she'd had enough sense to do it. Josie had made it clear several times that she wasn't in the habit of doing what other people wanted.

"Then Josie could have untied him after they left."

"I expect they're on Gardner's trail right now. I want you to keep a close watch on the way into the canyon.

I'm going to make sure nobody tries to circle around behind us."

The rocky slopes above the canyon were covered with enough juniper and pinyon pine to provide cover. Hawk hoped Zeke would arrive before Gardner's men had time to work their way into position above them. As his gaze swept the slopes, he cursed Gardner for causing Suzette to be caught in a gun battle. She had responded with courage and determination, but she didn't know a thing about having to fight to defend her property—or herself. But was Gardner *really* the one to blame? If Hawk hadn't let himself fall in love with Suzette, she wouldn't be in this position. It was his fault she was here.

No, dammit, it wasn't his fault. Even a half-breed deserved the right to have a home, own property, marry, and have a family without fear it would be taken away or destroyed. He'd followed the white man's rules, so the rules should protect him, not put him at the mercy of men so riddled with prejudice they'd lost all sense of right and wrong. He had a right to own a ranch in Arizona, and he had a right to live on it with Suzette. Dammit, he wasn't going to let anybody drive him away.

"Can you see anything?" Suzette asked.

"Not yet, but I expect they'll move soon."

"What will you do?"

"Stop them."

"What are you going to do when we come up behind them?" Josie asked Zeke.

"One of two things," Zeke said. "We can capture them and take them into Tombstone, where they'll probably be released before we can get back to the ranch."

"What's the other option?"

"We can shoot it out with them."

Chills ran down Josie's spine. She would love to see Gardner and the sheriff in jail, but she didn't want Zeke to kill either one of them. She was certain that people would find some way to convict him of murder.

"What if I'm the one who kills them?" she asked.

"It won't make any difference. Hawk and I will get the blame."

It rankled that she couldn't take responsibility for her own actions, but this was no time to worry about the unfairness of life. "I used to hunt coyotes that were after our chickens and pigs. I can shoot them without killing them. Will that help?"

Zeke grinned. "It'll help a lot. Now let's get a move on. I expect they'll be trying to circle around and come at Hawk from above."

"What will he do?"

"I'm not sure. He's got no idea what Suzette can do in a fight."

"She'd face the devil himself before she'd let anybody hurt Hawk." She knew because that was the way she felt about Zeke.

"Hello up there. We've got you blocked so you can't get out of the canyon. You might as well give up."

Hawk recognized Gardner's voice. Apparently, he rather than the sheriff was directing this attempt to take the horses.

Suzette turned to Hawk, her eyes revealing tension and fear. "Don't let him spook you," Hawk told her.

"He knows he can't get to us without some of his men getting hurt, so he's trying to convince us to give up."

"What if they come after us?"

"We'll abandon the horses if we have to, but they'll never catch us."

"But they're your horses."

"We can always buy more horses. I'll never find anybody else like you." He caught sight of a man moving through the rocks well within range. Apparently, Gardner wasn't willing to wait any longer. Hawk waited until he caught sight of a leg behind a pinyon pine, then took careful aim at the man's thigh. They heard the man scream over the noise of the shot ricocheting off the canyon sides. "One out of action and five to go."

The sound of a shot told Zeke the fight was about to begin. He had to get closer quickly if he was going to be any help. "Stay close behind me," he said to Josie as he urged his horse into a rapid trot. He'd figured out which canyon Hawk was using. Now he needed to locate Gardner and the sheriff. He'd be at a disadvantage, because he was below them. Zeke altered his direction and moments later caught sight of a man peering up from behind a boulder. "We'll go the rest of the way on foot," he said to Josie. They dismounted, ground-hitched their horses, and started forward.

"What are we going to do?" Josie asked as she dodged around a large barrel cactus with a few yellow flowers on top.

"We have to find cover before they know we're here. I'm heading for the rocks at the base of that shoulder."

That didn't look like enough cover to Josie, but Zeke

knew more about gun battles than she did. He'd been fighting for his life since childhood.

"Hurry."

The urgent whisper was unexpected. "What's wrong?"

"One of the men is circling out of Hawk's sight. We need to get to cover before I take a shot. Once I do that, they'll know where we are." Moving forward in crouched positions, they ran for the nearest cover. When they reached it, Zeke fell on his stomach and pulled Josie down beside him. "Don't stand up unless I tell you."

"I can shoot."

"I know, but so can they, and I don't think they'll balk at shooting a woman."

"Do you think Suzette is okay?"

"Hawk would abandon the horses before he'd let anything happen to her." He didn't take his eyes off ·the man trying to circle behind Hawk. "I'd do the same for you."

Then he calmly raised his rifle, aimed, and fired.

"Zeke's here." Hawk was relieved he didn't have to carry this fight any longer by himself.

"How can you tell?"

"That shot came from behind Gardner's position."

Just then, one of the men stood up with his hands in the air.

"Get down, you fool."

It sounded like Gardner's voice, but the man didn't move. Instead, he tossed his rifle aside and came out into the open. Hawk was shocked when he heard a rifle shot and saw the man crumple.

"Gardner shot his own man."

"He must be crazy," Suzette said. "How does he expect to get away with that?"

Hawk fired several shots into the rocks where Gardner was hiding in hopes a ricochet would hit him. The only result was to send two men searching for new hiding places. That exposed them to Zeke, who fired off quick shots at both of them. The men turned and ran from the rocks toward Zeke with their hands in the air. Hawk fired a couple more shots into the rocks to keep Gardner from shooting them before they could surrender.

"What's happening?" Suzette asked.

"Gardner and the sheriff are the only ones left. They don't have any choice now but to give up."

But it didn't happen right away. For the next hour, Zeke and Hawk took turns firing shots into the rocks where Gardner and the sheriff were pinned down. Feeling certain the two men couldn't escape, he sent Suzette to keep the horses calm. After about forty-five minutes, Hawk heard a grunt. He thought one of the men had been hit by a ricochet, but neither came out and both continued to return fire sporadically. Finally Hawk decided the stalemate had gone on long enough. He called Suzette back.

"I'm going to work my way down. I want you to fire an occasional shot into their position to keep them tied down."

Suzette looked scared. "I can't do that. I might shoot you."

Hawk couldn't help smiling. "I know enough to keep out of your way. They'll be shooting up here as well."

"What if I fire into the air?"

"They'll know it. You have to shoot into the rocks where they're hiding." Hawk wanted to take Suzette into his arms and kiss away her fears, but that would have to wait until later. He knew she had the courage to do what was necessary—she just had to convince herself. He gave her a quick kiss. "I'm counting on you. Can you do it?"

She swallowed hard but nodded.

Hawk hadn't gone fifty yards before he caught sight of Zeke coming in his direction. Moments later they met.

"How'd you get Suzette to shoulder a rifle?" Zeke asked.

"She didn't want to, but she didn't like the thought of me with holes in my hide. What about Josie?"

"By the time I got tired of waiting for them to give up, she was so mad she was ready to go after them herself."

"What do we do now? We can't both go in from the same side."

"Your skin's practically the color of the ground, so you get the honor of going around to the other side." Zeke grinned. "I'll wait right here. Just signal me when you're ready."

Hawk muttered a couple of curses but grinned once he was out of sight. It took him several minutes to work his way around the other side of Gardner's position. Once he did, he started grinning again. Choosing his position where he could see Zeke leaning against a rock, he shouldered his rifle and put a shot into the dirt at Zeke's feet. He chuckled when Zeke scrambled to his feet and crawled out of sight.

"Son of a bitch!" Zeke yelled. "You're supposed to shoot at Gardner."

"I had to make sure you were awake." He laughed aloud at Zeke's curses.

"Gardner, you and the sheriff might as well come out. We've got you covered on four sides."

"Liar!"

"Let's give him some proof," Hawk called out. Rifles booming from all directions nearly covered the sound of the sheriff's voice.

"Stop! I surrender, but I can't move. I've been hit."

"Send Gardner out, and we'll come and get you," Hawk said.

"I'll see you in hell first!" Gardner shouted.

Hawk decided the only way to get Gardner was to go after him. While the others kept Gardner pinned down, he worked his way through the rocks. Gardner and the sheriff were in a small ravine between two high walls of rock. The sheriff was seated on the ground, leaning back against a rock, his shoulder bloody. Gardner went from one side to the other, firing in both directions. Discarded shell casings littered the ground. Hawk couldn't rush Gardner because he was too far away. The sheriff caught sight of Hawk and immediately seemed to understand what Hawk needed. He called Gardner over to exchange his nearly empty rifle for a fully loaded one. When Gardner turned toward the sheriff, Hawk leapt over the rocks. Running on moccasined feet, he reached Gardner before the man heard him. As Gardner turned, Hawk's fist caught him on the jaw with a blow so powerful Gardner's eyes rolled back in his head and he sank to the ground.

* * *

"You can save yourselves the trouble of taking us to Tombstone," Gardner said. "I'll be out of jail in less than an hour."

Hawk and Zeke were headed back to the ranch with all six men securely tied to their horses. None of their wounds were critical. Hawk had packed them well enough to stop the bleeding until they could get to a doctor in Tombstone. Gardner was lucky he hadn't killed the man he'd shot, but he was insisting the man had been hit by a ricochet. Everybody knew it wasn't true, but Zeke didn't trust any of them to stick to the truth once they were out of his control.

"I'll go to Tombstone to testify against you," Josie said. She was still enraged that Gardner would shoot one of his men as casually as he would a wild animal. They halted before the ranch house.

"Nobody's going to believe a black woman," Gardner sneered, "particularly one who works in saloons. You might as well let me go right now."

The front door of the ranch house opened and a man with white-blond hair about Hawk and Zeke's age stepped out. "Maybe not, but I think they'll believe me."

Chapter Twenty-two

A wide grin split Zeke's face. He jumped off his horse and walked over to the man and pumped his hand energetically. "What are you doing here?"

"I thought I'd come see how my boys were doing before we headed home together. I didn't expect to see Jordy driving the herd toward my ranch, or Adam hiding down by the river. Why didn't you tell me you were having trouble? It goes against the grain to see my boys running from horse thieves."

"Who the hell do you think you are, calling me a horse thief?" Gardner demanded.

"That's Hen Randolph, you idiot," the sheriff told him.

Gardner's complexion lost color. Everybody in the Territory knew how Hen Randolph had faced down the whole Blackthorne clan of thieves and rustlers just over ten years ago. Nor had anyone forgotten that his whole family had come from as far away as Texas and Wyoming to back him up.

"We weren't trying to steal the horses," the sheriff said. "We just wanted these two to prove they owned them."

Hen walked over to the sheriff and looked up at him with the ice-blue eyes that had caused more than one seasoned gunman to suddenly decide he needed to be elsewhere. "Why?"

The sheriff looked at Gardner, then back at Hen. "Mr. Gardner believed it was unlikely they could have the money to buy horses of such excellent quality."

"I can assure you they had the money to buy their stud horse, because they bought him from me, and he wasn't cheap." Hen switched his gaze to Gardner. "As for the mares in question, they bought them from Luke Maxwell. You probably know him as Luke Attmore. I guess you've heard of his brother, too."

Gardner lost a little more color. For years Luke Attmore had been one of the most famous hired guns in the West. Chet Attmore's reputation might have been as well known if he hadn't retired so soon.

"They didn't tell me that," the sheriff said.

"As far as I can see, they weren't required to tell you anything. What are you doing so far from Benson?"

"Gardner's men tried to steal Zeke and Hawk's horses several days ago." Josie had dismounted and come up to Hen. "He tried to kidnap me, but Zeke stopped him. We took Gardner and his men to the sheriff"—she nodded to indicate the sheriff—"but he didn't believe us and let them go. Suzette and I overheard them planning to steal the horses, and we came back to warn Zeke and Hawk." Josie turned and pointed at Gardner. "He tried to kill one of his own men when he wanted to give up. I saw him do it, and I'll testify to it in court."

"I think we should all go to Tombstone together." Hen turned to Josie. "I'm sure the sheriff will listen to you this time."

As Zeke watched Hen Randolph and his boys ride down the main street of Tombstone, gloom settled inside him. He'd miss Jordy and Adam. They were nice boys, good workers, fun to have around. Gardner was in jail awaiting trial on attempted murder charges. The sheriff would lose his job once the citizens of Benson learned of his behavior, and the four other men would spend the next few months in jail for attempting to steal horses. With all the loose ends tied up, there was no reason for Josie to stay any longer. All she had to do was pick up her wagon, and she could come back to Tombstone or head south to Bisbee.

"Are you sure the sheriff will notify me when Gardner goes on trial?" Josie asked.

"He will as long as he knows where you're staying," Zeke said.

Josie's gaze narrowed. "What do you mean?"

"It won't be a problem if you stay in Tombstone, but if you go to Bisbee, he's got to know where to find you."

Josie grabbed his arm and turned him to face her. "Are you telling me I have to stay here in Tombstone or go to Bisbee?"

"I'm not telling you anything," Zeke protested. "I'm just trying to help you—"

Josie swung her purse at him, hitting him on the shoulder. "You're trying to get rid of me."

Zeke tried to grab her purse, but she yanked it out of reach. "I've never tried to get rid of you."

She switched her purse to her left hand and hit him on the other shoulder. "You think you can take advantage of me and then shove me off this way?"

Zeke was losing his grip on the situation. Aware that people on the street were beginning to stare, he grabbed her purse before she could hit him again. "I'm not trying to shove you off."

Ignoring him, Josie punched him in the stomach. "You can't get rid of me that easily. I'm going to marry you if I have to drag you in front of the preacher myself."

Zeke was so shocked at her words that Josie was able to land two direct hits before he had enough presence of mind to take hold of her wrists. "Do you know what you just said, or are you so angry the words are just tumbling out?"

Josie struggled unsuccessfully to break his hold on her wrists. "I don't care if you can do everything better than I can, that's no reason to push me away."

Zeke broke out laughing. "I'm not trying to push you away. I'm trying to keep from getting killed."

"Lady, do you need some help?"

Zeke became aware that three men, all scowling at him, had come up to them. "I'm the one who needs help," he said. "I'm trying to convince her I love her before she kills me."

"Looks to me like you're barking up the wrong tree, mister," one of the men said.

"Of course I love him," Josie told the man. "Do you think I'd hit him if I didn't?"

The man scratched his head and turned to Zeke. "You understand what she's talking about?"

Being careful to keep his hold on her wrists, Zeke managed to fold Josie into his embrace. "Yeah, I think I do."

"Prove it," the first man said. "See if she'll let you kiss her without scratching your eyes out."

"Don't you dare," Josie said, eyes wide. "Not in the middle of the street with everybody watching."

"I've got to," Zeke said, feeling a devilish satisfaction. "You don't want these nice men to think I'm a liar."

"I don't care what they think. If you dare—"

Zeke knew there was only one way to end this. He bent down and kissed her. Josie struggled for all of a second before throwing herself enthusiastically into the kiss.

"I guess he was right," the first man said. "Hell, we lose more good dancers that way."

"There," Suzette said when the telegraph operator finished sending the telegram to her sister. "Now all we have to do is meet her when she reaches Benson."

"Are you sure about this?" Hawk asked. "She may hate Arizona. We don't even have a place for her to sleep."

Suzette wondered why she'd ever hesitated to let herself fall in love with Hawk. He was the most thoughtful man she'd ever known. "If she hates Arizona, she can go back to Quebec. If she decides to stay, she can have one of the bedrooms. I've grown rather fond of sleeping under the stars."

Hawk's frown deepened. "I'm going to talk to Zeke about building more rooms, but that will take weeks."

Suzette slipped her arm around Hawk's waist and turned him toward the door leading to the street. "I've never been as happy as I have been sleeping out with you and the horses. I wouldn't care if I had to do it for the rest of my life."

Hawk's frown melted away. "We'll get started building right away."

"Don't do it on my account. I like having you to myself."

They emerged from the comparative gloom of the Western Union office to the brilliant sunshine of an Arizona afternoon. Suzette decided it was an appropriate metaphor for her life. Hawk was certainly the center of her world, the light of happiness that had illumined the dark corners and banished unhappiness. She knew there would be dark times ahead, but as long as she had Hawk by her side she could endure anything.

With a loud squawk of protest, the yellow grosbeak flew from its perch inside the wagon and came to a fluttering halt on the outstretched limb of a Fremont cottonwood. Angrily it trilled its irritation at the humans who had disturbed its rest and the quiet of the late afternoon. The sun was sinking over the Santa Rita Mountains in the west, time for all nature to rest. What were these creatures doing, laughing and splashing through the sun-warmed waters of the San Pedro River? Even the gray hawk had stopped circling overhead.

Joining with its neighbors, who were equally unhappy at having their rest interrupted, the little grosbeak angrily hopped from one branch to another, scolding the humans for making a ridiculous amount of noise and waking the mules from their afternoon snooze. As they extricated the wagon from the brush, something caused them to burst into laughter, sending a foolish vermilion flycatcher streaking into the night sky looking for a new roost.

Finally the noisy humans and their mules left the river and headed into the open countryside. The grosbeak flew to a higher limb and squawked a final complaint to hurry the intruders on their way, but they didn't seem aware they'd upset the quiet of the evening or deprived him of his resting place. They rode four abreast, talking and laughing like they were the only people in the world.

Gradually the sound of their laughter and the squeak of the wagon wheels died away until silence reigned once more. Even the river seemed to have slowed its flow. The grosbeak found a suitable limb in a willow thicket and settled in for the night. He glanced up to see the four figures still tightly grouped silhouetted against the setting sun. A final burst of laughter floated on the evening air before all fell silent. The evening shadows had brought peace to the San Pedro River Valley.

The grosbeak tucked his head under his wing and slept.

LEIGH GREENWOOD

The Reluctant Bride

Colorado Territory, 1872: A rough-and-tumble place and time almost as dangerous as the men who left civilization behind, driven by a desire for a new life. In a false-fronted town where the only way to find a decent woman is to send away for her, Tanzy first catches sight of the man she came west to marry galloping after a gang of bandits. Russ Tibbolt is a far cry from the husband she expected when she agreed to become a mail-order bride. He is much too compelling for any woman's peace of mind. With his cobalt-blue eyes and his body's magic, how can she hope to win the battle of wills between them?